ON ACCOUNT OF DARKNESS

The Summer Ontario Baseball Broke the Colour Barrier

ON ACCOUNT OF DARKNESS

The Summer Ontario Baseball Broke the Colour Barrier

D.M. FOX

The Publishing Shop
Petrolia, Ontario, Canada

On Account of Darkness

The Summer Ontario Baseball Broke the Colour Barrier

First Print Edition May 2022

Copyright © 2022 D.M. Fox

Book Design: Dawn Stilwell
Team Photo Credits

Chatham All Stars - Chatham Coloured All-Stars 1934 Championship photo," Breaking the Colour Barrier, accessed March 8, 2022, https://cdigs.uwindsor.ca/BreakingColourBarrier/items/show/960. Penetanguishene Rangers: L. Waxy Gregoire Collection

All rights reserved. No part of this book may be reproduced by any mechanical, photographic or electronic process, nor may it be stored in a retrieval system, transmitted or otherwise be copied for public or private use – other than "fair use" as brief quotations embodied in articles or reviews – without prior permission of the author.

Tradepaper ISBN: 978-1-989346-89-1
Digital ISBN: 978-1-989346-89-1

While every precaution has been taken in the preparation of this book, the publisher assumes no responsibility for errors or omissions, or for damages resulting from the use of the information contained herein.

Since baseball time is measured only in outs, all you have to do is succeed utterly; keep hitting, keep the rally alive, and you have defeated time. You remain forever young.
-Roger Angell

Hatred will steal your heart, man.
You don't have any fight left in you.
You accept what's around you.
That's what this country was like.
We thought it would change someday.
We just waited for it to change.
-Buck O'Neill

The following is based upon a true story. Excerpts from the Chatham Daily News, Midland Free Press, Barrie Examiner, and other Ontario newspapers were found during archival research, and have been re-printed verbatim, for the most part; due to a fire in the town of Penetanguishene archives some years ago, back issues of the Penetang Weekly Herald were unfortunately destroyed.

The people in this story are real. Some of the events were modified to fit the narrative.

The governing body of baseball at the amateur level in Ontario during the 1930s was known as the Ontario Baseball Amateur Association (O.B.A.A.), which was shortened to the Ontario Baseball Association (O.B.A.) in 1938. To simplify matters, in the story the OBAA is referred to as the OBA, the name which most baseball followers in Ontario used until the name was changed again to Baseball Ontario in the 1980s.

Disclaimer

The original newspaper accounts may contain terms and phrases which might be offensive to some readers.

Maps of Southwestern Ontario early 1900's

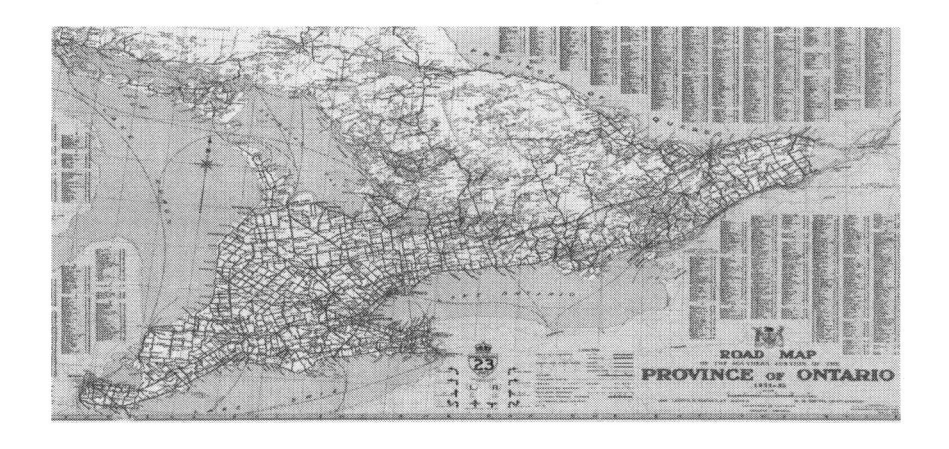

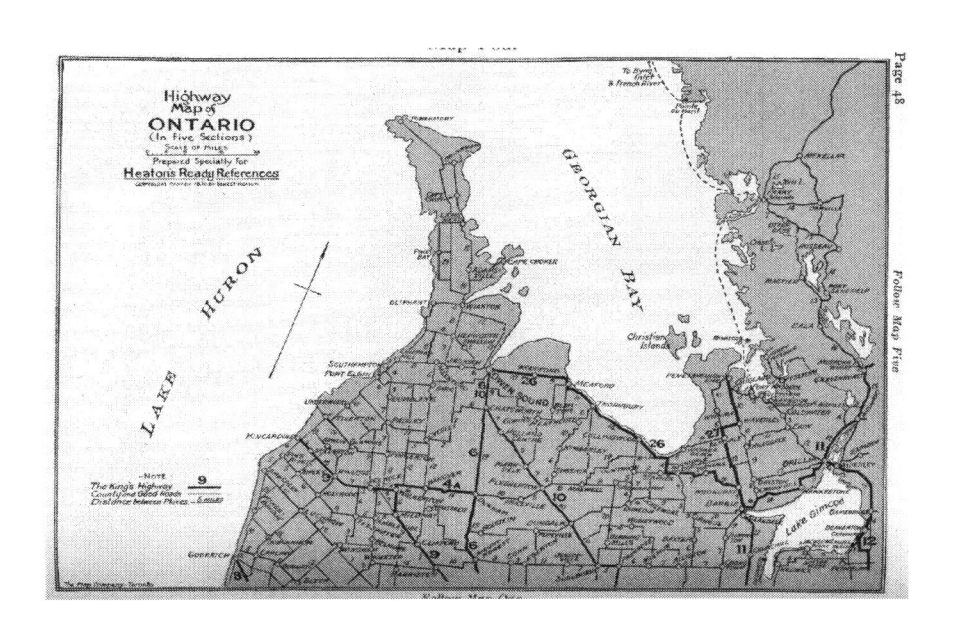

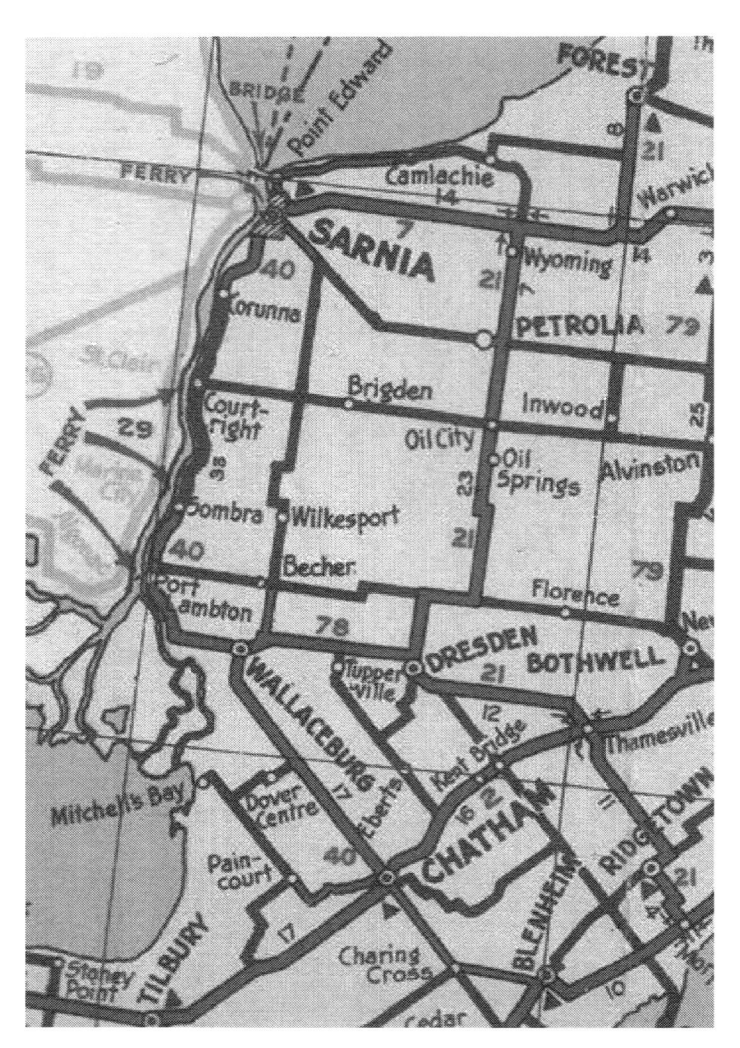

Ontario Highways 1934

Boomer Harding

Phil Marchildon

Stirling Park

Beck's Field

Front row L to R: Stanton Robbins, Jack Robinson (bat boy), Len Harding
Second row: Hyle Robbins, Earl "Flat" Chase, Kingsley Terrell, Don Washington, Don Tabron, Ross Talbot, Cliff Olbey Third row: Louis Pryor (coach), Guoy Ladd, Sagusta Harding, Wilfrid "Boomer"Harding, Percy Parker (coach). Missing: Joe "Happy" Parker, manager

Front row standing-Mervyn Dickey (reporter/statistician) Front row sitting-Fred Devilllers, Cy Richardson, Harold Crippin, Manager Jim Shaw, In front Jack Spearn(Batboy), friend of Jim Shaw, Phil Marchildon, Ivan Flynn (coach) Back row standing-Walter Spearn, Dan McCuaig, Unknown, Gerry Barbour, Bob Crippin, Harry Hale, Jimmy Bald, Marius Bald.

The Beginning

CHATHAM BOYS WIN IN LONDON
Coloured Team Trim Fellow Bell Hops in Six Inning Contest
Chatham Daily News Staff

London, ON - The Chatham Canadian All-Stars coloured team rode into London yesterday to hand the fast travelling Hotel London nine of the City Baseball League their first defeat of the season, when they went home with a 7-5 score tucked under the belt, "hot diggety-dawg."

Flat Chase, a boy who can really pitch and hit when aroused, hit a long Home Run which provided the margin of victory. Rookie Boomer Harding laid the lumber on a couple of pitches too.

Supporters of the local coloured lads saw their favourites DONE bow to the Chatham nine in a closely contested game.

A NOVEL RACE
Barrie Examiner Staff

With Phil Marchildon, Penetang pitcher and rugby star, breaking into print quite often these days, it was recalled that last summer he was one of the participants in a race at Payette's horse racing track in Penetang.

It was to be man versus beast versus machine, in a handicap race.

One of J.T. Payette's best horses was to race all the way around the track, a car driver was to race twice around, and Marchildon was to run halfway around the track.

Anyway, Marchildon came in first, beating both horse and car, although the handicap may or may not have been unfair, but Marchildon is an all-around athlete who counts speed of foot one of his many accomplishments.

1st Inning

Season Openers for both teams; brief histories of Penetanguishene and Chatham;Phil and Boomer both get their start behind the plate

Rangers Set to Open North Simcoe Season
By Mervyn Dickey
Penetang Weekly Herald
April 30th, 1934

The Penetang Spencer Foundry Rangers are in fine shape as the 1934 North Simcoe Baseball League season approaches. Runners-up to Barrie last season, the Rangers have a veteran lineup anchored by shortstop Hal Crippin, one of the more storied amateur players in the province. The Bald Brothers, Jim and Marius, return to man the right side of the Penetang infield, and seasoned backstop Fred DeVillers dons the tools of ignorance to provide leadership and defensive skills behind the plate. The Balds brought their young cousin Phil (Babe) Marchildon into the fold last year, and even though the high school hurler was one of the youngest players in the league, his skill on the mound belied his age, and hitters had considerable trouble catching up to his fastball, a rapid, darting pitch.

Local baseball man Jim Shaw brings a wealth of experience in his first season at the helm of the good ship Ranger. He should be a valuable mentor to the young phenom Marchildon.

This year, the team will move full time to its new home of Beck's Field, just off the entrance to the town, in order to accommodate the overflow crowds that flock to the team's games. The former cow pasture has been transformed into a first-class ball diamond by the players and a small army of rake-wielding local baseball fans. A snow fence around the outfield will help to prevent the odd wayward cow from getting a first-hand glimpse of the game or leaving a calling card for outfielders to dodge, as was sometimes the case last year.

Other teams in the league include Midland, Barrie, and Orillia. Teams will play each other twice at home and twice on the road, making for a twelve-game schedule. Tournaments and exhibition games will be added to Penetanguishene's slate of contests.

The North Simcoe League is quickly gaining a reputation as one of the most competitive loops in the province, and the Rangers will have their work cut out for them if they hope to capture the league title and advance in Ontario Baseball Association (OBA) play. All-in-all, it promises to be another season of winning and entertaining ball.

All-Stars Set for Second Season Success
By Jack Calder

Chatham Daily New Staff
May 4th, 1934

The Chatham Coloured All-Stars look forward to going all the way in city league play this year.

The collection of coloured players from the city's east end have gained considerable attention for their excellent and exciting ball, and have learned a great deal from their first season in the loop last year. The All Stars play a colourful and entertaining style, and never fail to put on a show for their fans.

The team is a collection of some of the best talent Kent County has to offer. A solid core, led by the Harding boys - Len, Carl, and young Wilfred, known better as "Boomer" (who may be the most promising of the lot), two-way stars Kingsley Terrell and Ross Talbot, and speedy outfielder Guoy Ladd, has been bolstered by a number of additions from the region. North Buxton's own Earl "Flat" Chase is an outstanding pitcher/shortstop who already owns the record for longest home runs hit at several southwestern ballparks. From Windsor, veteran catcher Don Washington has been brought aboard as a steadying influence, along with infielder/pitcher Donnie Tabron.

The All Stars play their home games at Stirling Park, an east end bandbox that draws huge crowds, and provides a raucous atmosphere that rivals any big-league park.

For this season, it has been decided that the winner of the City League will go on to compete in the Ontario Intermediate 'B" playdowns, involving teams from across the province. With such an accumulation of talent, the All Stars have to be considered a heavy favourite to represent Chatham.

Merv

Allow me to introduce myself. I'm Mervyn - Merv, for short - Dickey. Born and raised in Penetanguishene, the gateway to the 30 000 islands of Georgian Bay. As a newspaperman, I've always been somewhat skeptical about the accuracy of that total, but I've never taken the time to count.

I attended the old Penetanguishene High School, a stately two storey brick building that educated generations of townspeople until it met an unfortunate fiery demise. I tried out for all of the teams, but even in a tiny school like ours, I usually found myself at the end of the bench. Where I did excel was in the classroom, particularly in English. Words have always captivated me, especially in written form. I often have so many thoughts in my head that to others I seem lost, and I can have great difficulty expressing myself coherently in conversations. On those occasions, I'm a big-league scrub, a player who can barely get any playing time. On paper, where I have time to organize and express them in much more fluent fashion, I'm Carl Hubbell at the 1934 All Star game, striking out a half dozen Hall of Famers with ease, at least compared to my exploits on the playing field.

So, it was natural towards my senior years in high school that I drifted away from the playing field to the school newspaper. It was there that I became a star, filing dispatches on the goings on around PHS, including its many teams. After I graduated, a job was all but waiting for me at the Penetanguishene *Weekly Herald,* a small circulation paper that was at the hub of life in the town. I was assigned all manner of jobs at the paper, including covering town council meetings, special events, and, of course, sports in the town. We never lacked for stories to include in our sports section - if there's one thing that's vastly different about our society now compared to the early years of the last century, is that most people were active. It didn't matter if it was bowling, hockey, baseball, fishing, darts, curling, checkers, or harness racing at J.T. Payette's track. People were busy, and they were social in those days, and I was always getting results dropped off to include in the *Herald*. When I was growing up, there was no tv or radio, so people found activities outside of the house to take part in during the evening.

I had a long career across Ontario in the newspaper business, but I'm not going to talk about myself. I want to tell you about an incredible year - a history-making year in Ontario baseball -

1934, to be exact - and a very talented athlete and good friend by the name of Phil Marchildon. It was my very good fortune to watch Phil during the early 30s, and travel with the team as their statistician in that magical year.

⚾ ⚾ ⚾

Jack

Calder here. Jack Calder. Son of the Reverend A.C. and Mrs Calder, born in Chatham, proud graduate of Chatham Collegiate Institute. You name the sport in high school, I played it: football, baseball, hockey, track (I ran the 880 yds and mile), even a little boxing. I was not what you would call a star athlete by any stretch of the imagination, but no one competed harder than I did. As much as I loved all sports, baseball was truly my game. Playing, reading, and thinking about it has occupied most of my time since childhood. In grade school, I could not wait to rush to the variety store downtown every other Thursday to leaf through the latest issue of *The Sporting News*, the "bible of baseball." Stories about big leaguers, team-by-team news updates, and extensive minor league statistics waited for me as I walked down the store's ancient hardwood floor to the magazine rack. With my friends, I played a game called "National Pastime," a cards and dice board game version of baseball that was the most realistic thing on the market. I would play entire seasons in my bedroom on the desk my parents ostensibly bought for me to do my schoolwork on. I would keep track of my players stats on a piece of lined paper turned sideways, using each column to track the number of at bats, runs, hits, batting averages, et al. By the end of a season, the page would be full (I needed several, in fact), and it would tell the story of each player's year.

After high school, I landed a job with the Chatham Daily News, the local paper. Because of my youth and sporting background, I was assigned to the sports desk, and a year later (1932), I was appointed sports editor when my predecessor left. For a small-town newspaper, it was a busy post. Southwestern Ontario, and Chatham in particular, was a hotbed of all manner of sports in those days, and I covered it all. One of the first things my former editor told me was, "people never tire of seeing their names - or those of someone they know - in the paper," and I did my best to oblige him and our readers.

Shortly after I had taken over the helm of the sports department, I became aware of a ball team in the southeast corner of Chatham. Covering them was hard, because they played a lot of out of town games and tournaments. There wasn't much expense money available to travel and follow them when you work for a small-town paper in the middle of a Depression. They called themselves the Chatham Coloured All Stars - a team entirely made up of coloured players from that part of town - and they seemed to win just about everywhere they played. Their home field was Stirling Park, a quirky little bandbox of a ballpark wedged in between row houses stacked almost on top of each other, and they were enormously popular in that part of town and the outlying region.

Despite that popularity, the best competition in town was not available to them. Major League Baseball was still a long way from breaking the colour bar, and so, apparently, was the Chatham City League, and competing in the Ontario playoffs that followed a City League title. But in the winter of 1934, an enterprising and community-minded drug store owner by the name of Archie Stirling was about to change that. In their first year of play in the league the previous season, the All Stars took home the championship trophy. If they repeated that feat, they would be eligible (thanks to Archie's efforts) to take part in the Ontario Baseball Association Intermediate 'B' - the second tier of amateur play behind Senior - playdowns against other teams from across the province. A young star by the name of Boomer Harding was going to be front and centre of it. It was a rocky road that young Boomer and the All Stars travelled, and I had a seat near their bench for most of that ride. This is his story.

⚾ ⚾ ⚾

Merv

Phil was called Babe, or Bé, even though he was the fourth of seven children born to Oliver and Elizabeth Marchildon on a chilly late October day in 1913 in Penetanguishene, Ontario.

Penetanguishene and vicinity has a strong French-Canadian heritage, and while the name of the town itself sounds French, it's actually First Nation - it means "place of the white rolling sands," in the language of the Anishnaabe people who once fished, hunted, and camped on the shores of a long, protected, fjord-like inlet off of Georgian Bay, an extension of Lake Huron sometimes called "the sixth Great Lake." At the entrance of Penetanguishene Bay on the north side is a series of sandbars that boaters and swimmers alike have known about for generations, and it's those shifting sands that gave the town its name.

The first white settlers to the area had followed the British Navy, which was anxious to make certain after the War of 1812 that the tiny capital of York (now Toronto) would not be attacked a second time by American troops should hostilities between Britain and the U.S. flare up again. A naval base was built at the entrance of Penetanguishene Bay to allow Britain to patrol the upper Lakes, but that attack never came, and the navy left not many years later, followed by the army (who eventually pulled up stakes as well). But with the building of "The Establishment," as many locals called the base, a small support community developed, and stayed long after the military forces had left. There are reminders of the military everywhere - the Officer's Quarters (home to a well-known ghost dressed as an officer), and an Anglican Church built halfway between the fort and the town, are both still standing. There's even a pair of American warships at the bottom of Penetanguishene Bay, scuttled there after their capture by the Brits near the end of the War.

Penetanguishene was built on the side of a long, steep hill that descends down to the foot of Penetanguishene Bay. In the summer, with all the tourists arriving to boat off to fishing and leisure vacations along the eastern shore of Georgian Bay, the town dock down at the foot of Main Street was a hive of activity. The train tracks came right down to the waterfront. Summer cottages, fishing camps, and well-appointed inns beckoned. Main is bisected at the top by Robert Street, which runs out both east and west into the countryside. Close to the corner of Robert and Main is the town's Catholic Church, St Ann's. Its twin peaks tower out over the treetops, and are visible from far out into the Bay. For many years, when the church's bell rang at any other time than Saturday night or Sunday morning mass, you knew that it was a call for the volunteer firefighters, and Phil's dad - who served with the department for 55 years - would drop everything and race to the fire hall.

Penetanguishene's name was shortened to Penetang in the late 1800s, mainly because the arriving Canadian National Railway couldn't fit the town's full name on the station sign.

By the 1930s, Penetang (locals use the two names interchangeably) was a little town of 3 000 about a two-hour train ride - with connections - north of Toronto. The presence of First Nations people in this area dates back likely hundreds of years, if not more. The first white man to visit was the French explorer Samuel de Champlain, who was looking to build military and economic ties (mainly via the fur trade) with the local Wendat population. When I was in school, I remember a teacher telling us that Lake Huron on a map resembled a fur trader, with Georgian Bay the heavy pack on his pack. Penetanguishene was at the bottom of that pack.

Many from the first wave of settlers to arrive in the area came from the province of Quebec to the Penetanguishene peninsula in the mid 1800s. Free farmland and jobs in the local mills sawing white pine logs which had been floated down from the northern shore of Georgian Bay was the lure. One of those first settlers was a man named Hector Marchildon, and he began a family that is still there generations later. In his older years, Hector - who roofed his own house at the age of 87 - lived on a small farm on the outskirts of town, and would walk to Phil's house with a fresh pail of milk every night.

Hector's son Oliver Marchildon, Phil's father, was a tinsmith and a plumber. He did work for many wealthy Torontonians who had cottages along the shoreline and on the islands out in the Bay. Often, they refused to pay him for some or all of his services - which were usually done in an emergency - or drew the payments out over years. His wife Elizabeth - who everyone called Liza - took in laundry to help make ends meet and feed a growing family. Even Phil pitched in, rushing from school every day down to the town dock to meet the train with the evening edition of the Toronto *Star*, which he delivered up and down the hilly streets of Penetanguishene.

Like most people during the Depression, the Marchildons had to watch every penny. Liza stretched meals to feed nine mouths, and every fall, Oliver would supplement the family diet by heading out on the Bay to fish with his brother, bringing back a boat full of lake trout, which was stored in barrels of salt in the basement. Every scrap of those fish would be eaten - even the heads - then Liza would make stock from the bones, the intoxicating aroma of which you could smell up and down Maria St from their home.

The first few generations of Quebecois who came to the area retained their French language, but as the years passed and English became dominant in government, schools, and business, it became the language spoken in many homes of their descendants. Phil's parents grew up speaking French as well as English, but he and his siblings spoke only a few words and phrases of their grandparents' first language. Later on, when Phil went into pro ball with the old Toronto Maple Leafs of the International League, he was treated like royalty the first time he went to Montreal to play the Royals. The reporters there naturally assumed a guy with a last name like Marchildon would be able to listen and respond to their questions in French, but they were greatly disappointed that he couldn't. So was Phil.

Despite the lean times, Phil said that Penetang was a great place to grow up, and even though my newspaper career took me to the farthest reaches of the province, I couldn't agree more. The Marchildon clan was a huge one, and Phil could hardly walk a couple of blocks in town without running into kin. He thought that everyone grew up surrounded by grandparents, aunts, uncles, and cousins, and he got a bit of a shock one day when he moved to Toronto and found out that wasn't the case. Like all Penetang teenagers, Phil took part in all the usual local teenage hijinx: in the summer, rowing out to Whiskey Island just off The Establishment to drink beer and soak in the sun; in the winter, tobogganing down Main Street, and hoping a car didn't run the stop sign at one of the side streets. From December to March, there always seemed to be a rink shovelled off down by the docks, and all Penetang boys would play shinny there for hours. If it snowed, they would just bring a shovel along with their skates and sticks.

Because money was tight in the Marchildon home, Phil didn't play any organized sports until high school. The school had the equipment, coaches, and facilities for a wide range of sports, and he played almost all of them. I remember the first time I saw Phil on a playing field. It was at football tryouts after the first day of school. I was starting Grade 13, my final year, and Phil was a brand-new Grade 9. I knew who he was, because he was the bratty younger brother of my friend Norbert. He was about half the size of everyone else, but there was Phil trying out for the varsity team, even though he had never played the game before. We had no equipment on, so the coach had us play touch, and organized us into a scrimmage. "I hope your little brother Babe doesn't get hurt out here," I said to Norbert as we lined up for the first snap. "Oh, just you watch," said Norbert with a smile. The quarterback handed the ball off to Phil, who raced through our entire team to reach the end zone. No one came close to putting a hand on him. He wasn't just fast; he could change directions in mid-stride, and was at his top speed after only a couple of steps. I'd never seen someone that fast, someone that elusive, and I had played (more like watched from the bench) on some good teams in my years at good old PHS. He was just explosive, and not only was he fast, he seemed to be able to see the defence converge on him before it happened, and was able to cut back against the grain to avoid being touched - without losing a step. We had lost our starting running backs to graduation, but after watching

Phil race his way around would-be tacklers, the coach pointed to him and said, "boys, meet your new starting half back."

Phil was a natural, a gifted athlete at just about any sport. One of his proudest moments was when he won ten first-place ribbons at a school track meet. What made this accomplishment all the more impressive was that because it had been a lean month at the Marchildon home, he had gone to school without breakfast. He won a cup as the top overall athlete at the meet, and the cup sits in a local museum today. It was one of his most prized possessions.

Jack

Chatham was named after the English town of the same name, which was named in turn after William Pitt the Younger, the 1st Earl of Chatham.

Like its British namesake, Chatham's location on the Thames River was strategic in nature. A naval dockyard planned for the Canadian version, however, never materialized. The British root of Chatham, *cheto*, means forest, while *ham* was the Old English word for settlement, and when the first white settlers arrived in the area they set about clearing the Carolinian forest that covered the area. When the lumbering business faded, area residents turned to agriculture in an area with some of the best soil and climactic conditions (Chatham is roughly on the same latitude as Northern California) in Canada.

The Battle of Moraviantown was fought in the region in the War of 1812, a decisive American triumph early in the conflict that resulted in the death of the famed Indigenous warrior Tecumseh.

Located far enough over the border to assure feeling saves safety, Chatham became well known was the terminus of the Underground Railroad in the early to mid 19th century. The abolitionist John Brown planned and carried out his ill-fated assault on Harper's Valley from Chatham. Chatham became known as the "Black Mecca of Canada." By the mid 1800s, over one-third of the town's population was black, and the black community held significant economic and political clout in the growing town. In 1847, Chatham was designated as the seat of Kent County, prompting the construction of a grand stone courthouse in the town centre. Seven years later, the Great Western Railway came to town, and the community was soon booming. With some of the best farmland in Canada surrounding the town, the escaped slaves and their descendants grew and prospered, building Chatham and Kent County into one of the most prosperous places in the country.

By the late 1800s, Chatham was flourishing, the leading centre between London and Windsor, largely thanks to their efforts. But not all of them shared in the wealth.

Before the days of super highways, Chatham was on the main east-west transportation artery between Detroit and Toronto. With access to a huge labour force and proximity to American markets, manufacturing began to grow in the town by the late 1800s (Chatham was incorporated as a city in 1895). During the early 1900s, Chatham was a major automobile manufacturing centre. Being only about 50 miles from the U.S. border, Chatham has an affinity for things American that much of the rest of the province does not have. Chathamites cheer for teams from Detroit more than they do for those from Toronto, which is several hours to the east.

Sandwiched between Lake St Clair to the north, and Lake Erie to the south, Chatham's winters tend to be milder than other places in Ontario, although we don't always escape the snow. Because spring arrives a bit earlier and fall lasts a little longer compared to places north of Chatham, the baseball season tends to be longer. Maybe it's not a huge advantage, but Chatham ball teams can get on the ball diamond earlier, and stay on it later than many other places in Canada.

Wilfrid Harding was born August 6th, 1915, one of 8 kids to Bill and Sarah Harding. He was a loud and boisterous toddler, so much so that one of his sisters gave him the nickname Boomer, after a comic strip character she read in the *Daily News*.

The family, along with many others, was squeezed into an area in the south east corner of town bordered by Queen Street on the west, the Canadian Pacific Railway tracks to the south, and the Thames River to the north and east. It was an old land grant that the government had given to direct descendants of slaves. Houses were squeezed in cheek-by-jowl in a manner you didn't see in the rest of the town.

Boomer and his siblings were a rarity for their times - a product of a mixed-race marriage. His father was black, the ancestor of runaway slaves who found freedom in Canada. His mother was white, daughter of a long-established Chatham family. Her family highly disapproved of her marriage to a black man, and she was disowned as a result. Boomer recalled when he was young that if she was walking down the sidewalk in town and one of her family members approached from the opposite direction, they would cross to the other side to avoid her. He said that when that happened, she would pick up her pace, hold her head high, and continue on as if nothing untoward had taken place. Boomer remembered his mom once saying, "you sure find out who your friends are when you marry a black man."

Boomer's dad, Bill, was a fine athlete in his youth, but he had to put sports aside to feed a growing family shortly after the arrival of their first child. Every day he drove a horse and wagon down to the coal docks on Lake Erie. He would be gone at first light in the morning, returning with a load around noon, then spent the rest of the day making deliveries around town. It was a hard way to make a living, putting in a close to twelve-hour day, six days a week, with considerable physical labour, and dealing with the odd customer who was not able to pay for their delivery on a sub-zero January day.

On Saturdays and holidays, Bill would take his sons Len, Carl, Andy, and even young Boomer with him on his route down to the Lake. It would take about an hour and a half to drive the horse-drawn cart down bumpy roads across the flat, treeless, and windswept farmland to get to the harbour at Erieau. It was cold, bone-rattling, and boring as hell for the boys. When the cart got back to Chatham, they were put to work helping to fill buckets of coal before handing them over the side to Bill. It was hard and often cold work, and they always went home with aching muscles, and had to take their dust-filled clothes off in the woodshed attached to the back of the house before they could enter. Boomer told me that his parents had always stressed the importance of education, and to him there was no greater teacher than that long haul to pick up and deliver coal. The experience made him work that much harder in school.

Work was scarce for folks from Boomer's part of town in the Depression. About the only jobs available were hotel or train porter, mechanic, labourer, or farm hand. Despite the large black population in the area, there were no blacks in prominent positions in town: no black police, no black public servants, and certainly no black newspaper reporters. As the century turned, more and more black families eyed the country their ancestors had come from for employment, and Detroit was often the destination. It was only about an hour away from Chatham, and many people made the journey there looking for work. Canada had been the land of freedom, but apparently America was now the land of opportunity.

With 8 kids in the house, Bill and Sarah Harding had to be wise with his meager earnings driving the coal wagon. They always managed to have good food on the table, and decent (if not stylish) clothes to wear. Boomer had to wear his brothers' hand-me-downs, which included skates and ball gloves.

Sports were huge in the Harding family, as they were in that part of town. Boomer's brothers were all outstanding athletes, and he followed them eagerly. In high school, he excelled at pole vaulting, basketball, baseball, soccer, and hockey. His parents figured that if school did not provide a better life for the boys, perhaps sports would. But opportunities to play organized sports were few and far between for black youth beyond high school. As Boomer said, "if a young fellow from our part of town didn't get himself into baseball or hockey or some other sport, he generally would find himself in jail." The white youth of Chatham could make a whole lot of mischief, and usually get off with a warning from the local police. Such was not the case with kids from Boomer's part of town.

Boomer was a great forward in hockey, playing on the left wing. He was fast, and was unafraid of going into the corners to mix things up and go after the puck. More than one opposing defenceman who beat him to the puck would cough it up at the sight of Boomer barrelling in on him. I do not know how many assists he gathered from scooping up those loose pucks and passing to a teammate in a position to score, but I am certain he recorded more than his fair share. He took that competitive and fiery demeanour to all sports he played, and to the surprise of no one, was a star in all of them.

In his first year of high school, when Boomer went out for the baseball team, the coach put him at catcher, mainly because he was the biggest kid on the field. He could snap a throw to 2nd faster than anyone, but he always felt his best contribution to the team was with his bat. He loved to hit, loved to have a pitcher challenge him with his hardest stuff. Being a catcher really helped him with his hitting, though. He learned to pick up the ball out of the pitcher's hand to determine its spin and ultimate destination. "If the stitches were spinning forward fast," he once said, "that meant it was a curve with a sharp break, but if the stitches spun slowly because the pitcher didn't get a good snap on the ball as he released it, I would load up and get ready to hit that ball a mile." At a young age, he was already a student of the game.

⚾ ⚾ ⚾

Merv

In many ways, Penetanguishene and Midland, the town minutes away on the next harbour over, are twins. They share a common geography, climate, and history. But as time passed, the military left Penetang for good, and the white pine logs stopped floating down the Bay, and Midland surpassed Penetang in many ways. Because it had a deep, natural harbour, and a railway connection to the east before we did, Midland grew much faster and dwarfed our little town of 3000 by the 1920s. As the demand grew for Great Lakes freighters to ship prairie grain to the elevators that dotted the lakes (Midland had four in operation by the '20s) grew, Midland started their own shipyards, creating even more employment and prosperity for the town. They even had the money and political connections to build a new arena with artificial ice and heated dressing rooms, despite the ongoing Depression, an admittedly grand edifice that had the only man-made ice between Toronto and Winnipeg at the time. But the differences between the two towns was slight in many ways, most of all geographically. For outsiders, it seemed that the two towns were almost one; it was not uncommon for an individual to work in one, and live in the other. But if you ever wanted to start a debate in either town, suggest a common municipal government for them.

At first, the two teams were sporting partners. When the North Simcoe League was established in 1930, the two towns combined forces to challenge the larger centres in the league like Barrie and Orillia. The joint Midland-Penetanguishene entry featured stars from the former like Kirby Chalk and Herb Beauchamp, while the Crippin and Bald brother acts came from the latter. After two seasons, Midland decided to go on their own, and formed a team. Neither of the former partners was strong enough to knock the powerhouse Barrie squad off the top, and there was some resentment in town over the Midlanders' decision to field their own entry.

In many ways, Penetanguishene was like Midland's poor cousin. The Midland kids had more, and on the playing field, they tended to let us know that, which made an already heated rivalry that much more intense. Midland always seemed to have new uniforms and the latest equipment, while Penetang teams had mis-matching jerseys and hand-me-down gear. Whenever the two towns played in any sport, it was like a war - a tradition that carried on for decades. And in the early years of those battles, Penetanguishene won more often than they lost - a fact they didn't mind reminding the Midland kids about.

Organized baseball in Simcoe County, bordered by the towns of Alliston, Orillia, Collingwood, Midland/Penetanguishene, with Barrie in the middle as the seat of the County, was slow to develop, but by 1930, when the North Simcoe League began, the game took off. Sponsored by local business man J.T. "Jake" Payette, owner of the race track in town, the Penetanguishene Spencer Foundry Rangers at first played on an old softball diamond behind St Ann's, then a year later moved to a beautiful field on the southern edge of town donated by Charles Beck, a German immigrant who made his fortune in the lumber business. Named Beck's Field in his honour, it wasn't much more than a cow pasture when it was first opened, but as the team grew in popularity, improvements were made, and there was greater room for spectators. Other teams in the league were still playing on makeshift diamonds, but Penetang had a glistening little jewel of a ballpark, which the town was justifiably very proud of.

It didn't take long for the Rangers and Beck's Field to become a huge attraction for the people of the town. Hundreds of fans would jam Beck's tiny benches, and crowds would spill out down the base lines. Guys in their pickup trucks would drive in from a back road and park behind the outfield fence, sitting in the beds of the trucks while they smoked British Consols and drank Carling's Black Label as they watched the game. After the game, some of the Rangers would wander out to the outfield and talk baseball with the guys in the trucks, who always seemed to have a couple of bottles left over for thirsty players.

⚾ ⚾ ⚾

Jack

If you like to be outside, there are few places better than Chatham. Fishing abounds along the Thames River and up into Lake St Clair. The sun-soaked beaches of Lake Erie are just a short drive through the countryside south of town away. Hockey, baseball, soccer, rugby football, cricket, and lacrosse have been popular in town for decades.

Stirling Park is a small, oddly-shaped parcel of land right in the middle of Boomer's old neighbourhood that the town gave to the local community. Its dimensions were quirky - it was well over 400 feet to straightaway centre field, about 80 feet less than that to left, and as it was on an irregular-sized lot because of the railway tracks, it was only about 250 ft down the right field line. Shortly after the park opened, poles had to be constructed and netting strung across the right field fence to keep balls that cleared it from hitting houses or pedestrians out for a stroll on Payne St. But there was a charm to Stirling's unique dimensions, and there was hardly a summer night that failed to have a ball game played on it.

The park was named after the family of local merchant Archie Stirling, a businessman who believed in giving back to the community long before it became fashionable. The Stirlings donated the land, built a ball diamond, a pool, and a playground. In the winter, the ball diamond outfield was flooded to make a rink for skating and hockey. An area down the left field line was cleared, with benches huddled around a potbellied stove to warm up frozen skaters. Generations of east end kids learned to swim, skate, and play ball at Stirling Park. Archie was a big supporter of Chatham baseball in general, and of teams who played at the park which bore his family's name. Any hometown player who hit one out of the park at Stirling was welcome to two bricks of ice cream from his store. A Chatham team that won a provincial title received a ride in a fire truck through the streets of the city, and a free trip to the soda bar at Archie's store.

Stirling Park was the centre of the universe for its local residents. There was no TV, hardly anyone owned a radio, and even fewer owned cars. Stirling provided nightly entertainment. Since the town could not afford the funds to maintain it, a local business provided some lumber, chicken wire, and grass seed, and the community provided the sweat equity. The infield was dirt, and the outfield was grass that became increasingly patchy over the course of a dry southwestern Ontario summer, but it was Yankee Stadium for all its players and spectators cared.

Many of the games played in the early 30s at Stirling were of the pick-up variety. As time went on, the better players got together and formed a team and began to play tournaments and exhibition games against other teams in the area - other black teams, because even though they would have more than held their own, the Chatham Coloured All-Stars, as they called themselves, were not permitted to play against the white teams in the prestigious City League.

One time, a team from Detroit came to play at Stirling, with some players who had played for the Stars, a negro league team that had folded during the tough economic times. They only narrowly defeated the Chatham All Stars, in front of a crowd that filled just about every nook and cranny of the Stirling grounds. Admission wasn't charged, but in the 5th inning, one of the players who wasn't in the lineup took his hat off and went through the stands to take up a collection, so that each could pay what they could afford. The proceeds would be split 60/40 with the visiting team after the game, which would usually help pay for the umpires, game ball, and gas money for the visitors' ride home, and maybe something to eat on the way. That arrangement gave the All Stars added incentive to put on a good show on the road to help attract fans, and motivation to win, because 40% of the take would not pay for dinner on the drive home.

Because there were not many places in that part of town where people could gather, Stirling Park became like a church, community centre, and playing field all rolled into one. People came to Stirling not just to watch the game, but to socialize, catch up on the gossip, and sometimes just to be seen. Several generations of families would attend the games, and it was not unusual to hear a young voice yell, "Hi Grandpa!" at any point during a game. Bleachers built by the hands of the community ringed the infield, and went up several rows. The first row was always reserved for the elders, whose knees balked at climbing up the steps. The old-timers would be decked out in their best straw hats, wearing freshly ironed button-up shirts, with suspenders to help keep their pants up under the weight of sagging bellies. They would lean on their canes with gnarled, working man hands as they watched, talking about old times, old ball players, and the time Satchel Paige came to Windsor. For weekend games against travelling teams from places like Windsor or Detroit, fans would flood in from the countryside, and would be everywhere, filling the bleachers then spilling down the foul lines. Railway cars which had been shuttled off to one of the spur lines beside the park offered a better view for the fans willing to climb and sit atop them. To bring in a few more fans, and raise some money for the team, a draw for a box of groceries was held at every Stars game; fans dropped a few pennies or a nickel in exchange for a chance at winning a bit more extra food when putting dinner on the table was a challenge.

There were big wash tubs full of ice, with ice cold cans of RC Cola and Canada Dry Ginger Ale bobbing up and down for sale. One of the more enterprising fellows in the neighbourhood hooked up a propane stove on the back of his pick up, and grilled hot dogs for the hungry crowd. For tournaments, he hauled up pails of potatoes that he had peeled, hand sliced into french fries, soaked them in water to get the starch out, then fried them in oil. The aroma could be smelled everywhere, and even a passenger on a passing train must have wondered what the enticing smell was. Young kids would chase each other under the stands, and worried moms throughout the game were yelling their names to bring them to heel back in the bleachers. Young bucks would be watching the girls, and more than one first kiss probably took place under the stands at Stirling.

Because Stirling's dimensions were what could be best described as cozy, it was a tough place for visiting teams to play. The crowd was right on top of the action, and pitchers knew that if they caught too much of the plate to a left-handed hitter, that mistake could be easily knocked out of the park. Times were tough in the early 30s, but Stirling Park was a place people could go and forget about their worries for a couple of hours every night.

⚾ ⚾ ⚾

Merv

When Phil went out for the varsity baseball team in his first year of high school (the school wasn't big enough to have junior and senior teams), it was his first taste of organized ball. The team already had a pitcher, but because he showed great agility and a quick release on his throws, the Coach - Mr Wendling, who was better known as a track coach - put him behind the plate. But after a few games, when coach Wendling saw that the pitcher had to duck because Phil could peg throws on a line that passed over the mound by only a few feet to nab would-be base stealers, Wendling began to wonder about making a change to his lineup.

Phil said that he'd been throwing things his whole life up to that point; rocks at telephone poles, snowballs at his brothers, sisters, and cousins, just about anything that could fit in his hand. In the winter, on his way home from school, he would grab a handful and pack it into a snowball, then pretend he was a football quarterback, and throw the winning touchdown pass to a telephone pole a half block away. As kids, he and his buddies would ride their second-hand bikes out into the country (which didn't take long from just about any part of town) with a paper bag full of old soup cans. They'd set them up on a farmer's fence along the side of the road, then see who could knock off the most cans by tossing rocks at them. Phil won almost every single time. All that throwing, combined with his athleticism, gave him incredible arm strength by the time he was a teenager.

As I said, Mr Wendling didn't know a whole lot about baseball, but he knew an elite athlete when he saw one - Jean Thompson, a PHS middle distance runner he had coached a few years earlier went on to represent little Penetanguishene and Canada at the '28 Olympics. "Say, Phil," he said one day to Babe before after school practice. "That's a pretty good arm you have there - strong and accurate. If it was track and field season, I'd have you toss the javelin, but failing that, would you consider giving pitching a try?"

Phil had never thought of that before, but said, "sure - why not?" because few runners were even daring to steal on him anymore. Baseball was still very new to him at that point. Football was his game - from that first dodging moment on the gridiron in fall practice, he had been installed as our school team's star half back, and even took over as team punter. Penetang had a town football team in those days, playing against other teams in the county, and the coach had already lined Phil up to play for the team the following fall. He'd be a 15-year-old playing against grown men.

The first time Phil took to the mound in a game was in a tournament in Collingwood, a Georgian Bay shipbuilding town about an hour to the west of Penetanguishene. He had absolutely no idea what he was doing. Coach Wendling had to give him a quick lesson on the difference between the full windup and the stretch before the first game. After Phil completed his warm up tosses and the first batter of the game dug in, he had to call time to get the catcher to come out and tell him what the signs were, because he had no clue.

He really didn't need any signs, because his catcher just put his mitt in the middle of the plate, and Phil just reared back and fired. He got more and more comfortable as the day progressed, and the hitters got increasingly uncomfortable in the batter's box. Batter after batter would go down swinging, or weakly ground out, and when Phil got back to the bench after the inning, Wendling would slap him on the back and exclaim, "keep chucking them, Marchildon!"

Phil became a dominant pitcher over the next few years in the short Simcoe County baseball season. But it was as a football star that he made the most headlines, and gave him his eventual ticket out of Penetang. St Michael's College, a prestigious private school offering secondary and post-secondary education from Toronto, came up to the shores of Georgian Bay to play the first half of a home-and-home set of exhibition games with the Penetang footballers.

St Mike's was no ordinary institution. With a beautiful downtown Toronto campus, the school had high academic and athletic standards. They played in the Ontario Rugby Football Union, a league just a notch below The Big Four, which featured powerhouses from Montreal, Toronto, Ottawa, and Hamilton.

On game day, the field was covered in a foot of snow by a mid-October snow squall that had rolled in off the Bay. The only scoring in the contest came when Phil took a direct snap from centre instead of the quarterback, rolled to his right, then threw a touchdown pass to a receiver who was wide open in the end zone. He was left uncovered because he had pretended to head to the bench just before the play started, then raced to the end zone to await Phil's toss. Tiny little Penetang had just upset mighty St Mike's, who had a couple of future Grey Cup winners in their lineup.

After the return game a week later in Toronto, a St Mike's priest took Phil aside and offered him a full scholarship for the following year if he would come to the city and play football for them. It would take him a long way from home, but the idea of a free education in the midst of the Depression was not something he or his family could take lightly.

⚾ ⚾ ⚾

Jack

As someone who has spent many a summer night at a ballpark, I can tell you one thing without hesitation: the catcher is the hardest-working player on the field. He is involved on every pitch, has to know the strengths and weaknesses of each hitter, and what is working (and not working) for his pitcher on any given evening. He has to position his defence, block balls in the dirt, back up plays at first, and race to the backstop when his pitcher can't find the plate with a road map. All while wearing the heavy protective gear, the "tools of ignorance," a catcher dons.

Catching did not prove to be for Boomer. Foul tips, curve balls that hit the dirt five feet in front of home plate, and relays from the outfield that seemed to arrive at the same time as a runner rounding 3rd coming into home put an early end to his career behind the dish. He would still fill in on occasion, but one day just before his high school team was about to practice, his coach tossed him a 1st Baseman's mitt, and said, "Boomer, meet your new position."

From that point on, Boomer's bat, which had always been the strongest part of his game, became lethal - a game changer. That is not to say there were not some challenges to learning a new position, which took considerable time, practice, and patience, but without the rigours of catching, his bat gained new life, and he became a dangerous hitter, a guy the opposition did not want coming up in the order when the game was on the line. Boomer was always a guy who thrived in the spotlight, a player who wanted to be at the plate with go-ahead runs on base. I asked him once what went through his mind in those situations, and he replied, "nothing." He was not anxious in those clutch times; he figured it was the pitcher who should be nervous.

It did not take long for stories about Boomer's hitting prowess to spread. He continued to play other sports throughout the season - he was turning into one of the better hockey players the Chatham-Kent area had ever produced - but more and more it was baseball that was getting him noticed. Because he was so much more advanced physically than other boys his age, he was barely a teen when he was called upon to compete against older players. It started in high school, when after only a couple of games with the freshman team, he was promoted to the varsity squad, playing against boys three and four years older. He fit right in, and his hitting continued without missing a beat. His father Bill, standing next to me at one of Boomer's games when he had finished his coal route early one day, said, "if you're good enough, you're old enough."

Boomer quickly turned into more than a one-dimensional slugger, though. Opposing teams learned to pitch around him, and he was not afraid to take a base on balls. He was no plodding baserunner, and he showed smarts on the base paths from an early age. He did not go up to the plate looking to knock the ball out of the park. He was more adept at making hard contact. Late in the game, when your team needed a hit, there was no one you would rather see at the plate than Boomer. You knew something was going to happen when he came up to bat.

⚾ ⚾ ⚾

Merv
Race was a complex issue in a little town like Penetanguishene that had so many social and cultural influences over the years. The original settlers of the area were mostly French-Canadian Catholics, along with a presence of indigenous people (the original inhabitants of the land), and a recently-arrived growing Anglo-Saxon population that dominated the town's business and political affairs. There were also pockets of coloured people in the wider Simcoe County area, descendants of escaped slaves who had settled in the southern part of the

County near Barrie, in Collingwood and further to the west, in Owen Sound over in Grey County.

Penetanguishene had a mixed family when I was young - the Carters. Mr Carter was black, and worked as a millwright in the lumber mill. Mrs Carter was white. They had a neat two-story brick home on Fox St, just off the downtown, and they and their children were well accepted members of their church and the community. I can't speak to what they likely experienced in terms of prejudice, but my parents brought us up to accept everyone and treat them as equals.

Phil had that French-Canadian background, and he also had some Métis heritage. His grandmother Eleanor was of French Canadian and Ojibway descent, which was not uncommon in town. He inherited her dark hair and olive complexion, and was often asked when he left Penetanguishene if he was Indian.

A few miles northwest of town was the Christian Island reserve, where three hundred years earlier, Jesuit priests from a failed mission on the mainland fled with the surviving Wendat to make one last ill-fated stand in a land wracked by European disease and economic tribal warfare. The Wendat dispersed after 1650, and years later the Island became home to the Ojibway, who came to town often for supplies. There was something of an uneasy acceptance on both sides as far as their presence in town was concerned.

The Ojibway, for their part, were understandably distrustful of whites; they had moved into what became Simcoe County in the decades after the Wendat were driven out by the Haudensoaunee (Iroquois). In the 1830s, they were encouraged to settle on a 4000 hectare parcel of land near Coldwater, in the north-central part of the County. Surrounded by rich farmland and on the safest and fastest water route from Toronto to Georgian Bay (and points both north and west), the community flourished. With farmland for encroaching white settlers becoming scarce, in the 1850s the government split the band up, and moved half to a 650 acre reserve at Rama, near Orillia, while the other half was relocated to Beausoleil Island, a 1110 acre reserve just out in the Bay that crossed over into the rocky Canadian Shield. The Beausoleils, as they now were known, were moved again just a half dozen years later to Christian Island, that marginal farmland outcrop off the Penetanguishene peninsula that the Wendat had abandoned two centuries earlier. While they didn't go out of their way to be more than accommodating, the merchants in town recognized that the band was important to their business, but they did little to bridge the significant gap between them. The Beausoleils' reluctance to deal with white store owners, given their past, was understandable, but was viewed by some townspeople as aloofness. There was not a mutual feeling of respect between the two sides.

When Phil left Penetang to play in the Nickel Belt League up north in Sudbury in the mid-30s, he was reminded of his heritage just about every time he pitched by the hard-working and even harder-living miners who came to wager away their pay cheques on his game. "Goddamned Frog," and "Stinking Mick," were among the mildest names he was called.

Wilf Sheffield of Collingwood and Archie Thompson of Barrie were two black athletes who Phil faced many times across several different sports while he was in high school. Archie could really do it all - he was a star pitcher/catcher, a top-notch hockey and football player, and even boxed for Canada at the Empire (later Commonwealth) Games. Phil and Archie met up for the first (but definitely not last) time in a high school tournament in Collingwood. Word of Archie's reputation had preceded him, and Phil geared up to give him his best fastball with his first pitch. But word of Phil's newness to the position and subsequent wildness (an issue he would deal with for his whole career) didn't reach Archie, and he took Phil's first pitch in his front (left) shoulder. Archie went down in a heap, and the Barrie coach rushed out to check on his star player, but by the time he got there, Archie had jumped up, dusted himself off, and sprinted to 1st. He stole 2nd on the next pitch.

Later in that game, Archie faced Phil again. He didn't dig in quite as deeply as he did in his first at bat. Phil got ahead 1-2 on him, then threw what he called an "old sidearm country curve," from his rock-throwing days, and Archie corkscrewed himself into the ground as he swung right over the pitch for strike three. His next time up, he hit a ball so far into the gap in a fenceless outfield that by the time one of the outfielders had picked it up, Archie had rounded 3rd and was headed for home.

Phil and Archie crossed paths many times over the next few years, and became equally good friends and competitors. Barrie and Penetang developed a heated North Simcoe League rivalry, with the two players the star combatants for their respective sides. But while Phil was a slightly above average hockey player, Archie was head and shoulders above him in terms of talent. He was part of many strong Barrie teams, even won a provincial championship with Guelph - he teamed up with a couple of other strong black players, and they formed a forward line that was unstoppable - but he was never considered for a spot on an NHL team. Ontario was a regular pipeline to pro hockey in those days, and scouts combed the bushes for players (even places like Penetang), but there was no place for Archie Thompson in the NHL.

Jack

Even with a presence in the area for over half a century, blacks in Chatham - and other parts of Canada - had plenty of reminders that to some in the white majority they were second-class citizens. It was subtle, but as soon as you left the East End and crossed the northern set of railway tracks into the section of town that was predominantly white, the stares and whispers confirmed that.

Sarah Harding used to tell her children, "all people are created equal," but some appeared to be more equal than others.

It wasn't as blatant as in the Jim Crow states to the south, but Boomer and his friends knew that in the greater Chatham/Kent County area, there were certain places where they were less than welcome. Kingsville and Leamington had an unwritten "sunset" law that decreed that people of colour had to be off the streets by that time of day. Harrow's movie theatre was for whites only. In Dresden, in the north end of the county, there were signs in the windows of restaurants saying, "No Negroes Allowed." The cooks in those restaurants were often black, but the patrons were all white. Even though black people had been in the area for three quarters of a century, they often had to build their own schools, and frequent businesses in the East End of Chatham.

It was the height of the Depression, and jobs were scarce. Blacks were limited to jobs that usually involved heavy manual labour, like Boomer's dad on the coal wagon. Hotel and train porter were other jobs that were available for people of colour. After graduating from high school, the only job opportunity for Boomer was a bellhop at the Pitt hotel downtown. Many elders in the community were concerned that too many young men and women were leaving for job opportunities elsewhere.

Boomer attended Chatham Vocational High School, which in all reality was a school for black students - the whites attended Chatham Collegiate. It was not the Harding family's first choice, but segregation, while not an official policy, was a fact of life in southwestern Ontario - the last segregated school in Chatham/Kent did not close until 1965. In later years, Boomer would talk to competitors who grew up in cities in Montreal or Toronto, and they could not believe he was didn't attend a non-segregated high school. That did not mean there was no racism in those cities, but at least things were more equal in the classroom and on the playing field.

White boys during Boomer's youth would dream of growing up and becoming the next Babe Ruth or Walter Johnson. Boomer and his friends grew up hoping to be the next Satchel Paige or Cool Papa Bell. And dream of a day when they could all play in the same league.

Slavery in Upper Canada had been supposedly abolished by John Graves Simcoe when he became the colony's first Lieutenant Governor in 1793, but there was a loophole, one big enough to drive Bill Harding's loaded coal wagon through. There is no doubt that Simcoe was very much against slavery; he'd given numerous speeches railing against it in the British House of Commons when he was member of parliament before coming to Canada. When he came to Upper Canada, one of his first acts was to pass the "Act Against Slavery," the first of its kind in the British Empire, a piece of legislation banning slavery. That may sound like a monumental act, but it was not as grand a gesture as it might seem.

Britain's courts had freed all slaves in that country a decade and a half before Simcoe's law passed. There were many United Empire Loyalists in Canada - Americans who had to flee the country in the wake of the Revolutionary War because of their loyalty to Britain. Several hundred slaves were "owned" by these Loyalists who relocated to Upper Canada. In fact, the British parliament passed a law to ensure that these refugees would get to keep their slaves if they crossed over into Canada.

Simcoe's heart was in the right place when he passed this law, but he was not courageous enough to see the bill through to its proper, humanitarian finish. In order for his Anti-Slavery bill to pass, it would need approval from both the Legislative Assembly and Legislative Council. The Assembly was elected, but the Council, composed of the leading business and political men of the colony, was appointed. And most of the Council - at least five of the nine - owned slaves. Simcoe's bill would never pass without their support, so a grandfather clause was included. No new slaves could be brought into the colony, but those already in Upper Canada would continue to be enslaved, and their children would not be free until they turned twenty-five. To discourage owners from freeing their slaves, they were forced to ensure their financial security. So, in all practicality, slavery in Upper Canada wasn't abolished so much as it was slowly phased out. The British government finally abolished it across the Empire in 1834.

2nd Inning

All Stars and Rangers get ready to start the season; how the teams were formed. Archie Stirling has big plans.

Boosting Baseball
By Jack Calder
Chatham Daily News Sports Editor
May 25, 1934

This evening at Stirling Park the City Baseball League is to have its official opening. The game naturally demands and deserves your attendance.

The League provided excellent ball last year and broke no one. Baseball is well on its way back to being a position as a major sport in this city. There can be no doubt as to the loop's success from the standpoint of good baseball and from that of monetary returns.

The Chatham Coloured All Stars, '33 champions of the City League, hope to get off to a flying start by taking the R.G. Duns into camp.

If you haven't yet been to Stirling Park you've missed something for few of the accoutrements of a modern stadium are missing. The diamond is in dandy shape and the outfield is equally good. Facilities for the fans are tributes to the work of league officials and if you haven't heard about the brand-new dug-outs you don't talk baseball.

Today the only thing that stands in the way of a truly magnificent comeback for baseball locally is the cost of equipment for kids. The greatest ballplayers seldom come from well-to-do families. But if baseball gloves and bats were provided for kids at somewhere near cost price, don't think they wouldn't return to baseball in a hurry. To encourage the youngsters some interested individuals must provide them aid in securing equipment.

Talk it over with your neighbour at the ball game tonight.

HURLER FANS 19 BATTERS
Barrie Loses 8-0 Exhibition Game at Penetang on Holiday
Barrie Examiner
May 31, 1934

Phil Marchildon, Penetang's sensational young right-hander, fanned 19 Barrie batters on May 24, as the locals lost an exhibition game 8-0 to open the baseball season in Penetang. The 21-year-old pitching ace only allowed three hits and was complete master of the Barrie team at all times. Only two men reached base.

Barrie presented a team much below regular strength. Some of the boys used the holiday for other purposes than baseball, especially the pitching staff. Barrie's three hits, well scattered, were made by George Scott, Adam McKenzie, and Allan Tribble, outfielders. These three same players contributed seven strikeouts to Marchildon's total of 19. The rest of the Barrie players fanned the air with regularity and got no hits.

Penetang presented a youthful and scrappy team all around, in fact the best aggregation the northerners have shown yet. The usual loud and rabid crowd was out to cheer their favorites on. The noise started half an hour before game time and the razzing continued until the Barrie team were several miles on their way home.

Marchildon is easily 75 per cent of the Penetang team but he failed to show his usual power at bat. Much of this was supplied by Harold Crippin with three hits, two doubles and a scorching single in five times up. Crippin is also one of the finest fielding shortstops in the OBA intermediate class.

⚾ ⚾ ⚾

Merv

Despite the growing popularity of baseball, both nationally and locally, Phil's focus in his late teens was primarily football. Baseball was something to play before football practice started in the late summer. He was a huge pigskin celebrity in town. That didn't stop his cousins, Jimmy and Marius Bald, from trying to encourage Phil to join them on the Rangers.

The core of the team started playing ball about a decade earlier when they were boys. They tended to get into mischief around town - just stupid kid's pranks like turning over people's outhouses in those pre-sewage treatment plant days, or sneaking into the church tower to grab the bell rope and ring it before the priest could catch them. As the apples ripened on Mrs McElroy's Tolman Tommy tree in the middle of town one fall, it was too much of a temptation for the gang to resist. They raided the tree at night, and when Mrs McElroy caught them red-handed (literally) and threatened to call the town constable, enough was enough. Gerry Barbour's older brother was involved, and his mom flipped out. She told Mr Barbour that something had to be done to properly channel the kids' energy. He eventually figured that a softball team should be started to keep the boys occupied. They didn't have much money for equipment, so the good folks of Spencer Foundry, manufacturer of wood stoves and kitchen ranges, stepped in to buy some bats, balls, and catcher's equipment. Gloves were very expensive, so in the beginning, only the catcher had one - everyone else played bare-handed.

A couple of men who worked in the office at the foundry offered to coach the team. They had some tryouts and began to put a team together, but they couldn't find a pitcher who could throw in the windmill style. Joe Hale, who lived up the line toward the Establishment, brought along his grandmother when he tried out for pitcher, but he couldn't throw a strike to save his life. Grandma stepped in to show him how it was done, and struck out the next hitter. She wasn't eligible to play for the team, unfortunately.

The team, called the Lion Tamers, was very successful for a small team outfit, regularly punching above their weight against the bigger centres. They even reached the provincial final one year, facing a Toronto team with a lanky pitcher named Bill Durnan. Durnan's sport was hockey, though, and he later won six Vezina trophies in a Hall of Fame career minding the nets for the Montreal Canadiens. After a few years, with everyone talking about Babe Ruth and Lou Gehrig, baseball became the game in Simcoe County. There was a new game in town, and the Lion Tamers eventually became the Rangers.

The Rangers held their own in the new league, but they couldn't get over the top and win the pennant. Hal Crippin was easily their best player, but he was a better shortstop than he was a pitcher, and as Phil mowed down high school competition, Jimmy and Marius continued to put the squeeze on him to join the Rangers. But Phil was reluctant. "Getting high school hitters out is one thing," he told me. "But guys in the North Simcoe league know what they're doing at the plate. I might be no match for those guys, and before you know it, people might start saying, 'yeah, he's good at football, but he's not much of a baseball player."

Finally, the pressure was too much, and Phil agreed to come out for the Rangers in the spring of 1933. He was a little bit in awe at the first couple of practices, because now he was playing with a lot of the guys he watched when he was a kid. He started to get comfortable, and he knew maybe this was going to work out at one training session when Bobby Crippin, the team captain and one of the Lion Tamer originals, came out to the mound to talk to Phil while he was throwing batting practice. Bobby asked Phil if he could slow it down a bit so that the hitters could make some contact, and maybe the fielders could get a little practice, too.

Phil was still so new to pitching, and didn't do much beyond just reaching back and firing it in there. The team's catcher, Fred DeVillers, started to work with him on his curveball grip. He taught Phil to grip the ball tighter than he had been, which made the pitch faster, and harder for hitters to distinguish between it and his fastball. It took some time for Phil to master the new pitch, but he proved to be a quick study. In between games, he would work on his curve with his high school teammate Andy Vaillancourt, who worked in a barbershop on Main Street. When business was slow, they would slip out into the alley behind the shop, and Phil would pitch to Andy. Before long, he was learning how to use the pitch in games; sometimes, he would throw the ball toward a right-handed hitter, and have the ball drop in over the heart of the plate as the hitter's knees buckled, thinking a fastball was coming. At other times, he would start it outside to a lefty hitter, dropping it in on the outside corner for strike three. There would be games that first year Phil played on the team that he couldn't command that curve, and threw fifty-five-foot breakers that bounced in front of home plate and had DeVillers scrambling. Luckily, he had that fastball to fall back on, a pitch hitter's had trouble catching up to even on Phil's slowest day.

There was much to pitching beyond being on the mound that Phil had to learn, and his teammates took him under their collective wing to teach him. DeVillers told him to keep his pitching arm covered by a jacket while his team was at bat, or if he was on base, even on the warmest North Simcoe summer nights. His cousins taught him to play long toss in the outfield if his arm felt a little sore or tight. Hal Crippin had him jogging up and down the long Main Street hill in between games to strengthen his legs.

Penetanguishene finished first in the North Simcoe League that year, but failed to advance in the final against a powerful Barrie outfit, led by Phil's old rival Archie Thompson. But the town - and the league - had begun to take notice of the Rangers' hotshot new pitcher, who was routinely striking out a dozen or more batters a game. Phil's status in town grew even more, and the Rangers began attracting standing-room only crowds. When Phil walked downtown during the week, shoppers and store owners alike would call out, "great game last week, Babe!" or "go get 'em on Saturday!" as he passed by.

DeVillers and Hal Crippin were the heart of the team. Phil fit right in between them in the heart of the Rangers' batting order. The Bald brothers, who anchored the right side of the Penetanguishene infield, were on-base specialists at the top of the order. Chuck Sheppard rounded out the infield at 3rd, while Dan McCuaig, Joe Hale, Gerry Barbour, Peg Spearn, and Cy Richardson shared duties in the outfield. Bobby Crippin and Andy Vaillancourt were subs who could fill in at several positions; Bobby was a clutch pinch hitter, while Andy was a valuable late-inning pinch runner.

Phil learned a lot that year, and with much of the '33 team set to return the following year, optimism ran high along the shores of Penetang Bay as the March snows melted, the days grew longer, and baseball season was on the horizon.

Jack

In many ways, 1934 was a landmark year. Hitler consolidated his power with the Night of the Long Knives, inching the world closer to war. In the States, the FBI led widely publicized and ultimately successful ends to the crime sprees of John Dillinger, Bonnie and Clyde, Pretty Boy Floyd, and Baby Face Nelson.

As the Depression tightened its grip on the world economy, a new house cost just under $6000 on average, a gallon of gas 20 cents, a new truck about $650, and the best steak sold for 22 cents a pound. Drought in the middle of North America turned the prairie provinces and midwest states into a dustbowl, and unemployment bottomed out at 22%. There was a general feeling of hopelessness as governments were slow to enact relief measures, while politicians were certain that a return to prosperity was just around the corner.

The onset of the Depression brought a great demand for inexpensive forms of entertainment, and Stirling Park more than helped to fill that bill.

The guys in the East End had formed the core of the team several years earlier and played in tournaments all over the southwest of the province, travelling to those places in an old truck which Taylor's Flour Mill had loaned them for the occasion. It was not the most stylish of rides, but Boomer said, "it got us to where we were going."

Stirling Park hosted its fair share of tournaments and exhibition games, too. It was handy for people from that part of town, as well as the small farming hamlets that surrounded Chatham.

Boomer's brothers Len and Carl and a group of other players from their neighbourhood formed the first East End team. They were joined by King Terrell, a unique left-handed 3rd baseman and pitcher. Ross Talbot could play several infield positions and could pitch as well. There was speed aplenty on that first team in the form of outfielders Willy Saganosh, Cliff Olbey, and Guoy Ladd. It was a team that could beat you with its pitching, speed, and defence. Word spread quickly about the strong team in a tucked away corner of Chatham; a team from Detroit even challenged them to a game after the regular baseball season had ended. Several members of the Tigers were on this squad, looking to stay in shape and pick up a few bucks in the off-season. When the Detroit Manager found out he was playing a team full of blacks, he pulled his team off the field and threatened to call the game. He took one look at Saganosh, who was from the nearby Walpole Island reservation, and asked who that was. When told Willy's ancestry, the Manager said the whole Chatham team better become Indian in a hurry, or his team would not take the field.

So, they called themselves the Chatham Indians for a day, and played the game.

But for the rest of the time, they were known as the Chatham Coloured All Stars. They were an easy team to identify from a distance, because unlike the other teams in town who had sponsors who outfitted them in matching uniforms, the All Stars wore a collection of mismatched tops, pants, and socks. And from what Boomer told me, they did not mind the "coloured" part of their team name; it reminded the players of who they were, and where they were from.

Word of the Stars' success had spread far and wide, and the executives who ran the City League decided to invite the team to join their loop for the 1933 season. Maybe they thought the addition of the Stirling Park team would increase attendance; what they had not counted on was the team winning the league title over a couple of clubs stocked with veteran players.

It was late one February night, when I received a phone call well after 10 pm. It was Archie Stirling. He had called to inform me he had just gotten a telegram from the Ontario Baseball Association informing him that after having been nominated as convenor for Southwestern Ontario at the OBA's annual meeting in Toronto a few weeks earlier, he had successfully been voted into the position. "I will now have final say over all matters relating to amateur baseball in Kent County, Windsor-Essex, London, and Lambton County," he told me. His influence over baseball matters in the area had always been significant; now he would become an even bigger player in the game on a provincial level.

"And what grand changes will you make?" I asked, not expecting much from him in his first year.

"We plan to hit the ground running," Archie responded. "And I would like to invite you to a meeting at my store after the close of business next Monday."

"Sounds interesting, Arch," I replied, reaching for my pen and notebook. "Any hints as to what's coming?"

"Monday night is when you will find out," he answered, and then promptly hung up.

I was intrigued. There had been talk for some time for a Southwest super league with entries from Chatham, Sarnia, Windsor, London, and a few places in between, but that seemed like a longshot in those tough economic times. The Chatham City League had become very popular in town, with teams playing in front of huge crowds at Athletic Park. Maybe Archie had something in store for it. There was an air of mystery as well as excitement in his voice. He had something big in mind.

⚾ ⚾ ⚾

Jim Shaw of Port McNicoll - Fifty Years in Baseball
Special to the Toronto Telegram

Jim Shaw is well known in Toronto, and will be remembered as the Toronto Maple Leafs' Baseball Club's most famous lucky mascot in their drive for the International League pennant in the summer of 1926.

He first started his baseball career in Kemble, Ont., but at the age of 19 went west, and played with Portage La Prairie, Fort Francis, Rat Portage, and Qu'Appelle. In 1919, he moved to Port McNicoll, where he managed the C.N.R. Elevator team to a championship in their first year of organized baseball. Since then, Mr Shaw has managed great ball clubs, from Midland, Victoria Harbour, and now Penetang.

Dan Howley, then Manager of the Leafs, met Shaw on a fishing trip to Port McNicoll. Dan and Jim became great friends, and the Leafs' mentor invited Shaw to Toronto. The Leafs were in a slump at the time, but on the very day that Shaw appeared on the bench, the Toronto club took a double-header from Baltimore, then went on to win 14 straight games and the pennant. Howley always maintained that the presence of Shaw in the dugout meant victory.

⚾ ⚾ ⚾

Merv

After making the playoffs but losing the title series to Barrie, there was considerable enthusiasm about the Rangers' '33 season, and plenty of optimism about the upcoming one. But there was a nagging sense among folks who knew their baseball that the team, which just came up short of a title, was out-managed throughout the year. A.J. Fitzgerald, who ran the Spencer foundry for owner J.T. Payette, had managed the team going back to their softball days, assisted by one of his fellow employees. He was very organized and treated the players well, but there was a general feeling that the Rangers were lacking in fundamentals, made a fair number of mental errors (throwing to the wrong base, forgetting how many outs there were), and they tended to play a very conservative game on offence. It was automatic that when Penetang got the leadoff hitter on, the next batter - no matter where he hit in the lineup - was expected to bunt that runner over. A.J was not fond of the stolen base or the hit-and-run. And there were a number of one-run losses suffered by the Rangers that year that may have turned if he had been willing to roll the dice a bit. There were also whispers that perhaps he was not the best mentor for the talented but sometimes temperamental Phil Marchildon, a phenom with exceptional talent whose wildness in terms of balls, strikes, and emotions may have cost the team a game or two along the way. A feeling was also present that Phil wouldn't be a Ranger forever; player mobility was quite common in those days, with teams from bigger centres and higher leagues regularly plucking the top talent from small towns. A change was needed, so it was felt.

I was invited by several businessmen who helped sponsor the club to join a delegation to approach Payette to convince him to make a change. J.T. was an expert horseman, and was recognized as one of the leaders in harness racing in the province, but he knew when he was out of his element. "Boys," he told us after he had presented our plan, feet up on his desk in his office at the foundry, a cigar clamped into the corner of his mouth, "I inherited this foundry from my uncle. I know nothing about the cast-iron business, to tell the truth. I own several other enterprises in town which I can say much the same about. But here's one thing I know - people. I know how to hire the right people to run my businesses. And if this fellow you're telling me about knows how to run a ball team, then you have my blessing to install him as manager and bring a championship to this town."

"This fellow," was Jim Shaw, legendary local baseball man. From Grey County, Jim supervised the construction of grain elevators all around the Lake Huron and Georgian Bay shoreline as wheat exports from the Canadian and American midwest had exploded in the late 1800s and early 1900s. He seemed to take his ball glove with him everywhere he went, and played on a number of championship teams in his travels. By 1919, he had told me, he was tired of moving around from project to project, and settled with his family in Port McNicoll, the next town over from Midland, to run the CPR grain handling port there. He brought excellent organizational and management skills to the Port McNicoll elevators, which quickly became one of the most efficient and productive handlers of grain on the Great Lakes. Under Shaw's supervision, several thousand railroad cars each fall and winter would be filled with prairie wheat at the Port McNicoll elevators, which had received their bounty from heavily laden ships that loaded up at the top of Superior. The cars would trundle over the Hogg's Bay trestle, a wooden structure that spanned over 2000 feet, where they would connect with the main rail lines to eastern Canada and the U.S. In his spare time, Shaw organized and coached baseball; the Port McNicoll CPR team won a Georgian Bay title in his first year with them, and he oversaw the construction of the first curling rink in town. With his work ethic, eye for detail, and extensive baseball background, the sexagenarian Shaw was the natural choice to take over the Rangers and try to help them get over the top. And maybe he could be a calming influence over Phil, and get the best out of him.

⚾ ⚾ ⚾

Jack

It was after eight o'clock on the appointed Monday as I approached Archie's store. He ran a drug and confectionary store which served people over much of the southern half of the city, including the East End. The lights on the outside of the store were out, but lights and a few bodies could be seen on the inside.

Archie had made a makeshift meeting room in the middle of his store. Shelves of groceries had been pushed to the side, and all manner of stools and chairs were neatly spread in rows throughout the room. A fire roared in the pot-bellied wood stove in the corner, where many locals would sit and discuss the political and sports matters of the day during business hours.

The room was about half full, but it took me only a few seconds to realize that other than Archie and myself, the rest of the individuals present were connected to the All Stars. I was beginning to have a hunch about what Arch was up to.

Hap Parker had managed the team for several years, and he eagerly pumped my hand as I greeted him. "I don't know what old Arch is up to," he said, "but he told us it was something big. Told me to get the whole team here, said he was inviting you, too."

As the room slowly filled up, Archie stood at the front of the assembled group and asked for their attention.

Archie had been known as "Mr Baseball" in Chatham as far back as this reporter could remember. In the 1920s, he had fund-raised to build the city its first playground. He also founded the minor baseball league in town, and expanded amateur ball to other communities in the area. You name a community recreation event, league, or facility in town, and Archie spearheaded just about all of them. Archie was known as a strong supporter of the All Stars in particular. When they needed bats, balls, and catcher's gear, he either dipped into his own pocket or that of a network of contacts in the community to pay for it. If a fellow on the team needed a new pair of cleats, a pair would often be waiting for him before the next game or practice. He did not do it for the attention; many of his donations came anonymously, but most everyone knew it was Archie. He cheered for all Chatham teams, but he had a special rooting interest in the All Stars.

"Fellas," he began, "you all know I'm a big supporter of your team. Your skills are as good as any other team in this part of the province. And you also may know that recently I was appointed convenor by the Ontario Baseball Association for this area. I have the final say in all matters regarding amateur ball. And as such, I think it's time for us folks in Chatham to help bring baseball in Ontario into the modern world. Major League Baseball continues to bar black baseball players, even though many have more than held their own in exhibition games against white big leaguers. But here in Canada, while we're not perfect, our views about freedom and equality are more - enlightened, let's say. Everyone in our community - black and white - is justifiably proud of the terminus of the Underground Railroad being here in Kent County. There are pockets in this country just like ours, where there is some very high-quality ball being played by black teams. Our country is just so vast, you may not have heard about it. Black baseball has led something of a parallel existence alongside white ball in Canada. In my view, it's high time that ended. Change is coming to Major League Baseball. More and more owners are viewing the Negro Leagues as a potential pool of talent, even though Commissioner Landis is against it. Landis won't last forever, and we can do something here in Chatham to speed the whole process up."

Archie paused to clear his throat and let the weight of his words settle on the room.

"So, as convenor for the Southwest region of the Ontario Baseball Association," he continued, "I have decided that the Chatham City League, for the 1934 season, will have four teams. Not only will that make for a balanced schedule after we were down to three teams last season, it will ensure that the city will be represented in the provincial playdowns by the best team. The winner of the City League will go on to compete in the OBA Intermediate B playoffs, a tournament that will feature the top teams in Ontario. For the upcoming season, the teams will be…..Kent Bridge, R.G. Duns, Bragg's Insurance, and…the team from Stirling Park, the Chatham Coloured All Stars. Let's make that the Chatham All Stars. The 'Coloured' part, in my opinion, is not necessary.'"

Archie's announcement was greeted by a unanimous roar from the players and team officials that were assembled. Hats flew in the air, feet were stomped, and everyone took turns shaking hands and hugging at the news. A number of players even came over to shake my hand. Hap Parker looked like he was about to burst at the news. "Ain't that beautiful," he exclaimed, using his favourite phrase, one that would come to demonstrate so much about his character and outlook on life. Archie had done a good job of keeping his intentions under wraps when he became convenor, and his first move was a bold one, one that would be greeted with joy by the East End. The All Stars had the chance to play against the best teams in the province if they could successfully defend their City League title.

Hap took over the floor from Archie for a few words with his players. "Men, this is a brand-new day," he started. "You might not be welcome in the big leagues just yet, but thanks to Archie here, that day is comin'. We have a chance to make history, fellas. I have to be honest - I thought this day might never, ever come. But it's here. And ain't that beautiful," he added, beaming.

"It sure is, Hap!" shouted several from the audience.
"We have a huge challenge ahead of us, just the same. The city teams play tough, aggressive baseball, and so will we - if we want to compete with them. We're goin' to have to add some players, guys. Our schedule just got a lot longer, and we need a bigger roster. Guys have to work, guys get hurt - it's goin' to be hard to put the same lineup out on the field every game. And there's some high-level competition in this league, in this province, so we have to bring in high-caliber players."

No one was exactly certain what that meant, but it was fairly obvious that Hap intended to recruit some of the best black players in the area to augment the Stars' roster.

"In my mind, we have work to do," Hap continued. "We have to play good, solid fundamental baseball this year. There's a lot of good ball bein' played across Ontario. We have to pitch, hit, and field well, run the bases intelligently, move runners up, hit the cut off man, and take that extra base when we need to. We absolutely can't beat ourselves with mental mistakes out there. I've put the word out, and we're goin' to have at least three new players on the team that I should be up front and tell you about. We're bringin' in some guys from Windsor - Donny Tabron, a pitcher and shortstop, and Don Washington, a catcher. We're also addin' Flat Chase, a guy you all know about - one of the best hitters and pitchers anywhere."

Someone in the back of the room let out a low, long whistle. It broke the guys up. Flat Chase was a star, a local lad who it was said had a tryout with the Detroit Stars of the Negro National League a few years earlier, and was now a legend in southwestern Ontario. Hap had been busy, apparently.

"We have 18 league games, as well as exhibition games, tournaments, and hopefully city then provincial playoffs," Hap went on. "It's going to be a challengin' and busy year, but I think we have a group of guys that can meet that challenge. The teams we play this year already know how good we are, and they'll have somethin' to prove against us. They'll play hard, the crowds when we play at Athletic Park will be rough on us, and I'm not sure we can count on the umpires to be consistently fair. But this is a day we've all dreamed of - to be accepted on equal terms. And we're not just representin' ourselves, you know - we have a whole community to represent. We have to play this game hard and fair, so that generations of players after us will continue to be treated as equals.

Before you go, there's one more thing," he continued. "You all are used to being treated in some places as second-class citizens, but I know in the past you've mostly played in front of friendly crowds. I can't guarantee that will be the case this year. In fact, if we're good enough to move on from the City League, some of the places we'll play, they'll be downright hostile. Maybe even here sometimes in Chatham. My question to all of you is how will you handle it? Will you let it affect your play? I can't tell you how to respond, except to warn you that it's comin'. You're going to be called every name in the book, especially when you walk into the other team's park and beat them. The only thing I'll say is to remember who you represent, and who and what you're playin' for. You guys have a chance to go farther than any Chatham team ever has before. Don't let anything get in your way." Hap took one last look around the room, then a glance at Archie, who gave him a knowing nod. "Ain't that beautiful?" Hap said.

The meeting broke up shortly afterward, with Hap promising to book time in the CVI gym for indoor workouts to get a heads up on the season. As the room cleared, Archie came over to where I was seated, toward the back of the room. I was just taking down the last few details in my notebook when he sat down beside me, and asked, "Well - what do you think?"

"That was a pretty dramatic debut, Arch," I replied.

"Really - it's time," he answered. "The best players in the big league are all in favour of having the best coloured players in the game take their rightful place and join them. Judge Landis can only hold back the tide for so long. If we can do our thing in our little corner of the world to help speed that up, I think that's the right thing to do."

"Couldn't agree with you more, Arch. But I do have a question."

"What's that?" he asked.

"Who's going to sponsor the All Stars? The three other teams in the league are all named after their sponsors, and have all their equipment and expenses paid for, with matching uniforms to boot. Who's going to do that for this team? Will you step up?"

"Ordinarily, I would," Archie said. "But as convenor now, that would represent a conflict of interest. But I have gone to bat, to use a baseball term, for this team often in the past. I have supplied them with gear from my own modest means, and I had some heavy convincing to do behind closed doors at last month's OBA meeting to get the executive to accept my plan for the All Stars. I have never sought the spotlight, Jack - you know that. I don't need my business' name on the backs of their jerseys. But I give my word that I will encourage my fellow businessmen in the community to come forward and help outfit this team. It may take something of a conglomerate of sponsors, and the Stars will probably have to play some exhibition games to add to their revenues, but this team will have support."

"They were already pretty good, but if Hap adds more players like Tabron, Washington, and Chase, they're going to be fun to watch," I observed, closing my notebook.

"Oh, I think you can count on that." answered Archie.

⚾ ⚾ ⚾

Merv

The one thing about baseball that Jim Shaw admittedly didn't know a lot about was pitching. He liked pitchers who worked quickly, threw strikes, and got a lot of groundball outs. Phil

Marchildon could dominate hitters, but not in the fashion Shaw preferred. Luckily, he had an ace in the hole.

Since settling in Port McNicoll, Shaw had taken advantage of a perk offered by his employer to make regular trips to Toronto to watch the highest level of baseball available to Canadians at that time, the old baseball Maple Leafs (they had the name before the hockey team) of the International League. When the Leafs were home for a weekend series, Shaw and his wife would often travel down to watch. He was such a frequent sight behind the Toronto dugout that he became friendly with the Leafs Manager, a colourful character by the name of Dan Howley.

A long-time minor-league catcher who had a brief turn in the bigs twenty years earlier, after his playing days Howley turned his hand to coaching and managing. When he was a coach with the Red Sox, Howley offered to take one of their star young players under his wing. The player was enormously talented, but was becoming a headache to his manager, regularly breaking curfew and many team rules. Howley offered to room with the gifted but troubled youngster in order to help curb his nighttime habits, but to no avail. Years later, he joked, "I roomed with his suitcase, that's about all I saw of him on the road." Convinced the young budding star would never mend his ways, the Red Sox eventually sold him to the Yankees. The player in question was Babe Ruth.

Howley later coached with the Tigers, becoming player-manager Ty Cobb's most trusted lieutenant. Cobb let Howley implement some of his innovative ideas and drills, one of which was to have batting practice pitchers throw their best and hardest stuff to hitters in pre-game practice. Under Howley's guidance, Detroit posted team batting averages above .300 in his first two seasons with the club. In 1923 Cobb asked Howley to take the helm of the Maple Leafs, widely regarded as one of the best franchises in all of minor league baseball. The Tigers and Leafs had signed a player development agreement, and Cobb wanted his best teacher to work with the organization's top prospects. Howley and Shaw became good friends and fishing buddies, with Howley often coming up to Port after the season had ended to fish for Georgian Bay walleye and whitefish.

Dan Howley was a larger than life character. Some newspapers called him "Dapper Dan," because of his fondness for fine clothes and an uncanny physical resemblance to a famous mobster of the day. Others called him "Howling Dan," because of his booming voice, and a willingness to tell a long-winded story, which would be punctuated by howls of his own laughter at the finish.

Howley was in between jobs as the 1934 season had progressed. After leading Toronto to a Little World Series title in 1926, he went on to lead the hapless St Louis Browns. After three mostly unsuccessful years (his team finished 50 games behind the '27 Murderers' Row Yankees), Dan moved on to run the equally mediocre Reds, who let him go after three seasons as well. His career managerial record was an uninspiring 397-524, a .431 winning percentage.

Despite Howley's lack of success as a big-league manager, he was well respected as a coach and teacher. And it was in the latter category that Jim Shaw was hoping his famous friend might hop on board another train headed north to help him with a talented but raw pitcher.

Despite his prodigious talent, Phil could be temperamental, and more than a little wild with his fastball. Jim Shaw recognized early on in his tenure that he had a player on his hands that could benefit from some big-league tutelage and mentoring, and sent a telegram to his fishing buddy. He offered to pay Howley's way up to Port McNicoll, give him free room and board at the Shaw home, and maybe sneak out from work early in the afternoon to get in some angling with him. Howley jumped at the offer.

When Howley arrived in mid-June, the North Simcoe League was just nicely underway, so there was still a considerable amount of the schedule remaining. At Rangers practices, Shaw would work with the infielders and outfielders, while Howley took Phil and Fred DeVillers aside to share with them his knowledge from over a quarter century in the game.

I had long been accepted as a presence (if not a member) of the team by this point. I kept score and statistics, and wrote up accounts of each Rangers game for the *Herald*. I was welcome to watch practices, and Howley didn't mind me eavesdropping on his lessons with Phil and Fred. He knew the fastball was Phil's bread-and-butter pitch, but he realized after watching only a few innings of him pitch that Phil relied on it too much. "It's true - the better his fastball, the more advantage a pitcher has," he told the Marchildon-DeVillers battery in one of their first sessions. "Old Johnny Evers used to say, 'the batter doesn't hit at the ball - the human eye can't manage that - he just swings at where he thinks it's going to be.'"

In his later years, Phil did admit that the success and celebrity status he achieved as a teenager went to his head. Phil could be difficult to coach sometimes - he didn't always accept advice from people who he didn't think matched his level of talent - but he was all ears in that first session with Howley.

"The faster the pitch," Dan continued, sounding at first like music to Phil's ears, "The less time a hitter has to determine its location. But that doesn't mean you should try to tear the mitt off of Fred here with every pitch," he said, starting to change his tune. "Good hitters can foul off bullets if you keep firing them down the middle of the plate," he went on, "because hitting is all about timing. And pitching is all about disrupting timing. Every pitch has to have a purpose - even a curve ball in the dirt. Your fastball has a bit of movement on it, but it could have much more. And you need to learn to take a bit off of some pitches - disrupting that timing - and move the ball around the strike zone. Keep the hitter guessing, keep him off balance. Now, I haven't been here in Penetang all that long, but I've seen some of the older pitchers in your league, and the more successful ones do just that. Maybe they don't throw as hard as they used to, but they've learned to control their fastball, move it around, take something off. And so perhaps they don't strike out a dozen guys a game anymore, but they still lead their team to a win because hitters just can't seem to make decent contact against them. Sure, in this league, there aren't a whole lot of hitters who can catch up to your fastball, but as you move up - and I know that you will - you will run into more hitters that can. You get to the big leagues, even the top minor leagues, and just about every guy in the lineup can get around on a fastball. It's the other pitches, and the other things that a successful pitcher does that adds some deception, and makes it hard for hitters to square you up."

All that Phil really had at that point was the fastball he gripped across the seams, and the curve Fred taught him. Howley got him to drop down with his curve to a spot closer to where he released his fastball, which was between three-quarters and sidearm (like a lot of pitchers of the day). Phil had been throwing the curve from a nearly overhand position, and while it had plenty of spin to throw hitters off, because it came from such a different spot (we used to call the overhand curve a "drop ball" back then), they knew it was coming. Dan told Phil, "When you learn how to throw your curve from the same arm slot as your fastball, it will really mess with the hitters. Sure, that big overhand curve is hard for hitters to follow because it breaks so much, but that can make it hard for umpires to see, too, and it can be hard to get called strikes on it as a result. Throw your curve from the same spot as your fastball, and maybe you give up some spin and break, but you create more deception. Hitters can't decide what the pitch is until it's too late."

Howley believed in the importance of developing a whole arsenal of pitches. Sure, Phil could get North Simcoe hitters out with a fastball and the odd curve, but thirty years in the game had taught Dan to recognize potential, and he saw in Phil a diamond in the rough who could catch the eye of a big-league scout or two with some polishing. He also didn't want Phil tiring himself out throwing mostly fastballs in an age when pitchers were expected to finish what they started. "Old Matty said it himself," he said, referring to former Giants star Christy Mathewson, "save yourself in those early innings. Don't wear yourself throwing too many fast ones. Learn some other pitches, learn to take a bit off some pitches, and then if you need to reach back in an important situation in the 8th or 9th inning with the game on the line, you're likely to have it. Instead of throwing a half-assed fastball to their cleanup hitter with the game on the line because you wore yourself out earlier in the game, you'll have a little something left when you need it."

Howling Dan wasn't afraid to share the knowledge he'd gained from four decades in baseball, most of it from the strategic vantage point of behind the plate, or the manager's seat in the dugout. Much of what he said was for Phil's benefit, but he didn't mind eavesdroppers. "In or spin," he said one day while relaxing on the Rangers' bench in the midst of a workout. "Most hitters have a weakness," he continued. "I'm not talking about the guys at the bottom of the order, guys who go up there just hoping to get on base. I'm talking the heavy hitters, sluggers, guys in the middle of the lineup, players who can change a game with one swing of the bat. The big fellas, the guys like Jimmie Foxx, they don't like the stuff on the inside of the plate. They can't get those big, long arms of theirs around on those pitches, can't get the barrel out on time. If you jam the hell out of them, you have a better chance of getting them out, or at least keeping the ball in the park. Now, Babe Ruth is a big guy, there's no doubt about that. But he has such quick hands, he can get around on those inside pitches and hit them a mile. He's just up there hoping for a fast one he can get around on, doesn't matter where it's pitched. What he hates is the breaking stuff. He knows he can't hit those far, but if you give him a steady diet of curve balls, he gets impatient. He can't pick up the spin and follow it, though, because he swings from his heels. There was this southpaw relief pitcher we had with the Tigers, name of Ed Wells, and old Babe just couldn't do anything against him. First time Ed ever faced the Babe, his catcher came out to the mound and said, 'what are you gonna throw him?' and Ed just said, 'nothin.' By that, he meant his big old roundhouse curve, a pitch the free swinging Babe could just never time up. You could look it up - Babe barely hit .200 off of Wells for his career, and never hit a homer against him. In or spin, boys," he concluded to what by now was a sizable rapt audience. "That's how you get the tough hitters out."

Howley taught Phil different grips on the ball to create more movement on his pitches, and tried to teach him a change up which was more like a palmball, wedged deep into his hand, but the early results were not encouraging, and sometimes when Fred waggled his fingers as Phil peered in for the sign - the standard signal for a change up - Phil would shake him off. "The old change takes a while to master, Babe," Dan advised after one game.

After two weeks of Howley's instruction, the lessons were beginning to take with Phil. But Dan had been around the game long enough to know this was a long-term project. After one session I observed, Phil and Dan sat on the bench at Beck's while the other players headed to their trucks and cars for a post-practice beer. I did some more eavesdropping. "Phil, no one has pinpoint control. You have to focus on throwing to a location, as opposed to a certain spot - keeping the ball close enough to a hitter's hands on the inside, or far enough on the outside part of the plate to avoid the barrel of his bat, all the while keeping close to the strike zone. Pitching isn't like aiming a gun and firing - it's more a matter of controlling yourself, coordinating your body, your concentration, and taking control of the situation. All pitchers get into jams - a bad ball four call here, a broken bat single there, a routine grounder booted by an infielder - and before you know it, the bases are loaded, not necessarily through any fault of yours. The successful pitchers know how to stay in control and get through it, or at least limit the damage. Trying harder doesn't always work, but sometimes trying smarter does."

By the end of June, it was time for Howley to get back on board the train at Port McNicoll and head back to Toronto, where he had some real estate investments to look after while he waited for an opportunity to get back into baseball. The North Simcoe League was reaching its halfway point, with the Rangers solidly in first place. Phil's stubbornness had melted away - at least temporarily - in the presence of a former big leaguer.

⚾ ⚾ ⚾

Jack

We were unaware of it at the time, but we learned in the playoffs that Penetang had a former big-league manager working with the team. "Must be nice," Boomer said upon hearing this.

I can tell you how many one-time coloured big leaguers were working with the All Stars: none. Because, of course, there were none.

Younger guys like Boomer were taught by Hap, his brother Percy (who coached 1st Base), and some of the older guys on the team. Since it was mostly a veteran team, Hap did not have to do a lot in terms of teaching the finer points of the game. But when it came to tips, Boomer was keen to soak up as much as he could.

Hap continually preached to Boomer the importance of being a student of the game. "The best hitters," he said one day after Boomer had taken his batting practice swings, "are as good from the neck up as they are from below there. Sure, they've got strength and hand-eye coordination to get good wood on the ball. But the best hitters think the game, too. Babe Ruth, Lou Gehrig, and Josh Gibson, they all keep a little notebook in their heads. They watch the pitcher from the time he takes his first warm up tosses on the mound until his last pitch. They watch his delivery, keep track of which pitches he throws in a particular count, if he tips his off speed stuff, and they file that information away. In between at bats, they just don't sit on the bench chit-chattin'; they're studyin' the whole time."

Boomer took that advice to heart. Installed almost from day one in the middle of the Stars' batting order, he had a chance to see a pitcher for a few hitters before his turn at the plate came up. Even if he was a hurler he had faced before, Boomer watched the opposing pitcher right up until the moment he stepped into the box. He studied the pitcher to see what was working for him, and what was not. By the time he came up for the third or fourth time in a game, Boomer had a thick notebook in his head, and before long even the veteran hitters were asking, "Hey, Boom, what's he got today?"

Hap liked small ball, getting runners on and then letting them be aggressive on the basepaths to put pressure on the opposition defence. Just about every player in the All Star lineup could run, but the approach he wanted hitters in the heart of the order to use like Flat and Boomer was to be patient. "Those guys ahead of you in the order," he preached to them one practice, "their job is to get on base, set the table for you two. I want them to go up there lookin' to get on base, then get into scorin' position. Maybe that means workin' the count, maybe it means just puttin' the ball in play, let their speed take care of the rest. But I don't want you guys doin' that. I want you layin' off borderline pitches. You're not going to get solid wood on those balls, and the contact you make isn't likely to go for extra bases."

As word got around the City League after only two or three games about Boomer's lethal bat, pitchers began working the edges of the strike zone more, and the inexperienced Boomer began to get impatient, and chased a lot of those offerings. So, one day in practice, Hap instructed his batting practice pitcher (brother Percy) to deliberately throw pitches off the plate to Boomer. "But I don't want you takin' those pitches, Boomer," he told his young hitter. "I want you swingin' at everything and anything." Boomer was confused at first, but he began to see the method of Hap's apparent madness. He wasn't making hard contact on many of those tosses, popping many of them up, or hitting a weak ground ball. After a couple of those sessions, Hap instructed Percy to start grooving the odd pitch, and it didn't take long for Boomer to notice the difference.

"The secret to hittin' is to get a good pitch," Hap said to Boomer, "and not be afraid to take a walk if you don't get one." Boomer took those lessons to heart. Up until when he had two strikes, Boomer was selective. By late June, he was leading the league in both hitting and walks.

But the lessons from Hap did not end there. He knew the talent he had on his hands, and how players like Boomer do not just develop overnight.

Very early in the season, the two had developed a routine to give Boomer extra work at 1st base. He showed promise, but was far from a finished product, so before a game or practice, Hap would close his barber shop early and meet Boomer at an empty Stirling Park. The two would work on fundamentals in a private tutoring session for close to an hour before any of the other players arrived for the workout.

It was something of a comical sight for those who were not aware of what was going on. Rather than stand at home plate and rap out ground ball after ground ball to Boomer, Hap was more likely to be standing just a few feet away from 1st Base toward the pitcher's mound, with a bucket of baseballs at his side. In one of their first meetings, Hap had Boomer work on catching the ball with more authority. "The baseball's not an egg, don't catch it like one," he admonished as he tossed ball after ball to Boomer. "You ain't gonna hurt it." Boomer had natural, soft hands, but he did tend to receive throws from his infielders like they were of the soft-boiled variety. "I want to hear that 'pop!' when you catch that ball," Hap admonished. "You know what? If I was a blind man, I would know a good pre-game infield just by the sound. The coach hits a grounder to short, yells out 'turn two!' then I hear 'pop!' as the 2nd baseman gets the relay, then another 'pop!' as the throw goes over to 1st."

Sometimes, when Hap was trying to demonstrate to Boomer a skill like setting up prior to taking a throw, he would get right over beside him and put his hands on his back or shoulders to maneuver him into position, the duo looking like mismatched dance partners. "Don't lean out with your chest," Hap would say. "That gets you off balance. Keep a good base of support, and try to keep your chest upright, so that if a ball goes into the dirt, you can move better to scoop it."

Week after week, these sessions would continue several times weekly. "Catch that ball with your face," Hap would encourage Boomer. "Get your head right in behind your glove, I call that catchin' it with your face," which was Hap's way of telling Boomer to look that ball right into his glove. Hap would slowly expand the distance between himself and Boomer as he continued tossing balls at him. If Boomer lapsed back into his old ways, Hap would yell out, "remember to catch it with your face! Don't be afraid of that old ball, you ain't that pretty!" An unaware passerby might have been tempted to stop in at the park to see what was going on. Or perhaps not.

What Hap was teaching Boomer tended to be little things, but they all added up. "Late in a game and we're ahead of a run, you catch that ball like you mean it on a close play, that ball goes pop! and that might get us an out. The ump is watching the bag and listenin' for that ball hit your glove. You reach out and catch that ball with your face, the ump can't help but hear that, and maybe we get that call. You do that on close plays, and maybe we get a couple of calls a week. That adds up to outs, which means you're savin' us runs." Hap was teaching Boomer the intricacies of selling a close play to the umpire, and by mid-season he had all but mastered the art.

Boomer told me that after one game when he'd had an uncharacteristically rough night at the plate, Hap said to him, "One thing I've learned over the years is that the best hitters have the shortest memories."
Boomer gave him a puzzled look.

"By that," Hap went on, "I mean that baseball is a game of failure, but it's those failures that seem to stick in most hitters' heads. You can go 0-4, work the count in two of those at bats, then hit two balls hard right at guys. You did everything right, but have nothin' to show for it. Now, weak hitters go into the next game thinkin' about that, and they're often out before their first trip to the plate. But good hitters wipe that from their memories, and they go into the next game thinkin', 'I know I can hit anything the pitcher throws at me.' When there are runners on base and the game is on the line, good hitters want to be up there in the box. They want the game ridin' on them. They know that as long as they stay patient, and hunt the pitch they know they can hit, good things are likely to happen. You hit that ball hard, you're going to win. Good hitters, even if they've gone 0-3, if the game is close when they come up the fourth time, they're not thinkin', 'oh my goodness, I can't hit that guy.' They're sayin', 'just try and throw a pitch by me, see what happens.' Ain't that beautiful?!"

⚾ ⚾ ⚾

North Simcoe League Meeting Stormy Session - Umpires Warned
July 14, 1934
Midland Free Press

The Special Meeting of the North Simcoe Baseball League held in Orillia Tuesday evening was a regular flare-up between

Barrie and Penetang representatives. While Barrie claimed that they were entitled to the game played in that town on June 29th, it was awarded to Penetang by Umpire Madden as a result of "deliberate stalling" by the County Town team. After considerable wrangling, President Roth pointed out that the league representatives had voiced their unanimous intention, at a previous meeting, to abide by the umpire's decision, and that was a time to show their good faith . Further, no official protest within the stipulated time had been entered by Barrie, and the umpire's decision was therefore adhered to.

At that same meeting, a by-law was passed which calls for automatic dismissal of any umpire who is reported to the league by any two teams in the group.

A Toronto man, who has both played ball and officiated in that city the last two or three years, stood behind the screen at a recent North Simcoe game with this writer.

He said that if Hedger (the man behind the plate that day) is an efficient umpire, King Tut is a modern high-class hockey player.

Tempers Flare in Leafs' Double Header Sweep
Toronto Globe
August 14, 1934

The high-flying Toronto Maple Leafs swept a pair of International League games from Reading yesterday, but emotions ran high.

Upon being called out on a close play, Leafs 3rd Baseman Bill Mullen jumped to his feet and struck Umpire Crooke in the stomach, earning an ejection. Later in that same game, Toronto hurler Lefty Faulkner took exception to a called ball four which walked in a run, rushing to the plate, knocking Crooke to the ground. The two wrestled without interference for some time. Mullen contented himself with jolting Crooke in the solar plexus region, but Faulkner was not so bashful, not only upending him with a solid crack to the chin but climbing all over his carcass in most artistic fashion after having done so.

3rd Inning

Rangers go on a memorable road trip; tensions rise in All Stars' City League games; both teams clinch their respective league pennants.

No Roads? No Problem. Local Sportsman Comes to the Rescue
By Charlie Paradis/Penetanguishene Herald
With files from Mervyn Dickey
August 28th, 1934

The prosperous logging, shipping, and railway community of Parry Sound is ready to flex its muscles and let the province know that they won't take a back seat to any other town when it comes to sports.

The Seguin River which flows through town and empties into Georgian Bay has produced many a good stickhandler on the ice. Now, they're eager to take on their baseball neighbours to the south, and after sending an invitation to all North Simcoe nines to travel north to play on the eastern shores of Georgian Bay, the Penetang Spencer Foundry Rangers have decided to take the Shamrocks up on their offer.

One of the drawbacks to travelling to Parry Sound is the lack of accessible roadways. The main gravel road heading north to the town in the heart of the Canadian Shield could be best described as a cart path. Motoring on it is not for the faint of heart.

As a result, the other teams in the league declined Parry Sound's offer. Mr J.T. Payette, owner of Spencer Foundry, and one of the province's foremost horsemen, has offered the services of his yacht Vacuna to ferry the team and a small collection of fans up the Georgian Bay coast.

Merv

The loggers and railway workers of Parry Sound wanted a game, and I was invited along for the ride. Travel to the Georgian Bay port was as difficult as it was expensive, which was mainly accessible only by water or train in those days. They wanted the Rangers to come up for a game on Labour Day weekend. Phil was already a top attraction around the province, and Shaw had to deal with a plethora of invitations to exhibition games and tournaments. The good baseball folks of Parry Sound determined that Phil would bring in enough of a gate to help the town ball team balance their books for the season. With Midland and Barrie engaged in a playoff series to determine who would meet Penetanguishene in the North Simcoe final, it was a good opportunity for Shaw to keep his team sharp. It was to be a memorable day, not necessarily for the baseball.

When Shaw announced the contest at the end of a late August practice, some of the players blanched at the thought of going up to the eastern Georgian Bay town on a holiday weekend. Even during the Depression, Parry Sound was doing well as an important rail, lumber, and shipping location. Getting there was not an easy feat, though. Not long after the end of World War II, drivers from Toronto could zoom up to cottages, camps, hotels, and other weekend destinations via the brand-new multi-lane Highway 400, and Highway 69, built not long after in the ambitious Trans Canada era of the 1950s. But in the '30s, getting to Parry Sound by car was an arduous process over very ramshackle roads, and no one was anxious to put their vehicle through what passed for that route.

Enter J.T - who everyone called Jake - Payette.

Jake's career as a harness racing owner - one of his many side interests - had taken off. In those days, just about every small town had a track - even Penetang had one (built and owned by Jake) at the east end of town. The track is long gone in favour of a residential development, but it lives on in street names like Sulky Drive and Bridle Road. And as his career flourished, so did his wallet. Jake was already known as one of the top breeders in the province, and his star pacer, Cream O'Tartar, was undefeated on Ontario tracks. The Dominion Day race card which he held in honour of Canada's birthday every July 1st attracted some of the top equine talent in the eastern half of the country.

Jake had used some of his new-found wealth to add onto the beautiful home he shared with his wife on Robert St, across from St Ann's. He also installed extra seating at this track to hold the over capacity crowds, bought himself shiny new cars, and a new 40ft sailboat, complete with crew, that he christened the *Vacuna*.

Long before the first Europeans came to the area, lived the Wendat (called Hurons by the French). The term Wendat, in their language, meant "peninsula dwellers," and they called their land Wendakay - the peninsula. For centuries, the Wendat had lived a life of farming, fishing, and trading with nomadic tribes to the north for centuries before the arrival of the first Europeans. The Wendat had many gods to explain how the natural world functioned; the most feared and respected was a god of war by the name of Kitchikewana. He was taller than a white pine, and stronger than the north winds that blew in off the Bay. Kitchi was a fierce warrior who protected his people from invading enemies, and Wendat warriors always offered a prayer and a small gift of tobacco to him before a battle.

Kitchikewana had a temper that would explode during battle, shielding his warriors from harm. During peaceful times, however, he had difficulty turning it down, and he could be dangerous for other gods to be around. The gods got together and decided that maybe a wife would be a calming influence on the powerful warrior. They assembled the most intelligent, beautiful, and single women from the land of the Wendat, and invited Kitchi to meet them at a council fire. Kitchi was smitten at once with a lovely young woman named Wanakita, who was unaware as to why she had been invited. Kitchikewana proposed marriage at once, but Wanakita refused, saying that she had promised to marry a young man from her village.

Kitchikewana's legendary temper boiled over immediately. He took one giant hand and scratched his fingers into the ground, creating Penetang, Midland, Hogg's, Sturgeon, and Matchedash Bays. He then took the tons of dirt and rock he had scooped up and threw it to the north, creating the 30 000 Islands. When he was finished, Kitchi waded into the waters off the Penetanguishene peninsula. He was so exhausted and despondent after his rejection that he laid down in the water, fell into a deep sleep of depression, and died soon later of a broken heart. The animals of the Bay area covered his body with dirt, making it look like a huge mound rising out of the water. The island containing his body became known as Giant's Tomb, which we would pass on our way to Parry Sound.

Most of the guys on the team thought the game would be a laugher. Having finished first once again at the end of the North Simcoe schedule, Shaw wanted to keep the team sharp without taxing them too much while they awaited the league final. An exhibition game would be a bit of a break; no one thought the Parry Sounders would offer much competition. The post-game party on board Jake's yacht was the part of the day that most of the team (and the small coterie of friends and fans who were invited to accompany the team) were looking forward to the most.

We had an 8 am departure scheduled from the town dock. I headed down the Main St hill at about 7:30, and was at the wharf shortly after. The Penetang dock was already bustling, full of boaters, fishermen, and cottagers off for one last long weekend at their vacation paradises. The train station was right on the wharf, and from May to September the arriving CNR train let out car loads of vacationers twice daily.

As I approached the *Vacuna*, I was greeted by the sight of dozens of cases of beer, stacked one on top of the other, ready to be loaded for the after-game festivities. Jake's crew and several volunteers were in the process of loading them below decks. The Rangers equipment bag, full of bats, balls, and catcher's gear, sat lonely and forgotten on the dock. I grabbed it and slung it over my shoulder before I boarded, lest it be left behind while the team sailed out into the Bay.

We were moments from departing when a loud car horn caught everyone's attention. It was Jake himself, in his brand-new Marmon Red Devil motor car. He had come to see us off. Nattily attired (as usual) in a three-piece suit, Jake climbed out of another of his latest toys to wish the team well. He strode past the remaining tower of beer cases as if they weren't even there. Jake stood beside the foot of the gangplank of the ship and briefly chatted with Jimmy Bald and Hal Crippin. Then he yelled out, ever mindful of his business empire, "Do us proud today, you Foundrymen!" Pressing business matters, he said, would keep him in town for the weekend (in the face of declining orders, the foundry had recently cut back from two shifts to one). Otherwise, Jake - who loved a party and was as big a supporter of the Rangers as anyone - would have likely come along for the cruise.

With that, Jake was about to return to his waiting Red Devil, when he stopped to address the crew, who were loading the last few cases. "No booze for you," he said loudly, waving a finger at the trio. "You take good care of my new toy. I paid one helluva lot of money for her. I expect her back by daybreak with nary a scratch on her. You get that?!" The crew solemnly nodded. Satisfied his orders would be followed, he spun on his heels and headed back to the car, while the crew readied to release the lines and head out.

Not many people would have loaned their brand-new yacht to a bunch of ball players, and in hindsight, maybe it wasn't the best decision Jake ever made. But Jake liked to live large, loved to be the life of the party. Everyone had a good time when Jake Payette was around.

⚾ ⚾ ⚾

Leaders of City Baseball League Lose Last Evening
Score Was 5-2 - Considerable Excitement After the Game but no Damage Was Occasioned
By Jack Calder
Chatham Daily News Staff

The R.G. Duns handed the Chatham Stars their first setback of the 1934 city baseball league season last evening by romping home on top of a 5-2 score, in a game at Stirling Park.

Archie Stirling Jr, young southpaw was on the mound for the Duns, although he was in difficulty on one or two occasions he pitched himself out on top of the ground. On one occasion the

Stars loaded the bases with one man away, and Archie came through with a couple of strike outs to retire the side.

Ross Talbot started on the mound for the Stars but retired in favour of Chase during the fourth frame. A total of seven hits were collected off of the Stars hurlers, but errors on the part of their mates proved costly.

There was considerable excitement just after the game ended and it looked for a few moments as though there would be a near riot. It started on one of the bleachers when two fans, each an ardent supporter of the respective teams, got into an altercation which resulted in one of them being shoved off the stands. Several of the other fans showed a willingness to "mix" but there was no damage. As the players were walking off the diamond, some of them got into an argument, and it looked as though there would be a general melee but peace was restored with no damage occasioned.

Jack

Yes, in case you are wondering - that was Archie's son Archie Jr on the mound for Dun's. But Sr's loyalty to the Stars was without question. Mrs Sterling always cheered for her sons, while Archie just hoped his boys would do well - just not at the Stars' expense.

Look, I think it's safe to say that the All Stars were not necessarily welcome by all teams and fans in the Chatham City League. There was an underlying tension to every one of their league games that always seemed to be just a spark away from igniting. Games against the Stars were rarely friendly competitions. The opposition had no trouble getting motivated to play the defending league champs.

When the Stars played, you could count on pitches against them that were high and tight, spikes would be up on any close play on the bases, and an air of intimidation would be present throughout the game. And the Stars rarely failed to respond. They had to in order to gain a measure of respect.

Flat Chase, who pitched much of the regular season until his arm started to get sore in August, was an imposing presence on the mound. He was tall and intense-looking, and would have a look of contempt on his face as each batter stepped into the box. He was never afraid to pitch inside; there were a lot of hitters in the league who did not enjoy facing him.

The Stars gave no quarter on the playing field. They went into 2nd hard on double plays, applied tags hard to baserunners, looked to bowl the catcher over on close plays at the plate, and drove the other teams to distraction with their daring on the base paths. "Take the extra base" must have been the team motto. It did not matter the play or the situation - several times a Stars runner on 2nd scored on a ground out, or tagged up at 3rd and raced for home on a shallow fly ball. Hap was reluctant to bunt very often, because every player seemed to have the green light on the bases, but he loved a good old squeeze play with a runner on 3rd. Sometime it would be a safety squeeze, where the runner did not break from 3rd until he saw the bunted ball roll up the 1st base line, other times it would be a straight up suicide squeeze, where the runner was on the move as the pitcher went into his windup. Hap used the squeeze with a runner on 3rd sparingly, but he had done it enough to make the opposition guard against it. The All Stars, all in all, were a tough team to play against, and many of the white players in the City League joked that they would rather play with the Stars than against them.

Before they joined the City League, the Stars had played mostly in front of friendly crowds, because all they could play - for the most part - were other black teams and their fans, with the occasional white audience. But now that they were playing white teams both in and out of Chatham, the crowds could sometimes be hostile. At first, the insults and racial taunts were unsettling to the Stars, but they learned that responding would often only invite more of it. As Boomer said, in cases like that the best thing to do was to get in, play the game, collect their share of the gate, then get the hell out.

I am sure that one of the many reasons Archie Stirling championed the cause of the Stars in City League play was because he knew they would be an attraction. And they certainly were. The other teams in the league were used to drawing a collection of family, friends, and fans that added up to about a hundred people per game; by the end of June, that had gone up to several hundred, with crowds topping a thousand the odd time during the summer. Fans of colour from the outlying farming communities like North Buxton flocked to Stars' games at Stirling Park.

But with those increased crowds came a more charged-up atmosphere, and things finally boiled over late in the season one night in a battle for first place with Kent Bridge.

⚾ ⚾ ⚾

Merv

With lines cast off, the *Vacuna* began a slow jog under the power of the ship's engine until we left Penetanguishene harbour for the open waters of Georgian Bay, when her sails would be unfurled as we cruised north along the eastern shore in the direction of Parry Sound.

I settled in on a deck chair beside outfielder Danny McCuaig, who already had his feet up on the teakwood rail. Soon after, Jimmy Bald joined us. It promised to be a beautiful day: a lovely sail on smooth morning Bay waters up to the Sound, a ball game, then a sunset cruise back to Penetang. What more could a fellow ask for?

Jake Payette had to have seen the pile of booze still to be loaded on the dock, but he appeared to take no notice of it. "Say, Jimmy," I asked my railing-mate, "what were you and Jake talking about before we left?"

"Oh, I just asked him if he didn't mind a little victory celebration after the game," replied Jimmy.

"And what did Jake say to that?"

"He said, 'go up and beat the pants off of those Parry Sound hicks, then enjoy the party on the way home, because this isn't the first booze cruise to push off from this dock, and it sure as hell won't be the last.'"

The *Vacuna* left the sheltered waters of Penetanguishene Bay, carefully swinging wide of those shifting sandbars that gave the town its name, and headed north into a slight breeze. The stretch of water between the mainland and nearby Beausoleil Island (named for its incredible sunsets) was called The Gap by locals, and the winds which funneled from the north down between those two points of land could be notoriously unpredictable.

But the waters that day were calm, and we passed through that section easily. As we left the protection of the mainland and approached Giant's Tomb, the crew began to loosen the sails. Soon, with the beer on ice and safely stored below, we were into the magnificent open waters of Georgian Bay, which was living up to its name - La Mer Douce (the peaceful sea) - originally given to it by French fur traders. Before long, we swung east toward the protected inside passage along the shoreline, gracefully gliding among the 30 000 islands Kitchikewana had flung far and wide there. "Kitchi could've been a pitcher. He must've had one hell of an arm," observed Jimmy.

We docked at Parry Sound an hour and a half later. A town similar to Penetanguishene in size, it too is a jumping off point for summer vacationers. Situated near the southern edge of the Canadian Shield, a partially exposed layer of precambrian rock pock-marked with countless lakes and pine forests covering almost a third of the country, Parry Sound is a picturesque little town. When we reached the ballpark, celebrations were already under way. A band was playing in a nearby bandshell. Booths selling all sorts of refreshments from hot dogs to cotton candy were serving hungry patrons. It was the end of summer, but there was a festive atmosphere.

Jim Shaw was already starting to keep an eye on Phil's workload. The previous season, Phil and Hal Crippin had shared the pitching about 65/35, but Hal had tossed only a few innings this season, as Shaw had decided early on that Phil was the Rangers' meal ticket. But the Parry Sounders likely had been clamouring to see this phenom Marchildon, whose legend was spreading across the province. Shaw started Hal Crippin on the mound and Phil at 3rd, with a plan to switch them after five innings to give the fans what they wanted.

The Parry Sound team put up a surprisingly good battle in the early innings. Their pitcher, a gangly fellow by the name of Campbell, held the Rangers to one run through five innings, and scored in the bottom of the 5th to knot the game at 1.

The Rangers broke the game open with a five-run sixth, and Phil came in to pitch in the bottom half of the inning to shut the door. The final score of 8-2 actually flattered the home team, as Shaw put his reserves in for the final three innings. Still, the local side had made a good impression, and the fans, having had a chance to see Phil work for a few innings, went home happy.

The Rangers repaired to a downtown Chinese food restaurant for a celebratory dinner before heading back to the boat. With all that beer waiting aboard the *Vacuna*, the players seemed to turn things up a notch in that extra frame in order to get the game over and the party started.

The day was running later than expected, but there was still plenty of time left to get out into the Bay and watch the setting sun paint a canvas of colours while we raised our bottles toward the western horizon and toasted the victory.

But there was one small problem: the crew. Unable to attend the game in order to stand watch over the *Vacuna* as she was tied to the Parry Sound wharf, the three men quickly became bored, and as the game went on and we went for a celebratory meal, they sought out a tavern that offered them a view of the harbour. When we returned, they were in no condition to sail the boat through the rocky waters of the sound after which the town took its name. True to Jake's word, they hadn't touched a drop of the team's supply; they had ventured into town to find their own.

Before we left that morning, a wag had joked that we should've all packed swimsuits in case the ship sunk and we all had to swim to shore, and everyone laughed. That didn't seem so funny now.

Jack

Like most games involving the All Stars, emotions ran high during the contest with Kent Bridge. In the bottom of the 9th inning of a tied game, Stars outfielder Cliff Olbey walked and stole 2nd. With one out, Boomer was at the plate, and he hit a flyball to the center fielder. It was not deeply hit, but Olbey was one of those guys who took Hap's word about taking the extra base to heart. He tagged up the moment the ball was hit, and was off for 3rd the moment it hit the fielder's glove. A strong throw to 3rd was made, but on a hop to the 3rd baseman, a fellow by the name of Millen. With a sliding Olbey likely distracting him, Millen was unable to handle the bounce, and it deflected off his glove and rolled away from the base. With the ball and Olbey arriving at the same moment, the two players got tangled up, with Millen soon sitting atop a prone Olbey. Millen made a very slow move to get up and go after the ball, most likely to keep Olbey from scoring, while one of the other Kent Bridge players retrieved the wayward throw. For any other team, an interference call would have been all but automatic, and Cliff would have been granted home. But no call was forthcoming, so Olbey took matters into his own hands, and even though he was giving up several inches and almost twenty pounds, pushed Millen off of him and raced home with the winning run.

Olbey's action, as you could imagine, set off a firestorm once he crossed the plate. The Kent Bridge manager came storming out of the dugout, yelling that Olbey had interfered with Millen (it was obvious to most that it was the opposite). He jawed back and forth with the home plate umpire for several moments before Hap came out to argue his team's cause - it wouldn't have been the first time an irate Manager had gotten an intimidated ump to overturn a call against the Stars. The Kent Bridge field boss became more and more agitated, and soon Millen and several other of his teammates had encircled the debate at home. Not long after that, both benches emptied, and skirmishes between fans started to break out in the stands. The season was only at its half-way point, but already the Stars had put up with so much - fielders blocking their way on the basepaths, 1st Basemen taking a short grab on the pocket of a Stars' runner who was attempting to steal, runners doing a full barrel roll at 2nd to take out the Stars shortstop who was making a double play relay - those sorts of things. Many games seemed like a powder keg that was ready to explode.

Just when the volcano of on-field emotions was about to erupt, Archie Stirling appeared from the stands. He was often at games, but you would not always know it, sitting quietly at the top of the bleachers behind home plate. Even though he was not the biggest of men, Archie somehow managed to work his way through the forest of players into the heart of the melee, and was able to diffuse the brawl that was about to erupt. He must have threatened lengthy suspensions for both sides to the respective managers if they could not get their players under control. But somehow the argument ended, the call stood, and the game was over, but not forgotten.

⚾ ⚾ ⚾

Merv

As we climbed aboard the *Vacuna* for the trip home, the smell of booze was unmistakable on the crew, and there were doubtful looks among the passengers.

As captain of the team, Bobby Crippin decided to say something to Charley Craig, the captain of the ship. One of the Rangers' loudest supporters, leather-lunged Charley was an experienced skipper, with many years of sailing the maze of islands that stretched along the Georgian Bay shoreline from the mouth of Penetanguishene Bay all the way up to Killarney. The two stood on the dock and had a fairly animated conversation that lasted about fifteen minutes. Charley must have convinced Bobby that he could all but sail the *Vacuna* home blindfolded, because at the end of their discussion, Bobby scampered up the gangplank and disappeared below deck while Charley cast off the lines and hurried up after him. I had my doubts, but soon we were motoring out of Parry Sound for the sometimes-unpredictable waters of the Bay. Daylight was slowly fading away, and now the chances of seeing the sunset were fading along with it.

We didn't get far.

In Parry Sound's rocky, island-dotted outer harbour, navigating a boat can be tricky at the best of times. Throw in approaching dusk and an inebriated crew, and you have a recipe for trouble.

We had been underway less than ten minutes, when we heard a loud "thunk!" under the *Vacuna*, and she came to a sudden halt. Jimmy and I had resumed our seats near the bow, and were almost pitched overboard. Handing his Captain's hat to the nearest bystander, Charley did a beautiful swan dive over the ship's railing into the murky water to inspect the damage. For a man who'd had a few, he could hold his breath for an astonishingly long time, and I was beginning to wonder if rescuers were going to have to jump in after him, when he resurfaced. Hands reached over the side of the boat to help haul him back in. "Boys, she's fine!" he announced. "No damage done, no planking stove in. She's just beached herself bow first on a giant shoal. You all get to the stern, I'll put her in reverse, pour the coal to her, and she'll just slide off like hot butter."

Unbelievably, Charley's plan to free the stranded *Vacuna* worked. We all moved to the stern, he put her into reverse full steam, and she slowly slid off the rock and back into the water. Charley received a thunderous cheer from us passengers, but Bobby, after conferring with his brother Hal and Jimmy Bald, decided enough was enough. It would only take a couple of hours, and even though the *Vacuna* left some paint in Parry Sound harbour, the crew should sober up and have her back before daylight. Charley initially balked at the plan, but three large ball players helped him change his mind.

With the ship anchored, and the crew safely below decks in their quarters sleeping it off, the party commenced full throttle. It was the last long weekend of the summer, and it was time to celebrate. The cases of beer, which had been on ice in the *Vacuna*'s galley, were attacked with gusto by thirsty, happy ballplayers, as well as myself and the fans who had made the trip with us. Darkness was now fully upon us, and it didn't take long before many broke into song. We sang songs we knew as kids. Some were from the movies. Some we'd never dare sing in front of our mothers.

It was probably the latter, which floated unimpeded on the damp night air into the town of Parry Sound and surrounding cottages which brought some visitors shortly after midnight. A small launch pulled up alongside the *Vacuna*, and a rope ladder was tossed over the side. Maybe some of the townsfolk wanted to join our singalong.

But these two imposing individuals were no townies seeking merriment. It was two of Parry Sound's finest. As Bobby and Jimmy helped them over the railing, there was a moment of instant recognition: it was Campbell, who had pitched his heart out a couple of hours earlier, along with shortstop Ketcheson, who had three hits. Except now they had exchanged ball uniforms for that of the local police detachment. They were not small individuals. And they weren't there to replay the events of the game.

Ketcheson did the talking. "Fellas, first of all - great game today, best of luck the rest of the season - look, I hate to break up the party, but we've had a lot of complaints from people in town who can hear your singing and carrying on. Sounds like some of the songs might be a little.... questionable. We think it's probably best if you weigh anchor and head for home."

"We can't, Constable," Bobby interjected.

"Why not?" asked Ketcheson with some irritation.

Bobby explained. The two police officers exchanged looks. Given the boat traffic Parry Sound sees in the summer, we probably were not the first yacht to present them with this dilemma. "Tell you what," offered Campbell. "You give your crew a few more hours to sober up, then haul anchor and be out of here before sunrise."

"We can do that," said Bobby.

They left after Bobby, Hal, and Jimmy agreed to keep the noise down. But after the cops left and the supply of beer continued to be chipped away, the party slowly returned to full volume. The players and fans went through the hit parade of 1934, as well as a stirring rendition of "God Save Our King," "The Maple Leaf Forever," and "O Canada." It was a holiday weekend, after all - the last one of the summer. When you put a bunch of ballplayers, their friends, and a newspaper reporter who was a proud member of his school choir together and sprinkle in a generous quantity of booze, reason tends to go out the window.

The continuing revelry brought about a return visit from our police friends at about 2 am. This time they weren't nearly as accommodating. "That's it, boys, time to call it a night and get out of here," said Campbell. By this time, Charley had woken up, and while he was still unsteady on his feet, he was ready to take command of the ship. "Officer, I am the Captain of this vessel," he said, "and we will make preparations to sail immediately."

"No, you won't," interrupted Bobby.

"Like hell I won't," replied Charley, staggering as he said it.

"You heard me," responded Bobby. "You're still too sloshed to get us home in one piece, and your crew - such as it is - is still passed out. You almost sunk us once. There's no way you'll get a second chance."

"But I got us off that blasted shoal that got in our way," argued Charley. "I've been sailing these waters since you were in short pants."

"And who got us on that shoal in the first place?" countered Bobby. Charley tried to protest further, but Bobby stopped him. "Jake said to bring this ship back without a scratch, Charley. When we meet him at the dock, should I tell him to have a look under the waterline?"

Defeated, Charley sighed, "All right. Just wake me before we get back to the wharf, so I can make things look good and bring her in." With that, he disappeared back below deck.

Jimmy had some experience piloting boats on the Bay. Not as much as Charley, maybe, but Jimmy wasn't a big drinker, and was in much better shape to take command of the ship's wheel. While the rest of us stayed very quiet, Bobby grabbed a lantern and headed up to the bow, and leaned out on shoal patrol. When he held the lantern to the left, Jimmy knew to gently steer the yacht, which was inching its way out of the harbour, in that direction. A lantern to the right had a similar meaning. After about twenty minutes, the pair had successfully navigated the *Vacuna* out into the Bay. Many of the players had sailing experience, so the ship's sails were quickly unfurled once more, and Jimmy turned the ship south, where a gentle breeze guided us south in the direction of Penetanguishene.

We pulled into the harbour a few minutes before 5 am, and Charley was awakened to take the helm. About fifteen minutes later, we were pulling alongside the wharf. Jake wasn't there to meet us - not that anyone thought he would - and he never knew what had happened to his toy on her trip north. Sadly, that was our only trip on the *Vacuna*, as Jake sold her for some less fancy (and probably less expensive to maintain) minesweeper from the Great War. That boat mysteriously caught fire while anchored in the Bay one night a year later, and the insurance company suspected some shenanigans, although after a lengthy investigation, none were uncovered. Jake cut back on the high living considerably after that, and if Parry Sound ever challenged the Rangers to a game again, they would have to find their own way there.

⚾ ⚾ ⚾

Jack

We were both strangers at first, Boomer and I.

I was the seasoned white sports reporter, he was the shy black kid. On the surface, we did not have a lot in common. If you looked deeper, we had some similarities, the strongest of which was a love of baseball. As the season progressed, I became close with several of the All Stars, perhaps none more so than Boomer.

For much of the season, travel to games for the team was not an issue. Stirling Park, where they played their home games, was right in the neighbourhood most of the team lived in, while games against the rest of the league were played a few city blocks away at Athletic Park. When it came to exhibition games out of town, the team piled into the old truck Taylor's Flour Mill had loaned the team. I did not travel with them on most of those trips (and didn't have a car of my own to get there), but I was invited the odd time.

The players mostly told stories or played cards in the back of that rumbling delivery truck. A white coating of flour from the fifty-pound bags the mill produced dusted the floor. Benches were placed along the sides for everyone to sit. Some chose just to lean their heads back and try to get a few moments of sleep. On one of those occasions when I had been invited, the conversation turned to many players' experiences with racism in Canada. Most white Canadians, the consensus was, were "polite racists." They would politely move away from a black passenger on a bus. Whites would refer to blacks as negroes, but would sometimes use the "n" word. If a black applied for a job or to rent an apartment, they would politely be told the job or room had already been filled. Racism wasn't, in most cases, blatant or overt. If the team needed to stay overnight somewhere when playing in a tournament, accommodations could be difficult to obtain. Hotels were to be found only in the bigger centres in those days; along the growing highway system in southwestern Ontario, many gas stations also doubled as motels, with their rooms being one-room cabins in the back. This was a popular way for many Ontarians who did not have a lot to spend to see the province. When the team stopped to inquire about those cabins, they were sometimes told (politely, of course) that there were none available, even though there were few that appeared to be occupied. Other times, when the team arrived after dark, they were reluctantly rented cabins, but under the condition they agreed to be out first thing in the morning before the white guests could see them.

One time, the team stopped on the way home from a game against the Walpole Island Indian Reserve team, because they were afraid all the restaurants in Chatham would be closed when they got there. The hostess at the restaurant greeted the team nervously, and said she would have to ask her manager if she could seat us. He came out and politely said, "sorry we don't serve coloured folk here." Some of the players began to give the manager a hard time, but Don Washington, one of the veterans on the team who had seen a lot in his time, just said, "Fellas, this is obviously a second-class eatery if they refuse to serve us. Their food isn't worth our money, you know? We'll go to someplace that appreciates our money. Let's just go back home, you guys don't need this." Because restaurants could be a gamble - some would refuse service, some would only offer take out - the team started packing sandwiches for the ride home.

The Stars lost only two league games all season. After their last loss, there was a near riot in the stands. Two fans got into an argument that quickly got out of hand; one of them was pushed by the other off the top of the stands. As is often the case in situations like that, others quickly chose sides and rushed in, threatening to turn the steaming cauldron to full boil. Cooler heads prevailed, but even as the two teams were leaving the diamond, some of them got into an argument, but nothing came of it. Was this another example of racism, or fans getting too heated in the aftermath of a close game? Probably some of both, and to the All Stars, it was more of the former than the latter.

Every game the Stars played seemed to be a battle. The competition was intense, the other team sometimes dirty, the umps often biased, and the fans occasionally hostile. But the Stars found ways to respond without upsetting the apple cart.

If opposing pitchers threw high and inside to a hitter too often, they soon came to learn that Flat, King, or Donny Tabron would respond in kind. Behind the plate, if an umpire was doing a one-sided job of calling balls and strikes, Wash would set up on one side of the plate for a pitch, but secretly give the signal to throw to the other side. The seemingly wayward pitch would hit the ump squarely in his big balloon chest protector, not injuring him, but delivering a message just the same.

Despite these setbacks, the players were feeling good about the season and the approaching playoffs. People were taking notice of the team at the top of the City League standings, and the crowds were getting bigger when the Stars played. But it was an incident in Strathroy that had a devastating effect on the team.

This was one of the exhibitions the Stars played to make some extra money and face some tougher competition to gear up for OBAs, if they made it that far. But almost from the first inning, the white crowd was on them. Little kids threw rocks at the Stars on the field and on their bench, using the n-word at length, and generally acting in a vile manner toward them. No one put a stop to it: umpires, parents, or the Strathroy team. In fact, some of the parents laughed at their kids' antics. The kids finally tired of abusing the team mid-way through the game, but picked it up again toward the end. Boomer later said that it was one thing for adults to act that way, but it was another for kids to do so. "It was like we were circus animals in a cage," he told me, "and the kids were allowed to take turns poking us with sharpened sticks. At no time did parents step in to stop them - they thought it was funny. It was disgusting and heartbreaking at the same time. Kids aren't born with hatred in their hearts. They learn it. And then they grow up and teach their kids exactly the same thing."

⚾ ⚾ ⚾

Merv

Much has been said and written about life in a small town. Movies have portrayed an idyllic lifestyle. While there are some drawbacks, one of the biggest advantages that I have found over a lifetime spent in them is the sense of community you feel. You know many of the people, and you know the challenges they face. Life in a small town may be safer, real estate might be cheaper, but you are often far removed from specialized healthcare and economic opportunities. Penetanguishene was no different from a lot of other small Canadian towns in the latter category. The town was highly dependent on the seasonal tourism business for its survival. But in small towns there often is a collective positive outlook on life, and a willingness to work hard and make the best of things. There is a stoicism in small towns that you don't always find in larger centres. Wisdom, justice, courage, and moderation are traits common to many small-town residents. Certainly, there are some less than admirable traits, a backwardness perhaps to outsiders who felt small towners looked at them with mistrust, but on balance, life in a small town tends to be a more peaceful existence.

If there is one thing to know about the popularity the Rangers had by the 1934 season, it was that the town all but shut down on Saturday afternoons when they played a home game. If you wanted a haircut, gas for your car, a roast pork for dinner, or a new pair of shoes for church on Sunday, you best get them before 2:00 that day, because the majority of businesses were closed. Penetang was a town of only about 3000 year-round residents, but that year on a summer Saturday afternoon, almost two-thirds of them could be found at Beck's Field to cheer on their Rangers. The team had done well over its first three seasons, and with the maturing of Phil Marchildon and the addition of manager Jim Shaw, there was a palpable feeling of excitement in the air. The team seemed on the verge of big things, and many residents wanted a front row seat to watch.

There wasn't a whole lot to do for entertainment. You could go to the movies, but the selection didn't change very often. Some people had radios, but generally mostly only the wealthier people in town. Travelling shows sometimes came to town. But in the middle of the Depression during the summer, there was nothing like a ball game to help take your mind off of your troubles. At 25 cents for adults, ten cents for kids, a game at Beck's was affordable for most people in town, and provided some good entertainment.

Penetang was always an outdoors, sports-minded town. By New Years' Day, the harbour was dotted with a growing cluster of ice fishing huts. There was a big arena down near the waterfront. If you grew up in Penetanguishene, you knew how to skate. There were also badminton courts upstairs in the building - the sport was huge in town at the time. Cross-country skiing was a favourite winter pastime of many, too. You could just take your skis and be out in the countryside in a matter of minutes from just about anywhere in town, then ski for an hour or so without ever seeing another soul. When Phil eventually turned pro, he would come back to Penetang in the off season and would often ski in order to keep up his conditioning and build up his legs. Luckily, Georgian Bay always obliged with several feet of snow from late November to early April.

When the snow melted and the long winter was over, people in town traded in their skates and curling brooms for bikes, ball gloves, and boats. There always seemed to be row boats or little skiffs out in the protected waters of Penetanguishene Bay. New equipment was hard to come by, so most people made do with hand-me-downs. After a long time spent indoors, people spent as much time outdoors as they could once the longer days and warmer weather came along.

By the end of August, the Rangers had clinched first place in the standings. Barrie was close behind, with Midland in tow. Orillia was something of a doormat that year. The playoff format would see the second and third place finishers square off in a best of three series, with the winner taking on the first-place club in the final. The winner would go on to represent North Simcoe in the Ontario Baseball Association playdowns. The OBA rule was that you had to live or work in the town you played for, but enforcement was inconsistent, at best. While we had heard that other teams in the province had brought in "ringers," talented outsiders who somehow skirted the residency rules, the Penetanguishene fans were rightly proud of the fact that every Ranger was a local.

With Dan Howley back in Toronto, Phil had started to fall back on his fastball/curve combo. He was still having trouble throwing his change for strikes, but there was little incentive to use it, as he was regularly fanning ten or more per game. And the Rangers were playing like a well-oiled machine behind him, playing solid defence, and giving him lots of run support. Phil was even leading the league in hitting at one point. But Jim Shaw wouldn't let the club get complacent - he was in for the long haul. "We haven't won squat yet," he'd growl after the club celebrated each win.

⚾ ⚾ ⚾

Jack

Boomer was understandably very shy when he first joined the team that included his older brothers and several players he had grown up watching. He said later he truly was happy to be there, and wanted to let his bat do the talking. He would be one of the last ones on the flour truck on road trips, letting the older players get the prime card-playing spots. He stayed on the margins of things, like those card games and the good-natured ribbing that is universal among ball players. He spoke only when spoken to.

I noticed it fairly early in the season, and so did Hap, who decided to do something about it as summer rolled around.

He asked Boomer one day why he was so quiet. "Just shy, I guess," was the response.
"Well, that's no way to play the game," lectured Hap. "Be alive, son! You have to love this game to play it, because we sure as hell don't play it for money. You're a part of this team - one day you're goin' to be a big part of it - and I know you're just being so reserved because you want to show you know

your place. But never mind that. Tell me something - do you love this game?"

"Yes, yes, of course I do," replied Boomer.

"Then play like you do!! Show some emotion out there. Smile, laugh, even get pissed off once in a while, show everyone that you care. Be a leader out there, and let us all know how much this game means to you. Show us all that you don't care about all the garbage you guys have to take out on the field sometimes, because your love of the game is bigger than all of that nonsense."

And from that moment on, Boomer did. He was already a fixture in the heart of the Stars' batting order, and he took on more of a leadership role. He took part in the card games, faring quite badly at first, but being the competitor that he was, he learned as much as he could, and before long was winning more than his fair share of hands. He talked constantly on the field - with teammates, umpires, the opposition, even some of the fans.

I congratulated Hap for his work on Boomer's turnaround. "Y'know, old ballplayers say that the thing they miss the most when they stop playin' is the whole being part of a team thing.

They miss the game, but they miss the guys and bein' part of something bigger than themselves even more," he responded.

Don Washington was an important member of the team, a valuable veteran presence who knew how to work with his pitchers. He also was a huge mentor to Boomer. A few days after the Strathroy debacle, he took Boomer aside. "You can't take all of this to heart, man," he advised. "Hatred will just tear you apart. It will just rip your guts out, if you let it. You got to save it all for the game. If you let hate take you over, soon you won't have any fight left in you. This is all going to change one day. You know, the best ball players in the world - the white ones, at least - they don't care about the colour of a man's skin. Maybe some of the scrubs do, but the greats like Babe Ruth, Walter Johnson, or Carl Hubbell? They only care about one thing - can this guy help us win? Dizzy Dean once said, 'I played against a Negro League team that was so good, we didn't think we had even a chance of beating them.' Someone asked Diz if he would play with black players, and he said, 'Hell, I've played exhibitions *against* them. What's the difference?' Maybe it hasn't worked its way to people who run big league ball clubs yet, but one day some sharp operator will figure things out and realize baseball has been missing out on a great big ocean of talent, and teams will be falling all over themselves to sign us. Judge Landis likes to say, 'there's no written rule banning coloured players from Major League

Baseball,' but that's a lot of bunk, because there's been an unwritten rule since Cap Anson yelled, "get that n———- off the field!" at the start of a game 50 years ago. But Landis is a dinosaur, and one day there'll be a commissioner who rips up that rule, written or not. Change is already starting to happen. I heard tell of a semi-pro team in North Dakota. A guy who runs a car dealership owns the club. He got tired of always losing the league championship to another town, so he started bringing in all kinds of high-priced talent - black and white - to help him win."

"Black and white guys on the *same* team?" Boomer asked in disbelief.

"Yep. Won a championship, packed their ballpark. Imitation is the sincerest form of flattery, they say, so their big rival up and did the same thing. Those North Dakota guys catch on quick, I guess. Maybe it won't happen tomorrow, but it's coming."

⚾ ⚾ ⚾

4th Inning

Rangers Clinch Simcoe Pennant, Meet Barrie in Final
By Charlie Paradis
Penetang Penetang Weekly Herald Staff

Despite stumbling down the stretch and losing three straight, including a pair to Midland, which pulled the Consols briefly into a tie with the Rangers, the Penetanguishene Spencer Foundry team topped Barrie 3-0 in their final regular season game to capture their first ever North Simcoe League pennant.

By virtue of finishing in second place, the upstart Midlanders had home field advantage in the best-of-three league semi-final against third place Barrie. The County Seat team's experience showed in the playoff, and after dropping the first game at Midland's Town Park, Barrie took the second game, played to an extra-inning tie, then won the replay to take the series, and with it the right to face Penetang in the final for a second consecutive season.

Led by ace hurler Phil (Babe) Marchildon and his fastball, the Rangers have been the class of the circuit, and will take on Barrie in the league final.

Barrie bested the Rangers in last year's final, but the Rangers have taken 3 of 4 against their southern rivals, and have clearly been the better team this season.

With the pitching of Marchildon, the excellent all-round play of Hal Crippin, and the two-way play of the Bald brothers, Penetang is poised to bring provincial recognition to this northern town.

The Rangers host the opener of the best of three this Saturday at Beck Field, with the series switching to Barrie on Wednesday. If necessary, a third and deciding game will be held in Penetang the following Saturday.

Playoffs Begin, Interest in Local Ball Growing
By Jack Calder
Chatham Daily News Staff
August 7th

Playoffs in the City Baseball League will begin Saturday of this week, with the Braggs and Stars meeting at Athletic Park. Interest in baseball is picking up considerably now that the playoffs have been reached and a big crowd is expected at Saturday's game.

The winners of the Braggs-Stars series will enter further Intermediate O.B.A. play. Chatham's representatives are expected to go far, for in games with outside teams this year City League outfits have compiled good records. The Duns gave Harrow a close run in one exhibition while the Stars walloped several district intermediate teams.

An endeavour will be made in the near future to match the Stars with an all-star team chosen from the Merchants and City League Nines. The game would be expected to help finances of the City Baseball League.

City League officials are going to leave no stone unturned in seeing that Saturday's playoff game at Athletic Park is well attended. The game promises to be the highlight of the City Baseball League play this season. It will be the first of a three-out-of-five series.

"Babe" Marchildon Pitches and Hits His Team to a 3-2 Victory
Barrie Northern Advance Staff

The Penetang ball team went home rejoicing with a 3-2 victory over their Barrie rivals Wednesday evening. The game meant that Penetang will go into the O.B.A. playdowns, with Barrie taking a back seat for the first time in four years. Penetang had won the first match (of the best-of-three series) in the northern town handily on the weekend. The largest crowd of the season was on hand to see a sparkling display of ball. At least half the citizens of Penetang must have been on hand for the game.

"Babe" Marchildon, right-handed youngster, and Bill McGuire, veteran southpaw, staged a real pitching duel. The former's team mates came through with a little better hitting and with it came the victory. Marchildon fanned 11 and let his opponents down with five hits and issued five walks. McGuire struck out seven, all of which came in the first five innings. He allowed eight hits and walked two. Marchildon was also his team's best batter, getting a triple, two singles, and a walk.

In the first of the 2nd Penetang got their first run on Marchildon's triple and B. Crippin's single. Barrie got their two runs in the last of the third when Thompson walked. Scott got a single to centre and both scored on Jennings' timely drive to right field.

Penetang won the game in the eighth. Shepherd batted for Richardson and walked, coming home on J. Bald's triple to centre. Bald came home on the squeeze play when M. Bald laid down a perfect bunt. In the last innings Barrie used three pinch hitters. Hook, batting for Ramsey, fanned; Reynolds, for

McGuire, walked; Tribble, for Clark, walked. With the tying run on second, Dobson grounded to short for the final out.

The game was a real battle from start to finish with the outcome undecided until the last man was out. The Barrie hitters failed to come through when a hit meant the game. They had nine men left on to Penetang's four.
Outside of Marchildon, M. Bald was the best hitter for the visitors, getting two safeties. Devilliers, J. Bald, and B. Crippin had one each. For Barrie Jennings got a double and a single. Scott, Walls, and Hare came through with one hit each. Both teams were charged with one error.

Marchildon Knew the Batters
Pitcher Marchildon uses his head on the mound as much as his arm. He attended all four games of the Barrie-Midland semi-final series and parked conveniently close to the plate. There he watched batters of both teams and took notes in a little book. He knew every batter's particular weakness and in the games with Barrie, the local players were continually fed the kind of balls they didn't like. Marchildon had every batter analyzed down to the moment. It is said that Marchildon had down regarding several Barrie players, "can't hit nothing."

Braggs Defeated in Third and Final Game of Series

Tyrell Relieves Chase and Allows Only 1 Run in Last Five Innings
As Stars Win 10-7; Braggs Lose Early Lead
By Jack Calder
Chatham Daily News Staff

The Stars, leaders of Chatham's City Baseball League throughout the season, earned the right to enter further O.B.A. Intermediate B Playdowns Saturday when they defeated Braggs for the third straight time in a three-out-of-five series by a score of 11-7. After assuming a 6-1 lead in the first two innings Braggs lost all the pep that is usually associated with a leading team and the Stars took the game in low gear. Constant delays stretched the affair out over more than two and a half hours.

The Stars used two hurlers Chase and Tyrell, while Joe Jordan sent three of his Bragg riflemen, Belander, Murray and Blackburn to the hill. Chase had trouble with his control as his regular catcher, Don Washington, was out of action and Robbins who started behind the plate was a poor target. It was the first time Chase had started in several games. Tyrell allowed but four hits and one run in the five innings he pitched. Belanger started well for Braggs but faulty support led to his undoing and he went to pieces in the fifth. Murray was hit freely until he retired with one man out in the ninth. Then

Blackburn entered the game to retire the last two men without giving up a run.

Dutch Scott of Braggs came out of a batting slump to get three of the losers' eight hits. He also turned a pair of smart fielding plays at shortstop. J. Robbins, playing left field for the Stars, hit safely three times in five attempts while Tyrell, Boomer Harding, and H. Robbins all had two hits.

The Stars do not begin their campaigning in the O.B.A until September 6, when they will play the Middlesex county champs Sarnia Red Sox. The series will be a homecoming of sorts for Red Sox 3rd Baseman Dutch Schaefer and pitcher Smoky Joe Allen, both of whom donned Chatham uniforms not so long ago.

Rangers Set to Take on North Bay in OBA Playoffs
By Mervyn Dickey
Penetang Herald Staff

After dispatching defending North Simcoe champs Barrie Wolves last week, the Penetanguishene Spencer Foundry Rangers have learned who their opponent will be for their OBA quarter-final series.
A strong North Bay entry will once again represent Northern Ontario in the provincial playoffs, with the first game set for

North Bay on Wednesday, with the second game a Saturday afternoon affair in Penetanguishene. If a third game is necessary, it will be played in North Bay the following Saturday.

Both teams are led by star phenoms on the mound, Penetanguishene by Babe Marchildon, North Bay by Harry Preston. North Bay's prior playoff experience should give them something of an advantage, but it's worth keeping in mind that much of the core of the Rangers lineup regularly advanced far in provincial play last decade when they were a fastball team.

The winner of the best-of-three series goes on to play the winner of the Meaford-Lucknow series.

5th Inning

Stars, Rangers enter OBA tournament for the first time; Marchildon heads off to St Mike's

Jack

Ordinarily, the start of the playoffs inevitably means the season is winding down. In the Stars' case, it was just beginning.

Sarnia Red Sox had qualified from their region, and would meet the City League champs in the first round of the OBA playdowns. The OBA did their best to keep the initial matches reasonably close in geographic terms, but that was a challenge, because the OBA covered a huge area.

The Stars were not all that concerned about this match up. Both the Duns and the Braggs had played the Red Sox in tournaments earlier in the season, and had beaten them handily. I asked Hap what he thought his team's chances were after he had put them through a light workout before the series started, and you could tell he was confident. "We don't want to take 'em too lightly," he allowed, "because they have a decent veteran pitcher, but some of the guys on the Braggs have given us the goods on Sarnia, and they think we can take'em, easy." I found that last part interesting - teams which had fought the Stars tooth and nail during the season did not mind giving them the scoop on the opposition now, maybe because they were representing all of Chatham now.

Smoky Joe Allen was Sarnia's ace, a player fans of the City League knew well, having pitched in Chatham previously. Smoky had moved to Sarnia, but there was a chance no teams in Chatham would have taken him on anyway, because he was getting on in years, and his fastball had lost a considerable amount of zip. He was pitching largely on smarts now.

Speaking of pitching, things were not going all that well for Flat Chase, the Stars' ace. He was tiring at a time when the team really needed him. Hap had tried to share the workload between Flat, King Terrell, and Donny Tabron, but he would probably admit that he saved his big gun for the toughest games, and maybe he had gone to the well a few too many times over the course of the season.

Game one would be played in Sarnia. Although the Red Sox had represented the Imperial City in OBA before, Sarnia was best known as a rugby football town. The Imperial Oil Company built a huge refinery there, and the Imperials, as their Ontario Rugby Football Union team was known, always seemed to be able to offer jobs to the best players in the province. The Imperials were an ORFU powerhouse, and hosted the Toronto Argonauts in the Grey Cup the year before.

The Red Sox had some decent players, but football was the sport the best athletes in town went out for.

The Stars piled into Taylor's truck for the drive to Sarnia. Archie Stirling, I learned later, had supplied the team with gas money and sandwiches for the drive home. It was a self-assured club that pulled away from Chatham, knowing that if they took the first game, a win on home soil in the second was all but assured.

I joined the team, getting in at the last minute, which assured me a drafty seat by the tailgate. The ride would be smooth for the first half of the trip up the paved section from Highway 40 to Wallaceburg, but then it would be a bumpy, pot-hole filled rattle of a ride along the remaining gravel highway to Sarnia.

Ross Talbot sat next to me. He was one of the team's veterans, something of an elder statesman (if you could call someone in their late 20s that). "I have to tell you something.... don't know if you've noticed it," he confessed a few minutes into the trip. "What's that?" I asked, curiously.

"I think things have already started changing, maybe only if a little bit," he observed.

I gave him a quizzical look.

"When we started playing a couple of years ago," he continued, "we had to be in the entertainment business, you know. The more fans we could draw when we travelled all over the place to play, the more coin we could take home with us. So, in the early days of this team, we tried to play what folks called a 'colourful' kind of ball."

I had used that term in the past to describe the team's play. All of a sudden, I realized that it was a much more loaded word than I had thought. A huge pang of guilt washed over me. Talbot appeared not to notice.

"In the beginning, we were kind of like the Harlem Globetrotters, you know. Had to put on a show, act up - that kind of thing. Give the fans what they wanted, especially the white ones. During infield practice, we would make fancy plays, catch balls behind our back, toss our mitts to 1st with the ball still in it. When it was our turn to bat, Percy would do a little dance down in the 1st Base coaches' box while the other team warmed up. And you know what?"

"What?"

"I hated every damn minute of it. Sometimes, it wasn't baseball. It filled the stands and paid the bills, but it made us look like a bunch of clowns. The fans, they weren't laughing with us - they were laughing at us. It was embarrassing. It played to the old stereotypes, and it sure didn't go far in helping us to be treated like equals. But now that Archie got us into the City League, we don't have to do that stuff anymore. We can still have fun on the field, but we can focus on the game. Fans may come out now to root against us, but more and more they're coming out to watch us play. Now here we are, travelling to another part of the province, with maybe more to come. I bet you even a couple of years ago no one in Chatham would even dare dream such a thing."

"Listen, about my use of the word you mentioned - 'colourful' - I have to admit I've used it to describe your style of play," I said, guiltily.

"I know," replied Ron.

"I had no idea......"

"Look, I get it," he interrupted. "But we're more than that. Much more. We're a good ball team, and more importantly, a collection of great guys."

"Of that there is no question," I agreed. "And this is such a great opportunity for you guys. Not only do you get to play a much better, much more challenging brand of ball, but there's a lot of civic pride in Chatham, and you've become a huge part of that. People all over town are talking about the All Stars. I expect a huge turnout at the second game."

A lot of eyes in Chatham had been opened. Including my own.

⚾ ⚾ ⚾

Merv

For some, life in a small town is like a pitcher in a bases loaded situation - they feel like they're in a jam, and can't wait to get out. For others, living in a tiny place like Penetanguishene is like a favourite old ball glove - it's comfortable, it's familiar, and they would be lost without it.

While we both loved growing up in Penetanguishene, by the late summer of 1934, both Phil and I knew we weren't long for the old place of the white rolling sands. Some of my stories in the *Herald* had been picked up by the wire services, and before long I had a job offer as an editor from a paper in Geraldton, way up north of Lake Superior. And Phil and his family had decided to take St Mike's up on their scholarship offer, which meant while I would be headed north, he would be going south to Toronto.

There had been a lot of debate at the Marchildon kitchen table. Pro ball was looming as a possibility - Jim Shaw and Dan Howley had a vast network of contacts that would likely land

Phil a tryout with a pro or high-level amateur team. But for a small-town Depression-era family, a free education just couldn't be turned down. Phil wasn't the greatest student in high school, but Oliver and Liza felt that maybe with some better teaching, maybe he could become the first in the family to graduate from university. Phil was more interested in sports, and if he had dreams beyond high school, it was maybe suiting up for the baseball Maple Leafs or the football Argonauts.

Complicating matters was the fact that with the Rangers having captured their first ever North Simcoe League title, the baseball season was going to be going on past Labour Day, by which time Phil would already have been in class at St Mike's for a week. The Geraldton editor who hired me as his replacement agreed to put off retirement until the Rangers' season was over. But the team had little chance to advance without Phil, so Jake Payette and some of the leading businessmen in town decided to pool their funds to send a car to pick him up and drive him to wherever the Rangers were playing, then return him back to the city after the game. On most occasions, Oliver was the driver. Between football, schoolwork, and travelling to ball games, Phil had a busy fall. His parents feared that he would suffer bouts of homesickness, but he barely had time for it.

The Rangers would be taking on the North Bay Pirates in the first round of the OBAs. The first game of the best-of-three series would be played on Saturday, September 8th.

The Pirates were a northern powerhouse. North Bay was a boom town in those days - a major railway hub, and the gateway to timber and mineral riches further north. Because of that, the drive up Highway 11 north of Orillia up to the west end of Lake Nippissing was fairly smooth and only took a few hours in the comfortable sedans several business owners had loaned the team for the trip. Jake Payette, in anticipation of the Rangers travelling far in the OBAs both in a literal and figurative sense, had rallied his fellow Penetanguishene businessmen to help transport the team. The team gathered at Beck's shortly after 8 am and piled into the borrowed vehicles.

But the skies turned dark shortly after the convoy had turned north at Orillia about an hour later, and by the time they got to North Bay near noon, a steady downpour was falling. The team had registered to stay overnight at the Continental Hotel in town before heading home Sunday morning, and after checking in, the boys headed for the hotel's front lobby to monitor the weather. Word quickly spread of the Rangers' arrival, and before long, much of the North Bay team had shown up at the hotel to check out their opponents. An unimpressed writer for the North Bay *Nugget* wrote several days later that Phil was "on the small side." At around 3:00, there was a break in the weather, and everyone rushed out to the ballpark, but a quick inspection revealed the field was unplayable, and before long all had to make a dash for their cars when the skies opened up once again. The game was postponed. Game one would now be played in Penetanguishene on Wednesday, with the second and (if necessary) third games played back in North Bay the following weekend.

⚾ ⚾ ⚾

Jack
It was the first weekend after Labour Day, and the weather had turned from humidity-filled warmth to crispy cool, from summer to fall in the blink of an eye.

A surprisingly small gathering of fans was on hand to take in the first game of the OBA playdowns between the All Stars and the Red Sox at Sarnia, proof again that maybe baseball was not the biggest game in town. Old Smoky Joe Allen was on form for the first two innings, using all of his pitches and his wiles to retire six of the first seven hitters he faced, while his teammates spotted him a two-run lead. Chase gave up hits to the first two Sarnia batters, but then got three outs in succession to get out of a first inning jam. A base on balls, single, and hit batter by Chase saw him in trouble again in the 2nd. He then proceeded to walk in the game's first run, and the second came in later when Talbot bobbled a routine grounder.

It was best to get to a veteran like Smoky early, because he seemed to get better as the game progressed, and while their own ace was continuing his scuffles, there was little evidence of panic from the Chatham side.

Smith got the first two batters out in the 3rd, but things quickly came undone for him. A ball booted by the Sarnia shortstop gave the Stars their first base runner, followed by another error on a routine grounder. All season long, the Stars had been able to capitalize on their opponents' mistakes, and today was to prove to be no exception. Even though none of the Chatham hitters had made solid contact with any of Smoky's pitches to that point, Boomer laced a triple to left to quickly tie the game up. He probably could have made it around for an inside park Home Run in the spacious Sarnia diamond, but he pulled up at 3rd with a charley horse. Under the rules of the day (it had happened in the All-Star game that year), a "courtesy runner" was allowed. Boomer briefly left the game for some ice, and Cliff Olbey took over at 3rd, but was stranded there. Boomer pronounced himself fit, and was allowed to retake his position at 1st when Chatham took the field.

The Stars struck again in the 4th, when Hyatt, the Sarnia backstop, had trouble getting a handle on Smoky's curveball. Hap had been playing some small ball to get his offence going: Washington walked, stole 2nd, and moved over to 3rd on Stan

Robbins' bunt single. Robbins himself later scored after swiping 2nd.

But somehow the Red Sox hung in there. Trailing 4-2, they got a run back in their half of the 4th when Len Harding inexplicably dropped a flyball. Bent but not broken, Smoky kept his team in the game until the 8th. With two out, Donny Tabron was briefly knocked out when he was hit in the head by a pitch, but he waved off his own courtesy runner, and made it to 1st under his own power. The next hitter, Guoy Ladd, smacked a pitch into the left-centre gap, and Tabron came all the way around from 1st to score, putting Chatham up 5-3. Maybe he was shaken up by hitting Tabron, or maybe he just did not have much gas left after the patient Stars' hitter had spent the day working the count on him, but Smoky threw a fat one to Len Harding, and he hit it far beyond the left field fence to give Chatham a four-run lead.

Meanwhile, Flat had found his groove, and had breezed through the middle innings on the mound. He loaded the bases in the 8th, but got a huge strikeout on Dutch Schaefer - another former City Leaguer - then doubled in Boomer with the 8th and final run of the game in the 9th.

Chatham won the contest 8-3, to take a 1-0 lead in the series. They had shown the strongest parts of their game: base stealing, bunting, timely big hits, and despite some rough patches for Chase, strong pitching.

⚾⚾⚾

Merv

History was made on a cool but sunny midweek afternoon when the Rangers hosted their first OBA game against North Bay. Once again, the town shut down, and carloads of watchers from Midland and the outlying areas as well ventured to Beck's to watch - a crowd in excess of 2 000 was in attendance.

As would be expected, Jim Shaw's network had provided him with a scouting report on the Pirates before the series started. "I'm going to tell my guys," he confided in me as I wrote out the Penetanguishene and North Bay lineups in my well-used scorebook before the game started, "that there are only two guys on this team who can hit - Preston, their pitcher, and Guenette, their 3rd Basemen. The rest of the lineup is a bunch of bunters and guys trying to work a walk. Phil's thrown a lot of pitches this season, and we still have a lot of ball left to play if we want to win this thing, so I'm telling him just to go after their hitters and not worry about working the corners, keep throwing fastballs, mix in the odd curve. With all due respect to our visitors from North Bay, the only hope for them is for Preston to shut us out twice, and by some miracle manage to scrape together a couple of runs. Preston's a good hurler, from what I'm told, but he's no match for Phil."

So, with Fred DeVillers setting up a nice big target almost in the middle of the plate, Phil went after the North Bay hitters. The grind of daily football practice at St Mike's had taken its toll on him, and he was grateful just to be able to wind up and fire, mowing down the North Bay hitters with ease. He didn't have to worry about working the edges of the plate and trying to command his change, giving him many quick innings. It was just rock back and fire away. Trouble was, Preston on the other side was just as effective; maybe he didn't throw as hard as Phil, but he had a big leg kick in his delivery, and hid the ball well from the Ranger hitters.

The Rangers threatened early; Phil led off the home half of the 2nd with a single up the middle, was sacrificed over to 2nd, and took 3rd on a wild pitch. But with the opening run of the game standing just 90 feet away with one out, Hal Crippin struck out and McCuaig grounded out to retire the side.

Phil hit the first North Bay hitter in the top of the 3rd, and then time had to be called when a dog wandered out onto the field. The players and the umpires tried to shoo the canine off the field, but Rover displayed some good open field running before disappearing down the right field line, providing the crowd with some comic relief. The North Bay runner was still chuckling about the dog's escapade when he took his lead off of 1st as play resumed. He must have still been quite distracted, as Phil turned and picked him off by a good foot.

Penetanguishene opened the scoring in the bottom half of the inning when Joe Hale led off with a single to left, advancing to 2nd an out later when Marius Bald's ground ball to short was muffed. Up next was Devillers, who lined a ball up the middle. Hale stopped at 3rd, waiting to see where the throw from the outfield went; Marius, who thought Hale was going to score on the play, took a wide turn at 2nd, and the North Bay centre fielder alertly threw to the short stop covering the bag. Marius was "hung up," and caught in a run down, but the shortstop decided to pursue Marius back to 2nd, successfully tagging him out, but allowing Hale to score the game's first and only run.

North Bay got a runner as far as 3rd in the 6th inning when Mussell reached on an error. With one out, he took off for 2nd on a swinging third strike by the hitter McDougall, and reached 3rd when Devillers' throw to 2nd was wild. But Phil struck out the next hitter to end the inning.

Phil was just plain dominant, not allowing a hit until the 7th inning, and striking out 15 North Bay hitters. Penetanguishene came away with a 1-0 win in the game and the series, but their Manager was not concerned about his team's offensive performance. "Maybe this Preston is better than I thought," mused Shaw after the game. "If we don't scratch that run across today, we may have played until dark. Our guys just couldn't get their bats going against him."

⚾⚾⚾

Jack

Archie Stirling decided to move all of the All Stars' remaining home games to Athletic Park. "It's not a decision I take lightly," he advised over the phone to me, "because the Stars' fans deserve to see their heroes at their home park. But they have drawn such huge overflow crowds that after consulting with police and city officials, because of safety issues, as well as those concerning parking and other matters regarding transportation, Athletic Park is a more suitable venue for their playoff games. Athletic Park is much more accessible, and is capable of holding crowds in excess of 1 500 people such as we saw for some of the Stars' last home games. If they progress beyond this series, no doubt more people will want to see them. Athletic Park will be able to accommodate those fans." It was a little sad to think that Stirling would not get a chance to host history if the Stars made it to the final, but the prospect of a packed Athletic Park was exciting.

The second game of the series proved to be anti-climactic, although the fans did not know it when the first pitch flew.

Sarnia came to the do-or-die game against the Stars with only nine players. Unbeknownst to the Chatham side, there was an important football practice scheduled back in Sarnia. It was the last try-out for the Imperials, and several Red Sox players were fearful of being cut if they weren't on the practice field. Football was popular in Chatham, but not to that extent; it would be unthinkable for one of the Stars to forgo a ball game with the season on the line in favour of a football try-out.

But that is how big the gridiron game was in Sarnia.

Sarnia showed up with nine players, but given the times, that was not all that unusual. Work commitments, injuries, and the like often reduced the rosters of some teams. And undermanned teams, with nothing to lose, can be dangerous to play. But it was the eagle eye of Archie Stirling that stopped the visitors from pulling a fast one.

Hap had decided to give Flat's arm a rest and went with the lefty King. Hap wanted more bullets in the chamber for the next series - opponent yet unknown - as this one was a likely triumph for his Stars. Flat had pitched well through the middle innings of the first game, but his start and finish were shaky. The hometown fans were a little disappointed that their hero Flat Chase did not take the mound, but they were eager to see their Stars clinch the series.

And clinch they did, but not in a conventional way.

When Archie surveyed the small contingent of Red Sox disembark from their cars, he knew something was amiss. As convenor, he knew the players of the area like the back of his hand, and something did not sit right with him. He let it pass for the moment, but still had an uneasy feeling as he settled in for the game.

Smoky Joe failed to even make the trip to Chatham. In his place was a sidearming southpaw named Chowen, who made life tough for the Stars' hitters. Sarnia scored a pair of runs to take an early lead, thanks to several Chatham miscues in the field. Suddenly, this scrappy nine-man contingent was looking like they might force a deciding game.

Enter Archie. With uncertainty gnawing away at him, he went down to the Sarnia dugout at the end of the 4th inning, confronting the Manager and demanding to see his player cards. The Red Sox Manager knew the gig was up, and admitted that he had an ineligible player in his lineup - his 1st Baseman, specifically, a young slugger who was signed with the Sarnia Juniors, and not eligible to play for the senior club under OBA rules. Archie was tempted to call the whole thing off right there and then, but given the size of the crowd on hand, after consulting with both skippers he decided to let the game continue as an exhibition affair. Sarnia won the contest, 8-3, but had forfeited the game and the series to Chatham. Hap felt bad - he would have let Flat start and pitch the first two or three innings to make the fans happy, had he known. After the game, Boomer said, "It's just as well - don't know why they didn't start Chowen in the first game. I sure am glad we don't have to face him again."

⚾⚾⚾

Merv

The fans of both the Rangers and the Pirates had to wait a week for the series to resume in North Bay. Phil was back in school in Toronto, trying to pay attention in class. One thing he'd said he noticed before the first game is that all the football training he had been undertaking since the last week of August was beginning to pay off. He felt stronger, and even though he was a little fatigued, he felt he had more on his fastball in that first game. After such a close opening contest, it was fair to say that the Rangers were a little nervous. As well as Phil had pitched, Shaw felt there was little margin for error behind them because Preston had mastered the Penetanguishene bats so well.

And sure enough, the second game of the series turned out to be even more of a pitcher's duel, although Phil ran into a spot of trouble, loading the bases in the 2nd with no one out. Mussell, the lead off hitter, slapped a single to right, and moved up to 2nd when Burnside walked. A passed ball allowed

Mussell to reach 3rd, and with runners on the corners and no outs, North Bay seemed set to plate a run for the first time in the series.

A fly ball or wild pitch would have scored Mussell, but the North Bay manager opted for a squeeze play. The batter, Berard, bunted the ball up the 3rd base line, and Phil was able to pounce on the ball, scoop it up, and make a diving tag on Mussell for the inning's first out. An alert Burnside took 3rd on the play. On Phil's next pitch, Berard, who had reached on a fielder's choice when Phil tagged out Mussell, took off for 2nd. Burnside over at 3rd came down the line to see if DeVillers would throw down to 2nd; Fred leaped out of his crouch after receiving the pitch from Phil, and faked a throw to 2nd. By then, Burnside had committed himself too far down the line, and Fred wheeled and threw to 3rd. Burnside was stuck in no-man's land between 3rd and home. He was caught in a rundown and eventually tagged out by Hal. But in the confusion of the rundown, Berard scampered to 3rd. North Bay had two outs, but still had a man a base away from scoring. But Berard took too much of a lead on Phil's third pitch to the next hitter, and DeVillers gunned him out at 3rd. North Bay had run themselves out of an inning: four hitters had safely reached base, but not one of them came around to score.

Marchildon and Preston matched scoreless frame after scoreless frame. Phil was getting many of his outs by strikeout, while Preston had Penetang batters harmlessly pounding his low pitches into the dirt for groundouts. The home town ump was giving Preston a bit more generous strike zone, but he seldom was in hitter's counts in the game.

Neither team could get any offence going through the middle innings, and the final three were blanks as well, and the game was scoreless after nine. There were a few sparkling defensive plays on both sides, but both pitchers were firmly in control throughout the game. Phil was never in difficulty after that rough inning, while Preston didn't allow a Penetang runner to get past 2nd. The Rangers were able to get a man on base in a number of innings, but couldn't get a timely walk or hit to move him along or mount any kind of rally.

Finally, with the skies darkening and the threat of a replay looming (likely meaning a doubleheader the next day), the Rangers broke the log jam in their half of the 12th. With two out, Hal Crippin hit a sharp grounder which ate the 2nd Baseman Fellman up, allowing Hal to reach. Phil was up next, just looking to put a ball in play. He hit a little flare, a pop up almost exactly between the right fielder and Fellman, who was looking to atone for his miscue moments earlier. Meanwhile, with two outs, Hal had been off at the crack of the bat, and was already rounding 2nd as the ball began its descent. Maybe it was the crowd noise and he didn't hear the outfielder call for the ball, or maybe he felt he was in a better position to get it regardless, but Fellman didn't give up his pursuit. At the last second, the two players nearly collided, with neither able to focus on the ball in order to avoid crashing into each other. The ball glanced off of Fellman's glove, and rolled several feet away from him. Hal had crossed 3rd, and was making a mad dash for home. Fellman scrambled over to the ball, picked it up and fired home, but his throw was high, and Crippin slid in under the tag with the go-ahead run.

Knowing that he likely had another week off before his next game, Phil came out on fire in the bottom half of the 12th, and retired the side in order, the last two hitters on strikeouts. The Rangers had another hard fought 1-0 win, and took the series in two games straight, gaining new respect for North Bay and Harry Preston in the process. "We got lucky," grumbled Shaw after the game. "Preston kept us in check the whole series, and we could only scratch out two runs in twenty-one innings. We were lucky to escape with that win. We needed a bloop hit and a couple of errors to win that game. We have to hit better in the next round, or it will be over early." What he overlooked, of course, was the utterly dominant performance of his ace, Phil Marchildon. Marchildon had kept North Bay entirely in check, tossing twenty-one scoreless innings, and striking out 32 batters over the two games. Phil allowed North Bay only four hits. When I totalled things up from my scorebook, North Bay hitters managed only a paltry .060 batting average for the series.

After their victory, the jubilant Rangers once again piled into their vehicles for the trip south. One incident marred the celebrations, though. After taking home a hefty (40%) cut of the gate from the first game of the series in front of a packed house in Penetanguishene, North Bay refused to make the same arrangement after the second game. This wasn't optional; it was an OBA rule. The sum from the North Bay contest wasn't as big as our home game's was, but the tradition was to send the visiting team home with their share in cash. North Bay promised to send a check to cover the amount. Fitzgerald, the Rangers' business manager, was unimpressed, but took the North Bay team at their word. Times were tight for everyone, and even the Rangers needed those funds to cover expenses. Little did we know at the time that the cheque would never arrive, and the whole affair would drag out over months.

⚾ ⚾ ⚾

Rangers Clinch Spot in Provincial Semi-Final
By Charlie Paradis
With files from the Barrie Examiner and Midland Free Press Penetang Weekly Herald Staff

September 18th, 1934

The Penetanguishene Rangers earned a spot in the O.B.A. Intermediate B semi-final with a pair of shutout victories over the North Bay Pirates.

The Pirates, winners of the Northern Ontario playdowns, were unable to put a run across against Penetang's ace Phil 'Babe' Marchildon in twenty-one innings of play over two games.

In the first contest played under sunny Indian summer skies at Beck's Field, a jam-packed crowd of over 2000 saw Marchildon dominate the visiting North Bay hitters, giving up only four hits and a pair of walks while fanning 15. North Bay's Harry Preston, who is Marchildon's equal in terms of age, was almost just as dominant. Penetang managed a lone run in the sixth inning when Fred Devilliers cashed in Jim Bald's lead off walk with a two-out double. That was all the support Marchildon needed, as he struck out five of the last six hitters he faced to secure the shutout victory and a one game lead for the local side.

The second contest was played under not so friendly conditions in North Bay. Rain delayed the start of the game by three quarters of an hour, and some swear they saw snowflakes among the scattered raindrops throughout the rest of the day.

Luckily, the game moved along quickly as Preston matched Marchildon almost pitch for pitch.

Through nine innings, neither side could muster much offence. Penetang had runners at 2nd and 3rd with one out in the 7th, but Preston buckled down to get out of a jam. For a second straight match, the North Bay hitters were unable to figure out Marchildon, who retired the last fifteen hitters he faced. The game went to the twelfth inning before a runner crossed the plate, when Penetang's Hal Crippin reached on an error, and made a successful daring dash for home on another error on a ball off the bat of Marchildon.

Marchildon slammed the barn door shut with a 1-2-3 bottom of the twelfth to complete another virtuoso pitching performance in leading his team to a series victory. The young hurler allowed only three hits, and fanned 17, including 15 over the last 7 innings of the game. Preston was nearly his equal, allowing just a pair of hits while collecting 14 whiffs.

Maybe Barrie Team Not So Bad
Barrie Examiner Staff

When the Barrie baseball team lost out to Penetang this year there were actually some local fans who thought the Barrie team was just rotten. Maybe the local team wasn't so bad after all. Isn't it just possible Penetang is pretty good? Events since the Barrie-Penetang series seem to bear this out.

Penetang eliminated the powerful North Bay team in two straight games, both by 1-0 scores. Last Saturday at North Bay, the game went 12 innings before Penetang scored a run and won the game.

Now there's a team that was highly rated this year, North Bay Pirates, good fielders, heavy hitters, and with two fine pitchers, Pyette and Preston. They couldn't even score a run off of Penetang's pitcher in twenty-one innings.

Barrie beat Penetang once this year 5-1 right in Penetang. We'll see how many other teams win in Penetang this year. Twice Penetang beat Barrie by one run this year in Barrie, and in each case the locals were outlucked.

It's beginning to dawn on baseball fans that the North Simcoe league as a whole plays about as good a ball as any group in the O.B.A. Intermediate B series. Barrie reached the finals in 1930, and the semi-finals in 1931 and 1932. Now Penetang is carrying on the prestige of the league in O.B.A. playdowns. There wasn't much difference this year between Midland, Barrie and Penetang. Just Marchildon. But we're pulling for Penetang to go right through even though there wasn't any love lost for them this summer.

In referring to the delay in the OBA playdowns in the games between Meaford and Lucknow, the series took two weeks, the OBA rules call for one week. The OBA Convenor in the Grey-Bruce district certainly took plenty of authority when he let Meaford and Lucknow get away with that. The baseball season has been set back by at least a week, and has left Penetang, who completed their series within the required time limit waiting for an opponent.

Stars Step Higher
By Jack Calder
Chatham Daily News Staff

Beaten here yesterday, Chatham Stars nevertheless go on into the next round of O.B.A. intermediate B-2 series for the simple reason that Sarnia is some hot stuff for rugby. The youngster who played 1st Base for the Red Sox yesterday is a member of the Sarnia Juniors who are aiming high this year, and if the game had been played as a regular OBA fixture he couldn't have played junior ball again.

Happy Parker, Manager of the Stars, claims he didn't know until the fifth inning that the game had been declared defaulted by Manager Bill Perry of the Red Sox as the declaration had been made to Archie Stirling, OBA Convenor.

So the Stars go on and anyone who saw last Saturday's game will agree that the Chathamites are a lot better than the Red Sox. They're better all-around hitters and Chase and Tabron are better pitchers than anyone on the Sarnia club.

6th Inning

Stars take on Welland in next round; Rangers start epic series with Meaford; Chase hits legendary blast.

Rangers Learn Next Round Opponent is Across the Bay
By Mervyn Dickey
Penetang Herald Staff
September 20th, 1934

The Penetanguishene Spencer Foundry Rangers, North Simcoe Champs and Ontario Baseball Association quarter final winners, have learned who their opponent will be for the next round of competition.

The Meaford Knights, winners of the Grey County league, knocked out Bruce titleists Lucknow to advance. Given that Meaford is only an hour away from Penetang by car, one would think they would have been logical first round opponents. In fairness to the OBA, the geographic spread of this year's entrants has not been even, and some teams (like the Rangers) had lengthy hikes to take on their first round matchup.

The Rangers-Knights will be under the gun to get their series completed in a timely manner after the Meaford-Lucknow *convenor gave the two teams a leisurely fifteen days to complete their series, instead of the usual seven.*

Merv

The break in the playoff schedule was not entirely welcomed by Penetanguishene manager Shaw and his team, who were worried about losing some of their sharpness with the enforced layoff. Meanwhile in Toronto, Phil had some time to catch up on his studies and focus on football. The good Fathers at St Mike's were not keen on Phil missing practice and classes to travel to ball games, but the priest at St Ann's was a St Mike's grad, and he put in a good word. So did J.T. Payette, who was rumoured to have made a donation to the school to make sure Phil's services would continue to be available to the Rangers in their playoff quest, although that was never confirmed.

Phil's dad Oliver confided that things weren't going all that smoothly for Phil, as far as St Mike's football was concerned. The Kerry Blues were a powerhouse with a lot of returning players, and Phil had great difficulty cracking the starting lineup. Missing practice and weekend games didn't help. I later learned from Phil that his studies weren't going all that well, either, although that was easy to understand. For the first time in his young life, he was beginning to have doubts about himself. He was definitely not used to sitting on the bench and playing second string. And despite how busy he was, a little bit of homesickness was creeping in. It's quite a shock to the system to go from the small-town confines of Penetanguishene to the middle of a bustling city like Toronto. The only saving grace for Phil at that point was the car trips with his dad, and the care packages he delivered from Phil's mom. The homemade cookies, squares, and preserves Liza sent made Phil very popular with the boys on his floor at the St Mike's dorm, and served as currency to help pay for the missed class notes they let him copy.

Although they were on opposite shores of the Bay, Meaford and Penetang had much in common. Both were small, waterside towns at the end of a railway line. In many ways, they were a jumping off point for other destinations, the kind of place you go through to get to somewhere else.

Getting from Penetanguishene to Meaford was something of a task. First, the team had to travel on a reasonably good highway south to the crossroads village of Elmvale, then west through flat farmland to the soon-to-be growing resort community of Wasaga Beach, and then on through the shipbuilding town of Collingwood. From there, they hugged the rocky northwestern Georgian Bay shoreline, where the water changed in colour from dark Penetang Bay blue to aquamarine, through the apple orchards of Thornbury, then eventually along the shadow of the Niagara Escarpment to Meaford. The Ontario government had made much of that stretch of highway a relief project, giving the unemployed workers room, board, and 50 cents a day while they toiled on the road. Given the tight finances of the time, the province was strapped for funds, and could only afford to pave half of the road. In this case, the team was travelling west, but only the eastbound lane was paved. Drivers would opt for the paved half no matter which direction they were headed, which made for an interesting ride. People called these half-finished roads "Hepburn Sidewalks," after the Premier who built them.

⚾⚾⚾

Jack

After dispatching Sarnia, the All Stars found out fairly quickly that their next opponent would be the Welland Terriers.

Welland is several hours east of Chatham, in the Niagara Peninsula. Since most people in Chatham headed west toward Windsor and Detroit for jobs and other opportunities, Welland was almost a world away. No one on the team had even been east of London before.

The traditional coin toss saw the first game hosting duties fall to Chatham, with the second match in Welland. A third game, if needed, would be played at a neutral site somewhere between the two cities. In a troubling development that carried over from the Sarnia series, the Stars couldn't pull one out in front of their home fans.

Flat Chase started the game, but was just that - flat. He walked the first two Terriers, then bounced a pitch in the dirt that got away from Washington behind the plate, and there were runners on 2nd and 3rd with no outs. A wild pitch brought in the first run of the game. Hap called time, and had a quick conference with his star hurler and his infield. Just about everyone in the ballpark heard him plead with his Manager to keep him in the game. "I've just got some nerves....I'll pull it together." Hap wanted to let his veteran ace continue, but facing an unknown opponent, he didn't want to let the game get out of hand early, either. As the home plate umpire walked out to the mound with his mask in one hand and chest protector in the other, the traditional baseball signal to wrap things up, Hap gave Flat a slap on the butt, and said, "Go get 'em, Flat!" As much as anything, his early trip to the hill was to give Flat a chance to breathe and regroup.

But Chase simply didn't have it. Three pitches laters, he uncorked another wild pitch to the backstop, and the second Welland run trotted home without the benefit of a hit. An error by the usually sure-handed Ladd in RF, another walk and an infield hit loaded the bases. A free pass allowed the third Welland run of the frame to score, and Hap signalled for Terrell to trade spots with Chase, who had failed to get any of the six hitters he faced in that inning out. King made an impact right away, striking out the first two hitters he faced, and was a pitch away from limiting the visitors to just that early pair of runs, but Boomer bobbled a hot grounder at 1st, and failed to get to the bag in time to record the out, allowing the fourth counter of the inning to score. The next hitter cleared the bases with a triple, and Welland was up 7-0 before Terrell finally got out of the inning.

It was, Boomer later said, the worst inning the team - himself included - had played all year.

The Stars got one of those Welland runs back in the bottom of the 1st, but the hit parade continued, and the Terriers shocked the home crowd into silence with a 17-7 win. In one of their biggest games of the year, the team came up with what Hap later called their worst game of the season. "Wasn't even close," he said after the team had committed nine errors, "We beat ourselves." And now the All Stars had their backs against the wall, facing elimination in Welland.

⚾ ⚾ ⚾

Merv

Baseball and fishing were two of Jim Shaw's biggest passions, and in the summer, when the grain shipping business all but came to a standstill, he was often able to indulge them both at the same time.

So it was that Shaw was able to take an early August fishing trip/scouting expedition to Meaford, which was not far from his hometown of Kemble. He knew the area well, including the best fishing spots and baseball towns. The Meaford Knights were a strong outfit, and he knew they would be a possible OBA matchup for his Rangers. Like his team, they relied heavily on a star pitcher, one who Shaw knew would make things tough for his hitters.

Warpy Phillips, according to the Barrie *Examiner*, was an "undersized southpaw." The *Examiner* also called him "one of the greatest southpaw pitchers in the province," and his Meaford team, "one of the favourites" to take the OBA title now that their city's team had been knocked out. The Rangers had experienced some trouble with the few lefties they had seen, and Shaw knew that Phillips would be no exception. The manager shared his personal scouting report after the North Bay series. "He's just a little guy, maybe 5'6", but he has the liveliest arm I've ever seen. He looks like his shoulder is going to come out of his socket on just about every pitch, comes from somewhere between three-quarters and sidearm, and can throw all of his pitches for strikes - fastball, curve, change, even a 'nickel curve,' which is like a curve, but with two fingers on the seam instead of one. When it's thrown right, it comes in looking like a fastball, but then drops away at the last moment. Warpy knows how to start it on the inside corner to back a lefty hitter off, then it catches the outside corner with the hitter standing there with the bat on his shoulders. We're going to be in tough against this guy." Shaw had no idea who prophetic his words would be...

Beck's Field was the site of the first game, and once again, the good folks of Penetanguishene filled the bleachers, and spilled down both baselines. Many in the overflow section stood or sat on chairs brought from home, with pickup trucks pulling in behind to allow fans to perch on their hoods. The game was held up to allow all the fans to get a good vantage point, and the umpires, concerned about fan interference, ordered the groundskeeper to chalk an "out of play" line down a few feet away from the right and left field lines, in order to keep the crowd back. In a season of growing crowds, it was easily the biggest to date. There were so many fans that the admission booth couldn't accommodate all of them, but estimates put the crowds at around 2 500.

Phil struck out the side to start the game, and Beck's went wild with a roar that could be heard across Penetanguishene Bay. But Warpy silenced the crowd by duplicating that feat in the home half of the 1st. Six up, six down, and not a ball put in play. No one knew it at the time, but that inning was a harbinger of things to come...

The two pitchers matched each other almost pitch for pitch, and strikeout for strikeout for the first four innings. Penetanguishene drew first blood in the 5th, when Marius Bald reached on an error by the Meaford 3rd Baseman that skipped into the crowd, and the base ump awarded Marius 2nd. Phil had a chance to help his own cause a batter later, but hit a one hopper to short that was hit hard enough to allow the short stop to look Marius back to the bag at 2nd, and still have time to nip the speedy Phil at 1st. Hal Crippin came through for the Rangers, though, smacking a two out base hit that allowed Marius to come into home with the game's first run.

Meaford tied the game up in the 7th. Phil walked the leadoff hitter, just missing the outside corner with a curve ball. He crouched down on the mound for the longest time, glaring in disbelief at the home plate umpire, before he received the throw back from Fred. Phil had learned to harness his emotions over the course of the season, but sometimes they still got the better of him. The next batter, as was expected by just about everyone in the park, squared to bunt. Fred called everyone off and leaped out behind the plate to grab it, but instead of taking the sure out at 1st, he fired to 2nd. Hal was covering 2nd on the play, but he was a step late in getting there, and the throw sailed into centre field, and the runner alertly took 3rd. Phil now had men on the corners and no outs. The next hitter was hopeful of just getting a ball in play to score the runner from 3rd, but Phil would have none of it, blowing three straight strikes by him. That brought up Warpy, who unlike Phil, was able to help himself out by launching a sacrifice fly to bring the tying run home. It was an impulsive play on that bunt by Fred, but Phil supported his catcher. "The guy dropped the bunt right in front of home, and it just died there," he said after the game. "In that situation, you want the hitter to get the ball down the baseline to avoid the defence getting the lead runner. Fred made the right play to throw to 2nd - his throw was just a bit off, and maybe Hal got there a little late. It was the right idea, but the wrong execution."

Neither team was able to mount much offence in the remaining two frames, and the game was headed to extra innings. Neither pitcher was giving an inch, and finally, with the sun setting, the umpires called the game in the 13th inning. The first game went into the books as a 1-1 tie, and the second would be played in Meaford.

Shaw confided to me he was concerned about his team's inability to score: "We've played thirty-four OBA innings now, and we've managed only three runs. We're getting runners on, but we're having a lot of trouble moving them over, or putting hits together in succession. Sure, we've faced some top-notch pitching, but we need some timely hitting."

Jack

It was a sleepy group of Stars that gathered at Stirling Park for the trip to Welland, a four-hour trek along the Lake Erie shoreline on Highway 2 in the days before multi-lane highways. But they would be arriving at the Rose City in comfort. Archie Stirling had said before the season started that he would rally local businessmen to the Stars' cause, and he persuaded local oil and gas retailer Peter Gilbert to loan the team three cars for the trip, and threw in money for gas and dinner on the way home. Even after their dismal performance in front of the home fans in the first game, support in the community was growing. "Well we learned one thing about Welland that game," Hap drily remarked. "They're pretty sloppy when they have a big lead."

The second game in Welland was to be a turning point in the All Stars' season. They would have to return to their crisp defensive ways. If there was a silver lining to the first contest, it was that they were able to solve Welland pitcher Shupe for seven runs. Now, he may have let up on the gas a little bit with such a big lead, but the Stars to a man felt they could tie the series. "If we get some pitching, this series will be coming back to Chatham," Boomer said before the team departed.

To that end, Hap had a decision on his hands. Should he go with his sore-armed ace, Flat Chase, or go back to King Terrell, who hadn't exactly set the world on fire in relief of Chase although his defence had a severe case of the butterfingers behind him? In the end, he decided to go with King, but probably wouldn't hesitate to make a switch if the game appeared to be getting out of hand.

The choice of Terrell looked like a smart move in the early going. He retired the first six hitters he faced, but the home side took the lead with a run off of him in the 3rd. Chatham tied the game at one in the 5th, scored in typical Stars' fashion. Washington reached on an error, then stole 2nd. A wild pitch moved him to 3rd, then he came in to score on a sac fly by Talbot. Chatham had specialized in manufacturing runs all season, a skill that came in handy in this tight potential elimination match.

The tie was short-lived, however, as the hometown Terriers scored in their half of the 5th to retake the lead. The game was far from over, but the visitors had to be feeling the pressure. They had never led a game in the short series up to that point. Welland always seemed to be able to score when they needed to.

In the 6th, Len Harding led off with a single, but Terrell popped out, and Boomer flied to centre, and a promising inning appeared to be fading away. Flat Chase was the next hitter.

Chase didn't say much about it, but he was clearly irritated that he didn't get the ball to start the most important game of the Stars' season. He was a man of few words to begin with, but he had even fewer after Hap told him he would be starting at shortstop. The legend of Flat Chase was known far and wide across southwestern Ontario, but Hap showed some courage in choosing King over him to start the game on the mound. But somehow, Flat was able to focus on the game, had already made a nice defensive play in the field, and was coming up in a key situation.

Welland pitcher Shupe had been sharp all day, a stark contrast to his last outing. How would he pitch to Flat? He had already gotten the Stars' other dangerous hitter, Boomer, out. With two out, would he go right after Flat to end the inning, or would he pitch around him, moving Len up to 2nd with the potential tying run? Hap had the team running from the first game of the season, but he anchored Len to 1st for a couple of reasons. If he had stolen 2nd, Shupe would probably be ordered to intentionally walk Flat with a base open. Also, leaving Len at 1st would force the 1st Baseman to hold him on, opening up a hole on the right side of
the infield for the left-handed hitting Chase. Finally, there was always the chance that Len could get thrown out stealing, thereby taking the bat out of Flat's hands. Hap had let Len run

at will all season, but this was one of the few times he flashed the "don't go" sign over in the 3rd base coaches' box.

And what about Flat, up at the plate? What would his approach be? Should he try to work the count, or should he be aggressive and go after the first pitch that he saw to his liking? Shupe was tiring somewhat, so being selective and trying to make him throw a lot of pitches might reward Flat in the form of a sub-par offering. But maybe Shupe had already decided he was not going to give Flat anything good to hit. Putting the tying run at 2nd by walking Chase was risky, but you could not blame Shupe if he pitched around the slugger, and took his chances with the hitters behind him. Flat wasn unafraid to take a walk, but he knew what the team needed at that moment was a big hit, not a walk. Welland seemed to have the Stars' number, and with the end of the season looming, Flat was looking to do some damage. If there is one thing that has not changed about baseball going back to the days when the pitcher threw underhand, five balls were a walk and four a strikeout, it would be that cat-and-mouse game between hurler and hitter.

Sometimes, the crack of the ball coming off the bat makes a sound so loud and sudden that everyone in the ballpark stands up and takes notice. For a moment, time is suspended as the sound hangs in the air - the earth seems to stop rotating. Birds stop flying, clouds are stationary, and the whole world seems to come to standstill. The crack echoes around the ballpark, lingering for a few seconds in the crowd's collective subconscious. People passing by on the street stop to crane their necks at the source of the rifle-like sound. After its ascent, the ball seems to defy gravity, floating along in the air before starting its return to earth somewhere beyond the outfield fence. For the team of the player that hit it, there is a sense of jubilation, a moment of incredible release, and teammates scamper out of the dugout to congratulate the author of the awesome flight. For the opposing team, listening to and watching the trajectory of the ball while the batter rounds the bases can be soul-crushing.

Shupe had tried to get ahead of Flat, attempting to sneak a first-pitch fastball. Being a pitcher himself, Flat was guessing that he would have done the same thing - they say the best pitch in baseball is strike one, because it gives the pitcher the upper hand in the battle. But Shupe caught too much of the plate, and Flat was ready. His swing was effortless, so easy, and the ball just seemed to explode off his bat like it was fired from a cannon. It cleared the right field fence - at the moment of contact, the right fielder had braced himself, making that instant mental trigonometry outfielders do to calculate where the ball is headed. He
turned heel and started a sprint to the fence, then after several strides turned to find the ball in order to adjust his route, and he

knew it was over - he just pulled up ten feet shy of the fence and watched the ball sail to parts seldom seen by a baseball before. Flat's clout cleared a storage shed beyond the right field fence, landed on a sidewalk and bounced between braking cars across a road. The local newspaper later called it a "Murderous Wallop." As he rounded the bases, the hometown crowd gave the visiting slugger a standing ovation. Flat broke into a huge grin as he touched home plate, the first time he'd smiled all series. He had put his team up by a run with his prodigious blast. The game was not over yet, but the Stars were up 3-2 as the game headed to the bottom of the 6th a batter later.

"That was the turning point of the series," Boomer later told me. "Welland had been ahead of us for the first game and a half, but when we get a lead, we don't tend to lose it. That shot Flat hit really seemed to break their spirit."

King Terrell crowned the Terriers the rest of the way. His defence even pulled off a key 8th inning double play behind him, and with the "go" sign back on and the Welland infield caught napping, Len Harding stole home in the 9th to give the Stars a two-run cushion. Terrell retired the side in order in the last of the 9th, and the series was tied.

Boomer said the drive home always seemed longer after a loss, but this trip had promise. The Stars celebrated a little, wildly honking the horns on their borrowed cars as they headed out of Welland and into the falling southwestern Ontario night. They stopped at a roadside restaurant about an hour out of town, having broken into their post-game sandwiches on the long drive to Welland. The team was stopped before they could be seated once again. They were given menus and told the restaurant was only filling orders "to go," even though there were several (white) patrons seated. There was a protest, but Washington stepped in again, and told the team, "It's a helluva long drive home, and you guys are hungry. Let's just order our food and get out of here." Boomer said although Wash was probably right, the experience took some of the joy out of their victory, and he said, "it showed us that we still had miles to go, despite how far we'd already travelled."

The third and deciding game of the series would be played on a neutral field at London. The crowd wouldn't be as big if the game was held in Chatham or Welland, but it meant there was less travel expense involved.

⚾ ⚾ ⚾

Merv

The Rangers had been on something of a roll, winning their last two games of the regular season, then sweeping both four-time defending North Simcoe champs Barrie and then North Bay in two games. But failing to come away with a victory in their opening game with Meaford put the team in an uncomfortable position. Sure, a win on the other side of the Bay would even up the series, and give the Rangers a huge advantage with game three scheduled for Beck's Field, but a loss would have them facing elimination as they passed the angels at the entrance of Penetanguishene on their return.

Maybe it was the toll that commuting to games was taking, maybe it was the dual football-baseball life he was leading, but Phil himself said, "I just didn't have it," after the second game in Meaford. His fastball seemed to have no life to it, and it was a challenge for him to find the strike zone consistently. He kept falling behind the hitters, a high wire act for even the best of pitchers. On top of that, his defence behind him developed a case of the fumbles. Phil's opposite moundsman, the inestimable Warpy, continued to have his way with Penetanguishene's hitters.

The final score was 5-3 for Meaford, and the score actually flattered the Rangers. Phil walked six, the team committed five errors, and only a ninth inning two-run rally made the score respectable. Meaford broke the game open early with a 4-run second inning, and with Warpy firing on all cylinders on the mound, cruised to an easy victory. It was a long drive back around the shores of Georgian Bay for the Rangers, and an even longer one for Phil's dad, who started his day at 6 am with a thermos full of coffee and the car he was loaned full of gas and pointed south for Toronto. After picking Phil up downtown at St Mike's, the pair headed back north up Highway 11 to Barrie, then turned to the northwest along Highway 26 to follow the Georgian Bay shoreline through Collingwood to Meaford. After the game was over, Oliver retraced his route to drop Phil back off at school, then followed his headlights back to Penetanguishene, where he arrived shortly after midnight. He clocked over 400 miles on the day.

⚾⚾⚾

STARS BEAT WELLAND IN FINAL GAME
Tabron and Chase Star;
May be Placed in Finals
By Jack Calder
Chatham Daily News Staff

LONDON, Sept. 27th - Their high-powered offence clicking in every department, Chatham Stars steam-rolled their way into further O.B.A. play here yesterday afternoon with an 11-7 victory over Welland. The game was the third of the third round intermediate B series each team having won one of the preceding two contests. The Stars will now meet a team from eastern Ontario since the teams still competing in that district are so remote from Chatham, the Stars may not be called on to play again until the finals.

Don Tabron was back with the Stars again after an enforced absence and went the distance on the hill in steady fashion. He was found for eight hits and walked six but in only two innings was he in much trouble and over much of the distance he was accorded brilliant support.

STARS SCORE EARLY

The Stars were quick to establish their superiority as they went into a 6-1 lead before a third of the game had progressed. A wild throw by King Terrell paved the way for a Welland rally in the third frame and Welland reduced the Stars' lead to three runs. The Chatham team struck again with three runs in the sixth, however, and another pair in the seventh iced the game. Shupe relieved Tufts in the seventh for Welland and held the Stars hitless over the last two and two-thirds innings. In the eighth, Welland scored three more runs, two Chatham errors setting off the spark. The Stars finished off the game with a lightning-fast double play in the ninth.

Again, it was big Flat Chase, who played at shortstop for the Stars yesterday, who predominated on the attack. The Koloured King of Klout rapped a triple, double, and single in five attempts. Don Washington, Cliff Olbey, and Gouy Ladd all contributed two hits while Upper and Hughey were the only members of the eastern club to hit safely twice. Tabron and Ladd bagged triples.

The game held nothing spectacular outside of the Stars' hitting, but the Maple City campaigners more than established their right to enter further play.

Bits About the Stars

From the Welland-Port Colborne Tribune:

"A word about the Colored lads. They made a big hit with the crowd. Especially Percy "Feet" Parker, who coached at first base, and was a whole show in himself. His 'my, my, my' observation after close decisions went against the Stars kept the crowd in high glee. Flat Chase's home run brought down the house and every good play by the visitors was applauded. Catcher Washington proved to be a backstopper of no mean ability and all in all, the crew performed in a style that caused general bewilderment in view of the top-heavy score the Terriers registered against the Chatham club last Thursday."

Merv

September was just a few days short of giving way to October, and Meaford was returning to Penetanguishene for the third (and what the visitors surely hoped would be the final) game of the series in the longest baseball season anyone in town had ever seen. It seemed odd to be playing ball with the trees starting to shed themselves of their spectacular fall colours.

As usual, a huge crowd flooded Beck's field, circling the park in a very vocal pro-Rangers ring several rows deep.

Phil was getting more than a little frustrated at the Meaford hitters, and maybe himself, too. He was still racking up those double-digit strikeouts, but their hitters always seemed to find a way to get on base. A walk here, a bloop single there, and Phil often had to work with runners on. The Rangers bats were still lukewarm at best, although they managed to scrape together a run in the bottom of the 1st to take an early 1-0 lead.

Meaford got that run back in the 4th, then tacked on another to take the lead. The way Warpy was pitching, that run may have been all they needed. But Hal Crippin, who was about the only player consistently delivering timely hits in the Pentang batting order, hit a towering home run in the 6th to tie the score at 1-1. Otherwise, the two teams couldn't mount a serious threat to score. Once again, extra innings were looming.

But Meaford recaptured the lead the next inning. Warpy once again helped himself with a two-out double down the 3rd base line to drive in the go-ahead run. Crippin's long ball had brought life to the home crowd, many of whom were equipped with cowbells which must have driven the visitors crazy, but Phillips' hit brought silence to Beck's once more. Meaford led 2-1.

As the Rangers took their at bats to start the bottom of the 7th, there was heavy tension in the air, as they were down to their final nine outs in a series where runs had been hard to come by. Warpy retired Penetang in order, then Phil replied in kind in the top of the 8th. For the third straight game, both moundsmen had 10 or more strikeouts by that point. The Rangers couldn't muster any offence in the 8th, and the Knights failed to add an insurance run in the top of the 9th.

Suddenly, Penetang was down to possibly their final three outs of the season. With their 8th and 9th hitters due to lead off the final frame, there wasn't a great deal of reason to be optimistic. Both Peg Spearn and Dan McCuaig were overmatched against Warpy during the series.

Before he headed down to the 3rd base coaches' box, Shaw gathered his team on the Penetang bench. "Listen fellas," he said, "I'm not one for pep talks, alright? But we've beaten teams as good as - or better than - this team we're facing today. We've come too far for our season to end. Every hitter has been trying to take the measure of this guy Warpy this series, and that approach hasn't worked. I don't want any heroes out there, I want a team effort. We need base runners, we need balls in play, we need to move runners. You guys have been down at the end of your bats, some of you swinging from the heels to try to belt one off this little guy. Now it's time to work the count, choke up a little bit, and just punch some balls, make some contact. Peg - you set the table for us. We just need a little bingle out there, and get you on base."

And Peg did just that. He worked the count even at 2-2, then hit a ground ball sharply up the middle that must have bounced ten times and died in the outfield grass before the centre fielder could scurry in and pick it up, but it was enough to get between the shortstop and 2nd baseman, and the Rangers had life. Shaw had been a fairly conservative manager all season, preferring not to take chances on the base paths, mainly because he had an ace on the mound who could make a few runs stand up more often than not. But he could also be unconventional. In a situation that all but screamed for a sacrifice bunt, he was willing to take a chance. Despite his struggles at the plate against Meaford, Dan McCuaig could handle the bat. He could lay down a decent bunt, but he also could put balls in play. Despite the risk, Shaw put the hit-and-run on. Several of the Rangers stared in disbelief as they saw him flash the sign.

As Warpy was about to deliver his first pitch to McCuaig, his corner infielders began to creep in, fully expecting a bunt. Spearn alertly took a huge lead off of 1st, judging that there was no way they could pick him off with the 1st baseman playing several steps ahead of the bag. As the pitch came in, Spearn was off, getting a huge jump in the process. But instead of squaring to bunt, McCuaig pulled a liner past the 3rd baseman, who ordinarily probably would have been able to field the ball cleanly if he hadn't been guarding against the bunt. The ball hooked past the bag at 3rd, fair by about a foot, but shortly after that it rolled into foul territory. As the left fielder raced over to pick it up, Peg rounded 2nd, and headed for 3rd on a mad dash for Home. The ball disappeared into the overflow crowd, over the chalk line the umpires had the groundskeeper make for the first game, and the left fielder held his arms up to signal to the umps that the ball had gone out of play. As he did this, McCuaig strolled into 2nd, and Peg crossed the plate with the tying run.

As you could imagine, there was pandemonium on the play. The Rangers faithful yelled, whistled, and stomped their feet madly as Spearn came into score, but there was a subdued element to their cheering, because the play was quite confusing. It was like they wanted to celebrate their team tying the game, but weren't sure if the run would stand on the unusual play.

The Meaford manager stormed out of the dugout to the home plate umpire, saying there was no way that Spearn should be allowed to advance three bases on a ground rule double. After a brief conference with the base umpire, the plate ump directed Spearn back to 3rd. Shaw, who knew the official baseball rule book as well as he knew grain elevators, trotted down from the coaches' box and pointed out that because Spearn had started on his way to 2nd as the pitch was being thrown, he was entitled to that base, plus two more as a result of the double. Meaford's manager - who clearly wasn't as well-versed on the rules of the day as Shaw was - got back into the fray, demanding an explanation. Once again, the umpires walked away to confer amidst the din and confusion. After they had discussed the play, the home plate ump went back to the two skippers, and explained, "according to the rules of the game, the runner on 1st is entitled to the base he was attempting to steal, plus two more as a result of the ball rolling out of play. Runner on 1st scores, the batter is awarded 2nd."

Meaford's manager blew his stack at the call, claiming this was a ground rule that should have been discussed in much more detail in the traditional pre-game meeting with the umpires. He let them know on the spot that he would be protesting the game. Personally, I don't see how there could have been any confusion.

Despite having a runner on 2nd and no one out when the game resumed, the Rangers were unable to bring McCuaig in with the winning run, and for the second time in the series, the teams were headed to extra innings. Neither side was able to get a run across in the 10th, after which the umpires had to call the game because of the approaching darkness. Meaford still held a 1-0 lead in the series, with the fourth game likely to be delayed while their protest was heard, prolonging the series and the season once again.

The whole affair tacked on over twenty minutes to a long, pressure-packed game. The Meaford manager couldn't actually protest the call on the field, so he filed one stating that the ground rules had not been properly explained. "There will be a dog and pony show with the OBA, but Meaford doesn't have a leg to stand on," said Shaw after the game.

⚾ ⚾ ⚾

Meaford Protest Was Thrown Out
Midland Free Press
October 1st, 1934

Meaford Black Sox Baseball Club has been notified by the O.B.A. that the protest lodged against the Penetang Club was thrown out at a meeting held Saturday night in the Royal York Hotel in Toronto. As a result, Black Sox have been ordered to replay the game with Penetang on Wednesday, October 3rd, and to play to a finish. Meafords having won a game and tied two. The protest was entered last week when a Penetang batter knocked the ball into the crowd scoring a runner that was on first base to tie the game, 3 to 3. Officials of the Penetang club were present at the sub-committee meeting when the protest was dealt with.

At the meeting, at which OBA Vice-President Smith presided, Meaford claimed that McCuaig had made only a two-base hit, according to the ground rules, and Spearn, who was ahead of him on first base should only be allowed the two bases, but he was sent home with the tying run. According to rule sixty-five National League, Spearn was entitled to the base which he was attempting to steal, and two others. Thus, he was allowed to complete the run and the score of the game on September 26th remains 3-3.

Merv

By the time all the various OBA executives and representatives from both teams could be assembled, we were into October, with plenty of baseball left to play for whoever moved on from this series. The protest, as was expected under the rules of the day, went for naught, and yet another game was to be played. The ordered replay by the OBA meant that the Rangers once again got home field, but they were still facing elimination.

The contest promised to be another close one. After playing 33 innings over the first three games, Meaford had scored only two more runs than Penetanguishene. It certainly was nail-biting for the fans, but nobody complained about getting their money's worth.

The umpires, Shaw, and the Meaford manager ironed out the ground rules before the game started so that there would be no question this time. In fairness to Meaford, ground rule doubles into overflow crowds were not a regular occurrence in the Grey League, nor was it in North Simcoe, for that matter, and when you factor in a runner on the move prior to the hit, it's understandable where the confusion came in. It was a wild play, probably never seen by anyone in the park before. Except for Jim Shaw, of course.

Once again, an over-capacity crowd showed up to cheer on the home team. Fans again ringed the park several deep. The game featured more offence than usual, with both teams starting to figure out each other's ace. Phil was also visibly tired from his breakneck schedule. Honestly, I don't know how he did it. Weekends were a time for most to catch up on leisure, but for Phil, who had spent most September and October weekends in a car, and was juggling a full post-secondary course load, there was little time for rest.

Phil showed more polish on the mound in the first three innings of the game than he had in the previous three games. The problem was that Warpy was just as effective at shutting down the Rangers' bats, and the game was a scoreless tie after three innings.

Phil was the first to blink in this pitchers' duel, giving up a pair of Meaford runs in the 3rd. Phillips continued his mastery of the Rangers, and with the visitors up 2-0 as the game headed to the last of the 7th, fans had to be wondering if their team, which had staved off elimination twice, was now running out of chances.

As dominant as Phillips had been, the toll on his left arm was becoming obvious in the middle innings. He was still piling up the whiffs, but he was obviously tiring, and the Rangers had made some hard contact against him, but the Meaford defence came through for their ace on several occasions. But balls started to fall in during the 7th to the relief of the Rangers' faithful, and by the time the inning was over, the home team had plated three runs, and took a 3-2 lead heading into the 8th.

But if Warpy was running out of gas, Phil was close to emptying the tank, too. The strain of pitching five intense games in two-plus weeks was exacting a heavy price on both pitchers. Meaford's ability to scratch out runs when they needed them was on display in the 8th, when they scored two more to take a 4-3 lead. Heading into the last of that inning, the largest lead between the two teams in over 40 innings of play now was two runs.

Once more, the Rangers found a way to fight back, and responded to Meaford's pair of tallies with two of their own to take a 5-4 lead. If Meaford found a way to come back in the 9th, it would be tough for a fatigued Phillips to take the mound again, because he was for all intents and purposes finished for the day. But the lead revitalized Phil, and with the home team similarly brought back to life by their team's late inning heroics, he retired the side in order to preserve the win.

The Rangers, with their backs against the wall, extended their season yet again, and tied the series up at one win apiece. Phil seemed to have rediscovered his fastball, and the Meafords truly had to be concerned that their own ace's seeming invincibility had cracked. As had been decided by the OBA, a fifth and deciding contest would take place Thanksgiving Monday in Barrie on a neutral field.

⚾ ⚾ ⚾

Jack

Having dispatched Welland on September 26th, on the same day (we learned later) that Penetang and Meaford played to a controversial tie, there was little for the Stars to do but sit back and wait. We did not know it at the time, but controversy seemed to follow Penetang around.

Archie Stirling informed the club that there was another ongoing series between Milton and Peterborough, and if it finished up within the next couple of days, Chatham would have to play yet another series before they made it to the final. As Boomer noted, someone was going to get the short end of the stick, and "It probably will be us," he said in disgust.

The truth is that several leagues opted out of OBA play that year because they could not afford the travel the tournament would entail. That left the organization with an unbalanced number of entrants in several divisions. It also meant that some teams would run up more travel expenses than others, most noticeably the Stars, who at least had Peter Gilbert helping to foot the bill.

Boomer had been a beacon of positivity since his talk with Hap earlier in the season, but the long grind and the likelihood of having to play in what the team viewed as an extra series did not sit well with him. "I get it, there's circumstances beyond our control," he observed, "but it seems like the powers that be want to do whatever they can to keep us from winning this thing. You know what? That only makes us stronger."

Merv

Thanksgiving is a time of celebration across Canada, a time to give thanks, celebrate the harvest, spend time with family, and hunker down before winter hits in the upcoming weeks. For Phil, there was little time for any of that, as St Mike's had a huge Saturday game. Oliver picked him up in Toronto on Sunday morning, though, and after a huge traditional turkey dinner and time spent catching up with all his Marchildon and Lavereau (his mother's side) relatives, Phil was ready to take on Meaford one more time the next day.

As was traditional, the fifth game would be played on a neutral diamond in Barrie, the largest centre in the county, and as a result, the only town that still had a ballpark in use, others having put their fields to bed for the winter weeks before. Collingwood, which would have been exactly halfway between the two towns along Hepburn's sidewalks, had a field that was in no condition to be played on. Because it was only about a 40-minute drive away, a sizable contingent of Penetanguishene fans made the holiday Monday trek to support their team. Meaford, who came from over an hour away, had next to no fans in attendance.

Before the game, Jim Shaw was seated on the Rangers bench early, waiting for his prize pitcher to arrive at the park. "Hey, Babe. I received a phone call from your old buddy," he informed. Phil gave him a quizzical look. "From who?" he responded.

"Why, none other than your mentor - your personal coach, Howling Dan"

That got Phil's attention. "What did he have to say?"

"He asked how things are going with you and the team. Says he reads about how we've been faring in the OBAs thanks to the Toronto *Globe*."
"Did you respond?" Phil inquired.

"Why, I sure did. Invited old Dan to get himself up here and help me with the salmon run this month."

Phil was not the least bit interested in the fishing talk. From the moment the two met, Phil knew Howley was a connection, a man who could use his ties in pro ball to land Phil a tryout, and maybe even a pro contract. He was quite concerned about what Shaw might have told him, because Phil had fallen back on some bad habits over the past few weeks, eschewing much of what Howley had told him in favour of just reaching back and trying to blow his fastball by every hitter. "What else did you two old coots talk about?"

Shaw turned serious. "We talked about your development as a pitcher. He asked if you were working on your changeup and some of the other grips he taught you."

"What did you tell him?" asked Phil, sheepishly. He knew.

"I told him," continued Shaw with his heart-to-heart, "the truth."

Phil was often equal parts cockiness and arrogance. Athletic success had come to him at an early age, along with accompanying celebrity status that had started to grow far beyond the Penetanguishene town limits. To his credit, after Howley left at the end of June, Phil had continued to try to implement the repertoire he'd been taught. But Phil was not the most patient of pupils, and after the Rangers went on a three-game losing streak in August and briefly gave up the North Simcoe lead, he junked most of what Howley had taught him, and had gone back to his fastball, with the odd curve mixed in. Now, with Meaford starting to catch on to his bag of tricks, Phil wanted to point the finger at anyone but himself.

"You can't just rear back and fire away," Shaw advised. "The good hitters - and even some of the average ones - will start to time up that fastball of yours once they've seen it on a steady basis. Dan worked with you on the art of deception, and personally, I thought you were coming along well with it in July. Then we hit that little skid in August, and you stopped using that changeup, and some of the other pitches Dan worked with you on. You have to mix things up, Babe."

Phil was about to say something - if I had to guess, it would be something along the lines of, "When you're striking out over a dozen guys per game, you don't have to 'mix things up,'" but he bit his lip and thought better of it.

Shaw knew Phil probably had a response teed up, but he let it pass. He knew this is what you would call a teachable moment. "Babe, I know that this is new territory for you. You've had your way with most hitters for a couple of years now. And while this isn't the big leagues, there are some pretty good hitters at this level of competition, and for maybe the first time in your life, this game seems hard. But this is a good lesson for you. You have to be able to think this game in order to play it well. You have to use your head as much as your arm."

Phil knew better than to disagree with Shaw. He also knew the team had brought both Shaw and Howley in to work with him this year, and that the pair were laying the groundwork and making plans for Phil's eventual pro career.

Shaw was right - for perhaps the first time in his athletic life, Phil was having an extended trial with adversity. During the week, he'd work his butt off in practice with St Mike's, only to see second-string action. His family had trouble following his pigskin progress in the *Star*, mainly because the reporter assigned to cover his games had mistakenly called him "Talbot," or "Marcellus," in his reports. Once a big fish in a little pond, Phil was now the opposite. And it probably didn't help his emotional state that Meaford was beginning to figure him out. He had always relied on his bountiful athleticism in the past to help him conquer opponents; for the first time, that wasn't enough.

Baseball players are creatures of habit, and the Penetanguishene ball club was no exception. Their pre-game rituals never varied: players threw warm-up tosses with the same partners, Shaw hit the same number of ground balls for infield, while his coach Ivan Flynn hit the same number of fly balls for his outfielders to shag. Phil would warm up alongside either the 1st or 3rd baselines (depending on which side the Rangers would be using for their bench), and stationed his Catcher DeVillers just off of home plate to receive his pitches. Phil and Fred did that in order to intimidate the opposition; Phil's fastball would zing in with movement you could actually hear as the wind bit into the ball's stitches, then would hit DeVillers' mitt with a resounding pop that made the opposition pay attention. The team's pre-game preparations would conclude with Shaw taking the team into the outfield along the baseline closest to the team's bench for some last-minute instructions. This was a private moment for the team, in which Shaw would go over the lineup, the ground rules (at a visiting park), and any special scouting notes on the opposition or the umpires.

But before this fifth and possibly deciding game, Hal Crippin stepped up. With his brother Bob hobbled by injury, Hal had unofficially taken over as the squad's Captain. He was the strong, silent type, more prone to lead by example than oration. As the team headed out for their outfield gathering, Crippin took Shaw aside and said, "If you don't mind, Jim, I'd like to have a players-only meeting. We have some things to work out."

Shaw was enough of a leader to know that when a veteran approached like that, he should take a step back. "Go ahead," he agreed, heading back to the bench.

As the team gathered, Crippin spoke. "Guys," he began, "you all know I'm a man of few words. I like to go about my business, and no one else's. But this has been a long, drawn-out affair, this series. It's been tough. We're tired, and every one of these games in the playoffs seems like it's been a battle

- because it has. But you know what? I think we have Meaford on the ropes. They filed that protest after the third game because I think they knew that we're starting to get to Warpy. Don't get me wrong - they're the best team we've played all year, but they don't want any more of us. We played about as well as we can last game - good plays in the field, Babe pitched his heart out, and we made Warpy work for every out he got. We can't let up, though - we have to battle every at bat, make the smart play in the field and on the bases - not beat ourselves - and get some hits when we need them. We've come too far to have our season end, fellas. The winner of this game goes on to the finals, and it's gonna be us."

From a clipboard he'd taken from Shaw, Hal read off the batting order (which had been the same for weeks - the only change was the addition of Chuck Sheppard, returned from a job in Toronto he was laid off from - back at 3rd). There was a collective, hearty, "Let's get 'em guys," when the lineup had been read, which was usually a signal that the gathering was over. But as the team headed off to their bench, Hal caught everyone's attention when he said, "Babe, just a minute."

You could've heard a pin drop. As the team headed back to the infield minus its two best players, who stayed out talking in short right field, even the crowd seemed to take notice, as a collective silence seemed to envelope the ballpark. It wasn't the first time, to be honest, that I had watched one of the veterans (who were all of three or four years older) on the team take the youngster Phil aside for some sage advice, but it was usually done in private. This time, though, with fans filling every nook and cranny of the park, the outfield was about the only place where a conversation could take place without being overheard.

It wasn't hard to figure out the topic of their brief discussion. Knowing Hal, it was a to-the-point part pep-talk, part big brotherly advice type of conversation. He wasn't one to preach, but all of the players on the team took his words to heart. Hal was likely reminding Phil of what had to be done to win, and what Phil in particular could do to make that happen: stay composed, don't get upset when the ump didn't give him the corner, and pound that strike zone, especially the bottom part of it. As the two walked back to the bench, their short conference finished, a cheer rose from the fans closest to the Penetanguishene bench, and was soon taken up by the rest of the crowd. It was a definite turning point in the series.

⚾ ⚾ ⚾

Penetang Put Meaford Out by Close Margin
Northern Advance
October 11th, 1934

The Penetang ball team, led by "Babe" Marchildon and "Sheik" Crippin scored the decisive win over Meaford at Agricultural Park on Wednesday afternoon. The game was a real exhibition, which ended in a 3-2 score in favor of the northerners, and was witnessed by 2,503 people under ideal weather conditions.

Five games were necessary to decide a winner between these two teams. The first game in Penetang went to 13 innings ending 1-1. The second game was won by Meaford on their home field 5 to 1. The third game went to extra innings and was a tie. In the fourth game Penetang won at home by a one-run margin. The fifth and deciding game between those two evenly matched teams gave Penetang the right to meet Chatham Colored All Stars or Milton in the finals.

"Warpy" Phillips, diminutive southpaw of the Meaford Black Sox, pitched winning ball and was his team's best hitter. After striking out fifteen men and pitching sensational ball throughout, Warpy got himself in a hole in the ninth and before he was able to crawl out the winning run had been scored.

Shepherd started the fatal night with a single, Hale whiffed, Crippin hit safely, Shepherd going to third. McCuaig was safe on a bunt, filling the bases. Phillips could not locate the plate with Bald up and forced in the winning run.

Marchildon, Penetang ace, was right on the bit. He held the Black Sox scoreless until the eighth, when they tied the score with two runs. Machildon depended more on his team mates than Phillips. He struck out ning and gave seven hits, all of which were well scattered.

Penetang got the jump in the first innings when Bell in left field made two costly boners which netted the winners their first run. Bell was suffering from an injury and after his last attempt on a fly ball, he retired from the game.

M. Bald was the leading hitter for the winners with two doubles and two walks out of four times at bat. Crippin had three safe blows. For the losers Phillips hit a triple, double, and a single, which all any pitcher should do. Wright had a perfect average with a single and three walks out of four attempts.

7th Inning

All Stars learn they have to play another series before the Final, defeat Milton in Semi; Penetang placed in Final; word of Marchildon's temperamental personality reaches far.

Jack

As the Stars awaited word of their next opponent, Hap scheduled brief workouts at Stirling Park to keep his charges fresh. He knew they had played a lot of ball, but he wanted their skills to remain sharp. At one of those sessions, Archie made the brief trip from his store to the park to deliver some news.

While Archie and Hap conferred behind the backstop, the team watched nervously. They knew that the news might not be good.

After their short meeting, Hap had the players go through the last few minutes of their practice, then summoned the team to the bench. "Fellas," he began, "Archie told me a few minutes ago. There was talk, so he says, from the OBA that after we beat Welland, we'd go straight to the finals. But this Penetang-Meaford series is taking forever to finish, so now we have to go and play Milton, who just beat Peterborough. Archie lobbied hard against that, but we're all up against Mother Nature now, so Milton it is."

There was a collective groan from the players at the thought of more travelling, but Hap was right. The calendar was the opposition as much as the other teams. October weather in Ontario can be unpredictable. The odd snow storm can take place - usually nothing that sticks - and the weather tends to be cold and rainy. Good weather for football, but not baseball. The ball can be slippery, footing uncertain, and the bat stings in the hands when you try to connect with a fastball.

Boomer was not his upbeat self when I talked to him about it, though. "It just seems like everyone is doing their best to make sure we don't win this," he complained. "If it's not bad calls from the umps, it's strange decisions by the OBA. But I guess we're lucky in one way - we don't have to go to Peterborough." He was right about that. The Electric City is an hour and a half east of Toronto, which would have worked out to a five-plus hour trip from Chatham. Milton, on the west side, would at least - at three hours - be a closer journey. "But now I have to ask for more time off from work," he added. "So, do the other guys that have jobs. My boss has been pretty good about it, but you hate to ask. Lots of people are out of work or have had their hours cut, and jobs are hard to come by right now. You worry about your own job a little bit, and I don't think the OBA cares at all."

One development that helped the Stars was the return of Donny Tabron from Windsor. He had found a job there, leaving the team just as the playoffs started, but was laid off after only a few weeks, and was freed up to play just as the team needed him. With Flat's arm troubles, Donny offered Hap another good arm to use on the mound. When Flat was healthy enough to pitch, Tabron represented solid defence at shortstop. The Stars were no doubt happy that Donny had rejoined the club; his return to the roster would prove to be a huge boost to the team's fortunes in the weeks ahead.

One thing was obvious as the fall progressed: the Stars were becoming the big story in town. In the stores and restaurants, the talk was about the coloured team from the east end. A Chatham ball team had never gone this far in provincial play, and it caught the sporting public's attention. Overflow crowds had flocked to Stirling Park, and packed the tiny ballpark.

The decision had been made in the Welland series to move the Chatham home games to the more spacious Athletic Park, which was close enough so that many of the Stars' faithful could get there by foot. There was some concern that attendance might suffer because the first game conflicted with the opening game of the St Louis-Detroit World Series - southwestern Ontario is Tigers country - so someone came up with the idea of piping the broadcast of the game through the Park's loudspeakers, in effect giving fans two games for the price of one.

That first game against Milton at Athletic Park was a standing-room only affair, likely the biggest crowd to ever watch a sporting event in Chatham. Attendance must have been pushing 2 000. Chase's arm was still balky, so Tabron took the mound for the Stars. But there was nothing wrong with Chase's bat, as he staked Tabron to a two-run lead with a Home Run in the bottom of the 1st. There was no fence at Athletic Park in those days, but many say that Flat's blow was the longest the old Queen St ballyard had ever seen. The outfielders gave frantic chase to it, but Chase crossed home while the relay was still coming into the infield.

The game was an old-fashioned barn burner after that point, with plenty of runners on, and both teams threatened to score almost every inning as they took turns with the lead. The two teams combined for 34 hits on the day; Milton had a hit in every frame, Chatham in every one but the 6th.

Milton tied the game 2-2 with a pair in the 3rd; Chatham responded with two of their own in the 4th. Milton answered with two more runs in the 7th, tying the game at 4. But the deadlock was short-lived, as the Stars scored three in the home half of the inning to take what seemed an insurmountable 7-4 lead. But Milton kept coming. They loaded the bases with no outs in the top of the 8th, and wound up scoring a pair and cut the Stars' lead to one, 7-6. The home side added an insurance run in the bottom half, and for the first time all day, the crowd seemed to breathe easily as the Stars took a two-run advantage into the 9th.

But the plucky visitors had no intention of letting up. Their first batter of the 9th singled, and two batters later, moved up to 3rd on another base hit. With one out, a slow roller was hit to Boomer's right at 1st. Tabron had broken quickly from the mound to cover 1st, which would have been the sure out, but Boomer opted to try to get the force at 2nd. His throw was late, and allowed the first run of Milton's inning to cross the plate, and now they had runners at 1st and 2nd with still only one out. If Boomer had taken the safe play and tossed to Tabron, Milton would be on the ropes, with a runner on 2nd but two out.

The next Milton hitter lashed a line drive single, scoring the runner on 2nd, and knotting the score at 8. On the next play, a ground ball was hit to the left side between Terrell at 3rd and Chase at short. Both expected the other to make the play, and as the ball rolled into the outfield, the go-ahead run came around to score, and the visitors had their first lead of the game. The Stars were able to get the next two outs to get out of the inning, but headed to the last of the 9th trailing 9-8. Another loss in front of the home fans was a possibility.

Chatham was able to knot the game up once more on typical All Stars' small ball. Talbot reached on an infield hit, stole 2nd, and alertly moved to 3rd on a passed ball. With the Milton manager inexplicably opting not to bring the infield in, Talbot scored on a groundout. The Stars were unable to mount any more offence, and with the game moving close to three hours in length, the two teams were headed to extra innings.

Tyrell took over for a tiring Tabron in the 10th, and retired Milton in order. Things were looking good for the home side going into their half of the frame, with the top of the order due up. Len Harding drew a lead off walk, but was thrown out trying to steal 2nd. With the heart of the order coming up, you had to wonder if that was the right play. The Milton pitcher, Clement, was clearly running out of gas. But after Len was caught stealing, he retired Terrell for the 2nd out, and the prospect of an 11th inning was looming. Boomer swung and missed at strike three, but so did the Milton catcher, and Boomer safely scrambled down to 1st to keep the inning going, bringing up Flat once again. The Milton manager ordered his outfielders to take several steps back, mindful of Chase's first inning clout. Flat worked the count in his favour, then blasted another fly ball to right. Even with the fielders playing back, the ball was over their heads, giving Boomer the opportunity to make a mad dash and score all the way from 1st with the winning run. He was mobbed by his teammates, and the crowd, which had been on the edge of their seats all game, erupted. It was a close one, but the Stars took the all-important first game of the series 10-9.

The Milton-Chatham game was not the only extra-inning affair that day. The Cards and Tigers went to 12 innings before Detroit scored a run to win the game, sending the Athletic Park fans home incredibly happy. Both of their teams were victorious, and they were able to watch one victory, while - thanks to the technology of the day - were able to listen to the other.

⚾ ⚾ ⚾

Merv

The Meaford series took so long to play that the OBA decided to have Chatham and Milton go ahead and play a series while they waited for the two northern teams to finish. Between the tie games, protest, and the three games decided in regulation, the Penetang-Meaford affair - which was supposed to take a week - lasted nineteen days. At the rate things were going, fans were going to need to break out the mitts and toques for the next series.

A fall along the shores of Georgian Bay is usually a reasonably warm one. Nottawasaga Bay, the shallow southern extension of the Bay, warms up slowly in the spring, but heats up with the intense July and August heat, and holds that warmth well into the fall. That moderates the southern Georgian Bay climate. Farmers near Penetang can leave their crops in the field a little bit longer, swimmers at Wasaga Beach can continue to go for dips after Labour Day, and the trees in the apple orchards between Collingwood and Meaford are doubled over with the weight of the year's crop long into September. But as the northern hemisphere continues to tilt away from the sun, weather patterns change, and a blast of wind from the arctic can sweep down the Bay. The cold winds pick up the warm moisture from the water, and in only a few hours, the whole Penetanguishene peninsula can be covered in a foot of snow as early as mid-October. At that time of year, the snow generally doesn't stick because the ground has yet to freeze, but there will be plenty more where that came from.

With the two other teams playing their series, the Rangers had a chance to rest and regroup after the grind that was the Meaford experience. Phil was able to catch up on some assignments and work hard in football practice to try and win a starting spot with St Mike's. A few days after their decisive victory, Shaw had the team meet for a late afternoon workout to get some tuning up before the sun set, but nothing too strenuous. Grain ships were starting to pull into Port McNicoll harbour, so he generally returned to the elevators in the evenings to supervise the unloading.

⚾ ⚾ ⚾

Rangers in Provincial Final; Await News of Opponent
By Charlie Paradis
With files from the Barrie Examiner
Penetang Weekly Herald Staff
October 10th, 1934

Members of the Penetanguishene Rangers enjoyed some home cooking this past Thanksgiving weekend, then after dispatching the Meaford Sox in five intense contests, they waited on news of who their opponent would be in the OBA Intermediate B final.

Milton and the Chatham All Stars were set to play the second of their best of three series this weekend, after Chatham took the opening contest at home. Results of the second contest were not available at press time.

The west side of Penetang Bay, which was awash in an artist's palette of colour these past few weeks, now is gray and barren as old man winter gets set to move in from the north and take up residence. Baseball has never been played in this area at such a late date, but civic pride has never been higher. By winning the North Simcoe title over a talented Barrie squad, then dispatching North Bay and then Meaford in nail-biting fashion, the Spencer Foundry Rangers have gone where no local nine has gone before.

More on Marchildon (from the Examiner) -
Here is the North Bay Nugget's impression of Phil Marchildon, Penetang pitcher:

"Just as Hector Goldsmith (who the Pirates faced in last year's provincial title series) is a tin god in Southampton so is Marchildon a tin god in Penetang. They just about worship him - and no wonder.

"Marchildon is extremely temperamental. Anything not in his favor openly bothers him. If he doesn't like the ump calls on one of his pitches he stamps his foot and mutters something. If one of his players does anything wrong, Marchildon tells him about it."

Marchildon has started classes at St Michael's College in Toronto. He plays rugby just as well as baseball, hence the trip to St Mike's. He is a smart backfielder who can kick and throw passes with the best. It was no surprise that he made a place on the St Mike's senior O.R.F.U squad. In the meantime, Penetang must have him for all ball games or their chances are zero so the club is sending a car down to Toronto to bring him home for each game.

The North Bay Nugget in commenting on last Saturday's game at North Bay said: "The fans gave young Marchildon a rather rude reception at the start and got a great kick out of kidding him about his reported offers to try out for the Pittsburgh Pirates. But in the dying innings, there was not one of their number that did not hold the utmost respect for him. He was mowing down the North Bay Pirates hitters almost with ease."

Jack

Once again, the Stars were headed east for the second game, off in a group of cars provided by and fuelled up by Pete Gilbert. And once more, he threw in a few bucks for a victory dinner on the way home, if the Stars could find a place that would serve them.

Pete's wallet was no lighter after the second game in Milton was over. The Stars put forth easily their most dreadful performance of the season.

At first, it seemed like Chatham was poised for an easy win and a series sweep after they scored three times in the top of the 1st. But the home side matched that trio of runs in the bottom half, added five more in the next inning, and the Stars failed to bring another run home. Hap used all four of his pitchers (Tabron, Chase, Terrell, and Talbot), but it did not seem to matter who was on the mound: Milton pounded them all, and the score was an embarrassing 21-3.

The Stars headed home with their tails between their legs, facing a winner-take-all third game only three days later. With the strain on both teams' limited finances the long season had added, the OBA decided the game would be played at a neutral site in London, which was roughly half-way between the two towns. It also meant a smaller gate for both sides, with fewer fans likely to be in attendance. Hap decided to go with his ace Chase, and after 3 innings, that didn't look such a good choice, as Milton had taken a 6-1 lead.

Despite the lopsided score, Hap decided to stay with Flat, who shut the visitors out in the middle innings, but the Stars' bats went silent, and as they came to bat in the top of the 6th, it was looking very much like Chatham's season was about to come to an end.

Before the game, Boomer and I had talked about the possibility that today might be the last game of the year. "There are few feelings worse than losing that last game of the year," he observed. "When you get knocked out of the playoffs, you get the whole off season to recall that last game, and how you felt when the last out was made. The season is over, you didn't win, and now you have to wait a whole winter for the chance to play again. It feels like a punch in the gut, honestly, and every time you think about it over the winter, that pain in your stomach comes back. Doesn't matter what you might have done in the regular season. That last out in that last playoff game just stays with you."

But the Stars' season was not about to be over. They scratched out a run in that 6th inning to cut the lead to four. Then came an explosion in the 7th; the Stars struck for five runs to take the lead, the key blow being a bases loaded triple by Talbot. Chatham added a run in the 9th to go up 8-6, and while the home team scored a run and threatened to add more in the bottom half, Chase held tight and rewarded his Manager's faith in him, getting the final out with the tying run on 3rd to preserve the win, and the series victory for the Stars. "You dance with who you brought," Hap reasoned.

For the first time ever, Chatham was off to a provincial final.

CHATHAM TEAM COMES FROM BEHIND TO DEFEAT MILTON

Talbot's Triple in Seventh Inning Scores Three Runners; Chase's Good Hurling and Clever Infield Work are Features

MILTON - Oct 13th
Chatham Daily News Staff

Ross Talbot's mighty seventh inning triple with the bases choked brought in three all-important runs yesterday as Chatham Stars defeated Milton in the third and deciding game of the Intermediate B-1 semi-finals by a score of 8-7. The Chatham team will now oppose Penetang in the final series for the provincial title.

PENETANG NEXT

Chatham Stars, having progressed to the provincial finals, will meet Penetang for the O.B.A. crown. Definite dates have not been received yet by Archie Stirling, O.B.A. convenor, but the game in Chatham is not likely to be staged tomorrow or the following Saturday as officials do not wish the clash with the football Red Devils' home dates.

Clearly outplaying their rivals after a shaky start, the Stars were convincing in their triumph. An air-tight infield; three members of which are included on the Stars' pitching staff, *helped Flat Chase along the way. Chase, big Chatham pitcher, made a remarkable return to form after several poor performances to hold Milton to nine hits.*

Errors played a considerable part in Milton's defeat but the Stars outhit the local team and played heads-up ball to take advantage of opportunities and finally overcome an early lead. Milton was leading 6-1 as the game went into the sixth inning.

Marsh, curve ball artist of the Milton mound staff, lasted the route and pitched good ball, striking out seven, but seven errors were made behind him, while Chase's mates were responsible for only one error.

Merv

Phil would be the first to admit that he was a perfectionist. It might take some encouragement, but he'd grant that he could be stubborn as well, and maybe even a little too cocky for his own good sometimes.

"When you grow up in a big family during tough times," he explained, "you learn not to waste things, and how to do things right the first time. My parents drilled into me the importance of never giving anything less than your best. To waste money, food, time, or even talent was a sin. You learn not to do anything frivolously, or 'half-assed,' as my Dad would say. If you did something, whether it was cleaning the dishes after dinner, delivering newspapers, chopping firewood, or playing a sport, you did it to the best of your ability. In my house, if you didn't, you'd be finding yourself doing it over and over again until you did. That way you learned to do things right the first time."

Because he had experienced success on the diamond, track, gridiron, and ice since an early age, Phil had been playing against players older than himself for quite some time. And that maybe lent itself to some cockiness, a sure-fire belief in his abilities. Phil's name had been in local sports sections for quite some time, and now stories of his prowess were moving to a bigger stage. But with that perfectionist streak, and with that success on the playing field came a huge dollop of temperamentality.

Many say the golden age of sports was in the 1920s. Newspapers were full of stories about Babe Ruth, Jack Dempsey, Red Grange, and Howie Morenez. Sometimes, our copy of the Toronto *Star* arrived later than it did to other houses on our street. When my father did a little investigating, he discovered that a certain paper boy was reading the sports section from our paper before he flung it on the front porch. That offending courier, of course, was young Babe Marchildon, who was no doubt reading about his heroes. Dad didn't mind that Phil was getting a little extra reading in.

The 1920s ushered in a boom time in the construction of stadiums across Canada and the U.S.A. Yankees Stadium was the House that Ruth Built. Closer to home, the football Toronto Argonauts were packing in
20 000 at Varsity Stadium for their Big Four games, owner Lol Solman moved the baseball Maple Leafs from Toronto Islands to a beautiful new 25 000 seat park - called by some the best in all of minor league baseball - at the foot of Bathurst St on the Lake Ontario waterfront, and Solman was experimenting with floodlights for night baseball. Even though it was the height of the Depression, Conn Smythe, the hockey Maple Leafs' owner, built a sparkling new downtown arena, "The Cashbox on Carlton St," the sportswriters called his filled-to-capacity Maple Leaf Gardens. Phil quickly realized that sports might be his ticket to fortune and fame, something that was very important to a kid who had to take on a paper route to help put food on the table for a family going through tough times.

That lesson was quickly brought home to Phil the previous summer. Horse racing was popular throughout small-town Ontario, with Jake Payette's Penetanguishene track one of the most popular in the province. Dominion Day - July 1st, Canada's birthday - was the official season opener for his oval, and was the most-attended event of the year in town. Jake offered the biggest purses around, and horsemen province-wide wanted both a crack at those prizes and a chance to see how their horses measured up against Jake's.

Crowds filled the huge wooden grandstand Payette had built along the homestretch; those who couldn't get a seat were allowed to fill the space along the railing lining the infield before the day's card started. Jake thought he would bring in a few extra race fans as well as support a local family when he dreamed up a special race for his 1933 event. Phil would race Cream O' Tartar, Payette's most prized up-and-coming standardbred, and Jake himself in his Marmon Red Devil - a car made more for touring the open road than racing, but it was the pride and joy of his growing fleet of autos.

Jake and his mechanical beast would have to circle the track twice, the harness racer and horse once, and Phil would run a half lap. The early betting was on Cream O'Tartar, who later that summer would set a Canadian record in the mile. Jake had offered a substantial sum of money to Phil to agree to race (which would have brought in a considerable audience on its own), with the incentive of more if he actually won. A crowd estimated at just under 10 000 flocked to Penetanguishene by train, car, horse and wagon, boat, and foot to watch the spectacle unfold.

At the betting window, Oliver Marchildon brought an old coffee can full of tips he'd been saving, and unbeknownst to Liza, had placed its contents on his son to Win. The undefeated Cream O'Tarta was a heavy pre-race favourite, and the funds in the can had been for emergency expenditures, but Oliver had a hunch.

The track was dry but had deep furrows in it, not necessarily the best footing for the human racer, but all three participants got off to a good start, with Phil on the inside where the track was firmer. Because they were running different distances, Payette had their starting points staggered: with the finish line located almost in the middle of the grandstand on the mile-long track, Phil lined up opposite the finish on the other side of the oval, while Payette and Cream O'Tartar started at the usual starting post. Fans in the homestretch could see the whole spectacle unfold. At the start, Jake slammed his foot down on the accelerator and slid into the first turn, losing some speed, but he took the next one wider and at a lower speed, putting his foot to the floor the second he came out of the turn like a seasoned race car driver. Cream O'Tartar kept up a steady pace, gaining momentum, as was her trademark, as the race progressed. As Phil sprinted down the homestretch to the finish, the horse and car were closing the distance on him quickly, and the crowd was approaching a frenzy. Payette flashed by the grandstand in a maelstrom of power and fury, a maniacal grin on his face as he pushed his car to the limit. Phil nosed them out at the end, coming in at 1:07, while Jake finished in 1:08.5, and Cream O' Tartar, thrown off by the chrome and steel horse on the track, came in a second later.

As Phil went to collect his prize, he passed Oliver near the betting windows. "Had them all the way, Babe," Oliver said, grinning as he fanned a huge wad of bills. The cash-strapped Marchildons could breathe a little easier over the next year with their combined winnings.

Phil could be emotional. His teammates, most of whom were older, tried to keep him in check, but that was sometimes a difficult task. The new grips Dan Howley had taught Phil had given him added movement on his fastball, a development that not only handcuffed hitters, but sometimes his catcher and North Simcoe umpires as well. When he didn't get a call he thought he should have had, Phil would stomp around the mound and mutter to himself. Things came to a head in North Bay. Word had gotten out to the northern fans that pro scouts had been looking at Phil, and his act on the mound drew boos and catcalls from the fans.

One of the reasons Jim Shaw had been brought on board was to break Phil of some of those habits. Rather than make a big display of things, Shaw taught Phil to glare at the umpire on a close call that he didn't get, and snap his glove with disdain while receiving the throw back from DeVillers behind the plate, all the while not taking his eyes off the ump, sending a more subtle message. The North Bay fans caught on to that one quickly, and gave him the dickens for it. The home plate umpire, perhaps emboldened by the fans, walked out from behind the plate after one such display, and told Phil in no uncertain terms to knock it off. As he walked back behind the plate, he called over to Shaw on the Penetang bench, "Coach, I hope you have another pitcher, because if this one causes me any more grief, you'll need him." Shaw shrugged his shoulders toward Phil, as if to say, "You heard the man," muttering, "calling some strikes would help" under his breath at the same time.

When Phil first came to the Rangers, he would call out a teammate for making a bad play behind him in the field. The Crippin and Bald brothers put an end to that fairly quickly, but word got around the league, and the fans in the other towns would taunt Phil if someone booted a ball, but he learned not to take the bait. A few words from Oliver and Liza probably helped in that regard.

Slowly over the course of the season, with the help of Shaw and Howley, Phil learned to harness the French-Canadian blood running through his veins, and he learned to keep a lid on his frustrations. But his reputation arrived in other towns before he did, and Phil often had to keep his cool as the opposition bench jockeys and fans tried their best to get under his skin.

⚾ ⚾ ⚾

Jack

They say a lie can travel halfway around the world while the truth is still putting on its pants in the morning, and much the same can be said for a man's reputation.

Such was the case for Phil Marchildon. Boomer and his teammates had already heard about his penchant for calling out umpires before they had even faced the man. Word was Marchildon could be something of a prima donna on the mound. A story even circulated that one time he went all the way to the outfield to yell at one of his players who had muffed an easy flyball. No one knew if those stories were true or not, but all agreed that in the team picture of life, some players only see themselves in the photo. Suffice to say an act like that would not play well on the Stars team.

That's not to say that Boomer was not an intense competitor himself. He had a fire that burned brightly on the inside. Boomer hated to lose, but he rarely let his emotions get the better of him in the heat of a game. But there was an underlying intensity that all of his teammates, no matter the sport, saw. If you played with Boomer, you took practice seriously, and learned that it was best to give him some space after a loss.

Even though he was one of the youngest players on the team, Boomer had become one of its quiet leaders. When the game was on the line, there was no one outside of maybe Flat that the team wanted at the plate when a hit was needed. He was also one of the hardest workers on the team, sometimes staying long after a workout to take extra ground balls, or take more batting practice from Hap.

While his teammates talked of Marchildon, Boomer privately told me that he couldn't bring himself to be critical. "First of all," he said, "I've never met the guy, never laid eyes on him, never seen his act. But I can understand if he's a competitor. So am I. He doesn't like to lose, neither do I. All I know is you have to show some grace under pressure, keep your head even when things are going against you. They say that this guy is the best pitcher we're going to face all year, and if that's the case, let's go, let's get started. You want to be the best, you have to play the best. And beat them."

⚾ ⚾ ⚾

Rangers Ready to Take on Stars in Ontario Final
By Charlie Paradis

Penetang Weekly Herald Staff

The Penetanguishene Spencer Foundry Rangers now go on to play the Chatham All Stars, a new outfit from the southwestern Ontario city that has drawn raves for their play across the province, in the O.B.A. Intermediate B finals. Entirely composed of coloured players, the Stars won the Chatham City title, then eliminated Sarnia, Welland, and Milton to earn the right to move onto the championship series. This will mark the first appearance for both sides in the finals.

Owing to the lateness of the season and the likelihood of huge gates, Rangers management has made overtures to both the O.B.A. and the Chatham team to expedite this final and host the entire series at Beck's Field. Game one would be played Saturday, the second on Sunday, and if needed, the third and deciding match on Tuesday. Home crowds of upwards of 2 000 have been on hand to support the Rangers during their provincial run, with their last home date against Meaford topping 3 000, and team officials are confident that fan attendance would easily surpass that mark for the final. This would cut down on travel and related expenses considerably, and would go a long way to helping both clubs balance the books after a long season.

Understandably, the Chatham side wanted some time to consider this offer. It's not unreasonable that they might want the second game played in front of their home fans. Given the fact that old man winter is about to come a-knockin' at Ontario's front door, time is of the essence in order to get this series in.

At press time, a response had not been received.

And You Asked For It

By Jack Calder
Chatham Daily News Staff
October 13, 1934

When it was voiced around town yesterday that the games of the O.B.A. finals might be played in Penetang, right away there was quite a kick raised for a big number of Chatham people wanted to see one of the games and Penetang is too far away. Added to that is the fact that Chatham had never been the scene of an O.B.A. game.

The real reason that one of the games will be played here - on Thursday - is that the Stars feel that they will do better with a home crowd doing the rooting and they are anxious to oblige those fans who have followed them all season.

Yesterday afternoon a telegram was received by Archie Stirling, O.B.A.
convenor, asking what sum the Stars would want to play both games in Penetang. Here was a chance for the team to pay off some debts and making sure of a well-equipped team for next season. A meeting was held in the afternoon but there was little sympathy for the proposal that both games should be played away from home and the man on the street who wanted one of the games to be played here was taken care of.

Archie Stirling last night dispatched a letter to Penetang, offering to play the first game in Penetang on Monday and the return game here on Thursday. This morning confirmation of these arrangements were received from O.B.A. headquarters. The baseball organization has been good enough to see to it that the Chatham game will not be played on the same day as the Red Devils' last home contest, against De La Salle Grads here next Saturday.

Today a campaign is being launched to make sure that the playoff series will be financially successful as far as Chatham is concerned.

Chatham people asked for one of these games. Now it's up to them to support the Stars who know how to play really brilliant ball. Attendance at the game in large numbers is

essential and a little help in the financial campaign will be welcomed.

It will be a great day for Chatham when her representative goes into Chatham's first O.B.A. final games at home. There's considerable time before the staging of the game but now is the time to arrange to be at Athletic Park.

Rangers Set to Vie for Provincial Title
By Mervyn Dickey
Penetang Weekly Herald Staff

The North Simcoe League Champs have certainly put Penetang on the sporting map. Newspapers from across the province have been carrying stories about the team's progress through the provincial playdowns. For a town known more for producing hockey players (three born-and-raised Penetang natives donned the rouge, blanc, et bleu for the 1916 Stanley Cup winning Montreal Canadiens), the Rangers have let the sporting public know that there are some decent ball players in the area, too.

Unlike other teams in the province who have found loopholes in the O.B.A.'s residency rules, Penetang's lineup is entirely homegrown. The Crippin boys were born in England, but raised in Elmvale then Penetang. The Bald brothers, Babe

Marchildon, Gerry Barbour, and Fred DeVillers (among others) are born and bred Penetangers. Big name pitchers or sluggers have not been recruited and offered jobs to come and play for the local nine. This is a roster that learned to play the game from an early age along the shores of Georgian Bay.

Leading the way for Penetang has been a righthander with an electric fastball and movie-star looks by the name of Phil 'Babe' Marchildon. The team has always been competitive, but the addition of the youngster has put the team over the top. Marchildon wields a potent bat in the Rangers' lineup, and in addition to leading the North Simcoe League in strikeouts by a wide margin, he also was among its batting leaders. Long-time observers of the provincial baseball scene claim that Marchildon is one of the best Ontario-born hurlers to come along in quite some time.

But while Marchildon was fanning double-digit batters throughout the season, baseball is a team game, and he couldn't propel the Rangers to their lofty heights on his own. The Penetang lineup is anchored by the core of the former Lion Tamers softball team, an outfit that was very competitive on the smaller diamond until the Rangers were formed late last decade. Included in that group are Harold Crippin and brothers Jimmy and Marius Bald, who hold down the top two spots in the batting order while holding the fort at 1st and 2nd, respectively. Jimmy played that position with the Lion Tamers, and like everyone on that club with the exception of the catcher, fielded his spot without a glove. From his softball days, Jimmy became adept at using his long arms and soft hands to cradle throws from his infielders bare-handed, and when he became the owner of a 1st baseman's trapper, he became even more of a silky-smooth defender, turning many of his teammates' miscues into outs.

Crowds have been growing as the team has progressed further and further in league and provincial play. Team officials expect the first game of the best of three series against the All Stars will be another box office success, as another overflow crowd is expected to jam the bleachers, foul lines, and outfield at Beck's Field on Tuesday.

8th Inning

Marchildon being scouted by the pros becomes widely known;
No scouts came through Chatham to scout Boomer.

Merv

Trying to keep a secret in a little place like Penetanguishene is like trying to hide the sunrise from a rooster, so it became widely known by the end of the summer that a number of clubs - both in the major and minor leagues - were looking at Phil. Word spread throughout the town quickly, then spilled out into the County and across the province like a swollen creek during spring snow melt.

Many of the minor leagues at the time were still independent entities, competing with the big leagues for fans and players, but fighting a losing battle just the same. Big league clubs were busy either buying up minor league teams, or sitting back and letting the minors develop young players, then offering to take those players off the hands of those cash-strapped teams. Branch Rickey, the father of the modern farm system, used to say that he liked to sign young players, then watch them ripen into money.

Baseball scouting was patchwork in those days. Most teams had only a handful of full-time scouts, criss-crossing America looking for the next Lefty Grove, scouring the countryside for the "arm behind the barn." Scouts of that era were called "ivory hunters", living a nomadic life in search of undiscovered talent, hidden gems, diamonds in the rough, or the next "arm behind the barn". There was no way a full-timer like Sinister Dick Kinsella, Paul Krichell, or Cy Slapnicka could ever possibly cover the whole continent on their own, so they relied heavily on a network of unpaid contacts who frequented the lesser-known ballparks of the country - "bird dogs" they called them - to keep them apprised of the latest upcoming prospects.

There were certainly a number of anonymous bird dogs who had watched Phil pitch that summer. They weren't hard to spot. Usually, they were older men who carried with them a notebook, stopwatch, and an air of self-importance. They didn't actually work for big league clubs, their reward often being only an acknowledgement of their efforts. Sometimes, that came in the form of tickets to a big-league game, or mention in the local newspaper if one of their tips resulted in the signing of a player. Most did it for the love of the game. If their tips were persistent or strong enough, sometimes the club for whom they reported would send a team official to check out the prospect in person.

In Phil's case, both the National League's Pittsburgh Pirates, and closer to home, the Toronto Maple Leafs of the International League came to watch him. The former sent a club official who reported to the Pirates' head scout, Patsy O'Rourke. He wasn't able to make it to a game, but Shaw set up a hastily-arranged workout at Beck's. Since the field was just off the road that was the main entrance to town, more than a few people saw the unusual site of Phil pitching to Fred DeVillers, with only a couple of men in suits (Shaw and the Pirates' employee) watching. You didn't have to be a Major League General Manager to know what was going on, and while Phil and his family would have preferred to keep things private, word quickly spread that he was being scouted. Thanks to Howley's connections, the Leafs were able to scout in more of a thorough manner; a couple of coaches made the short trip up to Barrie to watch Phil pitch in a playoff game there.

The Marchildon family was excited about the prospect of a pro team signing Phil to a contract; Liza was hopeful it would be the Leafs, keeping her boy close to home, instead of maybe signing with a big-league team that would ship him off to some far-flung place like New Mexico. She had a tough time at the end of August just seeing him off to St Mike's for ten months.

In the end, all the teams seemed to agree on one thing about Phil: he was good in the North Simcoe League and OBA Intermediate B play, but they needed to see him pitch in a higher league before they would make a commitment. There was no doubt about Phil's talent, but in many ways, he was a big fish in a little pond, and the competition for jobs in those days was so tough that no one was getting signed out of North Simcoe. To that end, both Howley and Shaw had been working their networks for Phil to pitch in a higher league, preferably a place that could offer him employment as well. He was still technically an amateur, but teams in larger cities could afford to pay him under the table, or find a less than demanding job that wouldn't make him too tired to pitch. It seemed like only a matter of time before he was gone to bigger and better things.

As the summer drew to a close, Phil knew that his time in Penetanguishene was likely coming to an end soon. If Howley and Shaw could find a spot for him on a higher-level team, even before he graduated from St Mike's, he would pack his clothes and glove and make the trek to wherever the baseball fates would take him. But he had reconciled himself to the fact that if he was to seek his fame and fortune, it would be far from the shores of southern Georgian Bay.

Being scouted by a pro team was no guarantee of anything in those days; with so many players looking to make it big, it was a matter of producing right away, or else you found yourself on a train back home. During the tough times of the Depression, not every guy was willing to give up a good job at home for the chance to play pro ball. Like Phil, the Maple Leafs scouted Harry Preston and offered him a contract, which he turned down. "He had a good job with a mining company," Phil explained. "He was in the union and everything, and he said with so many guys out of work, he just couldn't give up a full time paycheck to go chase a dream of playing pro ball." Jimmy Bald had a similar experience a few years later. A team in a semi-pro league in the States had offered him a contract, but he had just hired on as recreation director at a new mental health facility the province had opened in town, and he couldn't walk away from it. Like Preston and so many other men during the Depression, especially in the early years, when there was little government assistance, giving up a sure thing for a long shot was not a chance they were willing to take.

⚾ ⚾ ⚾

Jack

Not only did word of Marchildon's supposed mound antics reach Chatham well before he set foot in the Maple City, so did word that pro scouts were looking at him.

It is easy to tell you how many scouts or their representatives were scouting the Stars: as Boomer put it, "not a single damn one," even though there were players like himself and Chase who were certainly as good as any other amateur player in the province. Chances are if there were scouts in attendance during the Penetang-Stars final, they would not be taking notes on the coloured players.

The big leagues were all the buzz. The recently completed World Series - played over seven straight days - was won by the Cards, who came back from a 3-2 deficit to defeat the Tigers, who Chathamites followed religiously. But for Boomer and his teammates, as much as they followed the Series, it might have been played on another planet. Such was the distance they were away from playing in the big leagues.

Despite the Depression, the Negro Leagues were going well, except for Detroit. They had a team off and on for much of the '30s. Detroit did field a team in one of the Negro minor leagues, and there was some interest on their part in Flat and Boomer, but it was not reciprocal. They wanted to play in the big leagues, and one could hardly blame them.

Chase was a couple of years older, but I failed to see why a big-league team was not interested in Boomer. He was just 19 years old, and already was one of the most feared hitters in the southwest part of the province. He had not developed into a consistent long ball threat, but that is often the last tool in a hitter's kit to develop, and Boomer showed considerable promise to become that kind of batter. Boomer was not just some one-dimensional slugger, though. He could hit for average, get on base, run, throw, and field his position with the best of them. He was athletic, smart, and a hard worker - a coach's dream. There was no doubt that if he got professional coaching and a chance to play and work out every day he was only going to get better. You could not draw up a player from your imagination and have one that was any better than Boomer.

No disrespect to Marchildon - he was one of the top young pitchers in the province, and he deserved both the accolades and the scouting attention. But if he was worth looking at, so was Harding, who was one of the best young hitters in Ontario. One had a future in pro ball waiting for him, the other would be relegated to amateur ball for the rest of his playing days before the major leagues finally woke up. It was a double standard that should have ended years earlier.

Who can you point the finger at - who can you blame for this deliberate segregation of the game? Certainly, you can look at Cap Anson, who threatened to pull his team off the field 50 years earlier when the opposition had a coloured player in their lineup, and all the players after that who refused to play if a black took the field. You could point it at the owners, who put offending a fraction of their fan base ahead of putting the best team possible on the field for the rest. But I would lay it squarely at Judge Kenesaw Mountain Landis, who did his best to hold back the incoming tide of black players. Landis presided over the game when the Negro Leagues were growing exponentially in popularity. He liked to claim that there was no written rule barring blacks from the big leagues, but there undoubtedly was an unwritten one. Maybe he was afraid he would have to compensate Negro League owners after his clubs took their best players, or have bidding wars develop for their top stars, or perhaps he was afraid of offending Major League owners, players, and fans, or maybe he was just plain racist. But no one would even sign a player of colour until Landis died. When scouts were asked why they did not sign black players, it was because they were instructed to say they could not find any good enough. They did not overly exert themselves to find one.

Despite this, Boomer was not bitter that Marchildon had at least one tryout (likely more) and he did not. "Maybe that's why he's so intense on the mound," Boomer reasoned. "He probably knows at just about every game there are eyes on him, and every game, every pitch has huge importance for him. We're all dreaming of better times, and this guy probably has so much pressure on him to be dominant, show that fastball, and strike out as many guys as he can. Look, he better not try to pull that stuff on the mound when I'm at the plate, or I'll try to line one off his forehead, but that might be why he can get upset when he's getting squeezed by the ump, or someone makes a bad play behind him."

***

In a Foreign Field Today
By Jack Calder
Daily News Staff
Saturday, October 13th

Chatham's own constellation, the Stars, are in Penetang today for the first game of the O.B.A. finals.

They have gone further than any other Chatham team has ever done since baseball was put on a properly organized basis in the province. This evening the Stars will either be up one or one game down in their quest for the title. Whether they're a match to the good or are on the wrong end of a 25-0 score when today's game is over makes little difference. They lost the second game of the semi-final round to Milton by a score of 21-3, but went back to Milton a few days later to win the deciding contest 8-7.

The Stars blamed poor umpiring for getting off to a bad start in the first game against Milton, but probably the one big reason is that they didn't have to fight, and before they knew it they were out of contention.

The Stars are a mysterious team. Their infield this summer turned in finer games than any amateur ball team in this district ever did. At other times Boomer Harding, the Stars' first base, was stretching high and low, far and wide, trying to haul in glaringly bad throws; the infielders were all dropping easy pop flies and messing up ground-hit balls.

But the Stars are a remarkably good ball team. They're led by a master of the diamond, Don Washington, who really knows baseball, and who has brought along his pitchers this season in admirable style and he has done his share of work offensively and defensively too. In a district where good catchers are rare indeed, Washington looks to be just about the best there is. He bats in fifth position and has hit hard and regularly all year long.

Four pitchers are on the staff of this team. Flat Chase is the regular hurler, and when he is right he has a terrifically fast ball. Cold affected his arm for a good deal of the later part of the season but at Milton the other day he finally turned in an effective game and looks ready for the series. He brings a mean bat and bats in the fourth spot.

Wilfred ("Boomer") Harding holds down first base for the club and his hitting and fielding have been big factors in the Stars' march. He bats in third position in the lineup and is a hard man to keep off the base paths. He has a good reach and races far to the left or right to cut off hits.

Ross Talbot was shifted this year from first to second base and the change seems to have done him good. He is hitting and fielding better than ever before. It was his triple with the bases loaded that decided last week's important game in Milton.

Don Tabron is the team's most improved defensive player. He has a short underhand whip from the shortstop position and he's almost sure-death on the hardest of grounders. He has been known to hit home runs this season and his average in hitting has steadily climbed.

King Terrell, the Stars' third baseman, leads off the batting order and is the most dependable man on the team. He throws left-handed but this is scarcely a handicap to him. He is fast on the bases and usually scores the first run of the game.

Terrell, Tabron, and Talbot are the Stars' relief pitchers, and they round out just about the only four-man staff in the O.B.A. They add variety to the Stars' pitching offerings for Chase's deliveries are fast, Terrell's sweeps in from the left shoulder and Tabron's and Talbot's are mixtures of curves and fast-ball deliveries. They are great fielding pitchers.

In left field is Len Harding who covers acres of territory and brings a two-base bat. Harding's collection of doubles is the envy of many City League players. Harding is especially good at cutting off runners at the plate with long throws from the outfield.

Gouy Ladd and Sagasta Harding share the centre field duties though Ladd has seen more work of late because of his ability to cover ground. Next to Tommy McKie, Ladd is the city's best ground-covering outfielder. (Carl) Harding is noted for hitting in the pinches and he may be used to hit for the weaker batsmen on the team if crises arise in the Penetang series.

Stanton Robbins and Clifford Olbey alternate in right field. Olbey has the facility of turning hits at needed times while Robbins, because of his short stature, is frequently walked. Both men do their fielding jobs well.

The Stars have, true enough, been disappointing in home engagements, but they are going to fight for the title. And a provincial baseball final will be an innovation for Chatham people.

9th Inning

Difficult negotiations to start the series; game one goes ten innings, game two has a wild finish.

Already, rough play and disputes with umpires had marred the 1934 World Series. The trend continued in Game Seven. A seven-run third inning by St. Louis removed any doubt about the final outcome.

In the sixth inning, Joe Medwick hit a ball to the center-field fence. Thinking triple all the way, he tore around the bases and slid safely into third base. The cloud of dust that erupted may have caused some of the discrepancies about the incident. Some observers thought Detroit third baseman Marvin Owen stepped on Medwick or kneed him. Medwick may have kicked back with either one or both feet at Owen's legs. Others thought both players kicked at each other.

After the inning ended, Medwick returned to his left-field position, where fans in the temporary left-field bleachers began throwing debris at him. Medwick headed to the safety of the infield and joked with teammates about it. (Detroit player-manager Mickey) Cochrane ran out to left field in an effort to implore the crowd to calm down, but was unsuccessful. Medwick tried several times to return to left field. A loudspeaker announcement stated that the umpires would forfeit the game to St. Louis if the crowd didn't stop throwing items.

During the entire Series, the umpires had made reports detailing players using profanity against each other. Medwick and Owen were called over to speak to Landis. Landis asked both players if the other had sworn at him, which they both denied. Landis told Medwick that he was out of the game and wouldn't listen to (St Louis manager Frankie) Frisch's protests.

Society for American Baseball Research

Merv

The location and dates of the finals series games took quite a bit of negotiating, with no small amount of acrimony. Chatham had finished up their last series on the 11th of October, Penetanguishene on the 8th. Despite the lateness of the season and the urgency to settle on playing dates, it was difficult for the two sides to come to an agreement. As cool arctic winds swept down across the still relatively warm waters of the Bay, mid-October snow squalls were rare, but not unheard of. But the two sides were squarely dug in when it came to determining where the games would be played.

Rangers management had offered to host the first two games of the series, with the third - if needed - to be played (as was the tradition) at a neutral site suitable to both sides. The rationale from the Penetanguishene side was that even though the first half of October had been very pleasant weather-wise, things could turn around drastically in twenty-four hours. With crowds likely to be well in excess of 3 000 fans, both teams would do well financially, and it was rumoured that Rangers' management offered an extra $200 to Chatham, which would go a long way to help defray the expenses the team likely ran up on its journey to the OBA final.

Transportation was also an issue. With no superhighways in those days, the drive from Penetang to Chatham was somewhere in the neighbourhood of eight hours. Rangers management pushed to have the series start on the Saturday after Thanksgiving - the 13th - but Chatham, having just finished a series on the Thursday before, declined. The Rangers' brass thought they could simplify things if they offered to host those first two games.

Chatham, somewhat understandably, argued against the Rangers proposal to host the series. They wanted at least one game in the championship series in front of their home fans, because few - if any - would be able to make the long trip north. Telegrams went back and forth, as did long distance phone calls involving officials from Chatham, Penetanguishene, Barrie (where the local convenor lived) and the OBA.

Finally, both sides agreed that the first game would be played on Monday, October 16th in Penetang, with the second in Chatham three days later. A third game, if necessary, would be negotiated later.

⚾ ⚾ ⚾

Jack

Maybe it was the grind of a long, drawn-out season, and the prospect of more lengthy travel. Or perhaps it was the stories the team had heard about Marchildon. Whatever the case, the offer from Penetang to play the entire series up there was viewed as an insult. Having to play three elimination series to Penetang's two did not help matters. It could have been a combination of all of those factors, but whatever it was, there were some bad feelings between the two teams before a pitch had even been thrown in the series.

"The whole city is behind us now," Boomer remarked after the Stars' last brief workout before heading north to chilly Penetang. "There's no way we're not playing at least one game in front of our own fans, the folks who've supported us. That's pretty arrogant of Penetang to think that wouldn't matter. I get they're concerned about the weather, but what's fair is fair. Whether it's Stirling or Athletic Park, the fans who supported us deserve to see us one more time, and we deserve to play in front of them once more, too. Penetang hosting the series would be a huge advantage for them. Everyone in the city is behind us now."

And he was right. The Stars were the talk of the town. They were the first Chatham team to play for an OBA title, and there was a lot of civic pride because of it. Penetang, from what I was told, even asked the Stars to name their price to play the series up there, but Archie Stirling and Hap would have none of it. Penetang held this carrot out hoping the Stars might jump at the chance to balance the books, but as Archie pointed out, "by the time gas, food, and hotel rooms are paid for, there wouldn't be much left." Maybe it was not as great a deal as Penetang thought it was, and Stirling lobbied hard to make sure that the Chatham fans were able to see their Stars in action. The fans who had supported the team all season through thick and thin deserved no less.

"I don't know about all this talk of winter coming," Boomer confided as the team prepared to leave just after sunrise the day of the first game for the trip to Penetang. "It's been a beautiful October." And it had been, although most veteran baseball people knew playing ball in Ontario after Thanksgiving was pushing it. It wasn't the threat of snow or the temperatures so much, it was with the sun lower in the daytime sky, the playing fields didn't tend to dry well after a day of rain as they would in the summer. That's acceptable for a sport like football, but certainly not for baseball.

Pete Gilbert had once again come through with a couple of cars and some gas money for the long journey north, although most of the team opted to travel in the flour mill truck, likely for the sake of team unity rather than comfort. Hap and coach Percy and a few others travelled in the cars. Because of the short turnaround between games, Hap opted to start Tabron on the mound in the first game, and fan favourite but sore-armed Chase at home. He ordered Tabron into one of the cars to make sure he arrived in Penetang rested.

I hopped aboard the flour mill truck along with most of the players, and a few hangers on. Boomer had invited me on board. "You're pretty much part of the team now," he said. It was symbolic that I was invited for the ride.

The ride from Chatham to Penetang promised to be something of a cross country odyssey. The milk crates were quickly overturned and the cards came out, and King Terrell kept up a steady patter of commentary and jokes to help pass the time, not repeating the same joke twice. This was going to be a long ride of about six or so hours through the southwestern Ontario countryside, across Oxford, Waterloo, and Wellington counties, into the highlands of Dufferin County, and on to

Simcoe County and eventually Penetang on Georgian Bay. It was the longest trip most of the team had ever taken.

The team left Chatham and took Highway 23, heading east to London, then followed the road as it turned northeast. The surface had been paved four years earlier to Atwood, north of Mitchell, so there was relatively smooth driving for the first two hours of the journey. Palmerston marked the halfway point, and there was a brief stop for gas, bathrooms, and for the team to stretch their legs. It was still early in the morning, so there were not too many folks around to give the travelling team of coloured ball players strange looks.

From Palmerston, the roads became progressively bumpier. People take for granted today's smooth thoroughfares that get you comfortably from here to there, but there were precious few stretches of highway like that in the province during the Depression. We made reasonably good time on lightly travelled roads through the gently rolling countryside north of London, Waterloo, and Guelph. Fall colours were at their peak as we made our way north, with the maples and oaks providing a brilliant canvas of glistening golds and radiant reds in the mid-fall sun. The harvest was in full swing; various machinery, some powered by machine, others by horse, were busily gathering the tall stalks of corn and fields of waving wheat as we drove by. Some fields, already harvested, were being ploughed for next year's planting, flocks of shrieking seagulls following the path of the newly-carved furrows. Throughout the trip, there was a sense of fall about to give way to winter, and a need to tuck the land safely to bed before it was covered by a blanket of snow.

There was considerable banter and ribbing as the first hands of cards were dealt, but players soon drifted in and out of the game, and most lost interest as the long grind of the trip began to settle in. The chit-chat of earlier in the ride had subsided, so I thought I would try to engage some of the guys in conversation.

"Fellas," I began in earnest, "how about that Series?" The recently-completed seven game World Series between the Tigers and Cardinals had indeed been a memorable one. The Dean brothers won a pair of games apiece for the triumphant Redbirds in a Series that was broadcast nationwide for the first time. Fans were glued to their radios as they listened to the games, and for seven straight days, North America was firmly in baseball's grip. It brought baseball into the mass media age. One of the games, of course, had been broadcast over Athletic Park's loudspeakers as the Stars battled Milton.

There was little reaction from the players. I was shocked, to put it mildly. "To tell you the truth," offered Boomer after a moment of uncomfortable silence, "I was working most of the time. The hotel put the games on in the lobby, but I could only catch bits and pieces." Several players nodded in shared experience. The Series did not appear to mean all that much to them. Wherever you went in downtown Chatham - restaurants, offices, garages - the game was on a radio somewhere. But not everyone in town had access to the broadcasts. "Look," explained Donny Tabron, "a radio is not something everyone can afford, you know? Maybe you have a neighbour who has one, and maybe they invite you over to listen, but a decent radio can set you back over $100." That was true, and it stopped me in my tracks. That was more than 1/10 of the average Canadian's annual pay - for those that had jobs. I felt a little sheepish for even bringing the topic up - I was putting my baseball fan self in their shoes, and assuming that they had the same opportunities that I did.

But there was more. Leave it to Wash - Don Washington - who wasn't afraid to be outspoken. "Don't take it personally, Jack," he said, sensing my unease. "They say this was the 'World Championship' of baseball, and you know what? There were some pretty good ball players in that series. The Deans, Mickey Cochrane, Hank Greenberg, Frankie Frisch, they're all stars, but I don't see how a ball team can call itself the best in the world when they don't have *all* the best players. How can the Cards say they're the best when they didn't have to hit against Satchel Paige, 'Schoolboy' Jones, or Teddy Trent? And their pitchers didn't have to worry about getting Josh Gibson, Turkey Stearns, or Oscar Charleston out? Until a 'World' Series has all the best players in the game taking part in it, I can't get all that interested in it."

As was often the case, Wash was right. Some future Hall of Farmers took the field, but all the best players were not in that Series - in fact, when Dizzy and his brother started their barnstorming tour as the Stars were getting set to head to Penetang, some of them - who were denied a chance to play in the bigs because of the colour of their skin - were playing against the Deans. Guys like Paige, Jud Wilson, George Giles, Tom Young, Chet Brewer, and Bullet Rogan, to name but a few, made up the opposition for the brothers, and beat them more often than not. The Deans each took home, it was rumoured, well over ten grand each for their two weeks of work, travelled in comfort, and stayed in the best hotels on the tour. Their black opposition, of course, made a fraction of that, and had to stay in substandard accommodations - rooming houses, or hotels in the coloured part of town. The fawning press covered almost every detail of the Deans' exploits on the tour, and made only passing (if any) mention of their opponents. And to top it off, black fans who wanted to see their Negro League heroes in action had to sit in segregated sections

- usually far from the action - of the ballparks the tour played in.

The convoy headed northeast to Mount Forest, a beautiful small town full of broad, tree-lined streets. From there, we swung east onto Highway 89 through sparsely populated undulating farmland, the odd small farmhouse breaking up the mostly featureless landscape. The players had settled in for the trip, but with each passing mile there was an underlying feeling among them of being farther and farther from home.

At one point during the trip, someone asked Flat about the time he caught the great Satchel Paige. "He came to Windsor five or six years ago, I forget," he started. "He was going to pitch an exhibition against the team I was playing for. There was an accident in the tunnel to Detroit, and his regular catcher was stuck in a traffic jam there. Satch had to be back on the other side to pitch in a game in Detroit later in the day, so the other coach comes over to our bench and says, 'We want to get the game going. Anyone want to catch him?' I volunteered, even though I'd never caught a game in my life.

"Yeah, you ain't no catcher," said Wash. Flat was long and lean, while Wash was short and somewhat squat, a typical catchers' build that didn't stop him from stealing bases.

"Oh, you got that right, Wash," Flat responded, "but there was no way I was going to pass up that chance. I figured maybe I'd learn something from catching him. Besides, the game was already late getting started, and the organizers were worried Satch would take off if things didn't get moving, and the big crowd that came out to see him would be demanding a refund. So, I put the gear on, and get ready to go catch his warm up tosses, when the coach comes over with something wrapped in butcher's paper, hands it to me, and says, 'here, you may need this.'"

"Let me guess," interrupted Wash. "A nice big juicy sirloin?"

"It was!" exclaimed Flat. "How'd you know??"

Wash held out his hands for all to see. "Take a look at these," he said. I'd never noticed before, but his right hand - the one he threw with - looked fairly normal, except for his ring finger. "Took too many foul tips off of this one," he said, pointing to the finger. His catching hand was a different story. His thumb looked puffy and swollen, while his index finger took a sudden right turn at the knuckle. His middle finger was as crooked as the road we were currently on, while his ring finger was so swollen it almost hid his wedding ring. His pinky wandered off to the left, like it was trying to leave this hand full of banged up, misfit fingers.

"I've done the steak things a few times myself," he added, "But I can't quite pick up the price of beef these days. I sewed some extra padding into my mitt before the season, and it took the sting out a bit, but by this time of year it's getting pretty flattened out." Catcher's mitts in those days looked more like a sofa pillow with a baseball-sized pocket than the oversized gloves you see today, which are much more padded - and forgiving.

"So," one of the guys asked, "what was it like, Flat? Tell us what it was like catching Old Satch."

Chase was not one of the more vocal players on the team, but he knew when he had an audience, and he geared up to deliver a clutch performance like he was up to bat in the last of the 9th with the winning run on 2nd. "It was unbelievable," he began. "Never in my life have I seen a pitcher like him. He's tall and gangly, kind of all arms and legs, but he has the smoothest delivery, and the ball just explodes out of his hand. He makes it seem so effortless. And he can throw the ball wherever he wants to - it's hard to believe a guy who throws that hard has that kind of control. His act was to guarantee the fans he'd strike the first nine hitters out, or they would get their money back."

"Did he do it?" I asked, pretty much knowing the answer. You would have to be living under a rock not to know of the legend of Satchel Paige.

"Without hardly breaking a sweat," Flat replied. "After I finished warming him up, I trotted out to the mound to go over the signals with him, but he just kind of waved me off, and said, 'Son, you just put that mitt up, move it around the strike zone a bit, and I'll hit it. If I'm gonna throw the ol' bat dodger' - his curve - 'I'll let both you and the hitter know before I let it go.' So, I go back behind the plate, and did just like he told me. I would put my mitt up, he would throw right at it, and the hitters would just kind of wave at the pitch. They just couldn't catch up with it, no matter how early they started their swing. Satch had such easy gas, I'm so glad I didn't have to hit against him. First two guys go out on six pitches - all whiffs - and the third guy comes up, best hitter on the team, and you can tell he's just itching to get in and take his licks. Satch throws him pitches almost at eyeball level, but the guy just can't lay off of them, and gets a piece of both, but fouls them back. You're not getting good wood on pitches up there, but Satch knows how anxious the guy is. Satch throws a pitch waist-high, just off the outside edge next, but the guy lays off of it for ball one. On his next pitch, while he's winding up, Satch yells out, 'here comes old Uncle Charlie, now,' and he throws a curve that drops about a foot at the last minute, and the batter ties himself into a corkscrew trying to hit it. But he's so jacked up that he swings and misses by about a foot. Satch strikes out the side in the second - one guy actually pulled a ball foul down the line, but that was all the contact anyone made. Next inning, he strikes out the side on nine pitches, guys might as well as tied white flags to the end of their bats, because they had no chance against him. The ninth hitter was just a kid. He steps in against Satch, and he can't even get his bat off his shoulders on the first two pitches, so he starts to walk toward the dugout. 'Hey, batter, you've still got a strike left,' the ump says. The kid just looks over his shoulder and says, 'I didn't even see the first two pitches, what makes you think I hit the next one."

On the bench between the third and fourth innings, he slaps me on the leg and says, 'Now, son, I'm going to back off a little bit, because I have to get back over to Detroit to pitch a game at five o'clock.' So, he starts taking a bit off his pitches, guys get around on him, but because he could work the corners so well, no one does much damage against him. He gave up a couple of singles, I think, just ground balls through the infield. One ball gets fouled off into the parking lot and bounces around for a while before some kids brought it back. The ump gave me the ball to toss back to Satch, but it was all nicked and banged up. "Ump," I says, "do we have a better ball than this?" Well, Satch comes down off the mound, and when he sees what happens, he says, "Ump just give me that ball." He then motions for me to meet him halfway from home plate. We walk back to the mound together, he puts his arm around me, and says, 'Son, I can do everything but make a ball like this sing When Irish Eyes Are Smiling, so if it's all the same to you, let's just stick with it for a while.'"

His regular catcher shows up in time for the fifth inning, which Satch says will be his last. Before he throws his first pitch, he waves in his outfielders, and turns to the crowd and says loudly, 'I won't be needing these guys this inning." He gets the first guy on a weak grounder, then reaches back to strike out the next two guys. Satch walks off the mound to a huge ovation, picks up his fee from the organizers, then gets into a car waiting to take him back over the river to strike out a bunch more guys."

"You think he could pitch in the big leagues?" asked Wash.

"Look, I'm no big leaguer, but I think he would be the best in baseball if some team would sign him. He should be pitching in Yankee Stadium, not striking out guys for cash in places like Windsor. In the off season, they say he plays against big leaguers all the time and beats them. He struck out Rogers Hornsby five times in one game, Jimmie Foxx three times in another. He's the real deal. Walter Johnson, Lefty Grove, Christy Mathewson - I bet he's as good as any of them. Ol' Dizzy Dean said, "me'n Satch are like two peas in a pod,' except Satchel said, 'yeah, we're alike, but Diz is in the big leagues, and I was bouncing around the peanut circuit.'"

We passed through a succession of small, one church farming communities for some time, eventually winding our way into the small town of Alliston. From there we continued eastward to a hamlet called Cookstown, where we turned north at the main intersection in town onto Highway 27 toward Barrie. The inhabitants of these small towns had awakened by now, and gave strange looks to the passing caravan as it rolled along their main streets.

At Barrie, the team turned onto Highway 93 north (a former military route established by Lt Gov Simcoe almost 150 years earlier) toward Penetang - one of Ontario's first roads, according to one of my high school history textbooks. The road, apparently, had not seen much in the way of improvements since Simcoe's days. The players had tired of cards by that point, which was a good thing, because about the only game they could play on that bumpy backwoods highway was Fifty-Two Pickup.

As someone born and raised in the flat geography of Chatham and Kent County, it was interesting to me how the terrain changed as we progressed to the northeast. Judging by the strain of the truck's transmission, it felt as if we were going through a series of successively bigger hills, a testament to the effects of the last Ice Age on central Ontario.

At a quick rest stop in Barrie, we were told by a gas station attendant that we were less than an hour away from Penetang. As the team edged closer to its destination, with the banter and the card games stopped. What could be best described as an intense quiet overtook the flour truck. All season long, this was a team on a mission, one that was about to see its toughest battle.

There were many disadvantages to the Stars not having one main sponsor, and the accompanying group of executives that most amateur teams had. Funding for equipment, uniforms, and umpires often had to come from passing the hat at the game, as well as the players' own pockets. Fortunately, Archie Stirling found a way to contribute to that. For successful teams, travel-related expenses came into play, but luckily Stirling had brought Pete Gilbert on board to help. But there was no one to take care of the logistics of a ball team - things to do with scheduling, and in the case of the trip to Penetang, hotel arrangements. Before we had left, I had asked Hap if those had been made in advance, but he reasoned that we would just book rooms when we got there later Sunday afternoon. "Anyone who has booked a room for the weekend will have checked out by then, there should be plenty available when we get there. Not too many people checking in on a Sunday. That's worked for us in the past."

Except the team had never travelled to a small town like Penetang before, and to their surprise, when they went to check into the hotel on the main street, a place called the Canada House, they were told there were not enough rooms available to house the team. It came as a huge collective shock to the players.

"No rooms to rent, or no rooms to rent to us?" asked Wash with some bitterness when Hap came back to the team convoy parked on the street outside of the hotel to tell them the news. The guys had already unloaded some of their luggage, and after a long day's journey were looking forward to unwinding in their hotel rooms.

"I don't know, but they said that there would be rooms in Midland, which is just the next town over," Hap replied. He was truly perplexed, and had been thrown off guard. Hap hadn't anticipated rooms not being available. After asking for directions, the team made the short drive to Midland, which did indeed have rooms for the team to stay in. But the bad feelings that were already present among some of the players intensified. Several thought that they were turned away because of their skin colour, and the fact that they were the enemy, leading to considerable grumbling before the team got settled in Midland. Fortunately, they were treated well in downtown Midland, a bigger town that apparently was more used to out-of-town visitors, and were able to unpack and then find service at a nearby restaurant. There was some debate as to whether or not the team should book two nights' stay, in order to avoid making the long drive home in the dark after the next afternoon's game, but the prevailing sentiment was to not spend one more minute in the area than was necessary.

⚾ ⚾ ⚾

Merv

Word travels almost at the speed of light in a place like Penetanguishene, and it didn't take long for news of Chatham's arrival - and subsequent departure - to spread.

At the turn of the 20th century, Penetanguishene boasted several fine hotels. The Georgian Bay House, at the intersection of Robert and Main, was a majestic three-story building that housed several stores, a bank, and a billiards parlour. But it had burned to the ground when I was a grade schooler, just after the Great War. Similarly, the Penetanguishene Hotel, a grand wooden Victorian establishment on the bay at the end of Fox Street where the well-to-do from Toronto and northeastern U.S. cities vacationed, had been destroyed by fire a few years earlier as well. The hotel industry in town, which had boomed with the coming of the railway before the turn of the century, had started to fall off even before those two hotels met their fiery demise.

Bigger and better tourist hotels had been built along the east side of Georgian Bay, and Penetanguishene became more of a place tourist bypassed as they made their connection to those finer wilderness inns further north. By the 1930s, the only remaining place with guest rooms in town, the Canada House, was an older building that had fallen into disrepair. During the summer months, the owners rented rooms to visiting tourists, but that business dried up after Labour Day, so the rooms were rented out to men who worked seasonally in those resorts up along the Bay. The lodgers would then vacate the rooms the following spring as they headed north to get the shoreside inns ready for the season. A town like Penetanguishene did not see a lot of travellers in between tourist seasons, so the Canada House earned the bulk of its revenue as a tavern, restaurant, and catering business. My father called the Canada House, a place where men drank dark liquids out of frosty glasses a "beer parlour." Women were not permitted in the tavern side; my mother called it a "House of Sin." I can imagine the staff's surprise when a dozen-plus ball team members appeared at their door that October afternoon inquiring about rooms. No doubt the proprietors encouraged them to make the short drive to Midland, where they would find suitable accommodations.

I won't pretend to have any insight as to how the Chatham team operated, but it didn't sound like they had made much in the way of advance arrangements. Look, I wasn't there, but from piecing together tidbits of information I had heard, the Canada House staff did the team a favour. Midland had two well-appointed hotels in those days down by the waterfront, and the team probably stayed in greater comfort as a result. Some people, so I later heard, were upset that the Chatham team was sent "out of town" in order to find accommodation; Midland and Penetanguishene are more than neighbours. They're towns tied together by history and geography, and there's very little space between the two. While Penetangers are rightly proud of their hometown, the towns are practically one. You can get from the main intersection in one to the other in ten minutes. The Chatham team wasn't necessarily sent to another town; they were sent next door, where our neighbours took care of them.

And I can't speak for the owners of the Canada House, but I think they didn't rent any rooms to the Chatham team because they were embarrassed, quite frankly, about the state of their hotel, and had few, if any, adequate rooms to rent. They extended what they thought was a courtesy by referring the team to more suitable lodgings. Did people think Midland, a town very much Penetanguishene's twin, would have different views on race? My hometown was not perfect by any stretch of the imagination, but years after the series, we received a reputation that wasn't deserved, and wasn't grounded in fact.

It may have just been a misunderstanding, but the incident added to the growing enmity between the two teams.

⚾ ⚾ ⚾

Game One - at Penetanguishene
Monday, October 15th

Merv

Jim Shaw ordered one last Saturday workout prior to Monday's series opener. It was a light session, designed more to keep the team sharp. Phil would have to give the session a miss because of football, but Oliver would be dispatched Sunday morning to bring him home for Monday's game. Shaw had an added purpose in gathering the team together before the first game.

"Fellas, one last word with you, if I might," Shaw asked as the workout came to an end. "I want to talk about his Chatham team, and what we should expect from them. They've had a long season, too - they even had to play an extra series while we were involved with Meaford. From what I've been told, they've gone through quite a bit this season, their first season playing mostly against white teams. In some places, they've had to battle hostile fans and bad umpiring, and teams that have played downright dirty against them. They're a scrappy team, they have good pitching, and just about every guy in their lineup can run. I would expect they'll be trying to use their speed against us. But there's another thing I want to talk about today......" Shaw let his last sentence linger in the air for a moment before he continued. "Look, I've travelled all over Canada and the U.S. in my time. I've lived and worked in a number of different places, with people from all walks of life. And do you know what I've discovered? We may have some differences - some may speak a first language other than English, and some may not look the same as we do, or worship in the same church, but all of those differences are minor, in my opinion. We all have far more in common than we think. We want for ourselves and our families to be healthy, happy, and prosperous. We all want to laugh, sing, play games, and just generally have the best life we can. The Chatham team is no different, fellas. They love this game just as much as you do - they have to in order to put up with all the nonsense they've seen this season."

Shaw paused again. A thoughtful and well-spoken man, Shaw likely had these words in mind from the minute he learned that Chatham had advanced to the final.

"Guys," he went on, "I'm sixty-four years old. I've been around this game longer than any of you have walked this earth. When I started playing as a young buck over in Grey County, you needed eight balls for a walk, and pitchers had to throw underhand. I've seen so many changes in the game since I started chasing flyballs, but some things never change. Baseball is, has been, and always will be a game about connections. It's about playing catch with your Dad, playing recess pick up ball at school with your buddies, it's about reading the box scores in the paper, and passing around a copy of *The Sporting News* to read about your heroes until it was tattered and torn. Baseball is about going over to your friend's house to see their brand-new radio, and listening to the magic of a ballgame from some distant place dance over the airwaves on a hot summer night. Baseball is about connections to the past, great players from bygone days, like King Kelly, Cy Young, or Honus Wagner. There's a reason we play with a round object, fellas - this game is one big circle, so many are the connections, and so often do we talk about past players and games. People talk about World Series games from twenty years ago like they were there. History is really at the heart of this game. And mark my words, boys - we're making history this week, no matter the outcome. The days of the great coloured players taking their rightful place in the big leagues is coming. I can't say when, but it will happen, and maybe we're playing our small part in making sure the best players are always on the field. So, I respectfully ask all of you right now what you would like your place in history to be? Will you treat the Chatham players with respect, competing hard against them, or will you contribute to the name-calling and abuse they've become all too used to? To be honest with you, I would like to know your intentions now, because there won't be a place for you on this team if your intentions fall into the latter category. Take a step forward if you don't plan on playing this series hard, but fair, and don't want to act like a true sportsman."

There was a moment of silence, but no one came forward to take Shaw up on his offer. "See you Monday, fellas," he said, and headed to his truck for the trip back home to Port McNicoll.

Phil and I had conversations about race in the past. We had talked about Archie Thompson of Barrie, an athlete Phil was in awe of, a guy he had expressed admiration for on and off the field. Penetanguishene was not necessarily a town of two solitudes, but there was something of a divide between those with French-Canadian backgrounds like the Marchildons, and Anglo-Canadian families like the Dickeys. Sports helped to bridge that societal gap. Those with British heritage tended to be dominant in the business, financial, and political affairs in town, although that was slowly changing with each generation. Phil had competed against several athletes of colour during his upbringing, and to him, it was not a big deal. He wasn't even sure Shaw's speech was necessary when he later learned of it, which showed maybe an open attitude and some naivete. Phil's talents perhaps insulated him from what was going on in the world, but maybe he judged a teammate or a competitor on his athletic skills alone.

⚾ ⚾ ⚾

Jack

After the team breakfast at 8 am, Hap sent the team back to their hotel rooms to pack up before they headed to Penetang around noon. Despite having to double up on the rooms and beds, the team was well-rested and ready to go. Even with the issue over hotel rooms, it was a wise idea to make that long trip from Chatham the day before. The players would have fresh legs for today's contest. It was a rough start to the series, but if there was one thing this team could do, it was bounce back from adversity.

On the way into town the day before, we had seen the Penetang ballpark - Beck's Field, they called it. We had heard about the crowds the team had drawn throughout the OBAs, so the players expected some grand little stadium, and were slightly disappointed that there was but a small set of bleachers around a chicken wire backstop in some farmer's field, with huge hay bales along the first base side that were to turn into makeshift viewing platforms when the game started. So, it was with sheer disbelief that the team saw the cars lining either side of the road outside of the park already as the Stars pulled in shortly after noon. There may have already been a few hundred fans present, and someone was already having to direct traffic along the skinny main street to get us into the field. "Say what you will about Penetang", one of the guys on the truck said, "it sure looks like they support their team." Once the fans started arriving, they just seemed to keep on coming. A sea of humanity had washed up on this waterfront town.

The truck and the accompanying team cars got separated in the midst of so many other vehicles. When the team was finally reunited, some of the team was a little rattled. It was a mix of several factors: being in a place so far removed from home, with a huge crowd already gathering, and with a championship at stake may have been playing on their nerves. Some were not convinced they were all that welcome in town just yet. The players could not wait for the game to begin, when they could be on the ball diamond where they were much more comfortable.

The Stars took their warm ups as the overflow crowd continued to flood in. Someone said the mayors of both Penetang and Midland had declared the afternoon a holiday in honour of the first OBA championship game to ever be played in the area.

And a lot of locals appeared to take the opportunity to attend the game. Boomer was an island of calm during this wave of activity. "Hap said this morning just to take this all in, we've worked so hard to get here, we've gone through so much, and that's what I intend to do. No matter what roadblocks they've put in front of us, we've overcome them. We're just so fortunate to be here, and this season has been a dream, despite the negative things that have happened." With the World Series and all other OBA playoff series finished, the eyes of the province had turned to what was happening between the Stars and Penetang, and Boomer intended to enjoy his time in the spotlight.

⚾ ⚾ ⚾

Merv

With a crowd that had to be well over 3 500 wedged into Beck's, the Rangers wasted little time rewarding the home crowd. The October weather, always subject to change, had been reasonably warm in our part of the province, with no precipitation in the last nine days and none in the forecast. The field was in reasonably good shape, and the game time temperature was a balmy (for the season) 65 degrees, although it would drop quickly as the game progressed.

Phil retired Chatham in order in the top of the 1st to open the game, and then the visitors showed the butterflies they surely must have been feeling by making errors on the first two balls put in play. Shaw had altered the Penetanguishene batting order, putting Hal Crippin, who was the team's leading man at getting on base (according to the statistics I'd been keeping all year) at leadoff. With a nod to small ball, he had McCuaig, who usually batted near the bottom of the order, batting second, giving Shaw the flexibility to bunt or use the hit-and-run if the fleet Crippin got aboard. But he needed neither strategy in that 1st inning. Crippin's leadoff grounder to 2nd was bobbled by the 2nd baseman Talbot, who then threw wildly to 1st, allowing Hal to take 2nd. McCuaig then hit a ground ball to shortstop Chase, who took his eyes off the ball for a second due to the distraction of Crippin at 2nd, and the ball kicked off of his glove into short left field, allowing Crippin to move up to 3rd. Chase was obviously shaken by the error and the incredible din caused by the home fans, because he missed McCuaig alertly scampering to 2nd base after he had picked up the errant ball.

With two runners in scoring position and no one out, Chatham pitcher Tabron calmed things down by striking out the next hitter, Marius Bald. That brought up Phil, who came up to a standing ovation. With the count even, Phil lashed a ball the other way right between the legs of Boomer Harding, the Chatham 1st Baseman. As the right fielder tracked the bounding ball down, both runners came into score, giving Penetanguishene a quick 2-0 lead. Phil was forced at 2nd by

Jimmy Bald's groundball. Bald moved up to 3rd on a double by DeVillers, and the Rangers had a chance to break the game wide open early. But the next hitter, Spearn, popped out, in a sign of things to come. The Rangers would not score again in the game despite many chances.

Leading off the next inning, Chase atoned for his 1st inning error with a lead off base hit. In another sign of things to come, Chase was off to 2nd with the first pitch to the next hitter, but DeVillers threw him out. Chatham had brought their track shoes, and probably intended to use them.

⚾ ⚾ ⚾

Jack

The Stars got off to about the worst start you could imagine, and were clearly unnerved in the 1st inning. Maybe it was the after effects of a long trip the day before, or perhaps playing in front of such a huge crowd on a foreign field, but they played like an intimidated outfit. They looked nervous, skittish, and not at all like the confident team that had triumphed in three series to get to the final.

But this was a team that had simply had come too far and been through too much to fold in the opening minutes of the series. Watching behind home plate amongst the rabid Penetang fans, at no point did I think the Stars were anywhere close to out of it. They had a lineup that could manufacture runs in a hurry, and two runs was not an insurmountable deficit. I was confident that there was no panic on the Chatham bench. In hindsight, this start was almost predictable.

Marchildon had faced the minimum through the first two innings, striking out three, but in the 3rd the patient Stars' attack started to get to him. Tabron walked to open the inning, then stole 2nd, but was caught trying to steal 3rd. DeVillers did not know it at the time, but the Stars were going to run on him at almost every opportunity for the rest of the series. With two out, Stan Robbins singled, followed by another base hit by Len Harding, but both were left stranded. Nonetheless, the butterflies were gone, and the Stars were ready to get back into the game.

⚾⚾⚾

Merv

Phil was cruising through the first three innings, although Chatham mounted a brief two out rally in the 3rd that he snuffed out with his fifth strikeout. After Chase rapped his second hit of the day and successfully stole 2nd in the 4th, Phil notched another "K" on my scorecard, and looked to be on his way to getting out of the inning.

With two out, Chase at 2nd decided to do whatever he could to disrupt Phil on the mound. He danced back and forth, and bluffed a steal on Phil's first pitch. Now the cat-and-mouse game began. Phil took his time before starting his motion toward home, trying to "freeze" Chase at 2nd. But Chase continued his dance, so Phil stepped off the mound to force him back to the bag. Phil was clearly distracted, as his next pitch was wide of the strike zone, forcing DeVillers to make a lunging grab to keep it from going to the backstop. Before his next pitch, Phil had clearly had enough of Chase, and whirled to pick him off at 2nd. Since he had been away from team workouts since Labour Day and hadn't had much if any, time, to work with his infielders, the timing between Phil and Marius Bald, who had coverage of 2nd on the play, was way off, and Phil's throw to the bag arrived a second before Marius did, bounding into centre field. Chase didn't break stride as he approached 3rd, rounded the bag and headed for home, where the throw from the outfield arrived too late to nab him, and Chatham had cut the lead to 2-1. It was a daring and brilliant bit of base running, something the Rangers were not altogether used to, and the confidence they'd gained from taking an early lead seemed to be fading away.

⚾ ⚾ ⚾

Jack

Now it was time for Marchildon to get rattled. The Stars' running game was clearly distracting him, taking the crowd out of the game in the process. Even if they didn't steal, they were always a threat to do so. The Stars always looked to force the issue on the bases.

Chatham had four stolen base attempts in the first three innings. "Do all of their guys run fast?" someone in the crowd around me asked. "Yes," I answered, but only to myself. Marchildon had a compact frame and was obviously an excellent athlete, but he was new to pitching, and his inexperience at holding runners on, combined with his high leg kick and deliberate delivery to the plate meant that Hap could let the team run almost at abandon on Penetang. The fans around me were blaming Bald for not covering the pickoff attempt on Chase at 2nd, but Bald had a long way to go in order to reach the bag, and Chase's antics had thrown Marchildon's focus off. The Stars were having great difficulty getting good wood on Marchildon's pitches; everyone in the lineup save for Chase was having trouble getting around on him, and were late on a lot of their swings. As a result, the Penetang manager, with a right-handed hitter up, had Bald playing more toward 1st in case of some late contact. To be honest, I was surprised Marchildon even tried to pick him off. With two out, Flat was smart enough not to make the final out of the inning trying to steal 3rd when a hit would score him from 2nd, but he also knew he could disrupt Marchildon, and his plan worked brilliantly, as Chase was able to score and get the Stars back in the game without the benefit of a hit by one of his teammates.

The Stars scratched out another run and tied the game in the 5th. Tabron led off with a walk - Marchildon battled all day with his control, especially now that the temperatures were cooling, and the Stars were content to work the count and wait him out. Tabron then stole 2nd, advanced to 3rd on a groundout, and easily scored when Len Harding doubled.

⚾⚾⚾

Merv

After that fabulous start, the Rangers' offence went cold. Crippin hit a two out double in the 2nd, but was left stranded. The next five Penetanguishene hitters over two innings were retired in order before Sheppard knocked a two out base hit in the 4th. He was then thrown out trying to steal 3rd. You couldn't blame Sheppard for trying to make something happen, because Joe Hale at the bottom of the order was a weak hitter, but that caught stealing seemed to take some more wind out of the Rangers' sails.

After Chatham knotted the game up at 2-2 with their run in the top of the 5th, the Rangers failed to respond. Crippin collected his third hit in as many at bats to start the frame, but three straight force outs ended the inning. The game was only just past the halfway point, but missed opportunities by the home side was already becoming the story of the game.

Phil had recovered enough to strike out two of the three hitters he faced in the 6th, finally retiring Chase with one of them. The Rangers' ace had 10 whiffs through 6 innings. But Chatham's pitcher Tabron had really settled in, bending but not breaking, and all the Ranger offence could manage in the last of the 6th was a two-out, two-bagger by DeVillers, who was left stranded - yet another notch in my scorecard Left on Base column. The game was moving along quickly, but it had the makings of a long afternoon.

⚾ ⚾ ⚾

Jack

One of the keys to the Stars' game all year long had been getting the lead off batter on, a feat they managed in the 3rd, 4th, and 5th innings in the Penetang opener. Chase opened the 7th by reaching on an error, the third time he had reached base. But this time Marchildon ignored Chase's gymnastics at 1st, and the next three Stars' hitters went down in order to snuff out the promising start. No one outside of Len Harding had really squared up Marchildon on the day, but the Stars were getting base runners, and Tabron was pitching an excellent game, matching Marchildon out for out, if not strikeout for strikeout. The game remained tied 2-2 as the teams headed to the home half of the 7th.

⚾ ⚾ ⚾

Merv

Missed chances and mistakes. That was now the theme of the Rangers' day. Six runners, four of them in scoring position, had been left on base through the first half dozen innings. Phil's throwing error in the 4th allowed Chatham to get back in the game. And there was to be more of both in the 7th.

3rd baseman Sheppard, who had earlier made a fine defensive play to snare a pop foul to end Chatham's 5th inning, led off with a double. But Hale behind him popped out to short, and Sheppard must have been getting a little desperate again to try to create something, anything. Phil could make a one run lead stand up the way he was tossing, and that was likely on Sheppard's mind as Crippin came up at the top of the order.

Crippin hit one on the nose, but directly at the right fielder, Robbins, so Sheppard - who had gone half way to 3rd while the ball was in the air - quickly retreated to the bag as Robbins settled in under Crippin's drive. The crowd tensed as Sheppard tagged up. Robbins' throw to 3rd was letter perfect, arriving on one hop, and for the second time that day, Sheppard was thrown out on the bases, and the Penetang rally was over before it started. With the light-hitting McCuaig behind Crippin, maybe Sheppard thought he would take matters into his own hands and try to reach 3rd. There are at least a half dozen ways a runner can score from 3rd without benefit of a hit, so maybe that was on his mind. But it was painful watching Shep again make the third out of an inning at 3rd base, because a two out hit scores all but the game's slowest runners from 2nd. The Rangers had squandered yet another scoring opportunity.

⚾ ⚾ ⚾

Jack

Marchildon was as advertised. He was emotional on the mound, but his fastball was the real deal, and if the Stars hoped to score again, they would have to scratch that run out. There was no doubt about his competitiveness, nor his arm. As I watched him work that sunny, crisp fall afternoon, I began to understand what all the fuss was about. There was no denying his talent.

He showed no signs of tiring in the 8th, fanning Len Harding and Terrell before issuing a two out walk to Boomer. That free pass was about the last thing Marchildon wanted to do because it brought up Chase again, the only hitter in the lineup to have figured the fireballer out. And sure enough, Flat drilled a pitch to the gap in left-centre that easily would have scored Boomer all the way from 1st, but the left fielder McCuaig made the best defensive play of the day, a fine running catch to snare Chase's drive and retire the side. The huge crowd certainly was getting their money's worth

The bottom of the inning showcased Flat's superb defensive skills. Even though he was better known as a pitcher, Chase was a peerless defender at Short. The first two Penetang hitters of the inning hit sharp ground balls that he fielded flawlessly, then easily tossed them both out at 1st. For the final out of the inning, Chase made a sprawling dive to his left to rob Marchildon of a sure base hit.

⚾⚾⚾

Merv

The Rangers seemed to be gaining some strength and confidence in the final innings. Heading to the bottom of the 8th, the heart of the order was coming up, and those bats came alive that inning. The Rangers seemed to be on the verge of figuring out Tabron, and hit him hard in the frame, but only the fine glovework of Chase at shortstop allowed him to come out of the inning unscathed.

In the 9th, Phil struck out the side, giving him 16 on the day. He had struck out five of the last six hitters he had faced. The control issues he'd had in the early innings seemed to have vanished as his fastball command improved. He was dominating hitters, who were having trouble managing as much as a foul ball against him. Phil had fallen into a rhythm; now, if only his mates could scrape together a run.

But I was having a nagging feeling. Phil had only so many bullets in the chamber. He'd thrown a lot of pitches on the day, most of them with a lot on the line, and he had to turn around and pitch again three days later. He had already thrown a lot of innings since the season started in May, and he had pitched five intense games in 19 days against Meaford. Those missed opportunities for the Rangers were beginning to weigh heavily on everyone - the team, the coaches, and the crowd. The best thing to happen would be for the Rangers, with their fifth, sixth, and seven hitters coming up, would be to get a run across, close out the game, and save Phil for the next one.

And that appeared to be happening when Jimmy Bald led off the bottom of the 9th with a hard-smash right up the middle, but right into Tabron's glove. The Rangers just couldn't produce any offence, it seemed. The next two hitters went down in order. Nine innings failed to produce a winner. Off to extra innings, with the contest still squared at 2-2. The sun was getting ready to slip behind Blue Mountain on the other side of the Bay.

⚾ ⚾ ⚾

Jack

Marchildon certainly looked all but unhittable over the last few innings, but with the temperature having dropped suddenly as the sun made its setting trek to the west, he seemed to be having trouble gripping the ball in the 10th. He issued a lead off walk to Washington, who stole 2nd on the next pitch. An infield hit by Robbins put runners on the corners with no one out, and a big inning looked to be developing. Marchildon did some of that stomping around the mound before his next pitch, facing a pressure situation without having given up a hard-hit ball. But facing the top of the Stars' order, Marchildon regained his composure and struck out the next two hitters, Len Harding and Terrell.

Boomer was up to bat next. He had walked his last time up, but had gone hitless in his three plate appearances prior to that. Unlike most of his teammates, Boomer at least was making contact against Marchildon, hitting two flyball outs in those three trips. But because Boomer was a student of the game, he went up to the plate with nerves of steel because of the mental notes he had compiled in his previous plate appearances, figuring he was due to bang out a hit against a tiring Marchildon. He worked the count to 2-2, then ripped a drive to right-centre that split the outfielders. Washington easily came to score, followed by Robbins, who came all the way around from 1st to put the Stars up 4-2 as Boomer pulled into

2nd with a double. The Stars threatened to add to the total when Chase reached safely on a missed third strike by the Penetang catcher, but Marchildon struck out Talbot - his fourth of the inning - to end the rally.

⚾ ⚾ ⚾

Merv

The air in the Rangers' balloon started leaking out in the 8th inning, when they hit the ball hard but had nothing to show for it; the pair of runs Chatham scored in the 10th seemed to take most of the rest of it out. They barely raised a challenge for Tabron, going out meekly in the bottom half of the inning 1-2-3. After Sheppard was thrown out at 3rd in the 7th, Tabron had retired the next nine hitters he faced in order. He needed help from Chase in the 8th, but you had to tip your hat to the Chatham hurler. He wasn't overpowering, but he got the outs when he needed them most.

But this was a game the Rangers could have won, without question. After the first inning, they couldn't buy a clutch hit to bring in a run. They didn't even get a runner past 2nd after that opening frame. Meanwhile, Phil, despite that botched pick-off throw, pitched his heart out and deserved a much better fate. He struck out 18 hitters on the day, including eight over the final three innings. The Rangers had wasted a gem of a performance, and now faced elimination in Chatham. Three straight games in the previous round they faced elimination, but escaped each time. It was reasonable to wonder if that high-wire act was coming to an end.

⚾ ⚾ ⚾

Jack

The prevailing sentiment of the shocked Penetang crowd at the end of the game was that they were the better team, but the final score failed to reflect that, as if Chatham had somehow dodged a bullet.

As someone who had watched the Stars all season long, I had one thought: no, they did not, not by any stretch of the imagination. Yes, the home team left a lot of runners on, but all that did was to cause the visitors to bear down harder. With the game on the line, Tabron was brilliant, his teammates behind him flawless after a rocky start, and at the plate they were able to fight their way back from an early deficit. The Stars had found ways to win all season long; games in which they had given up a big early lead, games in which they did not particularly play well, or games in which the opposition outplayed them.

The Stars used solid pitching, timely hits, strong defence, and aggressiveness on the basepaths all year long to record wins. They capitalized on the oppositions' mistakes. The hitters in the middle of their batting order might hit the long balls, but there were no easy outs anywhere in the lineup; every hitter was capable of getting on base - the last three hitters in the Stars' lineup got on base six times in the game, while Penetang's were aboard only twice (Sheppard - who was thrown out on the bases both times). All of the little things that add up were on display for the Stars in the first game: athleticism, opportunism, and skill. Penetang had an ace on the mound, the Stars would acknowledge, but they still found a way to beat him.

And while the Stars faced a long drive home, the knowledge that they were a game away from a title, and would be sending out their own ace, playing in front of their home fans, made the cross-province drive tolerable. "It's always a shorter trip home when you win," Boomer observed.

⚾⚾⚾

Game 1 - 10/16/34	1	2	3	4	5	6	7	8	9	10	R	H	E
Chatham	0	0	0	1	1	0	0	0	0	2	4	9	5
Penetanguishene	2	0	0	0	0	0	0	0	0	0	2	6	2

Chatham	AB	R	H	RBI	Penetanguishene	AB	R	H	RBI
L Harding lf	5	0	2	1	J. Bald 1b	4	1	1	0
Terrell 3b	5	0	0	0	M. Bald 2b	5	0	0	0
W Harding 1b	4	0	1	2	DeVillers c	5	0	0	0
Chase ss	5	1	2	0	Crippin ss	5	0	2	1
Talbot 2b	5	0	0	0	Marchildon p	5	1	2	0
H Robbins rf	3	0	1	0	McCuaig lf	5	0	1	0
Tabron p	3	1	1	0	Spearn rf	5	0	1	0
Washington c	3	1	0	0	Sheppard 3b	3	0	0	0
S Robins cf	4	1	2	0	Hale cf	3	0	0	0
Ladd ph	1	0	0	0					

	IP	R	ER	H	BB	K
Tabron	10	2	0	6	0	8
Marchildon	10	4	3	9	2	18

Doubles - L. Harding (1), W. Harding (1), Marchildon (1), DeVillers 2 (2), Sheppard (1)

Stolen Bases - Chase (1), Tabron 2 (2), Washington (1), S. Robbins (1)

Caught Stealing - Chase (1), Tabron (1), Sheppard (1)

Umpires - Scott, Orillia, at the plate; Pearse, Midland, on the bases

Chatham Stars Home, Ready for Thursday Game
Chatham Daily News

October 17th, 1934

The Chatham Stars arrived home from Penetang about eight o'clock this morning after an all-night drive, tired but happy and confident they will be crowned provincial champions after the game with the northern lads here Thursday afternoon.

The trip from the northern town was somewhat hazardous as fog blanketed the highways most of the way through.

The boys left here Sunday afternoon and remained in Midland for the night, proceeding to Penetang yesterday morning. They report having received courteous treatment from the northerners. Half-holidays were declared in Midland and Penetang for the game yesterday.

Marchildon, who worked on the mound for Penetang, is a "submarine" hurler and caused the local chaps a lot of trouble. However, Harding got to him for that big hit in the tenth yesterday to pull the game out of the fire.

Penetang Dropped the First Game to Chatham All-Stars
Locals Had Early Lead of Two Runs, But Were Unable to Hold it. - Marchildon Turned in Good Game - Visitors Got Their Hits When They Did Most Good.
Midland Free Press

Although Chatham Colored All-Stars defeated Penetang 4-2 on Monday afternoon at the latter town, in the first game of the

OBA B series finale, they have yet to demonstrate that they are a better team than the local ball players.

Penetang grabbed off two runs in the first innings, after shutting the visitors out in their half. Marchildon, the locals' right-handed ace, was by far the better pitcher, having 18 strikeouts to his colored rival's eight, but his mates failed to come through in the pinches when hits were needed. They were only three hits behind the Chatham sluggers, but failed to bunch them up for tallies, and the All-Stars pulled up on even terms by runs in the fourth and fifth innings.

Marchildon had some hard luck in the 10th when the colored lads brought in two runs to clinch the game.

It was a tough break for the Penetang crew, but they have yet a chance and may turn the tide when they play the second game at Chatham.

It was an ideal day for the game and one of the largest crowds of the series turned out to watch it. Many of them were disappointed at the lack of spectacular plays which have featured Penetang's forward march, but it was probably one of those "off" days which at some time or another crop up to spoil a club's chances.

Game Two - at Chatham
Thursday, October 19th

Merv

Cars were a luxury that few in Penetanguishene could afford in the tough economic times of the Depression. To get around, you either walked, took the bus to Midland, or hitched a ride in someone's beat up old jalopy. I had taken more than a few rides in the back of Oliver Marchildon's battered model T pick up, competing for space in the cargo bed with stacks of pipes and Oliver's plumbing tools. The old Ford served as both Oliver's business truck and the Marchildon family vehicle.

The effects of the Depression were felt everywhere, but especially so in small towns. The main employer, Payette's foundry, had cut back to one shift, because people were just not buying new stoves during the uncertain times. The boatworks in town had laid off most of their workers, because there were few yacht orders. Gerry Barbour's father's store burned down, and the insurance company refused to pay. With no income, Mr Barbour found it increasingly hard to make ends meet, and when he could no longer afford the mortgage on the family home, the bank foreclosed. Politicians at the time pledged that a return to prosperity was just around the corner, and that there was no need for government relief, because that would just make people dependent on it.

Despite these tough times, the team travelled in style to Chatham, thanks to Jake Payette arranging for the loan of a

Willys Overland, a Studebaker, and a couple of Ford sedans to ferry the team to southwestern Ontario. Similar to Chatham before the series opener, the team arrived the day before Thursday's game, and stayed in the Roth Hotel, one of the classier inns in town, so we were told. One of the team executives had called ahead to make arrangements for our stay.

The drive was on the long side, but thanks to the rides Jake had arranged, it was a comfortable trek. When you live in a small town in Penetanguishene, you get used to long rides to larger centres for shopping or medical appointments. But only the Rangers had been from almost one corner of the province to another in the OBA playoffs. They had already journeyed several hundred miles in their trip through the playdowns. Phil had probably travelled twice that distance, his dad triple.

⚾ ⚾ ⚾

Jack
After a lengthy and sometimes harrowing ride home through dense fog for much of it, the Stars pulled into Chatham shortly before 8 in the morning after their Monday victory. At times the convoy slowed to a crawl as we made our way through the thick blanket. I had to rush to the office to write an account of the game before heading home around noon for some well-deserved sleep. Some of the players had no choice but to try to

get some sleep on the ride back from Penetang, because they were expected to put in a full day's work on Tuesday.

On Wednesday, the day before the game, the Penetang caravan arrived in town. They were staying at the Roth, where Boomer and several other Stars worked. After graduating from high school, Boomer resisted the urge to head to Windsor/Detroit to look for work like many of his classmates did, taking a job as a bellhop at the Roth. It certainly was not glamourous or high-paying work, but it helped the Harding family pay the bills.

There was no doubt the line of vehicles that pulled up to the Roth was the Penetang team. They had far fancier vehicles than the Stars traveled in, and there was no flour mill truck pulling up the rear. These guys arrived in comfort and style; no need to work out the kinks after a bumpy ride. Similarly, if there were any Stars fans in the general vicinity of the Roth's entrance, there was no mistaking who Marchildon was. He looked a little smaller than he did on a ball diamond, but he had those matinee idol looks and a shock of thick, wavy black hair. His teammates were joking as they opened up the car trunks and hauled out their luggage, but you could tell they were deferential to him, and he led the procession of players into the hotel to register. He was their meal ticket, after all.

Not one of the Penetang party recognized the tall bellhop who handled their luggage - Boomer, who they had played against just forty-eight hours before. There wasn't even a hint of recognition. Meeting Marchildon at the Roth's huge revolving front door, Boomer asked, "take your bag, sir?"

"Uh, sure," Marchildon replied, clearly not used to the routine of checking into high-end accommodations.

Rooms and keys were quickly assigned, and Boomer followed Marchildon and his roommate with their bags to the elevator. Not a word was exchanged between them in the elevator. As they reached their rooms, Boomer took the bags in, and said, "There you are, sir. Will there be anything else?"
"Oh, no thanks," Marchildon replied. There was an awkward silence as Boomer stood still beside the bags. Marchildon clearly was not used to the customs of the hotel like the Roth. Finally, after a few seconds, he clued in, and reached into his pocket to give Boomer a tip.

As Boomer left the room, he thought to himself, "he has absolutely no idea who I am."

⚾ ⚾ ⚾

Merv
With a little bit of down-time before the team's pre-game dinner, I had a chance to check out the work of my Chatham

counterpart. It was interesting to see the headlines he (or his editors) used: "In a Foreign Field Today," was the headline on the day of the first game; Phil was referred to as our "Northern hurler." The way people south of Georgian Bay view us and where we live is quite amusing. Sure, we're a little bit removed where we live, but we're not "The North." That's Parry Sound, Sudbury, North Bay, and all those places farther north. Compared to, say Thunder Bay, we're in the banana belt. A trip to Penetanguishene is not like an expedition to the Arctic, but for some southern Ontarians, that's what it seems like.

Manager Shaw joined me in the lobby while I was perusing the local paper. He had decided to shuffle his batting order once again ahead of the critical second game. "I wanted Hal Crippin at the top of the order because I wanted to get him the maximum number of at bats in the game, and it worked, in a way - he was the only player in our lineup to bat five times. But Jimmy and Marius Bald are just as good at getting on base, so they'll be at the top of the order, DeVillers crushed the ball yesterday, and has probably been our best hitter in the playoffs, so he'll hit third, followed by Crippin and Marchildon. I'd put that heart of our order up against anyone's. We need some production from the bottom half of the order, though - get some guys on when the lineup turns over, so I've dropped McCuaig down to 6th. Despite his troubles on the bases, Sheppard hit well yesterday, so I'm hoping he can do that again. I thought of maybe moving him to the 7th spot, but again, I want guys on when the top of the order comes up, so I'm leaving him batting 8th. We can all but count on Phil going out and pitching a beauty for us again tomorrow. We just need to tinker with the order, take advantage of guys' strengths....and maybe get some clutch hits. And the way to do that is to put your best hitters in a place where they're likely to come up with runners on."

Jim Shaw was ahead of his time. He thought about the game in ways that few people did. One by one, as the dinner hour approached, the Rangers began to filter down to the lobby. Jimmy Bald asked Phil about the bellhop who carried his bags. "Did you see who took your luggage up to your room, Babe?" he asked.

"No. Some bellhop, I guess," Phil replied.

"You didn't recognize him?" Jimmy asked.

"Why?"

"That was Chatham's 1st baseman. The Harding kid. Guy who had the game-winning double off of you on Monday."

Phil's face went crimson red. "Oh," he said with embarrassment.

⚾ ⚾ ⚾

Jack

Hap's plan to have Flat pitch in the second game did not get past the pre-game warmups. He took Chase and Terrell down the 1st Base line with Wash to see who would go that day. It was obvious that Chase was labouring with every pitch, and after only about five or six laborious tosses, he went back to the bench, put his jacket on, and sat with a glum look on his face as he waited for the game to start.

But Chase was enough of a team player to know that even if he was unable to take the mound in the biggest game of the year, he could help the club with his glove and his bat like he did in Penetang. If Terrell got into trouble, Tabron would be the first man up to replace him.

There was talk amongst the guys about Penetang's arrival the previous day. It created quite a stir in the downtown. We had heard the team's sponsor was a high roller with deep pockets, but they arrived in a veritable auto show, according to the players. "Hey, Boomer," one of the guys called out. "Is it true you carried that big shot Marchildon's bags yesterday, and he didn't even recognize you?"

Boomer was uncomfortable talking about it. "Look, guys, I don't know for sure. Maybe he's just shy, maybe he didn't recognize me, I don't know. All of us bellhops look pretty strange in those monkey suits they make us wear. It's no big deal."

"Did he leave a good tip?" someone inquired.

"Sure," Boomer responded, quietly. Actually, he and I had talked about the incident when we first got to the ballpark - one of my alert readers had heard about it, and had given me the heads up, so I had to ask Boomer. "Look, he comes from a big family, and I hear they hardly have two cents to rub together. Maybe as soon as he saw me, he felt pressure to give me a good tip, but the guy just didn't have much cash on him. I doubt he ever has." Despite Marchildon's reputation, Boomer couldn't bring himself to bad mouth him.

But his teammates were more than ready to use that as ammunition in game two.

⚾⚾⚾

Merv
It was the wildest, craziest, damnedest game that I ever saw.

A phone line had been set up at the ballpark to allow the Chatham reporter and I to relay scores back to our newspapers. Several car loads of Rangers fans had left before sunrise to drive down to Chatham for the game. Crowds were already forming outside of the *Herald*'s office back home, where updates would be posted on the front window to a waiting audience. Wire services across the province would pick up copy from the Chatham paper. No matter where they were, everyone was in for a wild ride.

Like Penetanguishene, it had been a glorious Indian summer in Chatham, from what we were told. They had gone without rain for weeks, and the temperatures earlier in the week had been in the 70s. While the field would be in very good condition considering the time of year, the arrival of the Rangers ushered in a period of cooler weather, and the game time temperature was barely above 50. There was considerable dampness in the air, as a day of rain was less than 24 hours away, so the ball promised not to carry as well, and the pitchers would likely have some trouble gripping the ball the way they would like late in the game. A crowd in the neighbourhood of 1 500 made their way into the park for the game, and empty 45-gallon oil drums served as makeshift bonfire pits at several spots behind the backstop where the fans could warm their hands.

The Rangers got off to a quick start in the last game, but after putting a pair of runners aboard in the top of the 1st, clutch hitting once again failed to materialize, and Penetanguishene left valuable potential runs on base.

Jack

This time, it was the Stars' who jumped out to an early lead. The Harding boys had both singled, followed by an infield hit by Chase to load the bases. Up to the plate stepped Talbot, hero of the deciding game against Milton, but a goat in the first game against Penetang, when he struck out five times in as many at bats. Talbot laced a triple to clear the bases and give the Stars a three-run lead. A big inning looked to be in the making, but Marchildon hitched up his pants and struck out the next two hitters to end the inning. Marchildon looked fresh on Monday, but today he looked tired. I think he was lucky to get out of that frame without further damage.

There was still a lot of ball to be played, but the Stars' fans were ecstatic with their heroes' quick start. Terrell took to the mound in the second to shut down the opposition.

⚾ ⚾ ⚾

Merv

Baseball wisdom says that the best time to score is right after the opposition does. Down 3-0, the Rangers did that - and then some - in the 2nd inning. Phil led off with a single, but the next hitter, McCuaig, hit a tailor-made double play ball to Talbot at 2nd. Talbot threw to Tabron, who had taken over from Chase at shortstop for the day, and had to deal with Marchildon coming full tilt right at him to break up the double play, and while he did his best to avoid making contact with the oncoming runner, Tabron's attention was diverted, and he dropped the ball. Both runners were safe; while Phil's slide was legal, and probably a play any Chatham runner would make in that situation, he was the recipient of some dirty looks from the home team, and catcalls from the home crowd. The hard feelings between the two clubs were not abated by that take out.

Spearn walked to load the bases, and the Rangers looked to be ready to rally. Sheppard clubbed his third hit of the series to bring in Phil and put the visitors on the scoreboard. Terrell regrouped and got the next two hitters out, but Marius Bald came through with a timely hit just when his team needed it, driving in a pair with two outs to knot the game at 3, and the middle of the batting order was coming up.

⚾ ⚾ ⚾

Jack

Hap had seen enough. Having given up a three-run lead, he showed the quick hook by replacing Terrell with Tabron with two out in the 2nd.

The decision to go with Terrell was a risky one. He had not pitched in several weeks, and he showed it. Hap was hoping against hope that he would not need to use Tabron or even Chase. Terrell was only an out away from getting out the inning, but today was not a day to let a pitcher work his way out of a jam, especially with how well Tabron had pitched on Monday.

Except asking a guy to come into a situation like that was maybe asking a lot. Tabron hit the first hitter he faced, a call the crowd hooted and hollered at, feeling the Penetang batter didn't do enough to get out of the way of the pitch. The bases were loaded once again. Up came Crippin, who had already established himself as the team's most dangerous hitter, a guy who could change the complexion of a game with one swing of the bat. With the bases now full, Crippin cleared them with a double down into the left field corner, and Penetang was now ahead 6-3.

There was more than a little grumbling from the home fans. The Stars had come up with some clunkers during the playoffs on home turf, and the crowd was mindful of that. There were also some hard feelings about Marchildon's slide to break up what might have been a fairly routine inning. To some, it was a baseball play; to others it was borderline dirty. The gridiron star barrelled into Tabron at 2nd like a blitzing linebacker. Either way, it opened the door to a big inning for Penetang, and did not improve the crowd's state of mind one bit.

St Louis' Joe Medwick's slide into 3rd of game 7 of the World Series against the Tigers typified the mindset of those times. Detroit had seen a 3-2 lead in the series evaporate after the Cardinals had tied the series in game six; St Louis then took a commanding seven run lead after the first three innings of game seven. With such a big lead, Medwick perhaps did not need to try to stretch a sixth inning double into a triple, but he did, and badly spiked Tigers 3rd baseman Marv Owen as he aggressively slid into the bag. The incident did not go over well with Detroit fans, and when Medwick took his position in left field in the bottom of the inning, the crowd pelted him with garbage. Commissioner Landis ordered him removed from the game. It had been a very rough World Series. Dizzy Dean earlier in the series was knocked out on a relay throw at 2nd that caught him square in the forehead; Tigers catcher/manager Mickey Cochrane had been spiked badly twice in the series. That was how a lot of ball players played the game in those days, and the Medwick incident was still fresh in the minds of a lot of Chatham fans, who were diehard Tigers supporters. You could not help but wonder if it was on Marchildon's mind, too.

⚾⚾⚾

Merv

There was a noticeable change in the crowd after that 2nd inning. The fans were on the umps after Phil's hard slide broke up that double play. And they, too, had heard of Phil's reputation, and got on him, too. The sun had disappeared behind grey October clouds, and the temperature had dropped, but the heat was rising at the Chatham ballpark.

One of the things Shaw had impressed upon Phil throughout the season was the need to keep his emotions under control, and show grace under pressure. In many ways, Phil was the wild bronco and Shaw the veteran horseman, brought in to break Phil of his wild ways. To be honest, the results from that mentorship were mixed throughout the season, but it began to show some of its effect in the second inning.

Phil had faced eight men in a long first inning, and he had a long wait to get back out to the mound while his team circled the bases in a six-run second inning. Not surprisingly, he struggled with his control on this dark, cold, and drizzly day when he went back out for the bottom half of the 2nd, and gave up the dreaded lead off walk. His difficulties continued two batters later, when he gave back one of the bounty of runs his offence had supplied him with by surrendering a triple to Terrell. Once again, Phil recomposed himself, however, and retired the most feared hitters in the Chatham lineup - Harding and Chase - to end the threat. Even though it was early in the game, I wondered there and then if that might be looked back upon as a turning point if the Rangers won. With their best two hitters up, Chatham had a chance to all but erase the Rangers' huge lead, but Phil mowed them both down. It was obvious to any seasoned baseball observer that Phil was wearing down, and was getting by on his pitching smarts as much as he was by his fastball. We'd played only two innings, and the score was already 6-4 in favour of the Rangers.

Phil settled in after that, and retired six of the next seven hitters. The Rangers were unable to mount any offence after that big second inning, after having gone out in order in the 5th. But more controversy came along in the inning. Marius Bald was nicked by a pitch in his turn at bat, but the umpire ruled the pitch a ball. The crowd did not react well, thinking Marius had leaned into the pitch. Two pitches later, he was nicked on an inside fastball again, and this time was awarded 1st. The crowd hooted and hollered in derision at the ruling, but the Rangers stranded Marius there and no further damage was done. Penetanguishene carried a 6-4 lead heading to the bottom half.

⚾ ⚾ ⚾

Jack

Even though Marchildon seemed to be settling in as the Stars took their turn at bat in the 5th, the middle of the order was coming up, and the crowd sensed some excitement was brewing.

Sure enough, Boomer laced a single to right to open the frame, and when the fielder bobbled it, he raced to 2nd ahead of the throw. Once again, the speed up and down the Stars' lineup was a factor. Like Chase had done in game one, Boomer did his best to distract Marchildon on the mound, and while he did not wheel around and attempt a pick off, a distracted Marchildon uncorked a wild pitch that sent Boomer to 3rd. Catcher DeVillers seemed to think he had a shot at Harding, but he threw wildly down to 3rd, and Boomer easily came in to score, cutting Penetang's lead to 6-5. This was turning into something of a game of errors, and the team that made the fewest would likely emerge the victor.

Marchildon seemed to come unglued after that. He retired Chase, but walked Talbot on four pitches. Talbot was off to the races on Marchildon's next pitch, successfully stealing 2nd, and putting the tying run in scoring position. Washington, the next hitter, chopped a "swinging bunt," a ball that came off the bottom of the barrel with plenty of spin but not much speed. Marchildon was about the only one in position to field the ball, but he failed to get to it in time to get the speedy Wash out at 1st. Marchildon stood perplexed with the ball in his hand as the crowd roared its approval. With the corner infielders and Marchildon converging on the ball, the Penetang shortstop covered 3rd in case there was a play to be made on the advancing Talbot, and the 2nd baseman had covered 1st. With

2nd base left uncovered, Washington alertly took off for the base and made it safely without a throw. The Stars now had two runners in scoring position and only one out. They had hit only one ball hard in the inning, but were on the verge of scoring a trio of runs. It was a huge mental error on Penetang's part.

Patience at the plate and aggressiveness on the basepaths were the keys for the Stars. With Marchildon now battling his control, the Stars kept working the count, piling up the pitches and hoping to take some of the steam out of his fastball. On the bases, Marchildon's difficulties controlling the Stars' running game were obvious, and everyone in the lineup had the green light. You had to give a tip of the hat to his catcher, DeVillers. He had wielded a heavy bat in the first game, all the while trying to harness Marchildon's wildness all series long to keep the Stars' from running amok on the bases.

With the crowd in full flight, Marchildon's fifth-inning mound breakdown continued when the next hitter, Tabron, hit a ground ball right back at the Penetang hurler. Tabron got down the line as fast as anyone in the lineup, and Marchildon, fully aware of Tabron's fleetness afoot, rushed his throw to 1st, landing in the dirt. With the ball arriving a split second before Tabron did, Penetang 1st sacker Bald took his eye off the ball and could not scoop the errant throw cleanly. Talbot easily scored, and while

Bald scrambled to retrieve his error, Wash - who, in typical Stars' fashion, did not stop as he rounded 3rd, then slid into home with the go-ahead run ahead of Bald's toss to DeVillers at Home.

Marchildon got himself back together to finish the inning with no further runs allowed. Walks and errors meant that the Stars scored three runs with the benefit of only one base hit, and a bunt single. The Athletic Park scoreboard read Chatham 7, Penetang 6, as we headed to the 6th inning in this topsy-turvy affair.

⚾ ⚾ ⚾

Merv

The Rangers tied the game back up in the 7th when McCuaig drew a lead off walk, went to 2nd on a passed ball, then came around to score on yet another hit from Chuck Sheppard. But the weather, which had not been a factor when the Home Plate umpire yelled, "Play Ball!" in the first inning, had slowly come into play. The temperatures had dropped into the 40s, and a slight drizzle - more like a mist - had enveloped the field. This game did not promise to become a defensive spectacle in the final innings, and the team that made the fewest mistakes would likely win the day.

Phil responded to the bottom of his lineup finally providing some offence and tying the game by shutting down Chatham in the bottom of the 7th. In the top of the 8th, it was time for the home team to boot the ball around. Chase, who had moved over to short when Tabron took over for Terrell on the mound, muffed a ground ball that put the lead off hitter on. One out later, it was Talbot's turn to misplay a ball at 2nd. With the tying run in scoring position and two out, Phil stepped into the batter's box.

There was no doubt that Crippin was the most feared slugger in the Rangers' lineup, while Marchildon was arguably their best hitter for average. He wasn't a threat to knock one out like Hal was, but Phil won the North Simcoe batting title, and had a knack for putting balls in play. And that skill was on display in that 8th inning at bat, as he lined a solid single up the middle to drive in the go-ahead run, and the Rangers took a 8-7 lead as the game went to the bottom of the 8th.

⚾⚾⚾

Jack

When Penetang scored in the 8th, it marked the fourth time the lead had changed hands in this back-and-forth affair. Tension filled the diamond, and flowed freely into the stands. There had been considerable grumbling all day long about the umpire's strike zone for the Stars' hitters compared to that of the visitors, who seemed to get the benefit of the doubt on close pitches more often than not.

This was not new to the Stars. The City League umpiring had been inconsistent, at best, but usually seemed to go in favour of the opposition, so the Stars felt. There was a great deal of complaining about the officiating in the Milton series. It seemed the Milton hurler was getting the calls on the edges of the plate, while whoever was on the mound for the Stars had to practically throw one down the middle to get a called strike. It probably was not a coincidence that the Stars pitching staff led the City League in walks; they seemed to consistently have to work with a shrunken strike zone.

As had been their custom all series long, the Stars tied the game in the 8th by scratching out yet another run. Stan Robbins drew a lead off walk - the sixth free pass the fast but erratic Marchildon had issued. Hap sent Cliff Olbey in to pinch run, but his base-stealing skills were not needed, as Marchildon hit pinch hitter Sagusta Harding next, putting two runners on with one out, and the top of the order coming up. In fairness to Marchildon, new balls were an expense not many teams could afford, so discoloured, soiled balls were replaced only as a last resort, and with the cold and dampness in the air, any ball hit on the ground acquired a coat of mist on it. Balls that were fouled off out of play were given a quick wipe with a towel before being tossed back to the home plate umpire. Both Marchildon and Tabron had trouble gripping the ball properly on the day; both had walked the same number of hitters by that point.

All in all, things were looking good for the Stars. The pressure was squarely on Marchildon.

Len Harding laid down a perfect sacrifice bunt to move the runners up 90 feet, and when Kingsley Terrell hit a slow roller to 2nd, Penetang had no play at home, and had to settle for the sure out at 1st as Olbey crossed the plate with the tying run. Boomer was up next and hit a promising fly to right, but he just got under it, and the Penetang fielder settled under it for the final out of the inning. The Stars had tied the score at 8, but for the third time that afternoon had stranded a runner at 3rd. Cashing in just one of them would have put the Stars in the lead heading to the 9th.

⚾ ⚾ ⚾

Merv

The oil drum bonfires were going full tilt by the time we got to the 9th inning. You could hear the crack and pop of the wooden pallets someone had taken apart for firewood. Those who were not standing around them sat in the bleachers wrapped in heavy blankets, while others passed flasks to ward off the encroaching winter weather. As the day darkened, so did the home crowd's mood.

The Rangers had Sheppard due to lead off the 9th, but he was unable to reproduce his earlier heroics, and when Hale behind him - hitless in the series so far - was unable to get on base, the top of the order was up, but there were two out. The Rangers' chances of scoring in that frame seemed awfully thin, and the prospect of extra innings with a race against a setting sun loomed once again.

But Jimmy Bald slapped an opposite field single to left, and his brother Marius bounced one under the glove of the slick-fielding Tabron up the middle for another, and with DeVillers due up, the Rangers had one last chance to retake the lead. Tabron had a tough choice to make - pitch to the red-hot DeVillers, who had a pair of hits on the day on top of the two he had in the first game, or work around him and risk the prospect of facing potential game-breaker Crippin with the bases full.

Tabron opted to go after DeVillers. The bulky backstop came through with a double - his third of the series - to cash in both Bald brothers, but he got greedy, and was thrown out at 3rd trying to stretch his hit to a triple to end the inning. The Rangers were now up 10-8 as the game went to the home half of the 9th, with Chatham down to their final outs. With his work on both sides of the plate, DeVillers had been one of the series' best players.

⚾ ⚾ ⚾

Jack

The final turn at bat for the Stars in the game would be one to remember, but not necessarily for the right reasons.

With Chase to start the inning at the plate, even a casual observer of the game had to feel that despite being down two runs, Chatham had a chance to tie things up - a slim one, maybe, but a chance just the same. This was a never-say-die team, a group that found ways to win. But it had to be weighing on the team's mind that, with a third game already scheduled to be at a neutral site, the Stars were once again on the verge of letting the home fans down.

What was going through Flat's mind as he stepped into the batter's box to start the home half of the 9th? He probably was looking for redemption. If not for a sore arm, Flat would have gotten the ball to start the game for the Stars, and if he had pitched anything like he had in the regular season, it most likely would not have come down to the team trailing by two in their last at bat. The error he made in the 7th inning was likely on his mind, as well. But Chase was unable to ignite things for the

Stars on this chilly late afternoon, striking out for the second time in a row. The next hitter, Talbot, like Chase, wanted to atone for his error two innings earlier. After his dreadful 0 for 5, five strikeouts performance in game one, Talbot was an on-base machine in the second, reaching base in all four trips to the plate up to that point. He was aboard for a fifth time after drawing a one-out walk.

That was when things started to unravel.

As Washington, the next batter, took his first delivery from Marchildon, Talbot - who had swiped 3 bags on the day already - was off with the pitch. It was a close play, but the base umpire - a fellow by the name of McFadden, who had been the subject of the fans' wrath all day - called Talbot out. To an observer in the stands, McFadden seemed to be a step or two late in getting to the play, and did not have the clearest view he might have otherwise had. It really did look from that vantage point that the runner had beaten the throw by a hair. Talbot, who thought he was safe on the play, was furious, and immediately went after McFadden. Hap and Percy ran from the coaches' boxes to try to restrain him, but the tension of a long day and even longer series had clearly gotten to Talbot. As they tried to push him back, Talbot let go with a vicious uppercut at McFadden, missing the umpire by inches. The poor umpire's cap fell off as he bent backwards to avoid Talbot's attempted haymaker.

Peace was restored shortly after that. Percy grabbed Talbot by the back of his belt and lugged him into shallow centre field to get him to cool down, while Hap pleaded his case with McFadden. Under the custom of the time, Talbot was allowed to stay in the game, most likely because his blow didn't connect. 1934 was a different time, as far as umpiring was concerned. Respect for the men in blue was at an all-time low, training for them was very limited, and incidents like this were tolerated. "Kill the umpire," was a phrase in use since the days of Casey at the Bat, and until baseball took some steps to protect them in the form of fines and suspensions at the major league level after World War II, umpires universally were subject to all kinds of player and fan abuse.

Under normal circumstances, Talbot was as thoughtful and mild-mannered as they come. He was an intense competitor, to be sure, but one of those players who left it on the field when the game was over. But with the pressure all of the Stars were under - months of poor umpiring, abusive opposition, and hostile fans - he cracked. Certainly, when Marchildon executed his barrel roll into Tabron to break up the double play earlier, there was a feeling of "so, that's how the umps are going to call things today," on the Stars' bench. All season long, the Stars had not fought back, preferring to let their bats and gloves do the battling. But in this situation, the umpire seemed to have made up his mind that if the play was close, Talbot would be out - I don't know how else to explain him making the call almost as the play was happening. Ordinarily, an umpire will wait for the completion of the play, but his "out" signal and the Penetang infielder making the tag were almost simultaneous. Like it was preordained. When Talbot pressed the ump for an explanation, McFadden just ignored him, and that's when Talbot let loose with a swing just as Hap and Percy were trying to rein him in. This really was out of character for Talbot, and while I do not condone what he did, I understood it. Five months of frustration let loose in a second of bad judgement.

Things were settled, the call stood, and with the help of several teammates, Hap and Percy were able to get Talbot off the field so that the inning could continue. Hap returned to the scene of the crime to plead Talbot's case further, but to no avail. But the incident did nothing to alter the collective frustrations of the crowd, several of whom continued to torment McFadden as the game resumed. Hap took his time returning to the Stars' bench to let the crowd tell the umpire what they thought of his call. Marchildon was probably affected by the chilly delay, as he promptly hit Washington with his next pitch, and with two out the Stars had a runner on. Undaunted by the previous call on

Talbot, Wash took off for 2nd, and safely slid under the tag. The crowd erupted in a blast of sarcastic cheering as McFadden finally got the call right. At the plate, Tabron then lined a single between 1st and 2nd - the Stars' first hit since the 5th inning - and Washington came in to score, cutting the Penetang lead to 10-9. Still down to their last out, the Stars had life.

The Stars lived and died by the stolen base all year, so it was no surprise to see Tabron on the move to 2nd with the next pitch, and like Washington before him, he was safe. It was the Stars' tenth stolen base of the day. But Tabron wasn't content with having stolen 2nd. With light-hitting Sagusta Harding at the plate, he took off for 3rd. It was yet another close play, but Tabron appeared to have beaten the throw and slid under the tag. But then it looked like he had overslid the bag, and Penetang 3rd baseman Sheppard reached over and applied the tag to a prone Tabron. He was called out.

For the second time that inning, the field - and the crowd - erupted.

⚾ ⚾ ⚾

Merv

The afternoon had turned ugly in more ways than one. When Talbot was caught stealing on that close play, he went after the umpire and had to be held back by his manager and coach. That wasn't something we hadn't seen before, but I for one had never been comfortable with the sight of a player physically accosting an official. And the mood in the crowd went from surly to downright dangerous as a result. Shaw stood up on the bench, ready to charge out onto the field and quote whatever section in the rule book which dealt with umpire abuse, but order was restored. "Unacceptable," he muttered, sitting back down. Even on a dull afternoon, the atmosphere at the ballpark was absolutely incandescent. Was it the right call? Who knows. Poor DeVillers behind the plate must have been developing a sore arm with all the base runners he had to try to cut down, and for McFadden, the base ump, it seemed like every call he had to make was a difficult one. The call on Talbot at 2nd was a bang-bang play, and from the benches it was far too close to call. The umps in the crowd seemed to think they had a better view than McFadden did.

The game had no sooner settled down again when Tabron attempted that steal of 3rd. In my mind, he should have stayed at 2nd, where a two out hit was all but assured to bring him in to score, but I guess with Phil's wildness, there was always the possibility a wild pitch could score Tabron if he could move up to 3rd. On the play, the 3rd base bag clearly became dislodged, and Tabron slid past it, and an alert Sheppard tagged him. The players had indicated earlier that the bag was loose, and the umps tried to fasten it back down. The long peg hammered into the ground probably came loose with the late fall rain, and a more secure method was needed. Apparently, there was no groundskeeper in sight. In a game that could decide a championship, that seemed - well, odd.

Tabron came up steaming, and Chatham manager Parker joined him in berating poor McFadden, who clearly had never dealt with such a situation before. Tabron and Parker, understandably, argued that Tabron had stolen the base, while Sheppard, just as logically, countered that Tabron had slid past the baseline, and had tagged him out. On the Rangers bench, Shaw observed, "He should be safe. According to Rule 5.09, I believe, if the impact from a runner dislodges the base after he has reached the base safely, no play can be made. What's disappointing to me is that neither ump appears to know this rule."

In those days, few parks had fencing down the base lines to both demarcate balls out of play, and to keep the crowd back. Many fans had been encroaching on the field all day, and several times the umpires, as well as both managers, had to stop the game in order to move them back. But this was like standing at the ocean shore and trying to hold back the incoming tide with a butterfly net. The fans had been getting bolder all day, and by the time this play took place, well over a hundred of them had overwhelmed the 3rd Base line and spilled out onto the field. This would prove to be very detrimental to poor McFadden. When Tabron jumped up arguing that he was safe, many fans instantly stormed onto the infield and encircled the gathering at 3rd Base. While the Chatham manager was appealing for the fans to stay out of the argument and move back, someone connected with a punch aimed at McFadden, whose knees buckled as he appeared to take the shot in his right shoulder. It was an absolutely shameful display, and for the first time all day, there was some fear on the Ranger bench that the unruly mob would break out into a riot.

Ultimately, cooler heads prevailed. Chatham manager Parker and his players were able to convince the crowds to move back out of play, so that the argument could at least continue without an audience surrounding it. The fans grudgingly agreed to do so, but a deluge of garbage - somewhat like Medwick faced - rained onto the field from the stands.

Shaken up from the blow he nearly received moments earlier, for the first time all day McFadden actually decided to confer with the home plate ump, who probably had a clearer view of the play to begin with. The question was whether or not Tabron had arrived at the base safely and then dislodged it before Sheppard's tag, and that was indeed a close one. As the umpires conferred, all hell was breaking loose in the crowd. The boos and the catcalls had reached the deafening point, fans were all over the field, and objects were being thrown. Finally, the umpires broke up their conference, with McFadden pointing to 3rd, and giving the "safe" sign to a thunderous cheer from the Chatham fans. Meanwhile, on the Rangers' bench, Shaw was unimpressed, and went out to argue with the umpires - not about the call, but about the threat to the players' safety that all of the unruly fans and garbage being tossed on the field represented. The crowd, anxious to get the game back underway with darkness approaching, seemed to think that Shaw was stalling for time, and the boos rained down once again. As Phil headed out to the mound to resume the game, a liquor bottle flew from the stands, missing his head by inches.

Shaw had had enough. "Time!" he yelled, and stormed out to the Home Plate ump. "Until you restore some order to this game, my team will not take the field!" And with that, Shaw ordered the Rangers off the diamond, and sent the team to their cinder block dressing room under the stands. The crowd, umpires, and opposition were dumbfounded.

⚾⚾⚾

Jack

I, for one, had never seen anything like it. After the overturned call that resulted in Tabron being called safe at 3rd, just 90 feet from completing a comeback of epic proportions and giving the Stars a championship, the Penetang manager pulled his team off the field. Confusion reigned, because no one else had seen anything like it as well. Fans stormed the field.

Why did he do it? Was it to protest the overruled call? Certainly, it was a close play, but it really did seem to a bystander that Penetang had been getting the majority of the close calls all game, especially on the bases. McFadden was certainly put to work by the Stars' running game, but the experts in the stands were not impressed by his calls. Over the crowd noise, no one could hear what the discussion was about, but given the timing, the Penetang manager had to be voicing his displeasure with the call that would have ended the game had it gone in his team's favour.

Or did Penetang manager Shaw think that the original call on the field stood, and that the game was over? How else could you explain his sudden decision to pull his team off the field, an act that could conceivably cost his team the game? It seemed like an impulsive, petulant decision, a childish act of defiance over a call against his team.

What would be the end result? Was Shaw forfeiting the game? Why on earth would he pull a stunt like that, when his team was an out away from forcing a third and deciding game? Things were being tossed on the field, but that was not an unusual occurrence in those days, at least where the Stars - who were often the intended targets - were concerned.

Was it wise for Tabron to take such a gamble in that situation? Certainly, he had a lot to lose. Making the third out of an inning at 3rd is a bad thing at the best of times, but it certainly would be magnified with a game and the title on the line. But Penetang had been overmatched by the Stars' running game all series. Marchildon had his troubles holding runners on, and I think he was spooked by that errant pick off throw that allowed Chase to score in the first game. After that, he was reluctant to throw over to 1st to keep runners close, preferring to step off the mound, or vary the timing of his delivery to home to try and keep them close. And with so many of his throws missing the plate by a huge margin, DeVillers did yeoman work behind the plate just to nab those tosses and still make a decent throw to try to throw base stealers out. But the truth is that the Stars had all but stolen DeVillers' shin guards in the series, and Tabron taking off for 3rd with two out in the bottom of the 9th with his team down a run was how this team played the game. They took chances, they put pressure on the opposition defence, and they ran at every opportunity. If Marchildon's personal pitching coach made a return the next year, there was a lot of work to do in teaching him how to control the opposition's running game.

To me, even in the heat of battle, it seemed like an unsportsmanlike move by the Penetang manager. The Stars had come back fair and square, and if he was protesting a call he did not like by taking his team off of the field, well - that just wasn't something that he should have been allowed to do. Certainly, if the Stars had tried that, the game likely would have been over right there and then. But the Stars had fought tooth and nail all season, and this game encapsulated their fighting, never-give-up spirit. If they were awarded the game and the championship because Penetang decided to take their ball and go home, well, that just didn't seem fitting at all. The game should be decided on the field, and while the crowd was probably hopeful that this would seal the Stars' victory, I was actually hoping that Penetang would come back out and finish this game the right way. The Stars and their fans deserved no less.

⚾ ⚾ ⚾

Merv

Shaw made sure that he was the last one in the room.

No one knew what to make of what had just transpired. Every man on the team had played in the face of hostile crowds before, but nothing like this. Yes, even the most die-hard Rangers fan would have admitted that the umpiring had been inconsistent at best on the day. It's hard to believe this was the best the OBA could come up with to rule over an important game like this. Something had to happen to keep this game from becoming an embarrassment for the sport's governing body in the province.

Shaw closed the door and addressed the team. "Listen, fellas," he began, "we're not done yet. We will not be forfeiting this game and lose this series in this manner after all the hard work you've put in to get here, but there is no way I will jeopardize your safety under any circumstances. This has been a tough game to call for a lot of reasons, but these umpires are in over their heads, and we won't be taking the field again until there are guarantees that they will have the crowd under control."

The room was quiet at this point. It wasn't the players' choice to leave the field, but they seemed to understand that Shaw had no choice. He had been through the baseball wars before, and had probably been through a situation similar to this a few times before. There was method to his apparent madness.

Several moments of silence passed. The team could still hear the roar of the crowd outside, which showed no signs of subsiding. Finally, a knock at the door - it was the home plate umpire, a fellow named Collier, who most likely wished he was anywhere else but at the ballpark at that moment. Shaw had obviously been expecting him, and knew in advance what he was going to say.

"Manager," Collier began when Shaw opened the door, "I believe we have settled the matter on the field, and you have two minutes to get your team back on the field, or a forfeit of the game will be declared."

"And you are in no position to make such demands or declare a forfeit," countered Shaw, "because of a failure on your part to ensure safe conditions on the field and for the players."

"I don't understand," Collier responded with surprise.

"I didn't think so," answered Shaw, pulling out a well-thumbed rule book out of his team jacket in response. "Several times today, both teams had pointed out that the 3rd Base bag had not been properly fastened down. Not only did it make things dangerous for the players rounding the base attempting to score, it led to that unfortunate last play that saw your colleague take a punch to the shoulder. If I might," Shaw continued, flipping to a dog-eared page in his book, 'Rule 4.08 (g)...the umpire-in-chief' - that's you - 'shall have control of groundskeepers and assistants for making the playing field fit to play.' That means once the game begins, you have the responsibility for directing the home team to keep the field safe for the players, and despite repeatedly being told about that bag, you ignored it. The penalty, according to the rule book, is 'for violation, the umpire may award the game to the visiting team'," Shaw concluded, snapping the rule book shut with one hand for emphasis.

Collier looked positively ashen. He tried to argue with Shaw, but he quickly realized that he was out of his depth. Shaw had built grain elevators designed to last over a century, and oversaw the logistics of one of the country's busiest grain ports, supervising the transport of millions of tons of prairie wheat to feed a hungry continent. Studying and memorizing the baseball rule book from cover to cover was not a difficult feat for him.

"I will go confer with the OBA officials," Collier said shakily, and quickly rushed out of the room.

"He'll be back," Shaw said confidently. "And if he brings some OBA bigwigs with him, I have more ammunition."

⚾ ⚾ ⚾

Jack

I moved over closer to the Stars' bench while Penetang left the field to protest the umpire's call. Hap, Archie Stirling, and several OBA executives had huddled to try to figure out what would happen next.

"Ever see anything like this before, Hap?" I asked.

"Never before in my life," Hap replied. "Nowhere. And we've faced some pretty scary situations this year. That game in Strathroy, fans were insultin' us and peltin' us with garbage, and the umps did nothin' about it. But we didn't walk off the field. We just ignored it all and took it out on the Strathroy team. Beat 'em by a dozen runs."

Archie and the OBA brass were tight-lipped, though, and didn't offer a comment. It was a tense time, and they were hopeful for a quick and peaceful resolution. Whether or not he was right in pulling his team in, Jim Shaw was a highly respected man in Ontario baseball circles, and they didn't take his actions lightly, and knew that he must have had a reason for taking his team off the field.

Collier, the home plate umpire, came over to the group to update them on his visit to the Penetang locker room. They spoke in hushed tones, but it was obvious they took his report seriously. Archie accompanied Collier back to speak with Shaw.

"Did you catch what they said?" asked Hap. "No," I answered, "but if Archie is involved, you know that the OBA wants to keep this thing from getting all blown out of proportion."

"Yeah," Hap agreed, "but you couldn't have a better man trying to reach a deal than Archie. He'll get 'em back out here, and we'll finish this off on the field, like we should. No one wants things to end this way."

⚾ ⚾ ⚾

Merv

Shaw's prophecy came true not ten minutes after Collier's attempt to bully him back onto the field. But this time he came with support - one of the execs by the name of Stirling, a Chatham official who, to be fair, had a good reputation throughout OBA circles. He had managed to negotiate favourable terms for the series for both teams prior to the first game, an act of telegram and telephone diplomacy.

Stirling was conciliatory in his tone. "Mr Shaw," he began, "what would it take for you to get your team back on the field? The fans and players deserve no less than to see this game played to its conclusion. You don't want your season to end this way, the fans don't, and the Chatham side certainly doesn't want it, either."

"Look, sir," Shaw replied, "with all due respect, Mr Umpire here has committed several rule violations today. The most egregious of these involves rule 4.07. The rule book says, and I quote, from part (a), 'no person shall be allowed on the playing field during a game except for players, coaches in uniform, and umpires.' That was broken during that disputed call, and the poor base umpire almost paid for it with his dental work. Furthermore, under section (b) of that same rule: 'The home team shall provide police protection sufficient to preserve order. If a person, or persons, enter the playing field during a game and interfere in any way with the play, the visiting team may refuse to play until the field is cleared: If the field is not cleared in a reasonable length of time, which shall in no case be less than 15 minutes after the visiting team's refusal to play, the umpire in-chief may forfeit the game to the visiting team.' The atmosphere has become very unsafe for my ballplayers, and the Chatham team has a duty to keep their fans in order, or under those rules they will forfeit. I will give them fifteen minutes in which to do so," he said, glancing at his wristwatch, "or according to the rules, we are awarded the game."

The Stirling fellow was flabbergasted by Shaw's instant recall of the rules, and his subsequent ultimatum. In fairness, he may not have faced this kind of situation before. But he regained his composure quickly; he knew that a settlement would only come about if he kept his cool. "I'll tell you what, Mr Shaw," he responded. "Your knowledge of the rules is impressive, and I do agree that the game has reached the danger stage. But I cannot reasonably guarantee police protection - in fact, I can't even assure you that their presence, if I call them, will do a great deal to reduce tensions here. What I can do is lobby the Chatham manager and players to do their best to keep the crowd calm, and move them well back from the field of play, then make them aware that failure to do so may result in the home team losing the game by forfeit - as unpopular as that might be. I can make no promises, but we will do our best to make sure it is safe for the resumption of this game."

Shaw agreed that such a course of action would be acceptable. With that, Stirling and Collier left to implore the Chatham team to calm the fans down. Best of luck to them, I thought.

"Men, I think it's important to give you a say in this," Shaw said after the pair had departed. "Is this agreeable to you all? I can't guarantee there won't be some more rough stuff out there, but I've done all I can do. I'm sure you don't want to win a game sitting in the dressing room. But if you don't think it's safe, then raise your hand - no repercussions - but I will only ask you to go back out there if the whole team feels it's safe to do so."

Not a hand went up. The guys wanted to settle this on the field. "Hell no, Jim!" thundered Crippin. "We're an out away from putting his game away. What do you say fellas?"

There was unanimous agreement that the game should continue.

⚾ ⚾ ⚾

Jack

A sombre-looking Archie emerged from the Penetang locker room to make the trek back to the field, umpire Collier in tow. He talked briefly with Hap, whose body language expressed some resignation. Hap came over to talk with his team. "Fellas, Archie has gotten Penetang to agree to come back and finish this game, but we have to all go and ask the fans to keep off the field and stop throwin' things."

"Hap, are you kidding?" asked Wash. "We're not responsible for how they act. And how about we get the umpires to hustle and get in the position to make good calls while we're at it? If I was in the stands, I'd be irate that I'd paid to watch these clowns ump a game."

"Look, I don't disagree with you, Wash," Hap replied, "but we as the home team have a responsibility - accordin' to the rule book - to keep the visiting team safe from the fans."

"That's a laugh, after what we've been through this year. It's like there's two sets of rule books," said Wash.

"Be that as it may," countered Hap, "if we don't get the fans to simmer down, we forfeit the game. We're 90 feet from tyin' it."

There was an air of disbelief on the bench. But the players realized they had little choice but to ask the fans who had backed them all year to keep things under control. It certainly didn't help foster better relations with the Penetang team. The team fanned out among the crowd, pleading for them to cooperate in order to finish the game, a game the Stars still had a chance to send to extra innings.

⚾ ⚾ ⚾

Merv
Stirling came back one more time, and asked to speak privately outside with Shaw. Their discussion sounded heated at first, but soon toned down. Moments later, Shaw came back into the room, and said, "Let's go finish this off, fellas." As the team trudged back to the diamond, the fans were comparatively subdued, but greeted the Rangers with a hearty chorus of boos. Once the game was over, the team had already planned on heading straight to their cars and making a quick getaway.

Phil was given some warm up tosses to try to get loose again, but doing so in the high-30s temperatures was next to impossible. The Rangers fielders took some warm ups as well, and Tabron, given new life, was back at 3rd. A hit or error would tie the game, and send the two clubs to extra innings once again.

After his warm up, Phil walked around the mound for a moment windmilling his pitching arm, still trying to shake off the stiffness from the prolonged break in play. For a moment, I wondered if Shaw's move to take the team off the field only one out from victory was such a good strategy. One wild pitch would tie the game, a real possibility considering that he had already thrown four of them on the day when he was warmed up.

⚾ ⚾ ⚾

Jack

Hap had pulled all the right strings all year, and had made all the right decisions when it came to deploying his players and in-game strategy. He had a feel for the game few other baseball bosses had, a sense to know when to make a move - or, in some cases, not make one.

However, with the game on the line, perhaps he indulged in some over-managing. When the game finally resumed, Tabron took a generous lead off of 3rd when he saw Marchildon was in the full windup. The Penetang catcher recognized this, and called time for a mound visit to get him into the stretch. Had he not done so, Tabron was likely on his horse headed for home on Marchildon's first move. The Stars fans met this meeting with derision.

The Penetang 3rd baseman was playing in a few steps to guard against the bunt, but he couldn't cheat too much towards home, because Tabron's lead was matching him. One would think Tabron, after narrowly stealing 3rd, may have been more conservative so close to home, but Sagusta Harding had not played a great deal, and was not one of the stronger bats in the Stars' lineup. The count was 1-0 to Harding as Marchildon readied to deliver in the resumption of the inning.

Then suddenly, out of the blue, and without blinking an eye, Phil stepped off the rubber, likely hoping to catch Tabron making a break for home. Tabron didn't bite. The boos rained like a downpour. The fans were in no mood to wait any further for this game's outcome.

⚾ ⚾ ⚾

Merv
Phil was about to throw his first pitch when Fred DeVillers alertly called for time in order to visit him on the mound. He reminded Phil about the runner on 3rd, and to pitch from the stretch. He also advised to go right after the batter, a weaker hitter. The top of the order was waiting if Phil failed to get him

out. In hindsight, that move by DeVillers may have saved the game.

As most of the Chatham runners had all series, Tabron danced off of 3rd, daring Marchildon to throw over. Phil didn't respond, but he stepped off the rubber to move Tabron back closer to the bag. The Chatham crowd didn't like that one bit.

Phil's next pitch was outside, not a surprise considering the stiffness he was feeling. Tabron broke briefly for home, in case Harding put a ball in play. For his part, Harding gave no indication of his plans at the plate. Phil's next pitch was better located, hitting the heart of the plate for a strike. Harding took the pitch, obviously not planning on swinging until Phil could get one across.

With the count even at 1-1, Phil looked in for the sign, glanced over at Tabron, then made his move to the plate. At that split second, Tabron broke for home, and as the pitch came in, Harding surprisingly did not square to bunt. A suicide squeeze would be a bold move, but this looked like either a straight steal, or a hit-and-run. Highly risky moves, given the circumstances. "What the hell?" I wondered as the play unfolded. As Tabron sprinted down the baseline, every Rangers player (and fan) in the crowd yelled, "HE'S GOING!!!"

Harding swung and missed the pitch, and the instant that he caught it, DeVillers lunged for the 3rd Base side of the plate, where he applied the tag to a sliding Tabron's foot before he could score. Umpire Collier, likely chastened by the events of the day, leaped out to get as close to the play as he could. He paused a moment to make certain that DeVillers hung onto the ball. Satisfied at what he had seen, Collier bellowed, "yer outttt!!!" and just like that, the game was over.

Unlike every other close call that game, there was no argument from the Chatham Manager, who probably realized it was a botched play. Tabron was fast, but he couldn't sprint home ahead of Phil's fastball. Game over, the Rangers had a 10-9 win and the series was headed to a third and deciding game. What a wild one.

⚾ ⚾ ⚾

Jack

The Stars' crowd was shocked into stunned silence when Tabron was called out at home. Athletic Park went from cacophony to deathly quiet in a split second.

Some fans loudly protested the call, but Donnie was out by a foot. The ball arrived clearly well before he did, and the catcher made a desperate dive to tag him before his foot could reach the plate. Marchildon must have been out of gas, but he somehow found his fastball on that last pitch. I felt for Sagusta Harding at the plate. He hadn't played much in the playoffs, and trying to concentrate on Marchildon's pitch while Tabron was steaming in from 3rd must have been very difficult for a guy who hadn't had a bat in his hands a whole lot over the last six weeks.

Boomer said, "Damn. I hate to lose, and especially like that."

It was true. But what exactly happened on that play? Maybe the logical thing to do in that situation was to try a squeeze play, but trying to lay a bunt down against a guy as wild as Marchildon was easier said than done, and Penetang was expecting it anyway, because they had the corner infielders come in a few steps. Maybe Hap was hoping Sagusta (who was pretty good at making contact) would put a ball in play, and maybe find a hole.

As much as Tabron getting caught stealing at home was the play of the game, the story of it had to be the Stars' missed opportunities. They left too many runners on, squandered too many chances, like those three runners stranded at 3rd. The team that found ways to win was left wanting on this occasion.

It was the damndest game I'd ever seen.

Game 2 10/18/34	1	2	3	4	5	6	7	8	9	R	H	E
Penetanguishene	0	6	0	0	0	0	1	1	2	10	13	5
Chatham	3	1	0	0	3	0	0	1	1	9	8	4

Penetanguishene	AB	R	H	RBI	Chatham	AB	R	H	RBI
J. Bald 1b	5	2	2	0	L. Harding cf	4	2	1	0
M. Bald 2b	5	2	2	0	Terrell p, 3b	5	0	1	2
DeVillers c	5	1	3	2	W. Harding 1b	5	2	2	0
Crippin ss	5	0	1	2	Chase ss, 3b	5	1	1	0
Marchildon p	4	1	2	1	Talbot 2b	1	1	1	3
McCuaig lf	4	2	1	0	Washington c	4	2	1	1
Spearn rf	4	0	0	0	Tabron ss, p	5	0	1	1
Sheppard 3b	4	1	2	1	S. Robbins lf	2	1	0	0
Halde cf	4	1	0	0	Olbey rf	0	0	0	0
					H. Robbins rf	2	0	0	0
					Ladd lf	0	0	0	0
					S. Harding ph	0	0	0	0

	IP	R	ER	H	BB	K
Marchildon	9	9	6	8	7	13
Terrell	1.1	5	3	4	2	1
Tabron	7.2	5	3	9	5	7

Two Base Hits - DeVillers (3)

Three Base Hits - Terrell (1), Talbot (1)

Sacrifice Hit - L. Harding

Stolen Bases - Terrell (1), Talbot 4 (4), Washington 3 (4), Olbey (1)

Hit by Pitched Ball - DeVillers, Washington, S. Harding

Merv

The team returned to their hotel while Shaw met with the OBA and Chatham to determine the date and location of the third game. It would in all likelihood be at a neutral site, if past precedent was any indication - it was just a matter of where. Jake Payette, recognizing how late the second game would end, had his foundry business pay for another night's hotel stay for the team, and they would be on their way back to the shores of Georgian Bay first thing in the morning.

For once, Phil would be travelling home with the team. He had made the trip to Chatham from Toronto with his dad, who had logged a lot of miles since Labour Day. As the players gathered back in one of the hotel rooms, the unmistakable clink of beer bottles could be heard, and additional were quickly passed around to the thirsty gathering. I clinked bottles with Phil, and said, "great game, Babe."
"Aww, it wasn't so hot. Thanks anyway," he said, taking a long pull from his bottle.

"Why so glum?" I asked.

"This should be a championship party. We blew that first game, plain and simple. We got off to a two-run lead, and couldn't score again despite all the runners we had on. We just couldn't buy a clutch hit. I threw one away to open the door for them. All we did today was climb the mountain just to get back to square one. We dug a hole for ourselves by losing that first game when we could have easily won it. We should be taking a trophy back home. And I have to tell you....if the third game is tomorrow, or even the next day, I don't know if my arm will be up to it. Three tough games in less than a week will be asking a lot."

⚾ ⚾ ⚾

Jack

The negotiations for the third game went on for well over an hour, a process that should have taken all of fifteen or twenty minutes. From what I was told, it was a bitter meeting, the bad feelings between the two sides fully on display. Chatham wanted the game played in Guelph, while Penetang advocated for nearby Galt, after reminding all in the meeting that the series would have been over days ago if it had been played up north. Guelph was a field and city familiar to the Stars; Penetang wanted the game in Galt because they believed a crowd of 5 000 would be on hand. The almighty dollar, apparently, was more important than a championship trophy.

After much wrangling, Guelph was to be the site of the third game. Fair and good. It would be almost exactly the same distance - just under three hours - for both teams to travel. Guelph was a huge baseball city, and there would be a decent field to play on. Availability, given that it was late October, would not be a problem. The Stars had no argument with that decision. That Penetang pushed for a different site just seemed to fit the pattern of controversy that filled the series. I'm not saying they did it just to be contrary, but everything seemed to be a negotiation with them.

The sticking point was when the game would be played. Chatham initially pushed for the very next day to get the series over with once and for all, but even the OBA was against that, in addition to Penetang, which would not hear of its star having to pitch 3 times in five days. Besides, rain was in the forecast, and had already started, which would have resulted in a postponement anyway.

Chatham then pushed to have the game played on Saturday. More fans could attend the game because it was on a weekend, and the Stars thought it a fair compromise. A day of rest should be sufficient for the players. Penetang, not unexpectedly, refused, trying to get as much rest for Marchildon as they could. Sunday baseball was banned in Guelph, as was a whole host of events under Ontario's blue laws. Monday was the day Penetang had been pushing for all along, and after tense discussions, the OBA took a "take-it-or-leave-it" stance, giving the Stars no choice but to agree. There was a brief meeting of the Stars in the lobby of the Roth; many wanted just to go home, but they also wanted to stick around to see what the decision would be. They did not take the news well, figuring that they would be playing on Saturday. Once again, the powers-that-be seemed to have their thumb on the scale of justice when it came to decisions involving the Stars.

⚾ ⚾ ⚾

Rangers Triumph in Dramatic Style; Historic Final Moves to Guelph for Deciding Game
By Mervyn Dickey/Charlie Paradis
Penetang Herald Staff
October 20th, 1934

Word was relayed by long distance telephone late yesterday afternoon of the Penetanguishene Rangers' wild, exciting, and improbable win to tie their best of three O.B.A. final series with Chatham in a contest that will not soon be forgotten by those who witnessed it.

Down three after only an inning, the visiting Rangers struck for a half dozen in their half of the 2nd against Chatham, who answered with a single run in the bottom half of the inning, and three more in the 5th to reclaim the lead.

Penetang knotted the game up at 7 with a run in the 7th, took the lead with another solo run in the 8th (which Chatham answered) then scored a pair in the 9th to put the game seemingly out of reach. The plucky, never-give-up Chatham squad scored a single run in their half of the 9th, and had the winning run at 3rd with two outs, but baserunner Tabron was thrown out trying to steal home.

Phil Marchildon did not have his best stuff on the day, as the game was played under conditions even colder and wetter than the first game at Beck's Field. Marchildon fanned 13, but walked 7, and hit 4 batters. Catcher Fred DeVillers was the hero of the game for Penetang, clubbing out 3 hits, coaxing a winning performance out of Marchildon, knocking in a pair (including the eventual game-winner in the 9th), and making an outstanding defensive play to tag the would-be base thief Tabron at the plate. After a disputed call in the 9th inning in an afternoon full of close plays, the Chatham fans littered the ball diamond, and Manager Jim Shaw briefly removed his squad until matters subsided.

Given the rapid approach of winter, and in order to help save on travel expenses, the third and deciding game of this series will be played at Guelph. Mr Bert Dubeau, owner-operator of Penetang-Midland Coach Lines, has offered to charter a bus to take any and all interested local fans to the game.
Whoever wins this game will make history for their community, for neither has ever brought home a provincial championship.

Chatham Stars Ready for Big Game Monday

By Jack Calder

Chatham Daily News Staff

October 20th, 1934

Chatham Stars will journey to Guelph on Monday to meet Penetang in the final and deciding game of the intermediate B-1 class of the O.B.A. A gruelling series that so far has seen each club win one game will be completed and a long season of baseball in which both teams have played well over thirty games will be brought to a close.

Chatham took first blood in the finals on Monday of this week when Penetang dropped a ten-inning game by a 4-2 score, Don Tabron doing the pitching for Chatham. King Terrell was batted from the box here Thursday and Penetang went on to beat Tabron and tie the series with a 10-9 score.

The Stars management was a little backward about starting Flat Chase, speed-ball king, on the mound for Monday's game for the supporters of the team claim that Chase lacks competitive spirit and the team would go better with Tabron, Terrell, or Talbot on the hill. Chase said after Thursday's game that he wanted to pitch in Guelph on Monday, but unless he satisfies the Stars' management that he is ready to pitch *winning ball he will start the game at one of the infield positions.*

Monday's game will begin at 2:15.

MANAGER COMPLAINS

Coach Flynn of the Penetang team that defeated the Chatham Stars here Thursday afternoon and several of his players have registered a complaint regarding a story that appeared in some of the Friday morning papers.

In Mr Flynn's opinion a person would gather by reading the story that Penetang won the game as a sort of gift on Chatham's part. He and his players take a different view and maintain they won on account of their hitting.

As proof of their contention that the game was won by hitting the visitors point out that Penetang collected 13 bingles as compared with 8 the Chatamites secured.

As regards Chatham's runs, the Penetang man claims that several of them were a result of errors. The error columns indicated that Penetang was even more generous than the hosts, as Chatham was charged with four while Penetang had five misplays chalked up against them.

The story complained of, according to Mr Flynn, did not give a true picture of the game because it did not mention that two of the Penetang basemen were spiked by Chathamites; that the short stop, Chase, tackled a base runner; that the umpire was mobbed, and that the umpire reversed a decision.

Game Three - Guelph, Ontario
Monday, October 22nd

Merv

After a brief hotel lobby confrontation between my Chatham counterpart and Rangers 1st base coach Ivan Flynn over an item in the local paper, the Rangers headed back to Penetang shortly before noon, Shaw having given the team time to sleep in after the previous day's game. To be honest, it was an argument that didn't need to happen, another product of nerves frayed by a season gone too long.

Both teams had the weekend to get some added rest before making the trek to Guelph on Monday. Rain was in the forecast for both Saturday and Sunday for that part of the province, which would make for even sloppier play than we had already seen.

The series had been a battle both on and off the field. Shaw wouldn't say much about the meeting to determine where and when the final game would be played, but he did say the discussions were very tense. Just like on the diamond, neither side was willing to give an inch to the other. It's doubtful that Phil could have pitched on Saturday, which apparently was Chatham's choice of dates, although he would have willingly taken the ball and pitched on two days' rest if need be. But there was no way Jim Shaw was going to let that happen. Chatham had at least two pitchers, of course, and could afford the luxury of trying to get the series over with as soon as possible. Shaw knew the toll a summer and fall of pitching had taken on his ace's arm, however, and had likely advocated in very strong terms to play the game on Monday. Interestingly, the Chatham side was not in favour of playing the first game of the series two days after their previous game, but now they expected the Rangers to do so. The weather may have had the final say, anyway, judging from the weather report for the weekend.

When the Rangers were formed a couple of years earlier, Hal Crippin had been their pitcher. The team was a middle-of-the-pack outfit until Phil came along. Shaw tried to be careful with his young phenom's innings, originally planning to use Crippin on the mound some games and put Phil at 3rd or centre field to keep his bat in the lineup. But in a short Ontario baseball season, every game counts, and Shaw wound up using Phil more often than not. Between regular season games, exhibitions, tournaments, games where bird dogs would be in attendance, league playoffs, and now the OBAs, Phil was past 200 innings pitched, certainly not an astronomical total for a big leaguer in those days, but a heavy workload on a young arm that hadn't thrown half that many before. Shaw knew legendary hurler Hec Goldsmith wasn't the same pitcher this year after leading Grey-Bruce champs Southampton to an OBA title last year; such was the risk of relying on one pitcher exclusively in a long playoff run.

⚾ ⚾ ⚾

Jack

If you asked the man on the street, the Stars had proven that they were the superior team, and that Penetang winning the last game had more to do with lousy umpiring than anything else. The team had truly become the talk of the town. The Stars had become Chatham's team.

Over the course of the weekend, there was still considerable bitterness among players and fans that the deciding game had been pushed to Monday. The Stars had a rotation of pitchers that they could use, but Penetang, of course, had only Marchildon, who was breaking down. A Saturday game just made sense, especially at a neutral site, because more Chatham fans could make the trip to cheer on the Stars. The short turnaround meant that Penetang could just stay at their hotel an extra day (which their sponsor surely could afford), avoid the travel, and be finished with this marathon of a season once and for all.

But it came as no surprise to Boomer and his teammates that the OBA ruled in favour of Penetang, despite intense lobbying by Archie Stirling. "It's like they said, 'OK, you can play in the OBAs, but you're just not going to win it,'" Boomer observed. And it was hard to disagree with him.

So, Penetang went home Friday morning, while the Stars made plans to head for Guelph on Monday, and the OBA lost a golden opportunity to play the game in front of a packed house on Saturday. No mind. "It does give Flat's sore arm a couple more days to heal," Boomer noted. True enough.

I had received word at the *Daily News* office that one of Penetang's entourage was unhappy with an article I had written about the game. I made the short walk down to the hotel to discuss it with him as his club was getting ready to make the trip back home. I asked coach Flynn what he disagreed with in my article, and his response indicated pretty much all of it. But when he was pressed about what was incorrect in the article, he could not name a thing. It seemed like no point was too trivial, no grievance too small to overlook for the Penetang folks.

Merv

The long season had certainly taken its toll on both teams. Players had to take time off from their jobs to travel to games, and the season was rolling on long past when it should have been finished - the World Series had ended ten days ago when Chatham and the Rangers took the field for the third game.

Once again, to save the players' legs, the Rangers left for Guelph on Sunday, so that they could put up in a hotel and be well-rested for the Monday game. Phil tried his best to catch up on some assignments during the trip, but with the fatigue he was feeling as a result of the workload he was under, he was asleep before the team reached Barrie. Later, Phil expressed regret at going to St Mike's for the year, and getting so far behind in his schoolwork over the first two months of the academic year did not help. He really never did catch up, and his low marks, coupled with his family's limited finances, put an end to any post-secondary hopes he may have had. After the relative freedom he had experienced growing up in Penetanguishene, he bristled at the regimented lifestyle the Fathers at St Mike's insisted upon - a life of school, football practice, and study, with little time for enjoyment. Free-spirited Phil chafed under the restrictions.

A bus full of Rangers supporters would make the trip south on Monday morning. One thing other teams in the province learned is that the sports fans of Penetanguishene were second to none when it came to supporting their teams. It would be a small contingent of maybe 30 or so, but they would be enthusiastically and vocally cheering on their Rangers. What they may have lacked in numbers they more than made up for in volume.

The team had become an enormous source of civic pride. Tiny Penetanguishene, a one-horse tourist town, was punching well above its weight class, taking on - and beating - towns and cities many times its size. Stories about Phil and the team had appeared in the Toronto *Globe*, *Star*, and *Telegram*, and the citizens of the tiny town dutifully clipped the articles out and glued them into scrapbooks.

Speaking of horses, several bottles of horse liniment, courtesy of Jake Payette, had been sent along for Phil's tired arm. This was serious stuff - you applied it with rubber gloves. DMSO was the active ingredient - Dimethyl Sulfoxide - and since it worked wonders for Jakes' stable of racehorses, the thinking was that it could help Phil. Phil said he got an overwhelming taste of garlic in his mouth seconds after applying it, and it smelled so strong that you couldn't apply it indoors without opening every single window in the house. "It may take a year off my life, but if it helps put some zip back in my fastball tomorrow," Phil said, "I'm all for it." His roommate for the night might not have agreed with that. It turns out Phil had been applying the substance after every game since the first game of the Meaford series weeks earlier.

⚾ ⚾ ⚾

Jack

The Stars set out for Guelph the day before the final game, Pete Gilbert having rounded up some more financial support for gas and hotel accommodations. As the team met prior to their departure, there was a buzz in the air, as Flat had pronounced himself fit, and ready to pitch the biggest game of the season.

The Stars had called ahead and booked rooms at the Wellington Hotel in Guelph, whose owner was a former Chathamite and one-time lacrosse star. The team pulled into the hotel early in the afternoon. When Penetang rolled in to check in an hour later, they promptly left and looked for another place to stay when they learned the Stars were already there.

Only a handful of Chatham fans would likely make the weekday trip to Guelph, which was a huge disappointment to the players. But as the team gathered in the Wellington lobby for dinner in the hotel restaurant (there would be no refusal of service for the Stars on this trip), a telegram was delivered that lifted their spirits tremendously.

The telegram was addressed to Hap, who, after needing to borrow coach Percy's reading classes, gave the note a quick scan. "Hey, fellas," he said loudly after reading it, "before we go eat, you might want to give this a listen. I have here a telegram from none other than the Mayor of Chatham. It reads, 'Dear lads: best of luck tomorrow. Go bring home that championship. You have all done Chatham incredibly proud. Regards, Mayor Davis.'"

The team was collectively awestruck by the gesture. Hap took off the reading glasses, looked around at the team, and broke out in a huge smile. "Ain't that beautiful," he beamed. The players let out a huge cheer, and there were many slaps on backs and congratulatory handshakes as the team headed to the dining room.

It's hard to put into words how important that gesture was to the team. Outsiders since the start of the season, they now carried the hopes of the city on their shoulders as they sought to bring Chatham its first baseball title. Even though only a handful of supporters would be on hand the next day, the Stars knew that they had a whole city behind them, and that tomorrow many fans would be gathered outside the offices of the *Daily News*, anxiously awaiting updates.

To a man, the Stars felt that they were the better team. Because of Flat's troubles with his arm and a couple of errors in the field, perhaps the two top Penetang players - Marchildon and Crippin - had outplayed the Stars' leading duo of Chase and Harding, but the edge was slight. As for the rest of the players, the Stars believed that they were better at every other position. And they had the added benefit of greater pitching depth and team speed. The series had been close, but the Stars felt confident that they would triumph on Monday. If this was a war of attrition, they had more firepower to outlast their northern opponents.

⚾ ⚾ ⚾

Merv

Unfortunately, the playing conditions were not ideal when both teams woke up on Monday morning. Saturday had seen a heavy downpour in Guelph, and cold temperatures. Sunday was slightly warmer (about 60 degrees), but the rain lingered off and on until shortly before the Rangers' arrival in town. There would be little chance for the ground to absorb all of Saturday's rain, or Sunday's relative warmth to evaporate it. The forecast for Monday was for cloudy skies, and a game time temperature around 53 degrees. If there was a saving grace to the overcast day, it was that the forecast low temperature was only going to be two degrees cooler.

Given the events of the previous game, most of the OBA executive were due in town to watch the game, so we were told. You had to wonder if that was necessary, and if because they were arriving from all points of the southern Ontario compass was why the game had a later starting time. In the 1930s, Daylight Savings Time started on the last weekend in September, and given the length of time each of the previous two games had taken, I wondered if a 2:30 starting time was all that wise, given that the sun would set by about 5:30, and a gray cloudy day would probably mean reduced visibility ten to fifteen minutes before that time. The sloppy and cool conditions the day promised would not translate into many neat and tidy 1-2-3 innings. The average major league game was played in about an hour and forty-five minutes in those days, but at a time of year when a mid-afternoon start wouldn't involve the risk of running out of daylight. An extra inning game on this occasion would likely not go far, which would necessitate the two teams having to replay the next day, a scenario no one wanted. It was curious why the game started at such a relatively late hour.

Shaw was relieved that his ace would have three days rest between games, but he was concerned that Chase, who his sources said was Chatham's top hurler, (but hadn't taken the mound yet due to a sore arm), would have that same rest, and he was convinced that his Chatham managerial counterpart would have Chase start the third game. To Shaw, the keys for his team, then, were to get off to a quick start, avoid making mistakes, and pray that Phil's arm held out. Some better umpiring might help, too.

⚾ ⚾ ⚾

Jack

The Stars' approach with Marchildon last game, as per Hap's orders, was to make him throw strikes. Unless he threw the first pitch right down the heart of the plate, the batting order (outside of Boomer and Chase) was to take until they had a called strike. And it seemed to be working, despite the outcome. Marchildon was frequently behind on hitters, which took his curveball away from him. The effect of this strategy was also to wear Marchildon out as well, and he threw a lot of pitches in the second game, on top of the ones he threw in the first. It was something of a cumulative effect, but that approach was beginning to pay off.

Then there was the Stars' running game. Not only did they drive Marchildon crazy on the basepaths, they put extra pressure on Penetang's defence. Every Star busted down the 1st base line on a batted ball, and the Penetang infielders knew they had to field the ball cleanly and get a throw off right away in order to get the out. Their outfielders also were more than aware that the Stars would go for the extra base at every opportunity. Fielders tend to make mistakes when they have to hurry, and the Stars were experts at capitalizing on miscues.

To avoid a repeat of the second game's drama, the entire OBA brass was coming into Guelph by car or train to watch. With a crowd only a fraction of the size of the last game's likely to attend, that didn't seem likely, although the tensions between the two teams were sky-high, and it might not take much for things to get out of hand on the field again.

It was not a surprise that Hap decided to give the ball to Chase to start the game even though he came up with another sore arm just prior to the last game. During the regular season, he was all but unbeatable. His sore wing had caused him some problems in the playoffs, but after his pre-game warmup, he appeared fit and ready to go. The leash Hap had him on would probably be a short one though, with Tabron having pitched so well in this series. At the first whiff of trouble, Hap would likely make a change.

Penetang had won the coin toss, and would be the home team for the game. Batting first didn't matter to the Stars, who wanted to get out to an early lead. Len Harding worked the count full to lead off the game, then fouled off a couple of pitches before ultimately going down on strikes. But that at bat set the tone for the afternoon: work the count, and make

Marchildon battle for every out. The battle took some steam out of Marchildon, who gave up a single to the next hitter, Terrell.

With Boomer due up next, the excitement was growing on the Stars' bench. It was still early in the game, but this was not the guy Marchildon probably wanted to see at the plate. Going back to the last game, Boomer had three hits in his last six trips to the plate, and of all the Stars he had gone the furthest in figuring Marchildon out.

Marchildon threw over to 1st in an attempt to keep Terrell closer to the bag, but Terrell easily beat the pick off attempt, and resumed his huge lead off of 1st. The Stars had found Marchildon's biggest weakness early in the series, and were exploiting it at every opportunity - even the guys who didn't run that much took larger leads off the bag than normal. But with the two heaviest hitters in their lineup due next, Hap decided to play things conservatively, keeping Terrell anchored at first. Boomer was unable to solve Marchildon, though, but a two-out triple by Chase behind him easily brought the runner in to score, and the Stars had an early 1-0 lead.

Merv

The Rangers got their first look at Chase on the mound, and it was easy to see why he was their ace. He had long levers that generated a whipping action, along with a smooth delivery, command of his pitches, and even with some arm troubles, Chase threw the ball hard. The ball seemed to explode out of his hand from that nice easy motion. With this different look on the mound, the Rangers would need to see him once or twice before they could take their measure of him.

Chase got through the first two innings easily enough, making the one-run lead he'd been staked to stand up, and got the first hitter out in the last of the 3rd. But the top of the order was coming up now. The Rangers, who had such a difficult time in the first contest mounting offence when they needed it, found their clutch bats in the last game, and they hoped to carry the hot sticks over into today's match. Jimmy Bald singled, and his brother Marius reached on an error to keep the inning alive. DeVillers struck out, but then Crippin drove Jimmy in from 2nd with a two out single before the inning ended.

The Chatham strategy of taking pitches to try to fatigue Phil worked in the first inning, but he began pumping in first pitch down-the-middle strikes after that, and had six whiffs after only three innings. Wrapped in one of Cream O'Tartar's lucky blankets on the end of the Rangers bench while they took their turns at bat, Phil battled his control over the next few innings, walking several hitters, but he kept Chatham off the scoreboard. Heading into the 6th, the game was tied at 1.

⚾ ⚾ ⚾

Jack

Chase rose to the challenge of trying to secure a title for the city of Chatham. He even found his old fastball, and while he was not piling up the strikeouts like Marchildon was, he was notching a few and headed towards double figures himself. Penetang had some runners aboard through the middle frames, but Chase found a way out of trouble every time.

The sun showed no sign of making an appearance, and dampness had started to fill the air. Conditions were not going to improve as the game progressed. It promised to be another error-filled game.

Talbot opened the top of the 6th by reaching on a two-base error by the Penetang left fielder. Washington behind him slapped a double down the 3rd base line, bringing home the go-ahead run. The skies were darkening, but with the way Chase was pitching, retiring Penetang in order in the bottom half of the inning, that 2-1 lead was looking like it might stand up. A championship was within their grasp.

⚾ ⚾ ⚾

Merv

It shouldn't have come to a surprise that the third game was yet another close one. There were only two runs total separating the two teams in the series through six innings of the third contest, with both teams having several good chances to score in that game, but the aces on both sides got huge outs when they needed them. Hats off to Chase, who pitched so well despite that tender arm.

When the Rangers failed to score in the 7th, things were becoming tense on the Penetanguishene bench as they came in to take their bats in the bottom of the 8th. When you're trailing by a run at that point in the game, scoring to either take the lead, tie it, or just get back in the game seems to give teams a huge lift; failure to do otherwise gives them next to no margin for error when they come to bat in the last of the 9th. Phil was due to lead off the last of the 8th for the Rangers, and he smacked a single, his second hit of the day. The ball was hit in the gap and Phil rounded the bag widey, looking for extra bases, but the ball just died, and was quickly retrieved by the Chatham outfielders, holding Phil at 1st. The combination of a soggy field and humid skies conspired to keep most hits to singles on the day. Nothing really would carry. Hal had joked on the bench between innings that maybe the team should put some of Phil's horse liniment on their bats to get them going.

While the Rangers had the lead off man on, they were now heading toward the bottom half of the order, a group that outside of Sheppard hadn't produced much offensively in the series. McCuaig was given the bunt sign to move Phil along, and he laid down a beauty. Phil had been off with the pitch, and he took a wide turn at 2nd as the Chatham 1st baseman Harding went to field the sacrifice between 1st and the pitcher's mound. The sight of Phil making that turn must have caused Harding to lose his concentration for a moment, because after he picked it up he bobbled it, and stepped off the bag, then had to turn and hurry to get McCuaig at 1st. What he missed when he turned was Phil taking off for 3rd, where he slid in safely after the throw over from 1st. The Rangers had the tying run just 90 feet away, with only one out. A hit, error, or even a sacrifice fly could bring Phil in. Phil had learned from watching Chatham's daring on the basepaths, and figured he could do it, too.

⚾⚾⚾

Jack

The game was not one for the ages from an artistic perspective, that is for certain. The poor conditions no doubt contributed to the two teams combining for nine errors on the day. But the Stars picked the worst time to combine several of them after taking that one run lead into the last of the 8th.

Marchildon's lead off single brought new life to Penetang, and their small but boisterous group of fans, who made up for their lack of numbers with their constant chatter and cheering. The usually sure-handed Boomer bobbled a routine sacrifice bunt to allow Marchildon to reach 3rd. Then Talbot booted a fairly easy grounder to let the tying run come home. Penetang likely would have added more in the inning if not for a fine stab of a line drive right through the box that Chase made to end the inning.

Once again, extra innings were looming. The Stars were starting to get frustrated, feeling that they had yet to put away a team that they were superior to. Marchildon was once again on fire, and while the Stars' decision to wait him out led to 6 Chatham walks on the day, Marchildon finished strong, setting them down in order in the 9th, and was up to 17 strikeouts. Maybe a bit of aggressiveness early in the count might have given the Stars some better pitches to hit, but Marchildon was able to get ahead in the count, and then his curveball became more of a weapon. He did not always throw it, but you had to watch for it, and if you watched too closely for it, he would blow a fastball by you.

Merv

A fielding gem - a rarity for this game - by Crippin got Phil the first out in the 9th, and Phil took over from there, fanning the next two hitters, sending the tied game to the Rangers' last bat. But Chase on the mound for Chatham shut the door, and this clash of the titans was coming down to the wire once again, which maybe was fitting. Each team had its strengths and weaknesses, but there was little to pick and choose between the two clubs. Phil certainly did a lot of the heavy lifting for the Rangers, but Crippin, DeVillers, Sheppard, and the Bald brothers had all put in strong performances, too. Chatham maybe had more balance on their roster, but the two teams were very evenly matched.

When Phil wasn't getting strikeouts, he was inducing a lot of weak contact, as evidenced by the 10 ground ball outs he had. Certainly, the weather had a lot to do with the hitters not squaring up many balls, as Chase had 11 groundouts as well - 8 of them comebackers fielded by Chase himself. There were no extra base hits on the day - the pitchers were too dominant, and the ball carried like a pumpkin - kind of fitting with Halloween coming up. Chatham kept up the running game, but Phil and DeVillers behind the plate were catching on - Chatham was no longer running at will, as Fred threw out two out of five would-be base stealers. With hits scarce and the footing not always reliable, both teams played things more cautiously on the bases.

Phil fanned another two hitters in the Chatham top of the 10th, bringing his total to 18 on the day. Crippin and Phil each rapped out singles in the bottom half of the inning, but McCuaig popped out to end the threat. The game was now over two and a half hours old, and with the sun already hidden behind dark clouds, the game was coming to an end one way or another.

⚾⚾⚾

Jack

The Stars hurried in off the field after getting Penetang out in the 10th, anxious to get what might be their last turn at bat. Washington, who had walked twice and singled, was the ideal man to get things started. And Wash came through once again, reaching with his third base on balls of the day. Tabron was up next, and with the way he handled the bat, he was the right man for that situation as well. Hap had been holding runners back, but Wash had stolen four bases in as many tries in the series, so he was off with Marchildon's next pitch, sliding safely under the tag at 2nd. The Stars had the go-ahead run in scoring position with no one out. Tabron did his job two pitches later, grounding a pitch to the right side of the infield.

Tabron was out at 1st, but he moved Washington up to 3rd. It wasn't something that showed up in the boxscore, but it was a huge at bat by Tabron.

Stan Robbins was up next, and without hesitation, he laid down a perfect bunt down the 1st base line. Wash was moving with the pitch, making it a suicide squeeze, but by the time Marchildon was able to field the bunt and toss it to home, Wash had slid in with the go-ahead run. Penetang had been expecting a bunt, but it was so well executed by both hitter and runner that there really wasn't much they could do. Robbins reached first on the play.

The Stars tried to play for more runs in the inning, and some wondered if that was the right strategy, given the fading daylight. To be fair, it was a situation they had not been in often during the season. But if the game was called because of darkness before Penetang had a chance to complete their turn at bat, the score would revert to what it was at the end of the previous inning - a tie. The tradition in those days was for tied games to be replayed. It was difficult for players who have competed so hard to turn it off and deliberately try to make an out. It is unknown if that was the case with the Stars, but they sent five more men to the plate without adding another run before the inning ended, and one cannot help but wonder if that ate up valuable time and daylight. It's hard to ask players who had been battling all season to go up to the plate and try to make an out, but the game was now a race against daylight - what there was left of it. Just the same, the way Chase had been pitching, he could make short work of Penetang in the bottom half of the inning. It was close, but things looked very upbeat for the Stars.

⚾ ⚾ ⚾

Merv

It was a bold move for the Chatham manager to order that suicide squeeze in light of what had happened at the end of the previous game, but his gamble paid off as they scratched out the go-ahead run. It was a textbook example of that strategy. The Rangers were all but helpless because the squeeze bunt was so well placed. On a day when conditions made the long ball difficult, it was the smallest of hits that might decide the game.

To be honest, things did not look promising for the Rangers heading into the last half of the inning. The bottom third of the order was due, including Spearn, who had recorded his first hit of the series earlier in the game, Sheppard, whose bat had gone cold after the first game, and Hale, who was hittles in the series and would likely be giving way to a pinch-hitter. If Spearn was unable to get on base, the hill the Rangers would have to climb to stave off Chatham's pending title would become much, much steeper.

Give full credit to Spearn. Trying to pick out a battered and discoloured ball the same hue as the skies that the game was being played under was no mean feat. Spearn battled Chase through a ten-pitch at bat, fouling off borderline pitches before ultimately striking out, giving the Chatham hurler a baker's dozen whiffs on the afternoon.

Sheppard was up next, and the Rangers were down to their last two outs. His bat had gone cold, but he was as productive as any hitter in the linuep through the first two games. Chase threw one pitch that Sheppard later claimed he never, ever saw, and the home plate umpire, a fellow named Almas, removed his mask and chest protector, came out from behind home plate, and yelled out, "Time! This game is called on account of darkness." This was not unusual for the Rangers, who had gone through this experience twice in the Meaford series, and once in the regular season. But it appeared this was brand new territory for Chatham, who were dumbfounded at the umpire's decision.

To say that chaos ensued once again would be an understatement.

⚾ ⚾ ⚾

10th Inning

The aftermath of the controversial third game; the teams prepare to play one more time

Jack

"It was like the umps had some kind of pre-arranged signal or something. They just called the game, then jumped in a car and drove off," said Boomer in the aftermath.

That the home plate umpire called the game was as astonishing as it was devastating to the Stars and their handful of fans. Flat Chase had mowed down Penetang hitters, and was two outs away from giving Chatham its first OBA title. Now it felt like the trophy had been ripped out of the Stars' hands. After Flat got the first out, he was ahead 0-1 on the next hitter when the umpire ruled the game over. Given the way Chase was working, he probably needed no more than five minutes to finish Penetang off, and to the assembled, there was more than enough daylight left for him to accomplish that.

Archie Stirling was out of his seat and on the field of play in seconds, but by then the umpires had collected their gear and were off to the base umpire Hogan's car, and they drove off into the twilight. There was no argument, no explanation. Not that it would have done any good, because the genie was already out of the bottle. The debate itself would have taken care of the remaining daylight. Hap, Stirling, Shaw, and the OBA brass were left to sort things out - not that there was much to be done in that regard. What was done was...done. The game was over, like it or not, and had to be declared a tie, which meant a replay. Again, the Stars were two outs away, now they had a whole nine innings (or more, the way this series was going) to play before they could take their rightful place as champions. This was unjust - a travesty.

Did Penetang stall, knowing that they were down a run, had the bottom of the order due up, and having the game called was probably their best chance to avoid losing the game and the series? Certainly, that was a tactic that many teams used in that situation during those games before fields had floodlights. And while the Stars hustled on and off the field once the game went into extra innings, Penetang seemed to take their sweet time, without the same sense of urgency the Stars had. The first batter in the last inning certainly paced himself during a lengthy battle with Chase. He stepped out after each pitch, intently looking down to 3rd at his manager for the signs - of which there weren't any - then knocked some dirt out of his spikes and
adjusted his cap before leisurely stepping into the batter's box. "Ah, c'mon, hurry up," was the refrain from both the players on the field and the fans in the stands. But I would guess you

would have to ask the Penetang players themselves if that was what they did, and if that was the sporting thing to do. The game belonged to the Stars at that point, and Penetang was doing about all they could to exercise the only option available to them. "It sure looked like they were taking their sweet time," Boomer said.

But what about the umpires? Why did they call a game when it appeared that it was almost over, and there was just enough light to squeak it in? One can only guess as to their motives, but one of the more sage Chatham fans had a theory about the men in blue. "Penetang's owner," so this man's story went, "is some rich guy named Payette. He owns all kinds of businesses, and has a huge stable of race horses. He hangs out with some unsavoury characters around the track, and they say he made his money running liquor to the States on one of his fancy boats. Maybe, just maybe, this Payette fella got word to the umps through one of the fans from Penetang here today, 'hey, you do whatever it takes to make sure those coloured boys from Chatham don't win, and Mr Payette will make sure you're rewarded'." Maybe that was far-fetched, but there was indeed something about the end of the game that smelled like a rat.

For the second time in the series, the Stars had a title within their grasp. They booted it away the first time, but it was wrenched away from them the second time.

Merv

This much is true - the home plate umpire called the game, and got into the base umpire's car and drove off with most of the mouths of the people at the ballpark still hanging open. There was little time for discussion - not that it would have solved anything. A long debate about whether it was too dark or not to play would've been rendered moot long before the argument was over. The umpires left the OBA to deal with the fallout. I wondered if they had heard about the fisticuffs of the previous game, and weren't interested in sticking around long enough to find out if those tales were true or not. It had been an emotionally charged atmosphere all afternoon.

Did the Rangers stall? That's a good question, and the answer is complicated. It was a common practice in those days for the home team to try to run out the clock in that situation. It was usually done in subtle fashion, but Barrie had been so obvious and deliberate in their stalling in a game back in June that the North Simcoe executive overruled the umpire of the day, who called the game because of darkness, and awarded the game to the Rangers. That was the risk a team in that situation faced.

When Chatham scored in the top of the 11th, they did send five more men to the plate in the approaching dusk before the inning ended. Some of the folks in the crowd were yelling at the Rangers to hurry off the field to go take their turn at bat when the top of the 11th ended, but I'm not sure any team in that situation would have hurried their game up in order to seal a loss. Peg Spearn battled Chase to start that inning, just as any other hitter would in that situation. The Rangers did what any other team would have done. Yes, the Chatham team was on the verge of a title, but the Rangers were still entitled to their turn at bat.

Tie games were a fact of life in the era before night baseball. Three times in the past, World Series games had been called because of darkness, and had to be replayed. But stalling by the home team, whether due to a setting sun or falling rain, was as old as the National League itself. The issue of the home team hoping to overcome a deficit by using the forces of nature had become so commonplace that baseball several years later replaced such games with "suspended games," that would simply be picked up where the original game had left off at the earliest opportunity. But that wasn't the case in 1934.

Phil, for one, didn't think his team stalled for the simple reason that there wasn't much to gain by it. "Look, everyone knew I was just about done," he said later. "If there was a replay, the chances were that the OBA would order it to take place the next day, and there was no way I would be able to answer the bell.

I mean, I would take the ball if Shaw handed it to me, sure, but I could barely lift my arm to comb my hair, and anyone who knew anything about the game saw that I was out of gas." This much was true. In the space of seven days, Phil had pitched three complete games, two of them having gone into extra innings. Over those three games, he had pitched a total of 32 innings, struck out 52 (including 18, plus two in the 11th of the third game), and walked 17. Because the Chatham hitters didn't give an inch when they faced him (nor should they have) and tried to work the count, there was a lot riding on just about every pitch he threw, meaning that a lot of maximum effort pitches came out of Phil's arm. There were very few easy innings for him. If a replay was to happen the very next day, Chatham had to be heavy favourites, because Phil had nothing left. The Rangers had to know that they had nothing to gain from a replay. Chatham had proven they would be able to start a fresh pitcher. The Rangers' backup hurler, Crippin, had not thrown a pitch from the mound since that Labour Day contest in Parry Sound.

What about the umpires? Was the fix, as someone had suggested, truly in? Again, that's a difficult question to answer. Phil would tell you that he didn't get a lot of borderline calls, especially on the pitch he threw with the count full to the hitter leading off the 11th for Chatham. If the umpires were intent on making sure the Rangers won, six walks on the day for Phil might suggest otherwise. At times, it did seem like the Chatham strike zone was a lot smaller compared to the Rangers'. There was also a rumour floating around that maybe someone on the Penetanguishene side had bribed the umpires to do everything in their power to ensure a Rangers' win. The Black Sox scandal of almost fifteen years ago was still very fresh in many fans' minds, and the history of the game over the first few decades of the 1900s was marked by several betting scandals. But almost all of those involved players, and not umpires, perhaps for the simple reason that the players, by "laying down," could have more of an impact on a game than an umpire, and they could influence the game much more subtly. An ump cheating for one team and not the other would be fairly obvious. In the case of the Rangers, that "someone," of course, would be Jake Payette, and while it was said that Jake never met a wager he didn't want to put a fiver on, that was not how he rolled. In all the years that Jake owned a race track, there were never any allegations of race-fixing against him.

Did the umps just make an impulsive decision? Baseball had been shaken to its core over a decade earlier when Cleveland's Ray Chapman was killed after having been hit in the head from a pitch by Carl Mays of New York. In those days, pitchers were pretty much free to doctor the ball up at will. The spitball was legal, and umpires rarely penalized a pitcher for defacing the ball. Many pitchers of that era threw sidearm, or even underhand. Phil threw mostly three-quarters, but even the Chatham paper had commented on how tough he was to hit when he dropped down. The ball moves differently from a sidearmer, but the wisdom became that such a style of delivery caused a lot of stress on a pitcher's arm, which is why many by end of the War had moved to an overhand windup. It can be very hard for a hitter to pick up the point where a pitcher releases the ball in a sidearm (or "submarine," like Mays) delivery. In the aftermath of Chapman's death, baseball phased out the spitball, and umpires were much quicker to put new balls into play. But amateur teams in the Depression didn't have a lot of money to spend on new baseballs, especially teams without sponsors like Chatham. The tradition in amateur ball was that the home team provided a new ball at the start of the game. If it became too beaten up to use, the home team often dipped into its bag of used baseballs to come up with a replacement, rather than put an expensive new one into the game. So, with fading daylight, a battered ball, and pitchers whose delivery included some deception, if the umpires that day did act prematurely, they may have been doing so from an abundance - or maybe even an overabundance - of caution.

The Chatham OBA rep, Stirling, was furious in the aftermath of the game's suspension, and I certainly wouldn't have blamed him. But many years after the game, many called into question the umpire's decision, and when I've been asked whether or not it was in fact too dark to continue, I point out some facts about the game. The two teams combined for eleven hits over the course of ten innings (all results reverted to the last completed inning), nine errors, the same number of walks, and the two pitchers accumulated thirty-one strikeouts between them. That's a lot of pitches, which takes a lot of time. Yes, games were played at a much faster clip in those days, when walks and strikeouts were fewer, and batters put more balls in play. But with Chatham working the count, and all the baserunners, errors, and strikeouts in the game, it was a drawn-out affair.

The game started just after 2:30, once all the OBA brass were seated and the pregame festivities concluded (why the game didn't start earlier was beyond me), and with sunset at 5:25 DST, it's hard to see a game of that length being completed in that amount of time. The Rangers twice had extra innings games against Meaford called by darkness, but that was a month ago, when we were dealing with about a half hour more daylight at the end of the day. We couldn't get extra innings games in then - how could we get them in now? Night baseball had proved to be a boon to the Toronto Maple Leafs in 1934, but the days when amateur parks across the province had floodlights was still over a decade away.

⚾ ⚾ ⚾

Jack

The argument on the field continued on into the settling darkness, the lights of parked cars illuminating the field. The Stars and Archie Stirling justifiably felt that they had been robbed, with the championship just two outs away. The prevailing sentiment was that there was plenty of daylight left to complete Penetang's turn at bat. It was also felt, to a man, that Penetang had slowed down to a glacial pace that inning. "They had the bottom of their order coming up," observed Boomer, "and those guys hadn't done much against Flat all game, and the way he was pitching, it was hard to see them mounting a rally against him. I think it's just human nature - slow things down, take your time, and maybe the daylight will run out before the game is over. And a little help from the umps didn't hurt."

But now there was little for the two teams to do but return to their hotels, have a post-game meal, and wait for the OBA to make a ruling. Hopefully, the assembled executives would use their common sense and finally put
an end to this season, and give the Stars their justly deserved title. I am certain that Archie knew that there was nothing in his power to reverse the umpire's decision, but he would let the OBA know in no uncertain terms the mess they had made of the whole situation. The right and just thing would be to rule that Penetang did stall, and award the game to the Stars. That's

not exactly how anyone would have wanted it to happen, but at this point, everyone wanted this to be over.

Among the players, there was a huge feeling of injustice, that a tie had been snatched from the jaws of victory, and a sense of "here we go again." "It's like I said," Boomer reminded, "that the powers-that-be didn't want the coloured team to win." The Stars had to fight tooth and nail to score the go-ahead run in the 11th, and were giddy with excitement as the series finally seemed within their grasp, only to have it taken away in a matter of moments. It was gut-wrenching.

An hour and a half later, the OBA's decision was official: the umpire's decision was allowed to stand, the game would end in a tie, and would be replayed the following day. Boomer's prophecy had been realized. After an emotional roller coaster of a season, Archie Stirling looked worn out when I ran into him back at the hotel. It had been a long season for everyone, especially Archie. "What the hell happened, Archie?" I asked.

"Damned if I know, Jack," he answered. "I'm not a suspicious man by nature, but there was something awfully fishy about the way the game ended."

"Do you think Penetang was stalling?"

"Of course they were. That's what teams in that situation do. Same with rain delays. When a team is losing and the skies start to open up, you take your time, hoping the game will be called before it's official. But that's all academic at this point. What's done is done. What I want to do now is to ensure that the two umpires who cooked this up today aren't invited back to call the next game tomorrow, so that we don't have a repeat of this nonsense. The Stars were robbed, Jack."

⚾ ⚾ ⚾

Merv

A hotel in Guelph was about the last place the Rangers wanted to repair after the game. To a man, the team wanted to be on the way home, and some were expressing the sentiment that the season needed to be over. It was hard to argue with that.

In the face of some of the things we'd heard from the other side, I wondered why the Rangers had become the bad guys. They weren't the ones who called the game. They really had nothing to gain by stalling and hoping against hope for a relay. Even with the bottom of the order due up, only one man had to get on base before the top of the order came up. And with the Bald boys and DeVillers combining for six hits up to that point in the game against a pitcher who had to be tired, there was always a chance that the Rangers could string a couple of two-out hits together. Perhaps it was a long shot, but it wasn't out of the realm of possibility. The Rangers finally got their bats going in the last game, and even as they headed off the field and onto the bench for their last at bats, there was a feeling among the Rangers the game wasn't necessarily over just yet. Down two runs, Chatham came within inches of tying the previous game in their last at bat.

Phil was done, and the only reason he would get the ball to start the next game is that he persuaded Jim Shaw to do so, against Shaw's better judgement. Shaw had carefully managed Phil's workload during the North Simcoe campaign, working Hal Crippin in during blowouts or games against weaker opponents. But around the start of August as the Rangers began to gear up for their OBA quest, Shaw had gone almost exclusively with Phil. Just like Cardinal manager Frisch had ridden his ace Dizzy Dean through the last weeks of the season, Shaw had pinned all of the Rangers playoff hopes on Phil. But Frisch had Dizzy's brother Paul to shoulder some of the load, while Phil carried the burden by himself.

Phil convinced Shaw that it wouldn't be fair to go with Crippin, since he had not pitched in almost two months. "Jim, I can just drop down and throw sidearm all afternoon," he told his manager. Shaw relented, but reluctantly, and he secretly told Hal that he would be coming in if it seemed like Phil was faltering. While the team headed to their hotel restaurant for dinner, Phil was up in his room, his right arm and elbow covered in ice bags, waiting for room service. Young people do recover quickly, but over the past six weeks, Phil had pitched ten intense playoff games - two against North Bay, five versus Meaford, then three with Chatham, and asking him for one more in less than 24 hours was expecting a lot.

⚾ ⚾ ⚾

Game 3 10/23/30	1	2	3	4	5	6	7	8	9	10	R	H	E
Chatham	1	0	0	0	0	1	0	0	0	0	2	4	5
Penetanguishene	0	0	1	0	0	0	0	1	0	0	2	7	4

Chatham	AB	R	H	RBI	Penetanguishene	AB	R	H	RBI
L Harding lf	5	0	2	1	J. Bald 1b	4	1	1	0
Terrell 3b	5	0	0	0	M. Bald 2b	5	0	0	0
W Harding 1b	4	0	1	2	DeVillers c	5	0	0	0
Chase ss	5	1	2	0	Crippin ss	5	0	2	1
Talbot 2b	5	0	0	0	Marchildon p	5	1	2	0
H Robbins rf	3	0	0	0	McCuaig lf	5	0	1	0
Tabron p	3	1	1	0	Spearn rf	5	0	1	0
Washington c	3	1	0	0	Sheppard 3b	3	0	0	0
S Robins cf	4	1	2	0	Hale cf	3	0	0	0
Ladd ph	1	0	0	0					

	IP	R	ER	H	BB	K
Chase	10	2	0	7	3	12
Marchildon	10	2	1	4	6	18

Stolen Bases - L. Harding 2 (2), Washington (3), M. Bald (1), Crippin (1)

Left on Bases - Chatham 9, Penetang 11

Umpires - Almas and Hogan

GAME FOUR
Tuesday, October 23rd
Jack

The weather for what everyone hoped was the once-and-for-all deciding game was almost an exact copy of the day before. If anything, the skies were slightly lighter, but to be on the safe side, the game was scheduled to start at 1:15. No one was taking any chances on an extra inning game and encroaching darkness again.

Archie Stirling was pleased with the fact that the OBA had agreed on neutral umpires for this deciding game. We were told that two officials from the Toronto area had been contacted, and left for Guelph first thing in the morning. That the OBA had agreed to the neutral arbiters, Stirling felt, was an admission that the umpires had erred in calling the previous game. Whether or not that was the case, it was reassuring to know that the association had called in two highly competent umpires to preside over this game. The eyes of the province were on Guelph, and the OBA wanted no more bad publicity. The two teams should be settling this today, not the umps.

Despite the sore arm that had plagued him on and off since Labour Day, after watching him throw his pre-game warmup tosses, Hap opted to start Chase again, less than 24 hours after he had given it all in the extra inning game. I had asked Hap before the team had left the hotel who he was going with on the mound, and he said, "Flat, if his arm is sound."

"Aren't you concerned about his arm? He threw a lot of pitches today, don't you think he'll be tired?" I pressed.

Hap just smiled and said, "he's got all winter to rest."

⚾ ⚾ ⚾

Merv

Despite a regimen of ice, DMSO, and aspirin, Phil's arm was sore when he woke in the morning, and he likely knew he wouldn't have much. When I saw him at breakfast, he put on a brave face, and said, "we're going to finish these guys off today." But his body language suggested otherwise.

The Chatham side claimed that the OBA agreeing to the use of neutral umpires was an admission that the previous day's umpires were wrong to call the game when they did. Perhaps that was the case, but this was not the first time the Rangers had witnessed this. Neutral officials were called in to call the fifth game in the Meaford series, and it was a fairly standard practice. But as game time approached and the umpires made their appearance at the ballpark, Almas - the home plate umpire who had called yesterday's game - was there to work the bases. Chatham officials were not impressed.

This series, like the baseball season itself, had dragged on far too long. The hockey Toronto Maple Leafs had already started training camp, and playoffs were well underway in Canadian football, as teams fought for the Grey Cup. Shaw had vowed if he had anything to do with it, there would be significant changes to the OBA format next year, because the season had become costly for the two finalists, players had to take too much time off from their jobs, and the late October conditions were not conducive to high quality play.

Shaw knew that it would be something of a minor miracle if the Rangers pulled out a win in the fourth game. His prized pitcher had a sore arm, and much of his team was banged up. Phil was burning the candle at both ends with school in Toronto and commuting to Rangers, while the heart of the team - Crippin, DeVillers, and Sheppard, had done double duty with the Penetanguishene rugby football entry since Labour Day.

⚾ ⚾ ⚾

An Edge on The Series
By Jack Calder
Chatham Daily News Staff

From this distance it looks very much as if the Stars have a considerable advantage as they prepare to tackle Penetang in the fourth and deciding - maybe - game of the O.B.A.A. intermediate B-1 finals.

It is an understood fact that the northerners have but one dependable hurler. For that reason, the Stars did their utmost to have the third game of the series played on Saturday so that Marchildon would have to work twice in three days. They weren't trying to pull as fast one. The logical day for any game is Saturday and the Stars figured rightfully one day was as fair to one team as another. The season had been stretched long overtime too.

However, the third game was set by the O.B.A. for yesterday and Marchildon was given three days of rest before having to go to the hill against Chatham again. As a result, he compiled an amazing record of strikeouts and held the Stars to four hits. But he was facing a boy who can really pitch when he is aroused and Flat Chase must have been drilling the ball in there yesterday.

In the three games the Stars have scored only one more run than Penetang. Two of the games have gone into extra innings and the other was won in the 9th. Those results should just about prove that the teams are about equally matched. And they are just about as good as one another - when Marchildon is pitching. But with the two-delivery boy tired or out of the box, the Stars should snatch the series, with a fresh pitcher doing their hill-top task.

Jack

It was obvious almost from Marchildon's first pitch that he had nothing on his fastball; he dropped down with his delivery on almost every pitch because of what was likely an aching shoulder. Since the game was a replay, Penetang was the home team once again, but in a way, it worked to the Stars' advantage, because unlike their patient approach of the day before, the game plan was to try to jump on him right away.

Len Harding whacked the second pitch he saw for a base hit, stole 2nd, then came around to score two pitches later when Terrell belted a single. It was obvious that Marchildon had no bullets left in the chamber, that he had been hoping against hope that he could offer a different look with his sideram stuff. But the ball must have looked as big as a melon as it came into the Stars' hitters. Boomer slapped a single to move Terrell up a base, then both came around to score on a Chase triple. The Stars were up 3-0 before Marchildon retired a batter. He certainly wasn't fooling anyone. Somehow, he managed to get out of the inning without further damage, but the Penetang prospects looked dismal.

Merv

They say that the mark of a good pitcher is how well he pitches when he doesn't have his best stuff. If that is the case, Phil would be taking his finals in a course called How to Pitch on Guile. And if the first inning was any indication, Phil was about to flunk the exam.

Phil had a pained expression on his face since breakfast, and you had to feel for him out on the mound, because without his fastball he was in a shooting gallery. The Chatham hitters were not deceived in the least by his delivery, and Phil gave up some of his loudest contact in the series in that first inning. He was defenceless out there without his best pitch.

But Phil's teammates came up with four runs in the bottom half of the inning. The Bald boys and DeVillers had become the story of the series offensively, and when all three reached to start the frame, a big inning was in the cards. Fittingly, it was a wild start to an equally wild series.

Jack

Somewhere between the hotel and the ballpark, Hap had a change of mind about his starting pitchers. He wanted to go with Chase, but when Flat had all kinds of difficulty getting loose before the game (not surprising after having pitched over ten innings twenty-four hours earlier) he opted to start Tabron. That was a surprise to some, but other than the second game of the series, Tabron had pitched well all throughout the OBA playdowns. "Hap's the manager," Boomer said with a smile when I asked about the switch. "Flat will be there if we need him."

But when Tabron walked one of the Bald brothers to lead off the game, gave up a hit to the other, then loaded the bases with another walk, Hap didn't hesitate to put Chase in. The move backfired at first, though, because the Penetang carousel on the bases continued, and by the time the inning was finished, the Stars' three-run lead had vanished, as Penetang had plated four runs. An afternoon that started out with such promise threatened to turn into yet another nail-biter. An optimistic Stars fan was hard to find at that point; Penetang seemed to have found the solution to both of the team's top pitchers. Before the game, Penetang would have been considered heavy underdogs; everyone knew Marchildon was worn out. But after a marathon first inning, this game had the makings of a slugfest.

⚾ ⚾ ⚾

Merv

The long wait while the Rangers put four runs across in the bottom of the 1st may have done plenty to buoy Phil's spirits, but it did absolutely nothing for his ailing arm, and because of the long time between innings, he came out for the top off the 2nd only capable of throwing batting practice fastballs.

After showing patience at the plate all series, Chatham wasted no time pouncing on the meatballs Phil was throwing, and after he had thrown only ten pitches, three runs were in. Shaw had seen enough, and summoned Crippin. But Crippin, of course, hadn't thrown a pitch since the beginning of September. Not surprisingly, he struggled with his control, and by the time the inning was finally and mercifully over, Chatham had struck for four more runs to answer the four the Rangers had put up in their half of the first. After only an inning and a half, the score was 7-4, and many thought this was another game that would be pushing up against the sunset to complete.

Whatever momentum the Rangers had gained by coming back to take the lead in the last of the first was all but undone by Chatham's second inning outburst, and it showed at the plate when they came to bat. The Rangers were unable to mount any offence, and Chase seemed to be settling in on the mound.

⚾ ⚾ ⚾

Jack

What a huge lift it was for the Stars when Chase was able to shut down Penetang in the bottom of the 2nd. The game was far from over, but the team breathed a huge collective sigh of relief when their ace tossed a scoreless frame.

Penetang had to bring in Crippin to relieve Marchildon when the Stars batted around in the 2nd. You had to feel for both pitchers. Say what you will about Marchildon, he pitched his heart out, but he was simply worn out. That 11th inning yesterday, as difficult as it was for the Stars and their supporters, may have been the turning point in the series. It was obvious now that after a long season and a gruelling playoff grind, that inning had taken its toll on Marchildon. And Crippin obviously had not pitched in some time, because he could not find the strike zone with a road map when he came in.

After being aggressive with Marchildon's sub-par tosses, the Stars went back to their conservative mode against Crippin. He had managed to finally put an end to the bleeding in the 2nd, but the Stars made him work in the 3rd, and he loaded the bases with walks before recording an out. The rout was clearly on, and by the time the inning ended, the Stars had batted around once again, tacking on five more runs, increasing their lead to 12-4.

Back in the spring, Hap had stressed the importance of having more than one pitcher to share the workload. That strategy had more than paid off. If not for the work of Tabron (who logged the bulk of the innings) and Terrell in the playoffs when Chase was dealing with his sore arm issues, the Stars would not have advanced to the finals. And despite his inconsistency earlier in the OBA tournament, Chase was now relatively fresh (even though he had pitched the day before) right when the Stars needed him most. Penetang had only one pitcher, and his performance today showed the risk of riding one horse over such a long and bumpy road.

⚾⚾⚾

Merv

An enthusiastic busload of fans had made the trek from Penetanguishene to Guelph the day before, and had given the team a huge lift. There was no mistaking who the fans were supporting, with their cowbells, whistles, and assorted noisemakers. The bus had to return home after the game, however, and in the absence of those fans the atmosphere at the ballpark for the fourth game was quite subdued in comparison.

The Rangers had no response for the runs Chatham piled up in the 2nd and 3rd innings, and with Chase seeming to have rediscovered his fastball, the hopes for a comeback appeared slim at best.

Crippin had settled down on the mound for the Rangers, retiring the side in the 3rd and 4th, but his mates could supply no run support, and when Chatham tacked on another run in the 5th to pad their lead to 13-4, Phil volunteered to go back to the mound. Maybe he had been able to loosen his arm a bit when he went to shortstop while Crippin replaced him on the mound, or maybe the Chatham hitters, mindful of what had taken place as the afternoon melted away yesterday, began to take it easy on him, but whatever the case was, Phil shut down Chatham the rest of the way. The Rangers managed to score a pair of runs in the bottom of the 6th, and another in the 7th, but as the game headed to the 8th inning, Chatham had an insurmountable 13-7 margin.

Jack

Despite the high score, the game moved quickly, and by the 8th inning the Stars were six outs from a victory that had seemed so impossible six months earlier, a triumph that had been so cruelly taken away from them twenty-four hours before. Penetang had chipped away at the Stars' lead in the 6th, and when they threatened again in the 7th, there likely was a creeping feeling of panic among the players and supporters, but when the rally was snuffed out and limited to one run, the sense of relief on the Stars' bench was palpable. The end was near.

It's at times like these when the mind plays back the highlights of the whole experience, a tightly edited movie featuring snippets of all the ups and downs of the season. It's also a time when optimism dares you to look ahead, when you are close enough to think of the pending victory celebration. Six outs was all Penetang had left, and with Chase now dealing in mid-season form against a group of tired, dispirited bats, victory this time was all but assured. There would be no calling this game on account of darkness, no snatching the game away at the last moment.

When your pitcher is working ahead in the count like Chase was, it keeps you on your toes. It's no coincidence that pitchers who consistently pitch from behind and walk a number of hitters tend to have less than airtight defence behind them. Fielders tend to be back on their heels when that happens, their pitcher's struggles with the strike zone often causing them to lose their focus. With Chase going right after hitters, it was no wonder that Len Harding - already 4-4 on the day at the plate with three runs scored and as many stolen bases - made a diving shoestring catch in the outfield to end the 8th for Penetang, taking away the northerners' last hope of the day.

⚾ ⚾ ⚾

Merv

Being on the wrong end of a lopsided score is a lonely experience. You have moments of optimism, but that increasingly turns to despair as the game progresses and the inevitable conclusion draws nearer. You reach a point where you just want to get the whole thing over with and go home and hope for better next game. Except, of course, there would be no next game in this case.

That's where the Rangers found themselves as the bottom of the 9th started. Chatham had already packed up their gear over at their bench, the clinking of wooden bats as they're put into a huge canvas duffle bag representing the universal baseball death knell of the opposition's chances of mounting a comeback. When the other team starts putting the bats away when your team is hitting in the top of the 9th, you know you're facing an insurmountable lead.

As was the case the day before, the Rangers had the bottom of the order due up, a trio that was a combined 0-9 on the day. Unlike yesterday, this game would be played to its conclusion, unless the Rangers were somehow able to pull off a miracle. But with Chase having survived a rocky 6th and 7th innings by retiring the side in order in the 8th, he could clearly see the finish line, and made quick work of the bottom third of the Rangers' order in the 9th, and the game was over.

⚾⚾⚾

Jack

Given that the outcome was not in doubt for the last few innings, the final out of the game was almost anti-climactic. But the dam that had been holding back the Stars' emotions finally broke when the last Penetang out of the series was recorded. Gloves flew in the air, and the traditional dog-pile formed near the pitcher's mound atop Chase and his catcher, Washington. In the stands, hearty handshakes and outright hugs were exchanged among the die-hard core of Stars fans who had stuck it out to the very end. In the middle of the core of celebrants was Archie Stirling, whose smile lit up the dull day. I found it interesting that Penetang let Marchildon back on the mound, and I could only wonder why. The game was well out of hand by that point. Was there a scout somewhere in the stands, and he hoped to atone for the pounding he took early in the game? It really did not make any sense to risk hurting his arm in a blowout.

To say that it had been a long road for the Stars was an understatement, both literally and figuratively. They had traversed a rocky pathway, with trips to Sarnia, Welland, Milton, and Penetang, braving the abuse of fans, indifference of hotel and restaurant owners, ineptitude of the OBA, and the incompetence of umpires. They had triumphed despite all these difficulties. The team was the perfect example of resilience. The Stars would get knocked down time and time again, but they always got back up until they were the last ones standing.

It was a once-in-a-lifetime experience for all involved, and while it would be one that the participants would remember for the rest of their lives, the way in which it happened had been one none of them hoped to ever be part of again. There was a washtub full of ice-cold beer that one of the more thoughtful Stars' fans had thought to transport to Guelph, and the team devoured it quickly as they gathered for the traditional championship trophy presentation. The contents of the tub was adequate only to briefly slake the thirst of parched ballplayers; the real celebrations would begin in a few hours when the team returned to Chatham.

In their first year of competition, the Stars had done it. They were champions of Chatham, and now they were champs of Ontario. Archie Stirling's faith in the team had not gone unrewarded. The city of Chatham had their first OBA title. In the decades to come, the city would bring home many more titles at a variety of levels, breed big leaguers, and become a hotbed of baseball in the province, but it all began with the Stars.

⚾⚾⚾

PENETANG MADE GREAT SHOWING IN O.B.A. FINALS

Chatham Colored Stars Win Fourth and Deciding Game Tuesday

Midland Free Press

GUELPH - Chatham Colored All Stars are the 1934 O.B.A. intermediate 'B-1' champions. They defeated Penetang here today by a score of 13-7. After playing a 2-all tie game yesterday the teams went on a rampage this afternoon and did a lot of wild slugging and scoring.

The difference between the two teams today lay in the fact that "Big Flatfoot" Chase, the Chatham pitcher, was able to do a comeback within 24 hours, while Marchildon, the young Penetang hurler, was troubled with a sore arm. Marchildon started, was batted out, but later came back to the hill to hurl good ball. Chase didn't start bu had to come in after the Penetang team had put the first three batters Marchildon's bits of toil Shortstop Crippin assayed to hold the colored boys in check, but without success, being wild and unable to throw the ball where it couldn't be hit safely.

A running shoe-string somersault catch by L. Harding was the play of the game, but the work of Tabron at short was *outstanding. Spearn and Hale for Penetang had smart running catches in the garden.*

Coach Jim Shaw and his boys made a great showing this season and Midland fans congratulate them on their effort.

Jack

By the time the Stars had packed up, grabbed a quick bite to eat, and hit the road, it was getting late. They didn't anticipate pulling into Chatham until after 10:00 pm. The team knew that thanks to the latest advances in technology, fans outside of the *Daily News* were kept up-to-date of the score in Guelph. So, as the team pulled into the city, a small celebration was anticipated. But as they reached the ciyt's limits, it was nothing like what the players had expected.

It started at the Fifth Street bridge, which in those days marked the entrance to town. Fans were hanging off the bridge, banging on pots and pans they had brought from home, cheering for their heroes. The decision had been made to drive to city hall, where a short ceremony with the mayor would take place. But as the team got closer to the city core, more and more fans had lined the route, and by the time they were still a few blocks away from city hall, the streets were so blocked with traffic and celebrating fans that the team had to park and walk the remaining distance among the growing throng of well-wishers. The Chatham Kiltie Band had joined the festivities, and paraded in front of the Stars to herald the arrival of the team.

By the time the team reached city hall, a makeshift stage had been hastily set up, and the local radio station had set up a microphone and speakers for the assembled audience - said to be at least 2 000 in number, despite the late hour. Mayor Davis acted as master of ceremonies, and several town officials spoke before Pete Gilbert, as one of the team's unofficial sponsors, took the microphone. His speech was typical Pete - short, but sweet: "Folks, I had a lot of fun following these fellas all season. Well done!"

Archie Stirling was next to speak. "Everyone, I can't tell you how proud I am of this team," he began. "You know what they had to go through this year. They had their backs against the wall more than once, but they always got up off the mat and answered the bell. This was a team that never gave up, no matter what the circumstances, no matter if it seemed like the whole world was against them. They played hard, but they played fair. They were excellent ambassadors for the city of Chatham. The All Stars have put this city on the baseball map. They're the first champions from the Maple City, and this is only the beginning - I expect many more Chatham victory celebrations in the years to come."

The assembled audience responded to Archie's words with a rousing ovation. The Mayor added a few words, then it was time for Hap to speak on behalf of the team. "I'm not one for public speakin' and all of that," he started, and someone shouted, "but you sure love to talk, Hap!"

"No, I can't deny that," he answered. "But I have to tell you all that the support of this city was so important to us. We received a telegram from Mayor Davis here just before the first game in Guelph. It meant so much to the team to know the whole community was behind us. We set out this season with the goal of bringin' a championship to Chatham. We had no idea at the time just how hard that would be, but we did it." Turning to the Mayor, Hap was handed the OBA trophy, and, holding it aloft, he declared, "Mr Mayor - you told us to bring home the bacon. Well, here it is!"

The fans broke out into spontaneous applause and cheering. But Hap wasn't done, not by a long shot. Asking the crowd for quiet, he continued. "I want you to know we are just as thrilled as you are to bring a championship to this city. The support that you all showed throughout the season gave us such a big boost. We drew good crowds at Stirling Park, and then when we outgrew Stirling in the playoffs, you all came out in even bigger numbers to Athletic Park. A lot of people came to Chatham from out of town this summer to watch ball games.

And when they did, they would eat at our restaurants, fill up at our gas stations, and sometimes stay at our hotels. I don't know how you'd ever put a dollar figure on that, but the All Stars brought a lot of business to this town. The rest of the country isn't maybe doin' so well, but we're doing alright here in Chatham. The fellas on this team helped bring a lot of business to this town. Now maybe it's time to give them some good-paying jobs, because all they have right now is hotel work, or working in garages, low-paying jobs like that. It's time these men who have brought so much to this city share in the wealth. Maybe it's time for us to see our first coloured policeman, and our first coloured mailman in Chatham. These fellas played their hearts out for you all season, and it's time for the city to show them the respect they deserve."

The mood of the crowd had quieted with the impact of Hap's words. He took a moment to survey the situation, then continued. "Maybe my words are a matter of right place, wrong time, but these fellas are right to expect more from this community." Pausing again, he held the championship trophy up one more time, and as he looked at it, Hap's trademark grin broke out. "Ain't that beautiful," he said, and the crowd whooped it up one more.

⚾⚾⚾

The Whole Hog Brought Home
By Jack Calder

At last an O.B.A. title is ours.

The championship for which the Constineaus, the Pencratzes, the Conniberas, the Peters, the Morgans, and all Chatham's other baseball greats strove in vain was finally grasped yesterday at Guelph, when our good intermediate B-1 team, stepped all over Penetang.

It just crept up on us. Without the usual blaring, the mad back-patting, the whoops to high heaven Chatham has finished out a baseball season. And for once we ride the crest. Let there be no trace of stinting to our celebration.

The Stars cannot be said to have won their title at home. During all the playdowns they managed to win only one game here and the margin of victory in that contest was one small run.

That's not to discredit the team. In fact, those many triumphs on the road tell big things. Only once were the Stars beaten away from home. Sarnia, Welland, Milton, and Penetang all fell victim to the Stars' power attack on these teams' home lots. And Welland and Penetang were whipped on neutral battlefields.

Arrangements are already underway to do justice to one of the best road teams baseball in this province has known. Let Goldsmith dig his foot into that big mound in Southampton and mow down the rival batsmen. Let Fidler kick the dirt in Strathroy while the home fans applaud. Chase, Tabron, and Terrell like to win their games the hard way. They'll throw the ball down the mouths of the hostile fans and make them like it.

Chatham's champions. Those up and down Stars, who are fortunately better uppers than downers.

Town Honours Ball Team And Pacer
Manager and Players Congratulated by Prominent Citizens
SPECIAL STALL FOR HORSE

Toronto Evening Telegram
PENETANG - Nov. 21

A champion horse and a champion ball team were honored by Penetang citizens tonight, at a civic banquet attended by nearly 200 Penetang citizens and Midland supporters at the Knights of Columbus hall. The guests of honour were Mr. J.T. Payette's Cream O'Tartar, undefeated three-year-old champion pacer of Canada, and the Penetang ball team, winners of the North Simcoe League and runners-up for the Ontario championship.

Members of the team were given a place of honour at the head table with their coach and manager. Cream O'Tartar remained downstairs in a specially constructed stall off the main hallway, where he calmly munched his oats and eyed his many admirers with calm unconcern. The ball players missed the Ontario championship by a single game when pitcher Marchildon's arm gave out after gruelling series with Meaford and Chatham.

A host of dignitaries were seated at the head table, including local, provincial, and federal political representatives.

Following the usual toast to the King after dinner, Dr. G.E. Tanner, M.P.P, opened the program by proposing a toast to Our Country.

Manager J. Shaw said that he has been over 50 years in the baseball game, and had never managed a team more responsive to his wishes than the 1934 Penetang team. "They are a clean-cut bunch, and their parents may well be proud of them," he said.

Captain Harold Crippin thanked the citizens of the town for the banquet, and for their support during the season, and expressed the hope that all would meet again next year, when Penetang had won the championship.

Windbreakers were presented to each member of the team, and special prizes, the gift of the team manager, were given to the players with the three highest batting averages, Harold Crippin, Fred DeVillers, and Phil. Marchildon. Mr Norman Hawke, Cream O'Tartar's trainer, received a presentation of a curry comb and brush. It was 11 p.m. before the banquet program concluded.

After dinner, the tables were cleared away and a few hours of dancing were enjoyed before the gathering finally broke up.

11th Inning

Final thoughts; could some of the All Stars have played professionally?

Jack

In the years to come, Boomer played on various OBA powerhouse teams, and after the War, starred for the Chatham Panthers, the post-war version of the All Stars. But he didn't receive even a sniff of attention from pro ball teams. Could he have played pro ball?

Of course he could have.

Boomer and the Stars had proven themselves in that '34 season, defeating a pitcher who would go on to strike out the likes of Joe DiMaggio and Ted Williams in the big leagues. That certainly got some attention, but it wouldn't be until well after the War that scouts would make Chatham a regular stop on their routes.

In the mid-1930s, the game was getting ready for change. There were the usual holdouts, but many big-league owners and their general managers were realizing more and more that there was a huge talent pool they had been ignoring. Judge

Landis and WW II delayed that timetable, but there was a growing sense in the game that it was time that teams suited up the best players, regardless of their skin colour.

Boomer served in the War, and had an opportunity to play on integrated service hockey and baseball teams that featured some of the better players in the country. He attracted the attention of several hockey scouts, and after his discharge, tried out for - and made - the Windsor Staffords, a top farm club of the Detroit Red Wings, and became the first black player in the minor pro International Hockey League. Years earlier, Boomer had laced up the blades in order to take part in a public skate at the famed Detroit Olympia before an arena worker barred him from stepping onto the ice. Boomer pointed to a sign that said the skate was open to the public, but the worker said, "that sign doesn't mean what you think it does." Boomer was 31 years old when he made the Staffords; if he had perhaps been born twenty years later, he may have been part of the wave of black hockey players who broke the colour barrier in the late 40s and early 50s.

It took some time, but true to Hap's plea on that championship night, things did begin to change for the black community in Chatham. Boomer became the city's first mail carrier of colour, a position he held for 35 years. He continued playing ball into the 1950s, before transitioning to officiating baseball, hockey, soccer, and softball in the community. Even in his senior years, Boomer remained competitive, and became one of the top senior dart players in the country through his membership at the local Legion. In 1988, as part of the celebration of the Calgary winter games, he received an Olympic Gold Achievement Medal in recognition of his half century of sports excellence. He was one of only 18 Canadians to be recognized.

Despite missing out on an opportunity to play pro ball, Boomer was never bitter. To the people of Chatham (many of whom over the years knew him better as a mailman than an athlete), he was a gentleman, one of the finest people they've ever met. In his later years, Boomer expressed regret at not having an opportunity to see how far his diamond talents would take him, but he always looked back fondly on the times he had playing for the Stars. "Baseball is a game we played as kids," he recalled, "back when you played work-ups, and no one kept score. You'd play until just before dark, when all the moms in the neighbourhood would be standing on their front steps, yelling for their kids to come home. It was a game we played for nothing, and I don't regret that. After everything was said and done, it was the game and the fans at Stirling Park that mattered, the people who came out to forget about their troubles for a few hours while they cheered for you. The sound of the ball from the pitcher hitting the catcher's mitt, a freshly lined field, the roar of the crowd when you hit one over that short right field fence, a cold beverage with the guys on a hot summer night after the game. That's what it was all about."

For the 1935 season, the Stars recruited a speedy outfielder from Detroit who had come to work as a cook at the Roth. Ferguson Jenkins Sr was a fixture atop the Stars' batting order for the rest of the decade. His son, Ferguson Jr, made it to pro ball years later, and became the first Canadian named to the Baseball Hall of Famer after a career that included seven 20-win campaigns, and 284 career victories at a time when pitcher wins meant something. In the post-war era, integrated Chatham youth teams became a provincial powerhouse, winning OBA titles at every level. An important part of the legacy of Boomer and the Stars is that young Fergie and other Chatham kids of colour grew up playing together on those integrated teams. The Stars moved up to the Intermediate A level for the '35 season. They played in the highly competitive Western Counties Baseball Association and won that loop's title, but couldn't get past the first round of OBA competition.

I was sorry about the bad blood that had developed between Chatham and Penetang. But as time went on, we learned that the northern team had some trouble winning friends and influencing people across the province. We had heard that North Bay had refused to send Penetang home with their share of the gate receipts after their series. Penetang was not happy at the time, understandably so, but after the money they made the rest of the way, well, they were in very good shape financially, unlike all of their OBA competitors. North Bay did not do as well at the gate, and in hindsight, Penetang could maybe have afforded to overlook the sum they were owed. But they kept up the fight after the season, well into the New Year, threatening to petition the OBA to suspend North Bay for the next season until they paid up.

But here's the kicker: Penetang went after North Bay's star pitcher, Preston, for the 1935 season. I can't say that I blame them, because with him and Marchildon on the roster, that was all but a guarantee to return to the finals (I'd even heard a rumour they wanted to move up to Intermediate A). But they tried to persuade him to come south after the March 15th deadline for signing import players, so the OBA rejected their transfer request. Not only were they trying to get North Bay sidelined for non-payment of a relatively small sum of money, they tried to pry their top player away.

Penetang was a gritty team, and despite the obvious enmity between the two teams throughout the series, they played the game much the same way the Stars did. Maybe because they were from a small town they felt that they had to constantly prove themselves, but they did play with something of a collective chip on their shoulders. Did they play the game with a tough, ferocious intensity? Certainly they did. Did they play dirty? That's a difficult question to answer, and the best I can come up with is that they played within the rules, but they certainly pushed some boundaries. There was a grudging respect for Marchildon and his talents. The Stars knew he was tired heading into the series, and they did their best to wear him down with every inning, every at bat. Were there, perhaps, some misunderstandings? With two tired teams slugging it out to bring provincial glory to their towns (for the first time), undoubtedly there were.

The All Stars journeyed on a very rocky road all season long. I was lucky enough to have been a passenger for the trip. The season went on much longer than it needed to, but it only lasted a little over five months. Given the events of that year, it seemed much, much longer.

In the end, we're all travellers. Some of us get to our final destinations before others do.

⚾ ⚾ ⚾

Merv

Phil decided after a year at St Mike's, despite the chance to play varsity football and baseball, university wasn't for him. He returned home to Penetanguishene to pitch for the Rangers, but they couldn't get past Collingwood and their ace Smoky Smith in the North Simcoe League in 1935. Collingwood went on to win that OBA title that had eluded the Rangers the season before. Two years later, Warpy Phillips led Meaford to an OBA crown against that same Chatham All Stars club. Marchildon, Phillips, Smith, and Goldsmith: the 1930s was a golden age for pitching along the Southern Georgian Bay shoreline.

It was during an exhibition game in that '35 season against St Mary's that Phil learned from one of the opposing players about opportunities in the Nickel Belt League up near the northern Ontario mining town of Sudbury. Phil had hoped that the group of local businessmen who footed the bill for the team's lengthy playoff run in '34 would offer him a permanent full-time job to stay in town and play for the local team. "I didn't receive a single job offer," Phil said. "Some of my friends afterward told me that everyone in town thought I'd never leave, said I was too much of a home-boy, and I'd never leave Penetang." After Phil left the Rangers, sadly, they were no longer a force in North Simcoe circles.

It still took several years of pitching in the north, but Phil eventually signed a pro contract with the Toronto Maple Leafs, who sold him to the lowly Philadelphia Athletics a year later. His career was interrupted by WWII - he served two and half years in a German POW camp, but Phil came back to pitch in the bigs, winning 19 games in 1947, his best season in the majors. The following year, when Jackie Robinson broke the colour barrier with the Dodgers, the A's finished 4th, their highest finish in Phil's tenure with the team. But Phil said owner/manager Connie Mack was the reason they didn't finish higher. "If we had signed a pitcher from the Negro Leagues like Satchel Paige or Leon Day, that might have helped us win a pennant," he told me years later. "But old man Mack said didn't want to upset the other owners or the Athletics' white fans. He didn't want to spend the money, either."

I have thought long and hard about the 1934 series with Chatham in the years that followed. My mind replayed many of the events of that season, and of that epic battle between the two finalists. The Chatham team played hard but fair, there is no question about that. They had to prove themselves just about every time they took the field that year, which is why every game likely was a battle for them. They certainly gave no quarter. But that was to be expected, because the Rangers were cut from much the same cloth. As a team from a little town, they constantly were looked down upon by the players and fans from the larger centres, who certainly didn't like being upstaged by a bunch of yokels. During that series, were there things that happened that shouldn't have? The answer, sadly, is yes - unfortunate things were said and done in the heat of battle. The intensity of that series was at an all-time high, and the Chatham team's nerves likely had to be frayed to an end given what they had to deal with from umpires, opposing players, and fans all season long. The third game, when passions overflowed and fights broke out, was probably something of a breaking point.

Along the way in the 1930s, Phil's birth year was switched from 1913 to 1915, giving him a "baseball age." Had he been born in a different era and perhaps in a place closer to organized baseball, Phil may have had a much longer and more successful big-league career.

For twenty years, Phil Marchildon held the record for most wins in a season and in a career for a Canadian-born player. Both records were broken in the late 60s by Ferguson Jenkins, Jr.

As Jim Shaw said, this game is one big circle.

Postscript

Jack Calder's documenting of the Stars' championship season in the Chatham *Daily News* made for riveting reading, and as someone who saw the rise of the team from sandlot aggregation to provincial power, he was a logical choice to recount their title run. Like Boomer and Phil and many other players on both teams, Calder enlisted for World War II, serving as a Flight Lieutenant in the RCAF. He was shot down once, and injured when his plane crashed on a mountain top in Northern England. In between those mishaps, he filed several stories for the Canadian Press, before being killed when he was shot down once more over Germany in 1944. Mervyn Dickey, similarly, was a solid choice to relate the Penetanguishene experience. He's listed as the team statistician and as a hometown boy would have known all of the Rangers well. After his stint with the Penetang *Herald*, Merv went on to senior positions with newspapers in the Ontario towns of Geraldton and then Prescott (where he is still fondly remembered) before passing away in 1982. This book is dedicated in part to Jack and Merv's memories.

Jackie Robinson's big-league debut was still a decade-plus away, but there was a growing feeling across America that the best players were not necessarily in MLB. In 1934, even the best-paid major leaguers had troubles making ends meet, so barnstorming tours against top Negro League players in the off-season was a way to supplement their income. Dizzy and Paul Dean had to skip the Cardinals World Series parade, because they had a game in Kansas City against the Monarchs that day. Ol' Diz matched up against Satchel Paige in many of these exhibition contests, where Satch more than held his own. Dean would tell reporters, "if Old Satchel and I played together, we'd clinch the pennant mathematically by the Fourth of July, then go fishin' until the World Series. Between us we'd win sixty games." But major league baseball was far from ready for a black pitching ace; Dean and Paige may have been off-season equals, but Paige observed, "people used to say how Diz and me were about alike as two tadpoles, but Diz was in the majors and I was bouncing around the peanut circuit."

The Stars' success was celebrated in the city of Chatham. But in the larger scheme of things, systemic racism was still alive and well in Canada in the aftermath of their victory. A case in point: in 1936, Montreal chauffeur Fred Christie was refused service in the York Tavern, a bar located in the old Montreal Forum. Three different waiters refused to take his order - because he was black. Neither Canada nor the province of Quebec had specific laws at the time preventing discrimination, but Christie was able to persuade a lower court judge that the tavern had violated its duty, according to its liquor license, to serve all customers without discrimination.

On appeal, a higher court sided with the tavern owners, and the case went all the way to the Supreme Court, which said that Quebec's liquor laws did not apply, and the tavern had "freedom of commerce" to serve whoever they wanted. The decision has been called "the most significant statement of legalized racism" in Canadian history. This was a landmark case, one that allowed Quebec businesses to discriminate on the basis of race for another 40 years, until the province enacted its *Charter of Rights and Freedoms*.

A decade later, Halifax businesswoman Viola Desmond was forcefully removed from a Nova Scotia movie theatre after she refused to leave a whites-only balcony. Desmond was arrested, spent the night in jail, and was not allowed to call a lawyer. She was charged with a minor tax violation for the difference between the seat she paid for and the one she sat in - which was all of one cent. Despite taking legal action, Desmond was never acquitted of the charge in her lifetime before the federal government pardoned her in 2010.

Many Canadians have never experienced systemic racism, making it easy to deny its existence. In light of the murder of George Floyd and the Black Lives Matter movment, several

Canadian politicians have smugly suggested it's a problem that our neighbours to the south have, but we don't. That flies in the face of the head tax on Chinese immigrants after the building of the transcontinental railway - built with the help of thousands of Chinese labourers, and the internment of Canadians of Japanese descent in the Second World War, the forcible removal of First Nations from their homes to residential schools (the unmarked graves of many, much to our collective dismay, are now only being discovered), and a history of treaty violations. In our nation's largest city, black Torontonians are 20 times more likely to be shot by a police officer than a white resident. Immigration policies for many years made it very difficult for people of colour to move to Canada. One need look no further than the comments section on media articles dealing with racism to know that it is still very much alive and well in our country.

As Boomer noted after the Strathroy incident, children learn racism. They're not born hating people who are different from them. We've made progress in this country, but our legal, economic, and academic institutions have still far to go. Indigenous and black histories need to take their rightful place in our history curricula.

Washington Post baseball bard Tom Boswell wrote that "the Paige tragedy is that, by his excellence, he proved that 50 years worth of black-league players had been wronged more severely than white America ever suspected." Buck O'Neil had a different message for white America. "Don't feel sorry for us," he said in his eulogy to Satchel. "I feel sorry for your fathers and your mothers, because they didn't get to see us play."

-Larry Tye, "*Satchel: The Life and Times of an American Legend*"

The March to the Finals

OBA Quarter Finals (best of three)

Saturday, September 8th, 1934
Penetanguishene 1 North Bay 0
Chatham 8 Sarnia 3

Thursday, September 13th
Chatham 8 Sarnia 0 (forfeit)
Chatham wins series, 2-0

Saturday, September 15th
Penetanguishene 1 North Bay 0 (12 innings)
Penetanguishene wins series, 2-0

OBA Semi Finals (best of three)

Wednesday, September 19th
Meaford 1 Penetanguishene 1 (13 innings)

Thursday, September 20th
Welland 17 Chatham 7

Saturday, September 22nd
Meaford 5 Penetanguishene 3 (10 innings)
Chatham 4 Welland 2
Chatham wins series, 2-1

Wednesday, September 26th
Penetanguishene 3 Meaford 3
Chatham 11 Welland 7

Wednesday, October 3rd
Penetanguishene 5 Meaford 4

Thursday, October 4th
Chatham 10 Milton 9 (10 innings)

Monday, October 8th
Penetanguishene 3 Meaford 2
Penetanguishene wins series, 2-1

Thursday, October 11th
Chatham 8 Milton 7
Chatham wins series, 2-1

OBA Finals (best of three)

Monday, October 15th
Chatham 4 Penetanguishene 2 (10 innings)

Thursday, October 18th
Penetanguishene 10 Chatham 9

Monday, October 22nd
Chatham 2 Penetanguishene 2 (10 innings)

Tuesday, October 23rd
Chatham 13 Penetanguishene 7
Chatham wins series, 2-1.

Acknowledgements

A box score gives an incomplete summary of a baseball game; it tells you what happened in a game, but now how it took place. Similarly, in recreating the 1934 season, there was a box score in the form of articles found in newspapers from Chatham, Barrie, Midland, Brantford, North Bay, and Owen Sound, but there were few details beyond that.

So, with an outline of a story in place, it was up to the author to try to fill in the details. In that pursuit, there were several excellent sources. Noted baseball historian and Canadian Baseball Hall of Fame member Bill Humber was an excellent sounding board, and was very interested in and supportive of this project. Dr Miriam Wright and Dr Heidi Jacobs of the University of Windsor performed outstanding work in digitizing some old scrapbooks they were given that became the Chatham Coloured All Stars project and website. Dr Jacobs in particular was a fabulous resource in compiling some of the research that formed the basis of this book.

Mr Bob Bald of Penetanguishene, whose dad Jim played with Phil on the '34 Rangers was also a font of information. We had an extensive email correspondence, and it was a highlight when he invited me to tour the Penetanguishene Sports Hall of Fame to see the fabulous displays he and the board of the museum have put together. Mr Bald shared many stories about the Rangers with me, and was an enthusiastic supporter of my efforts. Unfortunately, Mr Bald passed away after a short illness during the writing of this book, which he had been keen to see in print. This book is dedicated in part to him, as well.

My wife, Sherry Taylor-Fox, is not a baseball fan, but she has put up with my obsession with it for 30+ years, and was invaluable in the writing of this book. She endured many quiet drives in the car when I was working out plot details and dialogue in my head, and she provided sound revisions and eagle-eyed editing of my final draft. Our sons Taylor and Liam also read a draft, and provided their thoughts.

I was fortunate to have several willing "beta readers" who are avid baseball fans themselves and offered suggestions, including Marty Wilkinson, Ken Lansing, Sean Lawes, and Tom Paradis. Tom is a childhood friend who has been one of the driving forces behind the Midland Sports Hall of Fame, and I relied on his research skills immensely. Kevin Crowley, a roommate from long ago and close friend, provided valuable insights which dramatically improved the finished product.

Toronto Blue Jays coach John Schneider managed Bo Bichette at AA in 2018. Bichette was having a difficult laying off of breaking pitches in his first few weeks at that level, so Schneider had him swing at everything in batting practice. It was a great story, Schneider told me, I adopted here.

Thanks also go to Amy Sultana of the West Parry Sound Museum for helping to piece together the Rangers' visit to Parry Sound. Nicole Jackson of the Penetanguishene Centennial Museum, Tom Barber of Huronia Centennial Museum, and Art Duval all helped provide important information. Mike Murphy of the Chatham-Kent Sports Hall of Fame, and Brock Greenhalgh (who has written his own book about the Stars), and Mr Ed Myers, who was a Chatham teammate of Fergie Jr, all contributed a wealth of thoughts and information. Thanks also to Dan Kelly (whose research paper about the Stars is a seminal work in the study of that time) for getting me in touch with Ed. Fred Osmon sent a very helpful envelope of clippings from the Chatham *Daily News*. Brian Kendall, co-author of Phil Marchildon's biography, was helpful with several aspects of writing this book. Eric Gray, David Firstman, and Del Jones offered great insight into the world of self-publishing. Thanks finally to Dawn Stilwell of The Publishing Shop, who expertly guided me through the process of putting this all together.

Bibliography

Bald, R. (n.d.). *The 1934 Penetanguishene Spencer Foundry Rangers*. Penetanguishene Sports Hall of Fame http://www.pshof.ca/uploads/6/8/9/5/6895306/the_1934_penetanguishene_spencer_foundry_rangers.pdf

Barbour, G. H., & Willer, B. (2003). *Huronia the Beautiful: A Peek Into the Past of Penetanguishene*. Memories of Small Towns in Huronia. Gerald H. Barbour.

Breaking the Colour Barrier. (2018). *Breaking the Colour Barrier - The Chatham Coloured All Stars*. http://cdigs.uwindsor.ca/BreakingColourBarrier/

Breslin, J. (2011). *Branch Rickey: A Life* (Penguin Lives). Penguin Books.

Bunch, A. (2017, September 8). *John Graves Simcoe's weird relationship with slavery*. Spacing Toronto. http://spacing.ca/toronto/2017/09/05/john-graves-simcoes-weird-relationship-slavery/

Cauz, L. (1977). *Baseball's Back in Town: From the Don to the Blue Jays-- A History of Baseball in Toronto*. Controlled Media Corp.

Chantler, S. (2019). *All Stars*. Amsterdam University Press.

Dixon P. S. (2019). *The Dizzy and Daffy Dean Barnstorming Tour: Race, Media, and America's National Pastime* (Illustrated ed.). Rowman & Littlefield Publishers.

Greenhalgh, B. R. A., Veronese, D., & Cupic, L. (2020). *Hard Road to Victory: The Chatham All-Stars Story*. Peppett Publishing.

Hawthorn, T. (2009, February 9). *Don Tabron, Ballplayer (1915–2008)*. Tom Hawthorn's Blog. http://tomhawthorn.blogspot.com/2009/02/don-tabron-ballplayer-1915-2008.html

Heidenry, J. (2007). *The Gashouse Gang: How Dizzy Dean, Leo Durocher, Branch Rickey, Pepper Martin, and Their Colorful, Come-from-Behind Ball Club Won the World Series-and America's Heart-During the Great Depression*. PublicAffairs.

Humber, W. (1995). *Diamonds of the North*. Oxford University Press.

Kahn, R. (2015). *Rickey & Robinson: The True, Untold Story of the Integration of Baseball* (Reprint ed.) [E-book]. Rodale Books.

Kelly, Daniel J. (1977, April). *The Chatham Coloured All-Stars 1933–34.* https://scholar.uwindsor.ca/cgi/viewcontent.cgi?article=1000&context=hardingpub

Kendall, B., & Marchildon, P. (1994). *Ace - Canada's Wartime Hero and Pitching Sensation.* Penguin Group (Canada).

Kepner, T. (2020). *K: A History of Baseball in Ten Pitches* (Reprint ed.). Anchor

Kerrane, K., Pease, D., & Goldstein, K. (2013). *Dollar Sign on the Muscle: The World of Baseball Scouting.* CreateSpace Independent Publishing Platform.

McDermott, T. (2017). *Off Speed: Baseball, Pitching, and the Art of Deception* (1st ed.). Pantheon.

McNary, K. (2013). *"Double Duty" Radcliffe: 36 Years of Pitching & Catching in the Negro Leagues*. Wooddale Publishing.

Miceli, Lauren A. (2016) *"The 1934 Chatham Colored All-Stars: Barnstorming to Championships," The Great Lakes Journal of Undergraduate History: Vol. 4 : Iss. 1 , Article 2.* Available at: https://scholar.uwindsor.ca/gljuh/vol4/iss1/2

Noël, F. (2009). *Family and Community Life in Northeastern Ontario: The Interwar Years* (Illustrated ed.). McGill-Queen's University Press.

Official Program: Chatham's Victoria Day - May 22nd · Breaking the Colour Barrier. (1960, May 22). Breaking the Colour Barrier: Boomer Harding and the Chatham Coloured All Stars. Retrieved March 15, 2022, from https://cdigs.uwindsor.ca/BreakingColourBarrier/items/show/957

O'Neil, B., Conrads, D., Burns, K., & Wulf, S. (1997). *I Was Right On Time* (Reprint ed.). Simon & Schuster.

Peterson, R. (1992). *Only the Ball Was White: A History of Legendary Black Players and All-Black Professional Teams*. Oxford University Press.

Posnanski, J. (2008). *The Soul of Baseball: A Road Trip Through Buck O'Neil's America* (Reprint ed.). William Morrow Paperbacks.

Robinson, J., & Duckett, A. (2003). *I Never Had It Made: An Autobiography of Jackie Robinson* (Edition Unstated ed.). Ecco.

Rust, A. (1992). *Get that N****r Off the Field!* Book Mail Services.

Sowell, M. (2015). *The Pitch That Killed: The Story of Carl Mays, Ray Chapman, and the Pennant Race of 1920* (Reprint ed.) [E-book].

Tye, L. (2010). *Satchel: The Life and Times of an American Legend* (F First Paperback Edition). Random House Trade Paperbacks.

Wencer, D. (2015, October 10). *Historicist: Hats off to Howley and his hustling horde.* Torontoist. https://torontoist.com/2015/10/historicist-hats-off-to-howley-and-his-hustling-horde/

White, B., Mays, W., & Dillow, G. (2011). *Uppity: My Untold Story About The Games People Play* (1st ed.). Grand Central Publishing.

Williams, T., Underwood, J., & Cupp, R. (1986). *The Science of Hitting* (Rev. ed.). Simon & Schuster.

About the Author

D.M. Fox grew up in Midland, Ontario, in the heat of the sports rivalry with Penetanguishene. When he played hockey in the latter, he was always intrigued by the huge black and white photo of an old ballplayer in the lobby, because for him, hockey was something to do between baseball seasons, not the other way around. He grew up watching his town team, eating crispy golden French Fries from John Deakos' stand behind home plate, and running the bases with all the other kids after the game. Growing up, his dream was to one day patrol centre field for that team, a dream that was dashed in the mid-70s by a spectacular fire that laid waste to the town's arena, and the ball diamond beside it.

Fox read Jim Bouton's iconic *Ball Four* as an adolescent, creating a passion for baseball literature that remains to this day.

Recommended to study journalism by his Grade 13 English teacher, Fox opted for a different route, and embarked on a 30-year career as an elementary school teacher. But he continued to be a voracious reader of any and all baseball works.

In 2011, he started writing a blog about the Toronto Blue Jays farm system called Clutchlings, and since 2018 has been the publisher and editor of the website Future Blue Jays.

On Account of Darkness is his first published book. He is currently working on a second book of historical baseball fiction entitled "Severn Sound: a Story About Health, Friendship, and Baseball." Fox lives in Nottawa, Ontario, with his wife Sherry and their cocker spaniels, Olive and Chelsea.

Manufactured by Amazon.ca
Bolton, ON